A Lady's Guide to Scoundrels and Gentlemen

THE HARP & THISTLE
BOOK 1

ARDEN CONROY

ARE YOU SIGNED UP FOR DRAGONBLADE'S BLOG?

You'll get the latest news and information on exclusive giveaways, exclusive excerpts, coming releases, sales, free books, cover reveals and more.

Check out our complete list of authors, too!

No spam, no junk. That's a promise!

Sign Up Here

www.dragonbladepublishing.com

Dearest Reader;

Thank you for your support of a small press. At Dragonblade Publishing, we strive to bring you the highest quality Historical Romance from some of the best authors in the business. Without your support, there is no 'us', so we sincerely hope you adore these stories and find some new favorite authors along the way.

Happy Reading!

CEO, Dragonblade Publishing

For my husband, whose support has been unending,
and belief in me unwavering.

Chapter One

Mayfair, London
October 1888

WHETHER ONE LIVED in Whitechapel or Mayfair, a policeman's knock in the middle of the night was always a concerning event.

Lady Vivian Winthrop had never been awoken in such a way before, and it was rather disconcerting. She had been deep asleep when the heavy brass knocker on the front door had pulled her from her slumber with its booming, metallic echo. Tying on her housecoat, Vivian hurried out into the second-floor hallway and hid behind a marble pillar to spy on the activity below. Her father, butler, and a police officer huddled in the entryway. Father was speaking in a hushed tone.

"He refuses to leave, Your Grace," the policeman replied, evidently not realizing his voice would echo in the large, opulent area.

Who was *he*? And where was *he* refusing to leave? Vivian cupped her hand around her ear to better hear her father's response but couldn't make it out.

"Vivian!" A frail voice called out from down the hallway.

Disappointed to be pulled away, Vivian followed the voice into a plush bedroom, where she found her grandmother, the dowager duchess, trying to sit up in bed. Vivian hurried forward with worry. "Gran! Here, let me help you." She placed a hand on her grandmother's back. "You know you can't do that by yourself."

"Oh, hogwash." Gran waved away her concern before tucking stray, gray curls back under her lace-edged nightcap. "Light me a cigarette, dear."

Vivian crossed her arms with a frown. "You're sick. You shouldn't be smoking. The physician said no alcohol, and no smoking."

"I'm not sick, I'm *dying*. Now light one for me. What's it going to do, kill me?" Gran cackled at her joke.

Vivian let out an audible sigh to show how much she disliked this, placed a cigarette in Gran's long cigarette holder, and lit it for her, ensuring Gran saw her face of displeasure.

With bony fingers, Gran placed the stick between her lips, took in an inhale, then exhaled with a long sigh of relief. "Thank you. Now. What's all the hubbub about?"

Vivian glanced back toward the door. "I'm not sure. There's a policeman downstairs talking to Father."

"Exciting!"

Vivian whipped her head back around, then flung her long, brown hair back over her shoulder. "*Exciting*? A knock upon our door at this hour means something bad has happened!"

"What did they say? And don't tell me you weren't spying on them. I know you far too well." Gran ended her accusation with a grin.

Feeling a bit sheepish, Vivian relayed what she'd overheard.

While mulling this over, Gran rested her head back against her satin pillow. "Interesting," was all she offered.

"Whom do you think they're talking about?"

"My word, Vivian. You really need to get out more." Gran, apparently understanding who was at the heart of the hubbub, motioned for her crystal ashtray. Vivian placed it within reach. "When is the last time you've been out somewhere, my dear?" Gran asked.

"Oh, not this again." Vivian groaned, hating the subject. "You already know the answer. The queen has ensured I cannot do anything. I am no longer included in anything that involves the aristocracy. She has always disliked me while adoring my brother, remember?"

"Oh, I remember. All because her silly husband made indecent proposals to me." Gran tapped her cigarette against the ashtray with a thoughtful look. "Five times."

Vivian's eyes widened. "You never told me *that* part!"

"I believe he did it after they had rows, knowing it would upset her. Begging a pretty American to be his mistress, the scandal! You should see how red her face can turn." Gran cackled again. "Anyway, that's why she has it out for you, because she has it out for me. You look exactly like I did when I was your age and Prince Albert became silly around me. But your brother is English through and through, like your grandfather. The good part of the family, in her eyes."

"And now we're being flooded with Dollar Princesses." Vivian was amused so many noble families were now being saved financially by American heiresses and their bank accounts.

Gran took another inhale from her cigarette holder. "I wish I could figure out how to best that woman, if only to annoy her." Gran then gave Vivian a long look over, as if an idea had begun to form in her mind. But whatever the thought was must have not materialized, as she changed the subject. "Enough about that, though. We need to have a discussion."

"Lovely."

"What are you going to do when I die?"

A queasy dread roiled through Vivian's stomach, and she braced herself for the discussion she had been trying to avoid for months. "Gran, please, I really don't want to talk about this."

"It's going to happen sooner rather than later. Are you planning on staying with your father? I know I'm here for my last days, but then it will be only you and him in this house."

That subject, Vivian tried not to think about too much. "This is where I grew up. Unlike you, I've never lived anywhere else."

Gran was American-born and her father had been a wealthy importer of European fashion and perfume. Gran's family had lived all over the United States before she'd moved to England to marry her late husband, the former Duke of Chalworth. "Where else would I go?" Vivian asked.

"You have any secret beaus you've been hiding from us?" Gran narrowed her eyes, as if she could discern the truth that way.

Vivian was shocked by the question. "Of course not!"

"That's too bad."

With a scoff, Vivian turned to the window beside Gran's bed and pulled the curtain to the side. As she gazed through it, the policeman left their house and climbed into the police wagon. "Once again, Gran, Queen Victoria has ensured that is an impossibility."

The horses trotted away, and the wagon was gone, leaving behind an empty, dark street.

Finding Gran's stretched silence strange, Vivian put her attention back to the frail woman. Gran was studying Vivian once again with an intense interest.

"Why are you looking at me like that?" Vivian asked.

"How am I looking at you?"

"Like you're up to something."

"Me? Never."

Vivian couldn't help but laugh and went to sit on the edge of the bed. "So, whom was the policeman talking about, since you already seem to know?"

"He was talking about your brother."

Vivian started at this. "Bernard? I can't imagine Bernard breaking the law." The Marquess of Litchfield helped their father, the current Duke of Chalworth, manage the ducal estate. He was also happily married, with two children. What kind of trouble could he possibly get into?

Before she could ask that question, though, her father came into the bedroom. Vivian secretly thought him adorable; he was short and everything about him was round. His face, his cheeks, his stomach. But his usual good humor was absent and he seemed to have something on his mind, though he did not appear overly worried, which relieved Vivian slightly. "I had a feeling you two would be awake," the duke said as he came to stand with them. "Unfortunately, I need to leave for a short time."

"Why?" Vivian asked. "What happened? Why was a policeman here?"

Father looped his hands together behind his back. "Nothing you need to worry about. Now get back in bed, and I will see you in the morning." He was turning to leave, but Gran wasn't having it.

"Stop right there!" Gran shouted while pointing her finger. "Don't you dare go anywhere without telling us what is going on. As your mother, I demand it!"

Despite Father's white hair and aged face, he looked like a small boy who had been scolded by his mother. "It seems Bernard got himself into a little bit of trouble at a pub."

"A pub?" Vivian repeated, surprised. When she thought of pubs, she imagined factory workers sitting along the bar drinking pints while someone banged at worn piano keys, a fight occurring somewhere in the background. "What is Bernard doing at a pub?"

"Apparently, he was betting on a fight."

Gran sat forward with interest. "A fight? You mean boxing?"

"That's what it sounds like. Something happened, and the pub owner wants him to leave without making a big fuss over it, which was why the policeman came here. To ask me to get Bernard out of the pub. Before a big fuss is made."

What had happened to Bernard? Vivian worried about him being so far out of his element. Had he been met with violence, perhaps? Picked on by other men at the pub?

"Take Vivian with you." Gran swept her hand toward the door, as if directing a servant.

Both Vivian and her father looked at Gran with surprise.

"Absolutely not." Father scoffed at such a ridiculous suggestion. "I refuse to expose the girl to such riffraff!"

"That *girl* is an adult woman!" Gran retorted. "And keeping her isolated from the world is not the way for her to live. It will suffocate her, and she will get more and more miserable as the years tick by."

"You make me sound like a recluse." Vivian clenched a hand into a fist upon her hip. "I do leave the house. I often go for walks, or to museums. And I see Anne at least once a week for tea."

"Go with your father." Gran snuffed out the cigarette in a way that told Vivian the discussion was over.

Knowing there was no use in arguing, Vivian turned to the duke for his final decision.

Father grumbled, also knowing it was fruitless. "Hurry and get dressed quickly, then," he said. "And remember, we will only be there for a short moment! We are not there to partake."

Vivian hurried into her bedroom. Knowing the household would be fully awake with the news her brother was in trouble with a pub, she rang her lady's maid and dressed as quickly as possible, choosing a boring, wool dress and a fur hat and matching coat.

SOMETIME LATER, THEY arrived at a pub called The Harp & Thistle. The street was dark and narrow, and the buildings looked tired. The pub's windows were small, but Vivian could see it was crowded even at this late hour. The loud crowd and banging of piano keys rang out into the night, just as she'd imagined.

Yet what energy it exuded!

"Wait here one moment." Father moved to exit the carriage. "You do not belong in there and will only invite trouble. A lady of the aristocracy would be very out of her element."

"Father, I'm a twenty-nine-year-old spinster," Vivian said

with little amusement. She was far from the beautiful aristocrat he was trying to make her out to be. That being said, Vivian did not want to cause trouble, so she agreed to stay safe inside the carriage.

Satisfied enough with her reply, Father climbed out when the driver opened the door and went inside the pub.

The minutes ticked by and gentle snores started coming from the driver. Still, Father and Bernard did not reappear. Vivian decided it best to let the man slumber, as they had roused him in the middle of the night. Recalling they were without a footman to keep the servants' gossip minimal, Vivian climbed out of the carriage despite Father's warning, prepared to rush back at the first sight of her family. Standing on her tiptoes, she was just able to peer through the pub's windows. Inside, people packed together tightly. Mostly men, but there were some women patrons too, which was surprising. She'd had no idea women went to pubs!

Vivian went over to the door that led inside. There was a poster on the door with photographs of two pugilists posed with their fists raised in front of them. In large, block letters, it read, "Bare-Knuckle Fighting," then "McNab vs. Burke" beneath that.

Vivian studied the two men. Both were bare-chested and wore light-colored, tight boxing shorts. They looked quite imposing with their scowls. The man on the left, whom she assumed was McNab, as his photo was under the name, held her attention. The photograph was small, but she was taken in by the sheer size of his muscles. His biceps and shoulders were rounded and large, and there was something frightening about him overall. His hair was darker and longer than Burke's, and he had hair on his chest and unfashionable stubble as well. And there was a determined glint in his eye—wild, untamed.

Curiously, there also seemed to be something on his face.

Vivian leaned in closer to get a better look. But before she could, the door flew open, nearly knocking her off her feet.

"Oh!" She jumped back as a man flew out the door and tumbled to the ground. As she had done earlier at home, she retreated into shadows, where the gas streetlamps did not reach.

The discarded man unleashed a string of crass, slurred curse words in the direction of the door he had just exited. Vivian assumed it was a general anger at being kicked out, until an imposing figure stepped forward.

"I've given you chances before, Murph." The man's voice was deep, and it gave her goosebumps. She'd expected a strong Cockney accent from the man, but, surprisingly, it was hardly there. In fact, he could have blended in quite well amongst her peers if they didn't listen too closely. How curious. "You throw a punch, I warn you. You try to rip me off, I warn you. But grabbing an unwilling woman? I don't tolerate that. No second chances for that."

Murph was somehow able to get to his feet and swayed as he tried to focus on the large figure. His face and limbs were thin, but he had a perfectly round stomach, a hint toward adoration for drink. "Aw, come on, McNab. She was only pretending she didn't like it—you know how women are. That's all it was."

"The woman told you to back off. You didn't."

Murph laughed. "They never know what they want. Trust me—she wanted me."

McNab grabbed Murph by the front of his shirt, lifting him up to stare him directly in the eye. The drunk man's feet dangled helplessly, and he whimpered with fear.

"I don't know how to make this more clear to you," McNab seemed to growl. "You're done and you're not welcome back. Ever. If you show your face, I'll rip you apart and throw you into the Thames, piece by piece."

Vivian swallowed and was quite glad to not be in Murph's place.

"All right!" Murph squeaked. "All right. Fine. Point taken. Let me go."

McNab let the man go and he crumpled to the ground, found his footing, and ran off like a dog with its tail between its legs.

McNab watched to ensure the man was truly gone, then let his shoulders fall with a sigh. He ran his hands through his hair with frustration.

Vivian couldn't help but watch with a strange interest. Beneath his shirt, which clung to him with sweat, the muscles of his arms and back moved in interesting ways.

Was this the same man who was on the poster? It had to be. He was even larger and more imposing than the photograph let on.

McNab headed back to the door, returning to the same shadows that shrouded Vivian. Unfortunately, she didn't get a good look at the front of his face, and she found herself wondering if he was handsome. Once he was inside, she would study the poster a bit closer to satisfy her curiosity.

McNab went to reach out to grasp the door handle when he paused.

And looked in her direction.

"Hello?" The tenor of his voice was cautious.

Vivian took several steps back, remaining as quiet as a mouse.

McNab headed in her direction, causing her heart to race. She could now only see the outline of his imposing form and it frightened her, as she was within his arm's reach.

"Are you all right?" McNab stopped walking.

"I—I'm sorry. Yes. I was standing here when you came outside, and I didn't want to be a bother while you were dealing with something." Her voice shook.

McNab took a few steps back to give her space. "I didn't realize anyone else was out here." There was a long pause as he looked her over. "Who are you?"

Vivian's family, of course, was well known to everyone. It would be unwise to tell him who she was. "No one of consequence, sir."

"Are you waiting for someone in the pub?"

"Yes."

"Who?"

Oh, now she would have to give herself away. *Blast!* She swallowed and used her brother's given name to be safe. "Bernard Winthrop."

The man seemed to still. "Are you the marchioness?"

So he did know who Bernard was, and this made her far more nervous. "As I said, I am no one of consequence."

A cold, autumn breeze kicked up, and the brown leaves strewn along the sidewalk began to spin and dance. The air between them felt strange and heavy, almost electric.

"Winthrop's father is inside gathering him," McNab said after a moment, and the outline of his head turned toward the door. "Looks like they're coming out now."

The pub's door opened and the sudden wall of noise from its patrons dissipated the strange air between them.

Bernard stumbled out, followed by their father, and came to a halt when McNab appeared in his line of sight.

McNab, whose back was now to Vivian, returned to the lamplight to approach the pair.

Vivian considered staying in the shadows. It wouldn't look good to follow McNab out of them, but she also couldn't stay hidden. They would discover her missing from the carriage soon enough.

Feeling nervous, Vivian stepped into the light, too.

"What are *you* doing here?" Bernard sputtered in her direction, no doubt quite surprised to see his sister. Vivian hid the shock his appearance gave her. Bernard looked a fright. His dark hair was disheveled, and his clothing hung loose, as if he'd recently lost noticeable weight. And he reeked of alcohol. She had last seen her brother only a few weeks prior and he'd looked well enough then. Like Vivian, he towered over their short father, as they both had taken after Gran, whereas Father had taken after their grandfather. Yet in the moment, Vivian was sure Father could knock Bernard over with a mere puff of air.

Father started upon seeing her as well and shot her a narrow-eyed look. But when a loud snore rang out from their driver,

Father thankfully suppressed his comments.

Instead, he turned to McNab.

"I apologize again." Father had to crane his neck to speak to the tall man. "My son knows better than to leave the house without his billfold."

Vivian shot a look over to Bernard. *That* was what all of this was about? She almost asked what he'd been doing at a ragged, working-class pub in the first place but didn't want to offend McNab.

"Paying up the tab for tonight is all that's needed for now," McNab replied cryptically.

Bernard's face twisted into a grimace, and Vivian wondered if there was more going on here being hidden from Father.

But it also was none of her business. Nor was it her place to say anything.

"Into the carriage, you two." Father made a shooing motion to his adult children. "The hour is late, and I would like to return to bed. I am also not going to ask why *you* were in the shadows with *him*." Father directed this question to Vivian with lifted eyebrows.

But before Vivian could respond—though she didn't know how to defend herself, as her behavior had been uncouth—*he* jumped in.

"I noticed a woman hiding in the shadows." McNab jutted his chin toward the spot he referred to. "I was simply ensuring she was all right, that's all."

Father made no reply, instead bellowing at the driver, who woke up by leaping three feet into the air and floundering down to the carriage door to open it. As she placed her hand on the open door, Vivian looked back over her shoulder, hoping to get a glimpse of McNab before she left his world and returned to hers. Half of him remained concealed by the shadows of night, but she could see wide shoulders taper to a small waist, the angles and planes of his face hard and unyielding. As soon as her eyes met his—a deep, beautiful green—something within her sparked. It was such a strange, strong sensation, she momentarily lost her breath. But there was a funny look in his gaze in response. Embarrassed, she immediately looked down at the ground, taking cover beneath her fur hat.

Oh, but he was indeed handsome. And she allowed herself a private smile.

Chapter Two

February 1889

THE CARRIAGE CAME to an unexpected halt, sending Vivian tumbling to the floor with a yelp of surprise. The Marchioness of Litchfield—or merely "Anne" to Vivian—helped her back onto the seat as a roar of shouts surrounded them. The street became so thick with people that the man closest to their carriage door had his cheek pressed up against the glass. Vivian's eyes were wide at the sudden rabid activity, and she shot a look of distress in her brother's direction, hoping he would know what to do. But Bernard merely laughed to himself while staring out the window, paying her no mind.

"Guess they found out." Father shrugged.

Vivian swung her head in his direction. "That's it? *That's* your response? We shall be *crushed* out there!"

"It was like this when the Dowager Duchess of Hilbury died ten years ago, too. Just shove your way through. You might get a few elbows, though. One of her sons had his nose broken by a rogue elbow, if I recall."

Vivian exchanged a look with Anne, whose pale-blue eyes were wide with worry, before staring out the window to the sea of hats. "But why do they care?"

"We're from the aristocracy. People are naturally curious about us, I suppose. You can either fight it or embrace it, like Queen Victoria does."

"Oh, yes, the queen." Her voice filled with sarcastic admiration. "It's because of her I was stamped *ye olde spinster*." Vivian frowned at this and readjusted her feathered hat with a huff. Queen Victoria publicly disliked Vivian, thanks to the existence of Gran, and had gone as far as ignoring her debut and snubbing her for social events. Without uttering a word, the queen had told the aristocracy a marriage to Vivian would not be met with approval. Still, the fact her father was a duke and the family had money tempted some mamas into introducing their spare sons to Vivian. However, over time, all of those men had married other women.

Ever since, her fate had been sealed as a forgotten spinster.

Bernard finally turned his attention to them. Over the past few weeks, he had begun to look and act more like his old self. At his worst during Christmas, he'd appeared quite ill, with concave cheeks and dark circles under his eyes. Vivian had expressed concern, but he'd told her to quit her worrying. Today, to her relief, he looked the best he had in months. "I can almost see Gran cackling at the ruckus she caused. It's a fitting grand, final send-off."

Vivian couldn't help but smile wistfully. "Yes, she would have been happy to go out with a bang like this, wouldn't she?"

Father cleared his throat, capturing everyone's attention. They began to bob and sway a bit as the crowd shoved against the carriage. "Before we go in..." Father tried to brace himself against the velvet-cushioned wall. "I want to warn you that your grandmother has left nothing of her property to me at my request, though I'm not sure she ever intended to include me. I have more than enough for myself. Other than that, I have no idea how she divided it. And I want to make a polite request to not fight. Wills have the uncanny ability to split families apart."

Vivian frowned. "Fight? Really now, Father, I think we're better than that." She shot a look over to Bernard, who was positively blissful in the moment with a dreamy, vacant gaze. Of course, she knew why. Gran's estate would go to him. He was the male heir, after all, if Father was being excluded. She only hoped that if anything, Gran had left her the seaside cottage—the former duke and duchess's second summer home—and funds with which to run it. Vivian would be splendidly happy, perhaps even live there year-round. It would be nice to finally leave Father's home for her own after twenty-nine years.

"Ready?" Bernard placed his hand at the door, his gaze over his shoulder at the family. Vivian swallowed, and Anne quietly took her hand. They held on tightly to each other.

The door opened and as soon as Bernard emerged, the shouting increased, and questions were pelted at them with alarming speed.

Vivian had thought they were surrounded by spectators. Curious, nosy people. But the reality was worse: it was newspaper journalists who were closing in on them.

"What will you do with the dowager's fortune?" one journalist shouted at Father.

Father grumbled at them and pushed past. "It's not going to me. Now out of the way!"

Journalists within earshot furiously scribbled this response onto their notepads and turned to Bernard, the rest of the family at risk of being swallowed up by the crowd.

"How does it feel to be one of Britain's wealthiest men?" another called out to Bernard, pencil held up in the air.

While Bernard slowly made his way through, Vivian followed Father, with Anne close behind, holding her hat secure to her blonde head, lest someone knock it off. Never in Vivian's life had she felt so claustrophobic. Someone elbowed her ribs, causing her to yelp with pain, and she glanced back at Anne, who clung tightly, pale with fear. They really could get trampled to death in a crowd like this.

Another question was thrown to Bernard, who stopped with a gleaming smile to speak with the journalists and shake their hands above the crowd. Unlike Bernard, Vivian was not amused by this attention in the least. In fact, she wanted to give the journalists her own elbow. Their grandmother had passed away!

Had they no shame?

As they inched closer to Gran's large Dower House, Vivian felt a tug on her skirt. She looked over, then down, to find a boy shoving his way alongside her, a pencil and pad of paper at the ready. "Yeah, uh, do you think you'll be getting anything, Lady Vivian?" He looked up with hesitance, as if unsure he had identified her correctly.

"Are you a journalist? How old are you?"

"I'm a cub reporter, fourteen years!"

"You are *not* a day over twelve."

He gave her a guilty grin. The boy still had to grow into his big front teeth.

"Well, if I get a penny, I shall be lucky: unlike my grand-mother, who was an American and thus able to inherit from her father, English women don't inherit." She stumbled, but with so many people around, she was in no danger of falling anywhere.

The cub reporter scribbled her response down. "If you get the dowager's entire fortune, what will you do?"

Vivian laughed as another person bumped hard into her. "That won't happen."

"But what if it did?" His brown eyes rounded in a plea, like an adorable puppy eager for a treat. Vivian suspected this was by design. "Come on, give me a good answer. You could send my career to the moon!"

Vivian laughed again. "Very well. If I received the entire dowager estate, that would make me Britain's richest spinster. What does someone with such a claim do? I suppose read books and drink tea all by myself in this house."

The boy gave her a loud thanks, tapped the brim of his hat, and crouched down to escape through the gaps between peoples' legs.

By the time the Winthrops had reached the limestone house, the Metropolitan Police arrived to control the crowd. Journalists were directed to the house-side of the street, and spectators were forced to the side of Hyde Park. Gran's butler, Heaton, hastened them inside while a footman yanked the front door closed behind them, sealing the Winthrops off from the wild ruckus. Startled by the sudden change in activity, the family glanced around at each other, wide eyed and out of breath, their hats and clothing mussed and askew.

As if perturbed himself, Heaton rushed a hand over his receding hairline to smooth out any out-of-place fine hairs before leading them into the drawing room where Gran's solicitor was waiting. The solicitor Mr. Northcott, who had deeply creased frown lines at his mouth and no sign of smile lines at his eyes, looked more like an undertaker than a respected law professional. As Mr. Northcott rose to greet them, he lifted reading glasses from a table and secured them over his nose and ears. Greetings were quickly exchanged before they settled down to business matters. Bernard and Anne sat on one sofa, and Vivian took the sofa across from them. Father sat off to the side on his own.

The solicitor began reading over the legal documents and for a long while, it was rather dry. He listed off the contents of the estate, including the dower house and seaside cottage, then explained the full process of passing it on. Gran had left a heartfelt letter he read aloud, causing eyes and noses to be dabbed gently with handkerchiefs. And then, as the solicitor reached the end, he shocked Vivian.

He shocked all of them.

"'And,'" the solicitor continued reading, pointing one finger for effect, "'it is all to be left to my only granddaughter, Lady Vivian Winthrop.'" As this was the end of the reading of Gran's will, Mr. Northcott stopped and pushed the glasses back up his nose as he eyed the family.

They sat in a stunned silence.

Vivian blinked, sure she'd misheard. But the quiet calm was short-lived.

"Excuse me?" Bernard shot up to his feet, his face purple. "Can you repeat that last bit? I'm sure I didn't hear you correctly!"

The solicitor obliged, clearing his throat over and over, a nervous habit. Bernard stormed over to him, demanded to see for himself, then shot Vivian an angry look and skulked to the other side of the room.

"This is preposterous!" Bernard's hands raked angrily through his dark hair. He began walking vicious circles around the room while Anne remained silent, her head bowed with defeat. "Vivian gets the entire estate? The *entire estate?*" His voice cracked. "This house, the seaside cottage, *and* the fat bank accounts? How in the blazes did Gran have all of that? They're part of the ducal estate!"

"In fact, that is not true," Mr. Northcott said. "Your grandmother was an American, which provided her the ability to inherit from her own parents."

"Yes, we know that!"

"What you must not have realized is everything she had was in a trust fund. With her father's help, she bought the seaside cottage, as well as the Dower House, *before* she married your grandfather. Her bank accounts were also in the trust and located in Boston until her passing. The trust was not subject to English law, which meant only she had ownership of it and the former Duke of Chalworth could not touch it. This was all done purposely. I believe she called it..." Mr. Northcott thumbed through the papers before him, stopping when he found what he was looking for. "'Scoundrel insurance.'"

Everyone looked at Father, as he must have known about all of this, but he was reading a newspaper, ignoring the entire saga.

"But... But Vivian's a woman! In England!"

"More specifically, a spinster." The solicitor peered at Bernard over the rim of his glasses. "And because of that, she can *also* legally own and possess all of the above."

As Vivian listened to this exchange, she wanted to jump to her feet and shout back to Bernard. He already had a house, his own bank accounts, even a family! He was titled, and he would one day be the Duke of Chalworth as well. Bernard had everything and she quite literally had nothing. But she didn't speak up—because she couldn't. Bernard was the older of the two siblings, louder, much more self-assured. A man, while she was a woman. Second in every possible way.

"It's not fair!" Bernard pouted.

"You sound like a five-year-old," Vivian responded dryly. Sometimes, however, her mouth spoke before her mind could stop it.

He glared hard at her. "You would be upset, too, if a Mayfair home slipped through your fingers! I won't have one of those now until Father dies!"

"I *can* hear you, you know." Father said this without looking up from his newspaper. "And you only live one entire minute outside of Mayfair. You're hardly in the slums."

Bernard restarted his circling around the drawing room, mumbling and cursing to himself. Finally, without a further word to anyone, he stormed out of the room, out of the house, forgetting the salivating journalists out front. They surrounded him like the vultures they were and quickly deduced what had happened. It was impossible to misread Bernard's outrage.

As if hoping to lift the air a bit, Father chuckled. "That went well."

But Anne, whom Vivian had previously noted had frozen stiff, suddenly jumped up with a choked sob. Without uttering a word, Anne then sprinted out of the room, trailing after her husband. She had not uttered a single word during the entire saga.

Mr. Northcott cleared his throat, bringing Vivian's attention back to the task at hand. He held out a fountain pen. "Anyway, Lady Vivian, could you please sign here and here?"

BECAUSE VIVIAN WAS a spinster, moving out of Father's home and into her own was hardly anything at all. The few dresses she had were wrapped in tissue paper and packed in a trunk, her toiletries secured in a box, and she was moved and fully settled in the day after the will reading.

Upon her arrival, Heaton opened the front door. As Vivian walked in, she clutched her handbag tightly against her chest as footmen moved her belongings past her and looked up at the enormous size of the place with wonder, as if she had never been there before when in fact, she had been there countless times.

But now, it was hers.

"Welcome home, Lady Vivian." Heaton shut the door behind her. The carpeting felt extra plush beneath her feet, and she followed the butler as he took her on a tour and introduced the entire staff, though Vivian was well aware of everything already. But he was solidifying her station, reminding the staff—and Vivian as well—that she was no longer the quiet little mouse who came by for tea on occasion, but the mistress of the home. It was such a small gesture, yet so thoughtful, Vivian immediately warmed up to the butler she had always thought so stoic.

Heaton's tour ended in the drawing room, where he left her to her own devices. Vivian glanced around the opulent, pistachio-green room. A large, marble fireplace with carved vines and floral motifs had a warm fire already lit inside of it. Oil paintings, which had been collected by her late grandfather many years ago, dotted the room with misty hunting scenes of the countryside. Her eyes hovered over the sofa, where she'd received the life-changing news yesterday, but that was not where she intended to go.

There was a chair near the window. She grabbed a book from the bookshelf—*Little Women* by Louisa May Alcott, a favorite of Gran's—and settled in as tea was brought in.

Yes, this is rather nice, Vivian thought to herself with a smile. *I absolutely could spend the rest of my life doing exactly this every single day.*

However, while Vivian quite enjoyed her solitude, just a few hours into her new life, Heaton walked in carrying a silver tray filled with calling cards.

As she had not seen any meant for her for so long, Vivian was a bit in disbelief about the sudden appearance of so many cards. She picked one up, the front of it an illustration of an ungloved hand holding a rose, a gentleman's name printed on the back. "What is all of this?" she asked after reading through a few, recognizing some names from her debutante days but unable to recall faces.

"Gentlemen callers, for Lady Vivian Winthrop," Heaton responded properly. "Those I allowed entry, anyway. Many more tried to pass through without a card. I assumed you would not associate with someone who didn't use calling cards." He sniffed at the idea.

Vivian gave him a questioning look. "But I didn't ask them to visit me."

"They are here to make your acquaintance."

"Because I moved in?"

He nodded, but something lay beneath the slight hesitance in the action.

"Heaton." Vivian took a patient breath. This was all new to both of them. "Please be forthright with me. Why are they here?"

Heaton looked directly into her face, a bit more casual in his stance. "Lady Vivian, you've been named *Britain's richest spinster* thanks to your American grandmother's money. These gentlemen are here with hopes of marrying you."

"*Marrying* me!" Vivian's eyes widened. "All of them?"

"All of them."

Vivian had had some gentlemen callers when she'd been a debutante. But now, she had a whole mess of them. Curious, and a bit in disbelief, she stood and hurried out into the hallway, Heaton trying his best to keep up. As she approached the receiving room, she could hear loud conversation spilling out past the closed doors. But as soon as she opened them and stepped inside, the room cut to silence and the dense crowd of men turned to stare at her. Bewildered, she froze and stared back. That is, until they began to shout like the journalists did, waving their arms in the air, no doubt hoping to capture her attention from the others.

"Lady Vivian! Our fathers are acquainted!"

"Lady Vivian, I played cricket with your brother!"

Lady Vivian! Lady Vivian! Lady Vivian!

Terrified, Vivian spun around and ran out of the room, her skirts billowing behind her—and the men actually chased after her! The poor woman sprinted as fast as she could down her hallway until she dove into the library, locked the door behind her, and pressed up against the wall as the stampede roared past. Heaton and the footmen began shouting above the noise trying to wrangle in the frenzied men like sheep dogs with a rowdy flock, yelling that Lady Vivian was not feeling well today and the gentlemen would have to call on her another time.

About ten minutes later, the house was awash in silence once again.

There was a knock on the library door and Vivian opened it to find Heaton. "Well..." He brushed off his sleeves with a stiff hand. "That was certainly something I've never experienced before. What shall I do with the calling cards?"

Vivian exited the library and looked along the hallway, worried a stray man could still be lurking. "Put them to the side somewhere. I don't want to look at them right now."

"Very well." He gave a small bow.

But her mind trailed back to the troubling words Heaton had said moments ago. "You said I'm being called *Britain's richest spinster*. Where did you hear that?"

"The newspapers, my lady."

Feeling dread, she recalled the brief encounter with the cub reporter. "Do you still have them? I would like to see, if so."

He confirmed he did and would be back with them in a moment. Vivian returned to the drawing room and pulled the sheer curtains aside for a clear view of the street. It was filled with carriages caught up in traffic by the departure of her chasers, as if she'd been holding a big, extravagant ball.

A rustle of paper caught her attention and she turned to find Heaton laying out an armful of newspapers on the table. Vivian went over to his side and gasped at what she saw. Somehow, her portrait was on the front page of several different newspapers, with headlines ranging from "Unmarried Daughter of a Duke Moves into Mayfair Home" to "Come and Get Her, Lads! Britain's Richest Spinster Ready for the Taking!"

"How vulgar!" Vivian pressed a hand to her heart.

Heaton folded his hands behind his back, his face remaining stoic. "Quite."

"What am I going to do about this?" she asked no one in particular, knowing there was no easy answer. "Any further visitors today, Heaton, please continue to tell them I'm ill."

He nodded once. "And what of tomorrow?"

"Tomorrow? You mean you think they'll be back?" The thought sent a chill through her.

"It's the season, Lady Vivian. This is what your life will be like for the foreseeable future. I'm sorry to say."

"Oh, blast." Vivian immediately covered her mouth and apologized.

But Heaton merely chuckled. "I've heard worse from your grandmother, and I worked for both her and your grandfather for many years. You don't need to worry about propriety around me."

Vivian let out a long breath. It was true; her grandparents had been known for being a bit rough around the edges, which was another reason why Queen Victoria wasn't very fond of the family. "Thank goodness. But yes, I need to figure out what to do about this. Frankly, I was expecting to spend the next few weeks relishing in my newfound independence, not chasing men off my property. I must be the only woman in human history to make such a complaint. Most unmarried women would find some shred of happiness or excitement in such a thing. Wouldn't they?"

Heaton, of course, had no response for this, as he was a butler, not a resource for romantic advice. She began pacing around the room, not unlike Bernard the day prior. Marriage would be stifling. A man dictating how she should spend her day? Expecting her to entertain the wives of the aristocracy? *She*! Throw dinner parties! The thought was laughable. And it caused her to shudder.

"I don't want to be married." Vivian lifted one of the newspapers, eyed the headline, then tossed it back down. "Especially not now. What would I get out of it? What could a woman my age possibly get out of being married now that I have my own home and assets? I can't very well climb much higher on the social ladder, either—not that I'm interested in that, anyway."

"Do you not wish for love, Lady Vivian? A family?" Heaton asked.

Vivian paused, her eyes trailing over to the crackling fireplace. How many times had she secretly cried in bed, staring at the fire that kept her warm, wishing she had a husband to snuggle up against instead? She pushed the thought away. "Everyone wants love, Heaton. But you know as well as I do, that's not something in the cards for a person such as myself."

He turned his eyes to the floor and didn't respond.

But it was the ugly truth of the aristocracy. Women and men didn't marry for love. They married to increase fortunes, to increase prestige. Perhaps some were lucky and truly loved their spouse, and a few times a century, there was a love match. But she was more likely to be struck by lightning than find love. To make matters, worse aristocratic men, whether married or not, were often scoundrels. And that was the rule, not the exception.

Aristocratic men had little to worry about in their lives. While their wives grew babies and upheld the household, the men were free to do as they pleased. Everyone, for example, had praised Prince Albert for being a doting, loving husband to Queen Victoria when he'd been alive. But Vivian had heard little snippets over the years that made her question their façade of perfection. Victoria had borne nine children, one after the other, and suffered greatly after each pregnancy with consuming melancholy and even hallucinations. There were rumors where, after child seven, the queen had begged Albert to let her stop having children, yet she'd gone on to have two more.

Vivian had lukewarm feelings toward the queen, but she didn't like women being taken advantage of by men, no matter who they were. Sometimes she wondered if Prince Albert had wanted so many children partly to keep Queen Victoria busy with a litter of them, thus out of his way to do whatever he wished.

It seemed plausible.

The thought of living like that made Vivian want to retch.

But as Heaton had predicted, the attention Vivian attracted didn't go away. Each day, she was "ill," yet each day, men descended upon her receiving room. And each day, Vivian asked Heaton to put their calling cards to the side, never to look at them.

One day, the solicitor reappeared unexpectedly. His was the first visit Vivian accepted.

Heaton led Mr. Northcott into the drawing room and left them to talk.

"Lady Vivian." Gran's solicitor, still as spirited as an undertaker, gave her a tight nod as she directed him to sit in a nearby chair. "It's nice to see you again. How was your first week here?"

"The house is infested and I'm looking to hire a rat catcher." Vivian ensured her voice conveyed vague irritation.

Mr. Northcott stared at her with horror.

"The men. It's a joke." She shook her head. "Never mind. What can I help you with today?"

Vivian noted he seemed nervous, frequently clearing his throat as he had last week. "I have a letter for you, from your grandmother," he said, lifting a sealed envelope to her in offering.

She took it with apprehension and gazed down at the blank envelope face before opening it.

Dearest Vivian,

Congratulations, my dear, you are now the wealthiest spinster in the country. Your daft brother is a gambling addict, and I didn't want his grubby paws on my money. And besides, you know I prefer you, anyway. You and I, we're two of a kind, two perfect diamonds in a pile of rubbish. That is precisely why I must do what I am about to. You will be angry with me, but you will one day forgive me, too.

*Now that my property and family fortune is legally yours, you have one year to marry for love or your inheritance will be relinquished to your brother. Yes, you will in fact lose the house, not to mention the seaside cottage, and will have to move back in with your father for the rest of time. Do be a good girl and find your crown jewel amongst the enormous pile of dog—*the following word was smudged, but Vivian had an inkling of what it was—*out there, because I am confident he exists, and you deserve a lifetime of love. Perhaps lighting a fire under your bottom will finally get you moving.*

Your grandfather and mother say hello, *probably.*

Hugs and kisses,
Granny

P.S. – Tell Victoria I'm watching her, ha ha!

Vivian stared down at the letter, her mouth dropped open and unable to form words. She could hear the woman's haughty voice as she'd read the letter, she could even envision Gran smoking from her long cigarette holder and blowing out smoke as she said *bottom*. There was no doubt Gran had genuinely written this. But it was also the most absurd demand Vivian had ever heard in her life.

"She…" Vivian couldn't continue.

"Yes, she did write that. May I?" The solicitor gently took the letter out of her hand and stuffed it back in its envelope before setting it to the side. "And yes, it's real. And before you ask, yes, it is enforceable. You can, of course, refuse to comply and lose everything now. That is a realistic option."

Vivian let out a long breath. Gran had been right—she was angry. Absolutely livid. "No, I don't wish to refuse to comply. But marry for love in one year? Was the woman mad? I haven't been able to find it in ten!"

"You know your grandmother."

Vivian could already see the life she'd envisioned melting away before her eyes. No more solitude. No more spending afternoons alone reading for as long as she liked. No more peace and quiet, for a noisy man would now be interrupting it all! "Yes. The answer is yes, she was mad. My goodness, even from the grave, she's going to ruin my life!"

The solicitor cleared his throat again, evidently eager to leave.

"Any other surprises I should know about?" Vivian narrowed her eyes as she stood up and began to lead him to the door.

"No." Mr. Northcott opened the drawing room door for her. "But I was specifically told to wait some time before giving you this letter. I had no choice. I apologize." It appeared to be a genuine apology, but it didn't make Vivian feel any better about the ridiculous situation.

"But why wait?"

"Partly to keep Lord Litchfield's influence out of your ear. She supposed, probably correctly, he would attempt to convince you into giving up without trying. But also, she wished to surprise you." The solicitor uncharacteristically bobbed on his feet.

Vivian couldn't help but laugh at this. Surprise? Surprise, indeed. But she knew Gran well enough to know another truth: Gran had wanted Vivian to get a taste of life with the inheritance so when it was threatened to be taken away, she would comply with Gran's demand.

Gran had clearly underestimated how many men would be pestering Vivian day in and day out. Thus far, the inheritance had added quite a bit of difficulty to daily life. Then again, it wouldn't be forever. But what she would do about the wretched husband bit remained to be seen.

She would figure it out.

Hopefully.

After the solicitor had bidden her good luck and goodbye, he ended with the advice that she keep Gran's one-year countdown concealed from her family. As Vivian didn't need their meddling in this situation, she wholeheartedly agreed and watched him leave, realizing how defeated she was in the moment. She already knew she would never find someone. One year from this moment, she would be packing up her belongings once again to return to Father's.

Vivian spent the rest of the day obsessing over the letter and worrying about her future. So, when Bernard showed up that night unannounced, requesting she not speak to him until dressed for the evening herself, Vivian complied purely out of curiosity. Her former lady's maid had gone on to work for a new family, thus Vivian had had Gran's lady's maid, Norris, stay on. Norris had an appreciation for color, Vivian had discovered, and dressed her in a lavender, silk gown with a deep, heart-shaped neckline, and elbow-length white gloves. Anticipation palpitated through her at the surprise.

As she entered the drawing room in her eveningwear, Bernard approached her looking smart in a dinner suit. "You drink whiskey, right?"

"Yes." Vivian came to a stop before her brother. She had yet to speak to Bernard since he'd stormed out of the house after the will reading. And Bernard had never before invited her to go out for the evening. She was happy to see he appeared to be reconciling with her. "Why?"

Bernard smiled wide. "I'll buy a round. Anne told me about your gentlemen chasers this week, and I thought perhaps you could go for a night at a wild pub, with whiskey, and fighting, and general debauchery. And all of that, of course, with zero expectations on propriety."

"My goodness, Bernard." Vivian looped her arm with his. He couldn't have arrived with a more appealing evening plan. "It's as if Gran herself sent you here."

✦

Chapter Three

DANTES MADE HIS rounds around The Harp & Thistle a few times each night. It was good to keep abreast of the general air of the pub, make sure there weren't any intense situations brewing, though that almost never happened. The Harp & Thistle always had a jovial atmosphere despite the mix of social classes. The pub sat on the razor-sharp edge between the upper classes and the slums, just like the McNab brothers themselves, and there was always something going on. Most of the time, though, the word of the day was useless gossip. Tonight, for example, everyone was abuzz about a spinster who'd inherited a Mayfair mansion. Something he could not give a single care about.

"Dantes!" One of their regulars, Billy, shouted over the loud noise and waved him over. As Billy was seated at the bar, and Dantes was about to head that way anyway, he followed the call.

As he squeezed through the crowd, Dantes crossed paths with a woman who, upon seeing his face, went wide eyed and pale, stammered an apology, and hurried the other direction while nearly dropping her pint in the process. Another patron, who'd witnessed the woman's severe reaction, looked up to see the cause, finding Dantes there. Fear immediately flickered in the man's face. Dantes scowled and continued on his path to the bar.

Billy, his cheeks and nose rosy red from the drink, gave Dantes a hearty pat on the shoulder. "Dantes, you'll win the fight for me tonight? I've got a lot riding on your name."

"Of course I'm winning tonight." There was no amusement in Dantes's voice.

"Jack here, he's betting against me." Billy nudged the man wearing a tilted bowler's hat seated next to him.

In response, Jack grinned from ear to ear, quite confident in his foolish bet. "Sullivan is bigger than you, Dantes." It was a claim anyone under Sullivan's shocking six foot, eight inches could make, even the McNabs. "And he's ten years younger, too."

Fair enough. But despite Jack's outward confidence, Dantes spotted the flash of doubt in the man's eyes as he studied Dantes's face.

Dantes shrugged. He was going to win—it was as simple as that. But he had to excuse himself as a form equally as menacing as Dantes stared him down. Dantes met his brother's irritated eye and slipped around the bar to see what grievance was on his mind this time. Despite the fact that his brother was the same size and nearly the same build as Dantes, the ever-present dark aura around him was intimidating. The perpetual scowl, the perfectly styled raven hair, the rigid spine. It always felt the man were on the verge of snapping, but he never did.

"Crowded tonight." Victor filled a pint until the frothy head rose to the rim. When he looked up, his green eyes, which matched Dantes's, were filled with contempt. "Everyone's itching to see you get knocked out. Including me." It wasn't a joke, but it made Dantes laugh, anyway. He didn't lose fights. Not now, not ten years ago. And it didn't matter how big the fighter was—it just made them fall harder.

Victor pulled another glass over to fill. "You hear about the spinster? It's all I've been hearing about this week."

"No." This wasn't true. However, Dantes didn't care about something so trivial and would much rather hear stories about his old school chums falling off their pedestals.

"They're calling her *Britain's richest spinster*. An aristocrat discard who inherited her American grandmother's estate. She's a Winthrop; her grandmother was the dowager duchess."

Admittedly, that got Dantes's attention. In the unending gossip about the spinster, he hadn't heard a family name mentioned until now. "Winthrop?" Dantes frowned, recognizing it.

Victor turned for a moment to slide the pints in front of two patrons, then wiped his hands on his apron. Victor was the oldest of the three brothers, and in this moment, Dantes noted the fine lines now permanent around Victor's eyes. He tried ignoring this, knowing he wasn't far behind.

"You think she's related to Bernard Winthrop?" Victor asked.

"Has to be." Dantes took a coin from another patron ordering pints and quickly filled them. "Maybe he can finally pay his debt." Bernard Winthrop, the Marquess of Litchfield, was another regular of theirs, or at least he used to be. The idiot had stopped coming by months earlier when he'd made a large wager with Dantes, lost, and couldn't pay up. Dantes didn't need the money; it was the principal of it. He would have forgotten about it if it were almost anyone else. Like Billy, for example, or even Jack, whom he barely knew. Those lads were all right. But Winthrop was everything Dantes hated about the aristocracy. Arrogant, pretentious—as if the world existed merely to serve him.

So when Winthrop walked into The Harp & Thistle moments later, Dantes was sure he was hallucinating.

"Speak of the devil." Victor's voice held as much surprise as Dantes felt in the moment. "And the cad came with a woman. You think that's his wife?"

Dantes stilled at the mention of a woman with Winthrop. The night Winthrop had made his foolish bet, a woman had come by with Winthrop's father to retrieve the idiot when he couldn't pay for his tab. Dantes had never found out who she was, but for weeks, he'd wondered about her, thought about her voice, that brief flash of her heart-shaped face before she'd looked away. He hadn't gotten a good enough look at her that night and had eventually stopped wondering about her. She had clearly not been of his ilk and would never give him the time of day.

Regardless, he tried to get a good look at the woman in the purple dress but couldn't see well, not in this crowd. "Winthrop would never bring his wife here." Dantes was certain of this. "Perhaps it's a mistress."

"Oi!" A voice caused the pair to turn and see the youngest McNab, Ollie. Unlike Victor, and even Dantes himself if he were being honest, Ollie always seemed to be smiling. He was several inches shorter than them as well, and as much as their family had tried, Ollie could not shed the heavy Cockney accent he'd acquired as a child. "The crowd is getting antsy," Ollie said. "When are we starting?"

A buxom woman clinging to Ollie's side giggled into his ear as she twirled a lock of his brown hair around a finger. Ollie was also by far the favorite of women. No matter their class.

"Half hour. I have to take care of something first," Dantes responded darkly. He turned to watch Winthrop weave his way over to the bar. Dantes grabbed a washed glass to dry off, needing to occupy his hands.

Ollie shot a questioning look to Victor, but as soon as Victor mentioned Winthrop, Ollie slipped away with his woman, clearly wanting nothing to do with the cad, either.

"Evening, lads." Winthrop took a seat at the bar right in front of them.

And so did the woman in the purple dress.

Winthrop introduced the McNabs to his companion using their surname only and didn't reveal who she was. And while Victor and Winthrop began chatting—Winthrop ordered two whiskeys—Dantes studied Winthrop's companion. She was dark haired like Winthrop, unusually fair in complexion like him, too. And she had dark eyes—so dark, they were almost black. But of course, no one had black irises. He wanted to know what color they really were, and who she was to Winthrop.

What struck Dantes most, though, was how she merely

looked at him the way she merely looked at Victor. As if Dantes were just another forgettable face blending into a crowd. There was no hesitating fear to hurriedly cover up, not even a vague sense of disgust.

It was peculiar, and his interest in this unusual woman began to grow.

Oh, he knew she saw the scar. It was impossible to miss. It started right past his hairline and went across his forehead, split over his left eyebrow, and went down his cheek, stopping at his jaw. It was deep and ugly and took up half of his face.

But this woman may as well have been looking at an eyebrow or a nose the way she glanced at it as if it weren't anything of note.

This had to be her. This had to be the woman he'd found in the shadows.

Who was she?

"Dantes, did you hear me?" Victor interrupted his thoughts. "You're by the whiskey."

Without further hesitation, Dantes poured out two neat whiskeys for Winthrop and his companion, sliding them across the bartop. Victor caught his eye as he did this, holding his gaze with warning.

"Dantes." The woman had finally spoken. Her voice was smoky. "That's an interesting name for someone with Scottish heritage. Is it as in, *Dante's Inferno*, perhaps?" She lifted her glass and gently swirled the contents. A lady nob who was comfortable drinking whiskey. Interesting.

Dantes looked her directly in the eye. Was she insulting him? Or making conversation?

"No. My name is Edmond." He intentionally said this to anyone asking about his nickname to see how they would react. Most of the time they paused, confused, wondering if they were supposed to call him "Dantes" or "Edmond." Or perhaps thought they had heard him wrong. Rarely, someone would figure it out after a long moment.

But to his pleasant surprise, she knew immediately. "I enjoy that book, *The Count of Monte Cristo*. Dumas is always a thrill."

Dantes actually smiled at that. Victor coughed.

"I'm curious to know why you received that nickname, Mr. McNab." She took a sip from her glass.

"Perhaps I'll share the story with you some day." Dantes held a protective blank face to give nothing away. But inside, his heart was pounding.

Winthrop, his conversation with Victor over, jumped in to finally introduce his companion. "This is my sister." He glanced between the McNabs. "Lady Vivian Winthrop."

She followed this up with a polite *hello*.

"Lady Vivian." Dantes repeated her name, sharp on his lips yet somehow like silk on his tongue. Unable to help himself, he gave her a quick once-over, though when his eyes came to her lips his attention lingered there. Her lips were full, pink, lush. In the shape of a heart. He imagined her eating a strawberry and enjoyed that they twitched under his gaze.

"Do you always look at women like that?" Lady Vivian asked, causing his eyes to finally lift to hers.

"No." He watched with pleasure as her cheeks flushed in response and gave him the tiniest flicker of a smile. But that was surely his imagination.

Winthrop jumped in, evidently realizing what was going on and no doubt eager to end the moment. He slapped both palms on the bartop, the sudden noise breaking the spell. "I came here tonight to make a wager. On the fight."

"You owe me plenty already, Winthrop." Dantes now had his full attention on the marquess. "I'm surprised you had the gall to show up tonight, to be honest."

Lady Vivian gasped, but it didn't seem to be at his language or refusal to call Winthrop by his titled name. She spun to her brother. "Is that why you brought me here? To use me as an excuse to go out so Anne doesn't know you're gambling?"

Winthrop leaned into her ear and said something low. "It

won't get to that, though," he promised with confidence, patting her arm dismissively before returning his attention back to Dantes. The smugness on Winthrop's face confirmed Dantes's suspicion: the cad expected his sister to pay off his debt. Lady Vivian, however, was clearly trying her best to not be upset by this. In fact, she looked ready to leave.

But selfishly, Dantes didn't want her to leave. Not yet, anyway. "All right, Winthrop." He met the man's eye. "One final wager, for the amount you owe me. If you win, you owe me nothing. If you lose, you owe me double. You're sure you want to do that?"

Winthrop grinned easily. "Of course. That's a foolproof way of canceling my debt. Sullivan is larger and heavier than you, McNab. And younger. You don't stand a chance."

"I won't lose." He never did.

"Lord Litchfield." Even Victor clearly didn't like it. "You can't be serious."

"Oh, I'm serious," Winthrop shot back before he took a swig of the whiskey.

"Can you even pay for that?" Victor motioned to the glass.

Winthrop reddened. "Of course I can pay for the drink!"

Dantes had his doubts. And it seemed like Lady Vivian did, too, based on the skeptical look on her face. Was Lady Vivian the Winthrop spinster who had the whole city talking? Perhaps it was another sister, or a cousin?

No.

Dantes didn't need to ask to know it was her. It was the sole reason Winthrop had brought her here. Now that she was swimming in money, Winthrop's debt was pennies to her. And as Dantes watched the pompous cad laugh over some inane story he told, Dantes decided he wouldn't accept Lady Vivian's money. He wasn't going to take advantage of her, even if her own flesh and blood would. Even Dantes possessed a small shred of decency.

"Have you ever watched a fight before?" Dantes turned the

question to Lady Vivian, though he could hazard a guess. Society women didn't go to fights, even the women society had forgotten about.

"No." Lifting her glass to take a drink, she didn't flinch at the burn. She set the glass back down. "I don't usually go to pubs, either, but Bernard knew I've had a taxing week and thought I would enjoy a night out. I didn't realize there were ulterior motives to the outing." She shot her brother a glare. He pretended not to notice.

"Would you like to watch right up front of the ring?" Dantes took a risk and looked at Victor, who lifted his eyebrows sky high at this.

But it seemed to pique her interest and she turned to Winthrop, as if asking if he wished to go, too.

"No Winthrop, though. Just you, Lady Vivian," Dantes added, eliciting a deep frown from Winthrop.

Lady Vivian seemed to notice how much her brother disliked this and gave Dantes a smug smile. "I would love to, Mr. McNab, thank you."

When it was time for Dantes and Sullivan to head down, Dantes led Lady Vivian along. Out of what to be habit for a proper lady, she placed her gloved hand in the crook of his left arm. It wasn't the kind of casual contact he was accustomed to, and it made him far too aware of her presence.

The crowd wasn't allowed through yet, so it was much quieter downstairs than up in the pub. He led her to his corner of the ring, where a towel and water already waited. He took a few deep gulps of water and noticed Lady Vivian eyeing Sullivan with evident trepidation, though he understood why. Sullivan wasn't called "the Irish Goliath" for no reason.

"How violent do these fights get?" Lady Vivian asked quietly, still studying his opponent. Unable to help himself, Dantes took the moment to admire the deep neckline of her dress. Why women wore clothing up to their jaws by day, only to reveal themselves by night, he could never understand. In this moment, though, he was glad to be on the evening side of fashion.

"Well, they're fights." He looked back up to her face just as she turned around. "And we don't use gloves."

Her mouth opened slightly in surprise. "Is that safe?"

He grinned. "Nope."

"Why do you do it, then?"

He shrugged, leaning back against the ring. "It's exciting."

"But doesn't it hurt?"

"Yes. It's not too bad, as long as you don't get pommeled flat, which I don't plan on doing."

Lady Vivian looked past him again to where Sullivan was warming up. Her eyes looked back and forth between the two men, only to land on Sullivan with a swallow. Dantes couldn't wait to prove her doubt wrong and see the look on her face when he did.

Dantes stepped over to a nearby bench, unbuttoned his waistcoat to remove it, and set it down on the seat. He didn't have a jacket, not in a hot, crowded pub. "You're the woman from the newspapers, aren't you? The one all those articles have been written about?" he asked as he began to unbutton the white shirt, noting with humor she looked away as she realized he was undressing in front of her. Her eyes forced their way up to his.

"Yes, I'm sorry to say." Her voice was strained.

"Why 'sorry'?"

"Because it's been nothing but a nightmare. I prefer solitude. Quiet. And my house has been flooded with greedy men."

He didn't like the sound of that. But he knew the nobs would think it grand. "Isn't that a good thing for an unmarried woman?"

"It's supposed to be, but I was stamped a spinster years ago and I don't care to give it up now." This was topped with a sigh of defeat.

Slipping his shirt off, he turned to toss it on top of the waistcoat. As he turned back, he caught her staring at him. He felt like a king in the moment. "I can understand that," he said, and her eyes flying back up to his. "I don't care to marry either. My life is this place. When I go home I don't want to hear a sound or see another soul."

She smiled gently. "Exactly. Unfortunately, now I have no choice but to marry."

"Why?"

"In order to keep the inheritance, I have to marry within a year. For love. I haven't been able to find that in almost ten years. I won't find it now."

Interesting. "Can't you marry anyone?"

She considered this. "Perhaps, but if I'm being forced to marry, I don't want to just marry anyone. Maybe it's silly, but even now, I hold hope someday I could fall in love." She glanced around the large, empty room. "This is a rather strange conversation for the setting, isn't it?"

Dantes laughed. He barely knew the woman, but from what he had seen, she was much more agreeable than her brother. If she held the same pompousness, he hadn't seen it. "Your brother, the marquess, he isn't a favorite of ours. But I like you, Lady Vivian."

All she said was, "Hmm."

Maybe he was laying it on too thick. "What happens if you don't get married?"

"My brother gets the inheritance instead. I would then have to move back in with my father. Don't get me wrong, I love my father, but..." She trailed off, not wanting to say the truth out loud.

"You want your own space. I get it."

"Precisely. I've never had it before, and I don't wish to lose it now. I suppose I could find a hermit to marry if I must. That way, we don't have to see each other." That seemed like the perfect solution to him, but what did he know?

Ollie shouted down the stairway that the crowd would be let through soon. Dantes confirmed he'd heard and began unbuttoning his trousers, slipping them down to the floor to step out of, not thinking.

Lady Vivian gasped and stepped back. "Excuse me, but what are you doing?!"

Dantes tossed the trousers over to the bench, embarrassed by her severe reaction. "I'm not fighting in a shirt and trousers. These are boxing shorts. I'm not jumping out naked in front of you."

She turned scarlet red and began looking around the room, clearly wanting to change the subject. "I'm assuming this is your pub? Do you own it alone?"

"No, with my brothers. You met Victor upstairs already, and my other brother, Oliver—we call him 'Ollie'—he's usually floating around somewhere and not behind the bar."

"I only have Bernard. Well, and my father, too. My mother unfortunately passed when I was a baby and Father never remarried. That's partly why I never married, I think. I didn't have a mother to help me with all of that when I made my debut. My grandmother did her best, but she was often perplexed by English society rules and directed me to do things acceptable in America but not here. Like, tell jokes. English noblemen do not like witty women, I quickly learned."

Considering the nobs he knew, he was not surprised by this bit. "What was it like, being raised by only your father?"

Lady Vivian took a moment to consider the question. "He was rather hands-off, letting nannies and governesses raise us while he hid from the world managing the estate. Then of course, my brother was sent to boarding school and wasn't around most of the time. My friends' fathers acted similarly but would still be present for many evenings as well as parties. Mine, meanwhile, was simply never home."

Dantes wasn't going to say this, but he remembered, before Ollie had been around, the long work hours his own father had put in and how much he and Victor had disliked it.

She continued. "Bernard and I once got into trouble because we stole from a toy store. It was nothing big—a small, wooden duck that fit in my palm. When our nanny realized what we had done, she pulled us by our ears up to his office, where he locked himself in the rare event he was home. Father politely told us not to do it again and gave the toy store a check for I'm sure was an exorbitant amount. That Christmas was the wealthiest Christmas we ever had, which is saying something."

"He solved problems with money," Dantes observed aloud.

Lady Vivian nodded. "We're much closer now. He's a good person with a tender heart, at least toward Bernard and me, but he still doesn't know how to solve problems that involve us." This ended with a light laugh.

Dantes held her gaze, feeling unsettled. "It was because of grief, wasn't it? He was drowning in grief."

She swallowed. "Yes."

"I immediately recognized it. My own mother died too, though when I was eight."

"Oh, I'm so sorry to hear that." Lady Vivian's voice and downturned expression seemed genuine in their regret for him, which was oddly refreshing. Dantes rarely shared this history with people because when he did, they always forced fake pity. Of course, he wasn't going to mention that his father was long dead too—it would only make this entire conversation far more personal and depressing. And yet something about her made him want to keep talking.

"Thank you." Dantes turned his gaze out over the large, empty room. While there were benches up front for their best guests—usually high-stakes gamblers, but occasionally, as in Lady Vivian's case, someone invited to the front—the room was mostly empty, concrete floor.

"What happened with your mother, if you don't mind me asking?" Immediately, he regretted the question. While he did want to know about Lady Vivian's mother since they shared that loss, she would likely want to know about his and he didn't want to tell her. It had taken many years for him to accept what had happened and to not be angry with his mother. Now, instead of anger, he felt strangely protective of her memory. People judged her on who she'd been the last few years of her life, as if she hadn't existed before then.

"No, I don't mind you asking." Lady Vivian clasped her hands together in front of her. "My mother perished of influenza when I was only a few months old." Her voice lowered to a whisper. "What about your mother?"

Frantically, he tried to figure out what to say and blurted out the half-truth, "Childbirth," before turning to his water. He took a long gulp, keeping his back toward her.

Lady Vivian was quiet, perhaps sensing something was being left out. But she passed over the moment, to his abject relief. "When I was a child, and after my nanny tucked me in for bed, I would stay up for hours daydreaming about a life with my mother in it. You know, her crouching down and buckling my shiny, black shoes. Walking me around the garden and showing me the different flowers. Taking me to her friends' tea parties." Dantes turned back around to find her smiling up at him. "I had quite the imagination."

It felt as if she could see into him. "I did the same thing," Dantes replied, feeling a kinship with this woman now. "But it was more going to football matches, not looking at flowers." And to his absolute surprise, he kind of, sort of, smiled.

And Lady Vivian's small smile became large and genuine, a beam of light, causing something within him to stir.

Dantes scratched his eyebrow. "My brothers and I were mostly raised by our grandparents. Really, I should say boarding schools. Believe it or not, you and I may have met during one of the seasons. What year was your debut?"

She blinked with surprise. "1878. But we didn't. I don't understand—how were you involved in any seasons? You're not from the nobility. I would have remembered you."

He ignored her question. "Why, because of this?" Pushing away the humiliation that wanted to rise, he pointed at the deep scar on his face.

"No." Lady Vivian watched where he pointed but didn't

elaborate.

"Hmm." Dantes lowered his eyelids halfway, winning another grin from her.

The sound of the crowd began to echo down the large stairway. They were still roped back at the top but being corralled to head down. Dantes needed to start warming up. "You know, Lady Vivian, your brother is going to be one thousand pounds in debt after tonight."

She looked at the ground. "That's why he brought me here. Well, I know that now, at least. I was surprised he wanted to spend time with me tonight, but he didn't really, did he?" She began to wring her hands together. "I'm sorry. I'm still emotional over losing my grandmother. Bernard doing this is hitting me when I'm still raw. Normally, I could give a rat's bottom what he does." She stiffened. "Goodness, I don't even know you. I shouldn't be burdening you with all of this silly stuff!"

"You're not burdening me." He meant it. "And it's not silly, either."

She studied him, as if a bit skeptical, but it was true. He liked talking to her, wished he could hear more. But unfortunately, he couldn't. "I do have to go now." He gripped the rope behind him. "But I know Winthrop expects you to cover his debt, and I won't accept your money. I don't care how much money you have—I'm not going to take it. I'll only accept payment from the marquess himself."

Lady Vivian's mouth opened ever so slightly, but she didn't argue.

He let go of the rope. "I hope you'll stay to watch the whole fight, but I won't be able to talk to you after. It gets too wild. Make sure to find your brother, get home safe, all right?"

She nodded. "Good luck tonight, Mr. McNab."

He gave her a crooked smile, but then his big mouth opened before his brain could stop it. "You know, it's customary for a fighter to get a good-luck kiss before a fight." It was, of course, rubbish. He had never asked for a good-luck kiss before. Had never heard of one of the other lads ask for one, either. Some of them maybe had a good-luck shot of whiskey beforehand, but that was it.

Unexpectedly, though, instead of a face twisted in offense, Lady Vivian gave him a grin of mischief. "Perhaps Mr. Sullivan would be up for your good-luck kiss."

"Let's find out."

"Oh, wait. I wasn't—"

"Sullivan!" Dantes shouted out over his shoulder. "How about a good-luck kiss before the fight?"

"Feck off, Dantes." The barrel-shaped man didn't even miss a beat.

Dantes couldn't help but laugh, but when he turned back to say goodbye to Lady Vivian for the final time, he found her staring up at him with wide eyes and fidgeting hands. Almost as if she *wanted* to kiss him? But there was absolutely no way he was going to try that. A woman like her would never want anything to do with him and the face he possessed, and surely, she would slap him for it. Which he would deserve, really.

As he had this thought, she seemed to snap out of the moment and let out a small chuckle. "Does that often work for you?"

"What do you mean?"

She knit her gloved fingers together politely. "When you ask women for a good-luck kiss before a fight. Do they generally acquiesce?"

"I've actually never asked someone that before."

Her gaze swept over him, clearly misbelieving, but mischief glinted once again when her eyes returned to his. "Well, that is quite the improper request, Mr. McNab."

Though she said it in a playful manner, he knew he was toeing the line. Then again, it wasn't as if he would ever see this woman again. He decided to toe the line further. "Very well." He stepped closer to her and she had to angle her head back to see him, lifting an eyebrow in response. "Would a kiss upon your hand be acceptable? Because unfortunately, everyone expects me to lose tonight, so I do need to get my luck from you."

"Why? Are *you* worried you will lose?"

"I don't lose."

"Surely, you could get your so-called luck from anyone else, then."

"No." He lowered his voice to a raspy whisper. "It must be from you."

Lady Vivian playfully twisted her mouth in thought before lifting the back of her white-gloved hand in offering. Holding her gaze, he gently placed his hand beneath hers, but then he did something he knew she wasn't expecting. With his other hand, he pinched the silk tip of her middle finger and gently pulled. Neither of them tore their eyes away from the other as he paused and left space for her to protest. Her eyes widened ever so slightly in realization of what he was doing and a faint blush swept across her cheeks. But she didn't protest—she stared back at him, waiting.

Slowly, he pulled the long, silk glove off and it dropped down and dangled from his left hand. He glanced down at her bare hand contrasting to his. Where his hand was rough, scarred, callused, hers was soft, flawless. Like every other person of the upper classes, this woman had never seen a day of work in her life.

Her long, dainty fingers curved around his and he swept his thumb over the top of her hand before lifting the spot to his lips. He watched her as he placed a gentle kiss upon it, letting the moment linger far too long.

VIVIAN COULD ONLY stare back, unblinking, completely stupefied by the moment. Mr. McNab had had the audacity to remove her glove and kiss her bare hand, and she'd had the audacity to let him!

Of course, it didn't escape her that he'd given her a moment to pull back, to stop it if she'd wanted. The only proper moment exhibited by either one of them in this whole silly game. But she hadn't pulled back, found she'd had absolutely no desire to, and in response, he'd given her a devilishly handsome smirk right as her hand had reached his lips, as his piercing, green eyes had locked with her own eyes, flashing the moment skin touched skin.

It was a mere kiss on the back of her hand, an acceptable greeting amongst polite society—that is, when the hand was covered. Innocent in the grand scheme of things. So why did it feel like the most intimate moment in the world?

As he lifted his face away and rose back up to his full height, letting her go in the process, she realized how close she stood to him in the moment. How had that happened? Moments ago, she'd been a few steps back. Now she was mere inches away.

Mr. Dantes McNab was a maestro of women, and she'd danced along with his tune without even realizing it.

The loud crowd began to head down the stairway, excited, drunken conversation echoing down and flooding the room. Vivian had mere seconds to respond.

She took back her glove and began to slip it on. As she pulled it up to her elbow, her attention lifted back up to Dantes. "Aren't you quite the charmer?"

"When inspiration strikes, I suppose."

She couldn't help but laugh. It was all in good fun, after all. "Goodbye, Mr. McNab. And good luck, again, with your fight."

Dantes gave her a tight nod. Vivian turned and began walking toward the bench on which she was meant to sit, but just like the first time she'd met him, she couldn't help but glance back over her shoulder to watch his powerful form walk away. Surprisingly, however, he remained rooted in place, watching her.

Upon this discovery, she turned forward again, this time with a large grin.

Moments later, the large room was packed tightly with people. Vivian glanced around in hopes of spotting Bernard, but he was nowhere to be found. She returned her attention to the raised platform of the fighting ring and began absently fanning herself, the room now stifling hot from the sheer number of people. Up in the ring, Dantes was jogging in place, stretching his arms. A man approached Dantes's corner of the ring—he was younger than Dantes, but as they talked to each other through the gap between the ropes, there was lots of back-and-forth laughter and deep discussion. It was clear to Vivian this man was his other brother, Mr. Oliver McNab.

Ollie reached up to clap Dantes on his shoulder and turned to head toward a bench farther down, catching her eye as he did this.

And he immediately tensed and looked away, scratching his jaw.

Odd, but surely nothing.

After the referee took his place, the bell dinged loud and the crowd began to cheer. Dantes lifted his bare fists in front of him, and a deep focus washed over him as he eyed his opponent. Across from him, Mr. Sullivan towered over the already towering Dantes, his own fists raised.

Sweat poured down both men as they began to circle each other, size each other up, trying to time the first hit. Dantes's back was now facing her, and she could see the cocky smirk on Sullivan's face.

She wanted to wipe it off him herself.

But what happened next seemed to move in slow motion. Dantes wound his fist back, the muscles in his back and arms flexing and cording with the movement, and he released his fist forward, connecting with Sullivan square in the jaw and stunning the enormous man. Sullivan's head whipped to the side, droplets of sweat and spit flying every direction, and then the man immediately collapsed to the ground.

He remained lying there, his limbs splayed out in every direction.

The room went completely silent as the referee slammed his

palm to the floor of the ring.

Counting out the seconds.

Calling out Dantes's win.

As the crowd erupted, Mr. Dantes McNab turned around and grinned with triumph directly at her.

Chapter Four

V IVIAN COULDN'T FALL asleep to save her life. Anytime her mind lingered toward the events of the evening, her heart rate leapt. And it wasn't only from that silly kiss upon her bare hand she tried not to think about. She'd practically had to *drag* a drunk, bawling Bernard out of The Harp & Thistle, though thankfully, Mr. Victor McNab had taken pity on her and thrown the sniveling man into their carriage.

Then he'd made a point to gloat about Dantes's winnings. That part hadn't been helpful to her.

The entire ride back, Bernard had mumbled incoherently to himself while his face had pressed against the carriage wall, and Vivian had eagerly hopped out as soon as they'd pulled up to her home. She hadn't even said goodbye to him because he'd been in the middle of asking himself, "How? How could it happen that way?"

She'd known what he'd meant. It wasn't even that Dantes had won the fight, though of course that had been a big part of it. It was how it had ended, a true insult to injury. Dantes had gone into the ring, hit Sullivan, and the Irish Goliath had immediately collapsed to the ground, out cold.

It had taken one single hit. Mere minutes for the fight to begin and end.

And when Dantes had turned to find her and grinned in that

boyish way, she couldn't help but return a grin herself and shake her head in disbelief.

Once it had sunk in, the room had erupted into chaos—shouting, whistling, wailing, sobbing. Her ears were still ringing, in fact.

Men had jumped into the ring, lifted Dantes into the air to more cheers, then taken him off somewhere. Probably a private party with beautiful women. Not that she cared—why would she care? She held no claim to the man. And it wasn't like she would ever see him again.

Vivian rolled to her side, tried pulling the covers to a more comfortable position. She thought about Dantes's comment about being involved in the seasons. How was that possible? Were there McNab noble families? The name seemed familiar. She thought through the Scottish nobility but only knew their formal titles. There was a duke from the Highlands, the Duke of Invermark, with a Mc- surname, but there was no possibility Dantes had ties to a duke. Nothing about him was gentlemanly. Though she did recall thinking his accent didn't match his appearance. His brother Ollie had a heavy Cockney accent, the one she'd expected Dantes to have. But Victor didn't have even a hint of a Cockney accent. Thinking of that, Victor could pull off being a gentleman. The way he spoke, walked, even stood perfectly reflected the gentlemen in her social class.

Now she was even more mystified. Was Dantes toying with her? He must have been.

Vivian turned in bed to her other side with a frustrated sigh. She could not get comfortable! Giving up, she glanced at the clock. Three o'clock in the morning. She had been lying in bed wide awake for two hours now. That was enough.

Vivian slipped into the drawing room to pour herself a splash of whiskey and went over to a window that looked out at Hyde Park. It was raining, and the gas lamps that lined the street reflected gold in each raindrop clinging to the window.

She took a sip as she stared out. The taste, the smell of the drink brought her back to The Harp & Thistle, to Dantes. Bronze-haired, green-eyed Dantes tossing away his shirt, his trousers dropping to the ground, revealing the most masculine body she had ever seen in her life. Not that she ever saw men's bodies. Did all men look like that underneath their clothing? But Dantes was a pugilist; his large, muscular frame had been built and was maintained for strength. His ancient ancestors had probably bred for strength. Strength that had taken down a man called "the Irish Goliath" with a single hit.

No, all men did *not*, in fact, look like that.

And the hair—heavens! The first thought she'd had when she'd seen the wisps of hair on his muscled chest had been to weave her fingers through it. She placed a hand over her face with a groan, completely ashamed of herself. No wonder she'd been so bashful from an innocuous kiss upon her hand. Dantes pulled out the deep-seated carnal instincts good breeding snuffed out.

She could *never* show her face to him again.

After letting out a shaky breath, Vivian threw back the rest of the whiskey. But right as she was going to turn to head back to bed, a carriage stopped in front of her house.

Vivian watched with guarded curiosity as a shadowy figure eased out into the cold, rainy night. Fearful of a visitor at this late hour, she was just wondering if she should ring for Heaton when skirts became illuminated by a streetlamp. The woman stopped, clearly considering if she should wake the household at this hour. The figure's face still shrouded in shadow, Vivian couldn't see who it was, but she had an inkling.

She ran as quietly as she could to the front door and opened it. The woman's stance tensed at first but relaxed when she realized it was Vivian. She rushed forward.

"Vivian!" Anne threw herself onto Vivian and began to sob into her shoulder.

Vivian tried to shush her and pulled her back into the drawing room, pouring out two small glasses of whiskey. Anne eyed it from the sofa with unease but took it, sipped it, and made a face. "You can't sleep, either?" Anne finally asked.

"No." Of course, Vivian couldn't tell Anne the real reason why. Anne no doubt assumed Vivian was just as upset as she about Bernard's fiasco.

"Bernard…" Anne stopped. Sobs took over again. Vivian went to sit next to Anne, pulling her close, and Anne was able to collect herself after a moment. "Bernard is at home, passed out drunk. I know he took you to The Harp & Thistle tonight."

Vivian remained quiet, unsure of what Anne knew. She was not going to be the one to break the one-thousand-pound news.

But Anne continued. "Bernard told me everything when he got home, Vivian. Everything. It was a marathon confession. He doubled his debt at The Harp & Thistle. He is thousands of pounds in debt."

"How much?"

"Five thousand."

Vivian's hand flew to her mouth. "I thought it was one thousand!"

Anne's lip quivered as more tears streamed. "No. He apparently visits several other places quite regularly."

It didn't escape Vivian that Anne had used the word *places*. What places? So, she asked.

Outside, the rain fell harder and tapped louder against the window. "It doesn't matter, does it?" Anne slowly rubbed her forehead, as if trying to settle a headache.

"It *does* matter. I'm assuming you came to me for help?"

Anne paused before giving a small nod.

"Then you need to tell me what's going on."

And the entire sordid truth came out. Bernard gambled most nights, owing money to numerous people at numerous gaming hells. He had open drinking tabs of large amounts at several pubs. But the hardest part for Vivian to hear was Bernard visited brothels—apparently, men could rack up debt there as well. Her brother was a monster. No—he was worse. He was a scoundrel, a woman's worst nightmare. The exact type of man she desperately needed to avoid if she didn't want a lifetime of heartache. Yet she couldn't even recognize it in her own brother. She'd known he'd had a bit of a struggle with gambling—the whole family had known that—but this? This went far beyond what she'd thought.

And if she couldn't see that scoundrel in her own brother, how was she going to be able to see it in every other man around her? The men who pursued her relentlessly? She was forced to find a husband now. How was she going to avoid the life Anne and, honestly, most women led?

Was it gambling? Drinking? Merely being the type of man who spent time at pubs? That could be an easy way to avoid a bad man. Avoid a man who went to pubs.

That must make Dantes the ultimate scoundrel. The man *owned* a pub. It was his livelihood, where he spent most of his life. And his brothers, his friends, his patrons—they were all scoundrels too. And as he was also the most gorgeous man she had ever laid eyes on, surely, the other women who went to The Harp & Thistle thought so too. In fact, he probably had a rotation of women who matched the day of the week. On Monday, he slept with Martha. On Tuesday, he bedded Theresa. Wednesday was Winifred. On and on, Dantes lived the life of the world's ultimate scoundrel.

And he'd kissed her hand in a way to say he wanted her to be one of those women. And she'd let him do it, hypnotized by his call.

Blast! She was a foolish, foolish woman!

"All right, here's what I can do." Vivian clapped her hands down to her knees. "Tomorrow, send me a list of the debts owed. Exact amounts and the recipients. I'll send it to one of my bank managers—one whom I trust with utmost discretion—and he will see to the payoffs." She paused. "He's an idiot." She shook her head at herself. "I'm sorry. I shouldn't be saying that."

"No. He is an idiot." Anne threw back the remainder of her glass into her mouth, choking briefly.

She began sobbing again and thanked Vivian, saying she had never felt as much shame as she did in the moment. "I'm jealous of you." Anne sniffed. "Normally, I'm too proud to say something like that, but tonight, I would gladly trade places with you. Bernard, I would do anything for him, you know? I grew his children. I went through the insurmountable pain and agony of that. I take care of them and him, running the household, while he goes around London sleeping with brothel women?"

Vivian looked down at her hands. "Has my father offered any help?"

"Bernard refuses to go to him. And in truth, I don't want the duke to know about any of this, either. We could lose everything from his debts, do you realize that? Our home, which would lead to losing our friends, our status, and reputation. Our children would be laughed at by the other children. I would never be able to show my face again in the light of day. And what can I even do about it? Bernard has a high annual income, but I don't ever see it and can't put any to the side. And it's not like I can go out and get a job. He doesn't love me, Vivian. No one could do this to someone they loved." Anne ran her hands over her skirt before looking back up.

Vivian stood to find the whiskey decanter again, adding a final splash to their glasses. She knew Anne was upset and thinking of the most catastrophic outcome. Vivian also knew it would never come to that. Her father, even Anne's parents, would never let it happen. But Vivian also understood Anne's need to fix this without getting any of their parents involved.

"Don't ever get married." Anne let out a watery laugh as she knuckled her damp eyes. "It's the surest way to misery." Anne accepted the glass back from Vivian but didn't take a sip. "When I debuted and Bernard came to call on me the first time, I was so excited. A future duke, could you imagine how exciting for a girl?" She took a hasty sip. "My parents were also thrilled, naturally. I still wonder why he chose me."

"You were quite pretty," Vivian explained. "And Father and

Gran approved of your family."

"I was also quite naïve. I believed everything he said to me. He could have come home with a kiss mark on his cheek, explain that a woman bumped into him on the sidewalk accidentally, and I would have believed it." A pause as Anne considered Vivian. "As I said, I'm a bit jealous of you."

From Anne's point of view, of course spinsterhood was wonderful. And truthfully, it had been once Vivian had accepted it. It would have continued to be wonderful if, beyond the grave, Gran hadn't nosed herself into Vivian's business. Though it was nice to no longer be a burden to her family now that she had her own home and money. For now, at least.

But spinsterhood could also be quite lonely. And this was a big house for a woman who had no family of her own, and who had lost all her friends. She had a too-big bed in a too-big bedroom in a too-big house. And everything around her, every moment of the day, was a stark reminder of how alone she was.

"Well, I would rather be me than you in this exact moment," Vivian admitted. "But it's not as wonderful as it may seem, so don't torture yourself by glamorizing my life over yours. Despite what you think right now, I do think Bernard loves you." He did, didn't he? Of course he did. "I don't know why he did all of this, nor do I know how to stop him. But… my life is rather lonely. As lonely as the bottom of the ocean, really, where even sunshine doesn't reach. There's simply nothing around me, and there never will be."

Anne didn't respond.

"Plus, you could always separate." Vivian nearly slapped herself as the words came out.

Anne straightened and her eyes widened, as if this thought had never occurred to her. "You think so?"

Vivian hurried to recover the suggestion. "Technically, you could, I suppose. It would ruin your reputation, which concerns you, so I would investigate it first before you think too deeply about it. Would you live in separate houses, for instance? A lot to think about."

Anne's lips pressed tight together as she thought about this. "On the subject of separation, there really should be brothels for women to attend. You know…" Anne lowered her voice. "With men inside."

"*Anne!*"

"What?" Anne laughed. "In the unlikely event our marriage all but ended, I'd be expected to be chaste forever. Which is ridiculous because we both know *he* wouldn't have that expectation—not that he would abide to it if he did."

Vivian had to agree with her on that, but also wondered if Anne was drunk, or if this was Anne untethered. Perhaps a bit of both.

"This whole conversation is shameful, but I don't care." Anne swept a hand up through the air. "I'm feeling a little better, though. Maybe it's the whiskey, but I think it's the conversation."

They sipped their whiskey, and exhaustion finally began to pull at Vivian's eyes.

"Do you think you'll ever get married?" Anne's question was hushed, as if she worried it was too intrusive.

Vivian stared down into her glass as she considered her response. Though she wasn't drunk, the effect of the evening's alcohol made confiding deeply in a friend far too appealing. "I'm not fully sure," she admitted. "But secretly, I do think I want to. Oh, why am I lying to myself? I want it more than anything. But only if it's true love. Otherwise, I couldn't be more uninterested. I don't want to be—" Vivian hesitated at how to finish the sentence without insulting Anne. "I don't want a loveless husband to add difficulty to my life."

Anne briefly smiled. "I understand. Look at me, living that life right now."

"Oh, Anne, Bernard loves you, though."

Anne, however, did not seem convinced. "What am I going to do with him?" She let out a loud sigh right as a clock rang four times. "Oh, my, is it really four in the morning?" Anne set her glass down and stood up. "I really should go. Tomorrow is not going to be a good day and I need all the rest I can get. Thank you, Vivian. For everything."

"Of course." Vivian gave the marchioness a hug and a peck on the cheek before they quietly went to the front door and whispered their goodbyes.

As Vivian watched Anne's carriage clip-clop away—if only Queen Victoria could see Vivian at the door in her nightgown—she recalled Dantes's declaration that he wouldn't accept her money if she tried to cover Bernard's debt. Frankly, she didn't understand why, as her money was as good as anyone else's. And though she hardly knew the man, she suspected he wouldn't waver in his decision. Which would make helping Bernard and Anne rather difficult.

But then an interesting idea began to prickle in her mind. Perhaps Dantes would be more willing to accept her money if there was a transaction involved, if they both received something out of it. Excitement rushed over her. There might be a way to get her out of her own predicament, and close the books on the issue between Bernard and Dantes as well. Vivian hurried up to her bedroom, scribbled the idea onto paper so it wasn't lost during sleep, and promptly succumbed to exhaustion.

Chapter Five

AFTER THE FIGHT, Dantes felt like a millionaire and he owed it all to Lady Vivian Winthrop.

Now, he'd known he would win against Sullivan—there had never been a doubt about that. At least, *he'd* had no doubt. He'd seen it in everyone else, though, even those who'd cheered for him. But ending the fight within minutes? Comical. All because of a good-luck kiss—he thought so, anyway. After all, he had the skill. But knocking Sullivan out right away was an outcome that had not once crossed his mind.

As soon as Sullivan had collapsed, Dantes had had to find her face, see her reaction. He hadn't cared about anything else. Had she known how unheard of that outcome was? Maybe not, but she'd figured it out by the reaction of the crowd. He'd seen her shake her head with amusement. And then he'd sworn he'd seen something else.

Pride. And that had felt pretty good.

The crowd had swept him up, he'd looked away for a few moments, and she'd been gone when he'd tried to find her again. Just as well. His father may have been from her world, and Dantes may have spent some of his own life in it, but he preferred grit over gold. For that fact alone, he could never be with a gal like that. No way would an aristocratic woman, with her elegant tea parties and balls, want anything to do with a hideous, hairy, bare-knuckle pugilist who lived above his pub.

Nor would he want anything to do with said tea parties and balls.

But as he lay in bed, his mind trailed back to the moment where he'd held her hand in his. Though it had been a bit daring that he'd removed her glove, a kiss upon a woman's hand was relatively innocent.

And yet, somehow, a mere "innocent" kiss had seemed to pause the world around him. Her touch… He'd quite literally lost himself in it. In her. He didn't even know the woman. How could something so simple and inoffensive be so consuming?

Granted, it wasn't even that he found her beautiful. The world was filled with beautiful women. But a thread had seemed to weave between them when she'd opened up about her mother's death and confided in him, a complete stranger, that she used to daydream about a life where her mother was still alive. He had never met anyone who understood this aspect of his life.

Dantes would never admit this aloud, but not only had he daydreamed like that as a boy too, he still did it. A grown man in his thirties, nearly the same age his mother had been when she'd passed, and he still imagined a life with her alive.

In that moment, he wondered what she would have thought about Lady Vivian. Probably would have called her a snooty tart or something. He couldn't help but chuckle to himself a bit, but the humor fell away immediately.

Dantes rubbed his hands over his face, then raked his fingers through his wild hair. It didn't matter. None of this mattered. He would never see Lady Vivian Winthrop again, which was for the best, and there was no use in dwelling on her.

By the time he'd cleaned up and gone downstairs to The Harp & Thistle, Victor and Ollie were already preparing for the evening crowd.

"It's about time you got up." Victor was behind the bar working on some kind of logbook. But when he finally looked up to see Dantes, he stilled. "You look like death, Dantes."

Dantes grunted in response. He *had* drunk a bit too much last night after such a quick fight and wanting to forget about Lady Vivian.

Victor watched Dantes make his way to the sink and fill a glass with water. "I'm only tolerating this," Victor started up again, "because fight nights bring in such a big crowd, especially when *you're* up in the ring. It's not excusable behavior otherwise. You're a grown man with—"

Anger flashed through Dantes's mind. "Usually, people follow that with 'a family.' I'm a grown man with a pub and two mind-numbingly infuriating brothers, both of whom are as family-less as myself, I might add." Dantes started chugging his water.

But Victor was unaffected. "I was going to say 'with responsibilities,' but since you're on the subject, the only reason *I* don't have a family is because I don't want one. Not because I can't get one."

Dantes narrowed his eyes. The two brothers had always grated at each other to some degree, a power struggle, and that hadn't changed as they'd aged. Dantes, as a child, had always been the wildest of the bunch while Victor had tried to reel him in—though there were a few times Victor had gotten into mischief *with* him, and while his brother would never admit it, he'd loved it. When they'd spent those years living on the streets, Victor had been the one who'd acted as parent. Kept them safe, fed, clothed. Well, as best as a twelve-year-old could, anyway.

"You make it sound like this happens all the time. Ten years ago, yes." Dantes washed the glass, setting it to the side to dry. Back then, at the height of his fighting career, Dantes would fight far more than he did now, would stay up drinking, would stay up with women, until well after sunrise. When he'd woken at supper time, he would be flooded with shame and melancholy. Rinse and repeat. "But when was the last time I slept in with a hangover?"

Ollie answered first with a wide grin. "Two years ago. You

idiots had the exact same conversation."

Dantes couldn't help but laugh. "See? Maybe let loose yourself every once in a while, too. Perhaps we'd be able to stand you."

Victor sighed and returned to what Dantes now realized was the inventory books. Knowing his brother preferred silence for the task, he grabbed a rag to wipe down the tables and a broom to sweep up. A bit later, Victor's voice cut through the silence, his voice softened from earlier. "A note came for you while you were still asleep."

Dantes turned to see Victor holding a piece of paper up for him to grab. "Who is it from?" He immediately crossed the room.

Victor hesitated, as if he couldn't believe it himself. "Lady Vivian."

Surprised, Dantes plucked the note from his brother's hand and read it, an odd caution snaking through him.

To Mr. Edmond McNab,

I take my pen in hand to write a quick note requesting your presence at your earliest convenience. I understand time is a precious commodity to al, and will patiently await your arrival. I have a pressing matter to discuss.

Yours sincerely,
Vivian Winthrop

He eyed the address she'd included. He really didn't care to make a visit all the way over there—he preferred it here, where he could *tell* someone he needed to talk to them instead of having to send a vague, flowery letter that left the true urgency of the matter in question. Then again, if she'd made the effort to send a note so quickly, it must have been something rather important. Hopefully, it would be worth the effort to visit.

WHEN HE RANG the bell at the address from Lady Vivian's note, a rather stoic-looking butler answered and gave Dantes a quick once-over of evident suspicion, his eye hovering over the long scar upon his face. The butler asked if he had a calling card, which of course Dantes did not, and the butler nearly slammed the door in his face. However, when Dantes revealed the note, he was led into the receiving room, where a large group of dandies were lounging about.

The butler didn't leave the room. Instead, he began to search for something in the drawer of a sideboard. Dantes turned his attention to the men about the room, recognizing nearly all of them. Many of them he knew from boarding school or university, the rest from the years his grandparents had hoped he would find a debutante to marry and settle into their aristocratic lifestyle. To their disappointment, however, not one grandson of theirs had embraced the life they'd tried to bring them into. It had been a valiant effort, but it never would have worked. The McNab boys were too wild, their blood too muddled, for the aristocratic vise.

"Look what the cat dragged in." It was Thomas Crosby, a cad he'd known from boarding school. The biggest cad of them all, really. "It's comical to even see you show up here, McNab. It doesn't matter your grandfather is the Duke of Invermark. Your father's legacy is a joke. And a duke's daughter would never choose a gutter rat over one of us."

Dantes coolly shoved his hands into his pockets, his wide shoulders loose and relaxed. "I received an invitation."

All at once, the room filled with raucous laughter. Crosby knuckled a tear from his eye. "You're so full of it, even now."

The too-familiar shame of being himself pounded against his heart, but outwardly, he shrugged without care. "All right."

Crosby stood to assess Dantes better, a cocky grin plastered on his face. Unwavering, Dantes eyed him back, his face level and at ease, but blood-red rage pumping through his body. He could take Crosby down—he always could have—but Crosby was constantly surrounded by his little weasels. Dantes may have been larger and stronger, may have known how to fight, but even the biggest man alive could not take on more than ten grown men at once.

Crosby sniffed, loudly. "Do you ever miss our Eton days, Edmond?"

Dantes kept his mouth shut. Boarding school had comprised the most miserable years of his life and Crosby knew this. He'd been the cause of the misery, after all.

"I remember those days quite fondly." Crosby looked over his shoulder to his weasels and received numerous chuckles in response. He then returned his icy gaze to Dantes. "Do you recall the time we tied you to a pillar in the dead of winter? What good fun we had together." Crosby ended this with hearty laughter, as if the two were old chums sharing a humorous story from boyhood.

Of course Dantes remembered. The only reason he hadn't died that night was because one of the older boys had snuck out to see a girl and returned later than intended, stumbling upon Dantes in the process. Nor did he forget the time they'd tied him to the foot of his bed, each of the boys unleashing punches and kicks to his face and body. That had lasted an hour, and would have been longer if the headmaster hadn't stumbled upon it. Of course, no one had gotten in trouble. Like Crosby had said, it didn't matter Dantes's grandfather was the Duke of Invermark. His father had abandoned his duties and married a commoner. A poor one, at that. To Crosby and his ilk, Dantes was a street rat.

Crosby grinned again. "How about Eleanor? Would you like to know how she is?"

Dantes made sure he did not move a muscle. "No."

Crosby responded with another cocky laugh.

However, Dantes was pulled away from the heart-warming reunion when a deep voice interrupted. "Pardon, Mr. McNab, but Lady Vivian is ready to receive you now." It was the butler. Dantes blinked. Had the man ever left the room? Had he heard the entire conversation? Dantes wasn't about to ask. But as he followed the butler out of the room, Dantes glanced back at Crosby—the man remained planted in place, looking utterly perplexed.

Lady Vivian was in her drawing room, an airy, light-green room awash in sunlight. As Dantes crossed the threshold, the butler turned and asked him to wait a moment at the door and went to have a private word with Lady Vivian. Dantes watched as she listened intently to words he could not hear, her hands clasped together neatly in front of her. As she paid no mind to him in the moment, he allowed himself to take her in. She wore a peach dress with a high collar that climbed up her long, delicate neck, her dark hair swept up to a soft and opulent bouffant, revealing sparkling, blue sapphires at her ears. He watched her lips move as she said something to the butler. When his eyes trailed up to hers, he realized she was now looking directly at him. And she was blushing.

"My rat catcher is here." Lady Vivian let out a recovering laugh. But when he only responded with a face of confusion, she turned to her butler. "How does no one ever get my jokes?"

"Your sense of humor is far more refined than ours," the butler responded with a smile.

Lady Vivian laughed again, a rather loud but bright sound that filled the large, quiet room. "You always know what to say, Heaton. Mr. McNab." She now had her attention back on Dantes as Heaton, the butler, left them alone in the room. "May I offer you tea?"

But he shook his head. He didn't want to be here any longer than necessary and was itching to escape post-haste. "No need to make a fuss over me, Lady Vivian. We can get right down to whatever is on your mind."

"Then, please, come sit." She seemed to float as she walked over to a sofa, extending a hand to where he was meant to sit. She took an armchair nearby, and he sat after her. "I prefer to get right to it as well. I dislike small talk. I've never been particularly good at it, and I find it tiresome." Her hands folded neatly into her lap. "I wish to discuss my brother with you. The marchioness came to me in tears quite late last night. I've learned my brother has been..." She took a deep inhale. "Leading quite the double life."

Dantes already knew all about it but waited for her to continue.

"I wish to discuss the debt Bernard owes you."

"I won't accept your money." He'd already told her this yesterday. Had he really needed to come all the way here to repeat himself?

"I want to make a deal. I will cover his debt—"

"No."

She ignored him. "In exchange for your help."

He kept his mouth shut, now curious to see where she was going with this.

"Heaton told me you knew the men in my receiving room."

"That's right." So the butler *had* been in there the entire time. Had she put him up to it, or had that been of his own volition?

"Are they gentlemen? And I mean in figurative terms. I know they all call themselves that."

"Not at all," Dantes replied immediately.

"Not one of them?"

"Not one."

Lady Vivian crossed one leg over the other and Dantes had to make a concerted effort to not watch her little slipper peeking out from under the hem of her skirt.

She released a sigh. "Last night, I mentioned my receiving room has become swarmed with men since I took over the estate. I don't speak to any of them, yet they return every day. I wish I could ignore them for eternity, but the fact remains I do need to get married, and I refuse to marry a scoundrel. I refuse to marry a man like my brother, a man who does secret things behind his wife's back. Other women, gambling debts, addictions, all those horrendous diversions that make a man a scoundrel. The problem is men are so good at hiding this aspect of themselves that I cannot pick out the scoundrels from true gentlemen. I couldn't even recognize it in my own brother."

Where was she going with this?

"I want you to teach me how to recognize a good man."

Dantes furrowed his brow. Was she serious? "What, you mean like some kind of matchmaker?"

Lady Vivian wrung her hands. "It sounds rather silly when you put it that way, but yes, I suppose that's what I'm looking for." As she said this, Heaton reentered the room with a silver tray. She thanked him as he set the tray down on a small table next to her and left the room again. "Let's say I'm at a ball. A supposed gentleman asks me to dance. I want to know if he is worth my attentions after the dance. How do I do that? Do I ask him what his favorite card game is and run if he says poker instead of old maid? Is there a certain way he carries himself, how he talks?"

That was what she wanted? That would be easy. "No, just ask me."

She tilted her head. "What do you mean?"

"If he gambles, if he goes to brothels, I'll know. I can tell you."

Lady Vivian gave him a look of suspicion before her eyes slid over to the silver tray and she lifted a random card. "Lord Jonathon Trundell. What can you tell me about him?"

"Alcoholic."

Her eyes widened and she set it to the side, grabbing another random card. "The Honorable William Baker IV."

"Womanizer."

Another card. "Mr. Arthur Greene."

"Got his sister's lady's maid pregnant."

"My word!" She dropped the card as she said this, hastily picking it back up and putting it with the rest. She grabbed one last card.

"Mr. Thomas Crosby."

That name, coming from her lips, made his skin crawl. Why

did she have to go and pick that one? "He's the worst of them all, Viv."

Her eyes flashed in surprise. At Crosby's label? Or at using such a casual nickname for her? He hadn't even meant to say it, either. It had just come out. Yet surprisingly, Lady Vivian—Vivian—didn't remark on it. "And why, may I ask, is Mr. Crosby the worst of them all?"

Dantes's gaze didn't waver from hers as he weighed what to tell her. It wasn't exactly a story to tell a lady, and he absolutely didn't want her to know about it. As he grappled with this, she seemed to understand he wasn't going to explain, that it was personal.

"Anyway, there is a ball coming up to which I've received an invitation. As much as I wish to decline, I can no longer avoid social events and the pressure builds for me to attend. I would like you to accompany me so I may identify any good men there worth my attention."

Unease roiled in his stomach. "A ball?"

Vivian nodded, somehow making such an innocuous movement graceful. "Yes, it is the first of many for the queen's seventieth birthday this year." As Dantes opened his mouth to respond to this detail, she hurried onto the next thought. "And I would request your expertise at any social events I must attend. I promise I won't command too much attention from you, and the events will be limited."

Letting out a breath, Dantes leaned forward to rest his elbows on his knees. He very much disliked the idea of having to reenter high society to help her find a true gentleman. But if he declined, she would certainly end up with the most idiotic of cads. And he definitely hated the thought of *that*.

Vivian moved from her chair and plopped down directly next to him, gently placing a hand on his arm, sitting so close, he got a whiff of her perfume. Roses. He wondered where she'd applied it.

"Please, Mr. McNab. I'm sure it sounds awful to you, and you couldn't have a more yawn-inducing companion. But I do need your help and you will get your money owed in return. Everyone wins." She smiled up at him.

The money. He'd forgotten all about that part, and he still didn't like it. But it was clear Vivian wouldn't give up until he accepted her money. For whatever reason, this woman was intensely loyal to her brother. And he hated that Winthrop was taking advantage of her and she didn't seem to know it.

"Also…" Mischief shone in her eye. "I will not let you leave until you say *yes*."

"You would hold me hostage?" He gave her a crooked smile.

"I would."

Dantes sunk back into the sofa and studied Vivian for a long moment, her long, delicate fingers remaining upon his forearm. Her touch branded through to his skin, a strange sensation that raised caution. He met her dark eyes, so close, he could see the long, dark lashes that framed them.

He *did* have the information she wanted. But he already knew which aristocratic men remained unmarried. Presuming she would be happiest with someone near to her age, excluding older widowers and freshly of-age men a decade younger meant there really weren't many left. And they were all men who'd either put off marriage to indulge in their favorite sins, or men with such awful reputations no title or amount of money, even these days when estates were collapsing, could win a bride. While Dantes was not a marrying man himself, not that she would even consider him—a true gentleman had manners, morals, and a bespoke wardrobe that made even the hideous marginally attractive, traits Dantes did not possess—the thought of putting her with any of those idiots made him sick.

Perhaps, though, he was unaware of the one perfect gentleman for her and would find him at one of the infernal events she thought she had to go to.

So, he agreed on her deal and promised to meet her at the insipid ball in two weeks' time.

Chapter Six

ANNE RUSHED INTO her entryway to greet Vivian, looking rather flustered. Several times a month, Vivian and Anne had afternoon tea together, and today was one of those afternoons. But usually, Anne was in better humor.

"I'm so sorry, Vivian." Anne gripped both of Vivian's arms as if she were about to share tragic news. "But your father is here talking to Bernard and I think Bernard told him everything. And to make it even worse, the queen is here for tea, too."

Vivian gasped with horror. She had not seen that woman since the public snubbing all those years ago and was not expecting to see her before the ball this upcoming weekend. "Please tell me you are joking," Vivian whispered.

But Anne shook her head with a forlorn expression.

"Oh, blast." Vivian wrung her hands. "I cannot believe she had an invitation sent to me for the ball this weekend. All those years of ignoring me, but now I'm in the newspapers, it's suddenly fine to have me around?"

"I know," Anne agreed on a whisper. "It doesn't make sense to me either."

Vivian sighed. "So, what, she just showed up here?"

Anne glanced back over her shoulder briefly. "Yes. She does that sometimes. Bernard fawns over her and you know how she is. She loves being fawned over, thus she loves Bernard."

"He does that even happen after what she did to me?"

Anne shifted with discomfort, not happy to be in the middle of this.

Somewhere in the depths of the house were the squeals and laughter of children. "That's all right, Anne," Vivian promised. "I'm sure it will be fine. She isn't the first one to suddenly remember I exist, and she'll probably be on her best behavior because of it. But she terrifies me, Anne! Always in black, with that forlorn face, no hint of humor anywhere."

Anne pressed her lips together in a tight line before continuing. "You know, when I'm forced to be around someone who makes me want to curl up in a corner, I think of something about them to remind me they're more human than they let on."

Vivian tried to search her memory for anything about the queen that cracked her terrifying shell. But the queen was known for keeping people at a distance, never letting anyone get too close to her. "I can't think of anything," Vivian said with defeat.

"How about this? Did you know she used to keep saucy diaries?"

Vivian blinked. "I beg your pardon? What do you mean, saucy diaries?"

"The queen used to write detailed diary entries about her and Prince Albert. You know…" Anne leaned forward. *"Being together."*

Vivian frowned deeply. This was ridiculous. "I've never heard of that before. I don't believe you."

Anne's pale eyes went wide. "Apparently, she wrote several pages about their wedding night. She would also write entries about how he looked after getting caught in the rain. You know, his shirt sticking to him and all that."

Vivian gasped. Queen Victoria had written that?

"And—apparently, Prince Albert once gifted her a marble statue of himself as a fully nude Greek warrior. She had it displayed at the palace, but people were so shocked by it, she had it removed. No one knows where it went, but rumor is she moved it to her private quarters at the Isle of Wight house."

Vivian tried to place this saucy diary in the hands of the stoic queen she knew, let out a little shriek, and slapped her hand to her mouth to keep any more noises from escaping. When she was able to control herself, she asked, "How in the blazes do you know this, Anne? I'm sure you're making this up to mess with me."

"I swear I am not! It's one of those widely known secrets. I'm not sure how it got out all those years ago, but there's too much detail for it to be false."

More tiny squeals of laughter grabbed the women's attention and as Vivian looked down the hallway, she spotted Bernard stepping out of a room with a child hanging from each arm. Her father exited the room as well but began heading toward the two women. Bernard roared out like a monster and stomped dramatically across the hall to another room, causing more shrieks of joy.

"Is Bernard playing? With the children?" Vivian was shocked. Never had she seen him do such a thing before, always worrying about getting dirty.

Anne wrung her hands. "Yes. Yes, he is."

"Isn't that a lovely change!"

But Anne didn't respond to this comment as Vivian's father stopped before them. He kissed Vivian on the cheek and immediately turned to Anne.

Father cleared his throat in preparation. *Oh, dear.* "Anne, I had a talk with Bernard and he told me about..." He glanced sideways at Vivian for a moment. "About his problems."

Both Vivian and Anne stared back in silence.

"Now, I know Bernard can get a little wrapped up in his...problems. And I know you're not happy with it. I suggested he spend the day at home with his family. And I may have suggested flowers, or something, so if he goes overboard with that at all, I apologize."

Anne stiffened. "What, exactly, did he tell you, Your Grace?"

Father glanced over at Vivian again and then covered the side of his mouth with his hand as he whispered, "Gambling."

Vivian wondered if her father had thrown money at the problem, and if Bernard would make Anne aware of it.

A small light of hope seemed to dim in Anne. "I see. Well, have a good rest of your afternoon, Your Grace."

Father, evidently unaware of Anne's change in demeanor, bid the two women goodbye and left.

Anne dragged Vivian into the drawing room, and Vivian immediately spotted the severe-looking Queen Victoria, bedecked in a black hat with the largest ostrich feather Vivian had ever seen in her life. As the queen noted their arrival into the room, she squinted and leaned forward, homing in on Vivian.

"Your Majesty." Anne forced brightness in her voice as both women curtsied properly, then the marchioness dragged Vivian to her seat. "You remember Lord Litchfield's sister, Lady Vivian Winthrop."

The queen's face pinched together. "Ah, yes, the forgotten girl everyone suddenly wishes to befriend."

No thanks to you. As Vivian took her seat, she shot a look over to Anne. However, Anne had taken a rather keen interest in pouring tea for everyone.

"I suppose that's an apt description," Vivian responded, not knowing what else to say. It was the truth, after all.

"I've been around long enough to see it all." The queen floated a hand through the air. "However, there seems to be a new type of woman emerging I have never before seen and I find it quite dreadful and fear for future generations!"

"What do you mean, Your Majesty?" Vivian thanked Anne for her teacup and saucer as it was handed to her and took a sip.

The queen looked Vivian over. "We shall use you as an example."

"Oh."

"I've never heard of a woman inheriting an estate. Quite frankly, your grandmother was utterly foolish for leaving everything to you when it should have gone to her grandson. *He has a family to look after!*"

Vivian merely stared, her cup suspended midair, rendered mute by the sheer irony that the queen had, in fact, inherited the United Kingdom. It took everything in her not to point this out. With haste, she took a sip of the hot tea. Did her entire worth as a human, as a woman, revolve around marriage and motherhood? If she never attained those milestones, would she cease to exist? Obviously not, but that was how it felt. "Your Majesty, I've been meaning to tell you. Gran mentioned you in a letter she left me."

Queen Victoria's eyes widened slightly. "Did she?"

"Gran wanted me to tell you, oh… What was it she said?" Vivian remembered quite well but took glee in making the queen squirm, if only for a moment, and made a show of it by tapping her chin. "Oh, yes, I recall now. She wanted me to tell you she's watching you. And added 'ha ha' after that."

The expression on the queen's face went from curiosity to dread, and she tried to covertly glance about the room, as if Gran's ghostly form were hiding somewhere.

Vivian was greatly amused and appreciated Gran's last joke.

The queen, evidently eager to move on, took a sip of her tepid tea before gasping at how hot it was and began to fan at it. "I was telling Lady Litchfield a moment ago how lucky she is to have such a doting husband. Anytime I'm out for a promenade or a drive through the park, Lord Litchfield makes a point to come chat with me. It doesn't matter what he's doing! Horse riding, cricket—he will immediately come to my side and provide the most captivating conversation. The marquess is a lucky woman." The queen shot a squinty smile to Anne. "As queen, I find it quite disconcerting the number of Americans marrying our gentlemen in these last years. A friend's American niece lives here now after marrying a destitute earl, and, unlike Lady Litchfield, the girl does not appreciate everything her husband has provided for her."

"Oh, how lovely for her." Vivian wondered how, exactly, a destitute earl provided for his presumably wealthy heiress wife and exchanged a look with Anne over the edge of her teacup.

"Yes, it was a good match. Unfortunately, she's spoiled so rotten by him, she thinks her life is dreadful and has been dabbling in that ridiculous suffrage movement. What folly that all is! She has a bee in her bonnet about women voting, which is utter nonsense. That's what I mean about this new type of woman. Women have so much to worry about as it is. Now some are going on to university and taking men's jobs away from them, becoming physicians and solicitors themselves and adding on that stress. And on top of that, voting?" The queen *tsked*. "It's *nice* for wives to unload work and dreadful politics onto the husbands. Lady Litchfield, for example, needn't worry about anything ever in her life. I know when her husband votes, he has his wife's best interest at heart. He is a lovely gentleman who takes care of his family."

Anne began to cough, hastily setting her teacup down, lest it spill.

"What about women like myself?" Vivian pulled the queen's attention back. "Unmarried women? Who is looking out for us?" Granted, Vivian would be marrying in the future, but that wasn't the point.

The queen gave her a tight, condescending grin and leaned forward to pat Vivian's knee. "No offense, but women like yourself clearly are incapable of making good decisions. A woman who doesn't follow the natural call of loving a gentleman and creating children is the least trustworthy type of person—and frankly has no business deciding laws."

Ire rose inside her and Vivian recalled Anne's advice, remembering that this frightening, stoic queen who only wore black had saucy diaries.

Vivian imagined the queen as a young woman, giggling and blushing as she daydreamed about her husband.

Something very human, and very relatable.

Surprisingly, it helped.

As Vivian wasn't one to create a fuss and disliked confrontation, she appreciated being able to stuff the ire back down and resume a pleasant demeanor.

But apparently, Anne felt otherwise. "I disagree," Anne suddenly jumped in, to Vivian's abject surprise. "I agree with your friend's niece that women should be able to vote. And quite frankly, I'm glad the suffrage movement has begun to gain steam in our country. Perhaps divorce will become easier for women to attain as well." She took a sip of her tea, looking quite pleased with herself.

The queen gasped loudly, placing a gloved hand over her heart. She quickly regained her composure, however, and forced a pleasant face. "Well. Isn't this tea lovely, dear?" She took another sip of tea as well, her back straightening severely.

Anne narrowed her eyes before returning her attention to Vivian. "Are you still going to the queen's first birthday ball of the season this weekend?"

"Yes, and, in fact, I'm being escorted by Mr. Edmond McNab, the one who…well, you know. Knows Bernard." She turned her attention to the queen. "Of course, if that's all right with you."

The queen replied, "Edmond McNab? Who is that?" Queen Victoria frowned as she searched her memory. "Ah, yes. I recall now. One of the Scots families. A duke. I do like the Scots."

Vivian and Anne exchanged looks of surprise. Surely, the queen was mistaking Dantes for someone else. "A duke?" Vivian wondered how much the queen would divulge.

"The Duke of Invermark. His only child, only son at that, was a bit of a rogue. Wanted nothing to do with the dukedom. Took money from his parents, ran off to London, and invested in a railway business. It was quite the scandal at the time."

"Is he still alive?" Vivian knew Dantes's father was long gone, but she still wasn't convinced this was the same family.

"I have no knowledge of his whereabouts. He hasn't been my concern for over thirty years." The queen paused in thought. "I suppose if you wish *those* McNabs to be present, I can add them to the list. Too many Americans these days—we could use more

Scots. Perhaps they will return to the rightful place within our kingdom and mend the duke and duchess's shattered hearts." She then waved her hand to indicate she was dismissing any further discussion on the subject.

Vivian was trying to remain calm with this revelation. So Dantes *was* the grandson of a duke.

Anne remained interested in Vivian's little tidbit about Dantes. "I didn't realize you had any interest in Mr. McNab. Or anyone, for that matter?"

Vivian laughed, feeling a bit lightheaded from the news. What had given Anne such a silly idea? "Oh, it's nothing like that. I simply don't have anyone else to accompany me and when I met him...that one evening...we got along well enough. He is easy to converse with, and nothing more." An image of him knocking out Mr. Sullivan, all raw strength and flexing muscles, flashed in her memory. She shifted in her seat.

Anne gave her a side-eyed look. "You are a terrible liar."

"Honest. It's nothing more. There is absolutely zero interest there. For either of us." One day, Vivian might tell Anne Dantes had helped her find her a husband for repayment of Bernard's debt. But now was not the time.

"How many dances are you hoping from him? All of them, perhaps?" Anne fluttered her lashes.

Vivian gasped. "You are terrible, Anne! No, of course not. I doubt I'll be doing much dancing, either. I'm far too old for that now."

Queen Victoria perked up, her eyes bright and merry. "Lady Vivian, am I understanding correctly, you are seeking a gentleman to marry? We could use more English brides!"

Vivian stammered. "But my grandmother—"

"Your mother was fully English and your father is half. You grew up here. Never mind that." With another hand wave, the queen dismissed this monumental moment as if she were deciding against a second helping of biscuits. "I am famous for my matchmaking abilities. So many lovely couples have been introduced by me. In fact"—she practically vibrated with excitement—"I already have several gentlemen in mind for you. I'll be sure to send them your way at the ball this weekend."

Vivian gripped her teacup so tightly, she was sure it would shatter.

DANTES GOT FIVE solid jabs in to the punching bag. He bounced on his feet, light as a feather. Sweat poured over him; his hair hung in his face.

He could do this all day.

Taking a deep breath, he readied again, focused on the worn leather bag, ignoring the large, empty basement room that surrounded him. Somewhere behind him was the fighting ring.

He circled the punching bag, then blitzed it with more heavy hits. His breathing was labored, his muscles tired. As he continued his dance around the bag, he fell into a calm trance, thinking about how sore he felt in such a short time. Only a few years ago, he would have been hours away from this level of soreness.

Frankly, that worried him.

Dantes made sure to keep up with training, made sure to keep as healthy as he could. But he wasn't getting any younger, and no one could outrun passing time.

Dread filled him like a warning sign alongside a road, but he tried his best to ignore it.

The swinging bag stilled between his hands and he took a moment to breathe before starting again. More sweat, more hits, until he thought he was going to collapse.

"Dantes? Are you down here?" Ollie's voice called out.

Dantes stopped, wiping the sweat from his brow with his forearm as he took in deep, restorative breaths. "Over here," he replied loudly so Ollie could follow his voice.

Ollie appeared a moment later carrying boxing gloves. He

eyed Dantes's bare hands. "You're using gloves, right? I'm not sparing with you and getting a black eye like that one time."

Dantes angled over to the ring where his water sat, then chugged it all down. "Yes, of course. We don't want to mess with your pretty face."

"Go ahead and laugh. But I don't think you'd be happy with me going to a ball with you while having a bruised face."

They both climbed into the ring, Dantes grabbing gloves he had tossed to a corner earlier. He slipped them on, hitting his fists together. "Don't tempt me. It would be nice to not be the one catching whispers."

The brothers met in the middle of the ring, their gloved fists raised. Dantes used to train with Victor, but that stopped several years ago when Dantes had gotten an especially hard hit to Victor's jaw and Victor's response had been, "I'm too old for this rubbish," before throwing down his gloves and storming back up to the pub. Dantes hadn't been challenged like that since. Ollie's strengths didn't lie in fighting, but he was also the only person who would spar with Dantes. And it was only because he didn't have a choice.

They began to circle each other and Ollie threw out the first punch. Dantes blocked it with ease, dodged the next one, and got a solid connection to Ollie's ribs. Ollie swore out loud but quickly regained himself. For a long while, they continued their circling, their uppercuts, right hooks, left hooks. Dantes held back his strength, while Ollie held back his mouth.

As their sparring continued, Dantes's mind trailed to Lady Vivian. He often found himself wondering what she did at any given time. While he cleaned pint glasses, was she drinking tea? While he swept the floor, was she writing letters? What she did in her day-to-day life, he found himself curious over. What did Lady Vivian Winthrop do each day? How did her elegant life differ from his own?

A solid hit to his stomach pulled his mind out of the clouds and knocked him to the floor, gasping for air.

Ollie let out a loud *whoop*, pumping a fist into the air. It was the first time Ollie had ever won a fight. "I may have broken my hand, but I finally got you down!" He let out a loud, obnoxious laugh.

Maybe *Dantes* was getting too old for this rubbish now, too.

Ollie sank down next to Dantes, a goofy grin slapped onto his face. He removed his gloves and tossed them to the side. "Wait until Victor hears about this."

Dantes shot him a withering look.

And Ollie lifted his palms in mock defense. "All right, I know I didn't truly deserve that win. Your mind was clearly off somewhere else. I wonder where?"

With a groan, Dantes sat up but didn't respond.

"It's your turn to clean the loo. Maybe you were thinking about that?"

No response.

"Or, perhaps, your thoughts dwelled upon a certain lady whom you're escorting to a ball in a few days?"

"No."

Ollie laughed and set his hands behind him to lean back. "Sure, sure. Now, I was wondering. When was the last time you went to a ball?"

Dantes let out a loud, long sigh.

"Over ten years now, yes?"

Irritated, Dantes began removing his gloves with hard movements. "Yes, you are already aware of that, though. What point are you trying to make, Ollie?"

"You're mere days away from taking Lady Vivian Winthrop to Queen Victoria's first seventieth birthday ball, where several hundred people will be attending."

Dantes stiffened as he set the gloves down.

"Ah, I see you haven't considered the fact that you will have to dance for the first time in twelve years in front of Europe's snobbiest set, with the woman newspapers obsessed over. Everyone will be watching you. And her."

Dantes swore. He should never have agreed to this.

"Come on, then. Up on your feet." Ollie hopped up.

Dantes stood, too, and Ollie stepped forward with an expectant look on his face.

"What the blazes are you doing?" Dantes growled out, disliking how Ollie stood practically in his face.

"You need to practice dancing." Ollie took Dantes's hand in his.

Dantes ripped it away. "Have you gone mad? I'm not dancing with you!"

Ollie shrugged. "All right. Good luck on Saturday, then."

Dantes watched as his brother started walking away. He ground his teeth, realizing Ollie was right. He had no business being in a ballroom after all this time, and he *would* be expected to dance. But it had been so long, he wouldn't remember how to. He couldn't simply dive in unprepared, either. He was supposed to help Vivian, not make everything worse. "Fine," he said simply.

Ollie spun back around. "Smart move. Unlike you, I still attend those fancy balls a few times a year."

"Which is precisely why you agreed to go with me."

His brother nodded. "Trust me when I say you don't want to be the lad who trips in front of everyone. You especially don't want that for Lady Vivian."

Ollie had a good point, as much as Dantes hated to admit it. "What are you suggesting, then?"

"We practice a bit every day. We can practice a waltz now, a quadrille tomorrow—keep at it until you know what you're doing again. Polkas are strictly forbidden; it shows too much leg, apparently, so you don't need to worry about that."

"I have to dance with you is what you're saying."

Ollie's mouth twisted into an obnoxious grin. "Well, yes, you can't really spin out your punching bag."

A flash of a memory arose, one of him in a garden. He and Eleanor were hiding from the rest of the guests. She giggled and looked up at him with clear, blue eyes, and in turn, he slowly spun her to the music. Dantes frowned deeply at the memory.

"Come on." Ollie waved Dantes toward himself. "Pretend I'm Lady Vivian. Take my right hand with your left." Ollie made Dantes hold his hand. "Now put your right hand on my back."

"I swear to God, if you tell anyone about this—"

"I'm not exactly eager for the world to know I dance with my smelly, sweaty brother in my spare time, either."

Dantes hesitated a bit before taking the proper stance, holding Ollie's giant hand in his and putting his own hand on Ollie's rigid back. "You couldn't play a duke's daughter if it saved your life."

Ollie laughed loudly at this but kept his attention on the task at hand. "Ready? Now left foot steps forward."

Dantes stepped forward, leading Ollie back.

"Now right foot to the side."

Dantes followed Ollie's directions, stumbling a few times, but as the minutes passed, he eased back into it, and eventually, it was like he had never stopped dancing and he no longer had to think too much about it.

He spun Ollie out, then brought him back in.

"*Oh, Dantes.*" Ollie used a false, high-pitched voice, fluttering his eyelashes. "You're so handsome. Can you please dance with me all night long?"

Dantes responded with a few choice words, though he couldn't help but let out a little laugh.

And then someone coughed to get their attention.

Dantes and Ollie froze in mid-step.

"If this is how you've been training for the last few years, Dantes, it's a wonder you win every match." Victor's dark, disdainful voice cut into the silence.

Dantes and Ollie stepped away from each other and turned to find Victor standing outside of the ring, his arms crossed tightly across his chest, a severe scowl chiseled into his face.

"I was helping him ready for Saturday," Ollie explained.

"I know what you were doing," Victor replied. "And I'm glad you two are going out for a grand time, leaving the Saturday crowd up to me."

"You said you found extra help."

Victor ignored this, let his arms drop, and began walking toward the stairs. "Stop faffing about and come upstairs. The night crowd is already trickling in."

Dantes watched Victor ascend the stairs and disappear. It didn't escape him the heir to the dukedom also refused to have anything to do with it. Someday, Victor's world would come crashing down around him and Dantes and Ollie would be helpless to do anything.

Chapter Seven

WHEN VIVIAN WENT to the dressmaker Claudette, the woman already knew Vivian was *Britain's richest spinster* and closed her shop for a few hours to focus solely on her. Claudette showed her the fabrics others had recently picked, explained how evening fashions had changed from her debutante days, but as Vivian looked over an unassuming, pale-gray silk, Claudette had other ideas.

"How open are you to something a bit different?" The elderly Frenchwoman puckered scarlet-red painted lips. Vivian had never seen anything like it before outside of actresses on stage, yet it somehow fit the woman quite well without being garish. "Something that would really stand out, make every gentleman trip over themselves?"

Vivian was not one for standing out, and she said as much.

"Chérie, you will stand out no matter what because of who you are. Let me show you what I'm thinking, anyway." Claudette disappeared for a moment before returning with black lace and a bolt of fabric. A fabric that somehow shimmered and flowed like liquid gold. "The majority of the dress would be gold." The fabric seemed to melt between her fingers. "With this black lace over the bodice, and down the back of the skirt." Claudette demonstrated the two fabrics together.

Vivian eyed it with trepidation. "It's truly stunning, and

unique, to be sure. But I can't imagine that on me."

Claudette met her eye in the mirror. "Is there a particular gentleman you have your eye on?"

Vivian lifted her chin. "No."

But Claudette clearly didn't believe Vivian and gave her a wry look. "Close your eyes then, Lady Vivian. The most handsome man you have ever seen turns around to see you. What dress are you wearing?"

Vivian closed her eyes and imagined herself in a pale-gray dress, lost in a crowd. It did nothing for her, except make her think of a drab cloud. Next, she imagined herself in shining gold layered with black lace, long, silk gloves past her elbows…and a sudden vision of Dantes's face as he turned around to see her. Her eyes flew open as she took a sharp inhale.

"You blushed." Claudette gloated in the mirror. "You *do* have a gentleman in mind."

Irritated by such an accusation, Vivian of course denied it. "Absolutely not!"

Claudette tilted her head and lifted an eyebrow.

Vivian shifted, eager to move on from the subject. "The man I thought of, for whatever ridiculous reason, is of no interest to me. Even if he were, he is unattainable."

"Why? Is he married?"

"No."

"Then he is attainable." Claudette gave Vivian a wise, knowing look. "I have had heard the most private details of every aristocratic romance over the past thirty years and know better than anyone the hard rules of men in matters of the heart are more malleable than pure gold—it just takes the right woman to hammer them into place." She smiled at Vivian's reflection. "Will you be going with the gold dress, then?"

Vivian put her eyes back on herself and allowed a small smile to break through.

SHRILL LAUGHTER RANG above the murmured conversation at the ball and Vivian looked down at the gold-and-black dress that cascaded below her. The discomfort of standing out so much in a crowd made her quite uneasy—she had received constant stares since the moment she'd stepped into the large, glittering ballroom—but she had to admit that, at least in this dress, she almost enjoyed the attention.

Almost.

"Vivian?" a man's voice rang out with surprise. She turned to find Bernard standing with their father and a few other men, all of their faces wearing the same open-mouthed, wide-eyed expression. Realizing this himself, Bernard grabbed her wrist and dragged her away in a huff to an empty corner of the room. Father followed as Bernard continued talking. "What in the devil do you think you're doing?"

Vivian ripped her wrist out of his hand. "What do you mean?"

"Showing up here looking like this!" Bernard looked her over with dismay.

Father nodded in agreement. "I do have to say this is a bit unusual, Vivian."

Vivian looked between them, dismayed. "What's wrong with the way I look? I spent a lot of time with the dressmaker, and I was looking forward to wearing this tonight!" Her voice was edged with distress.

"No, Vivian." Bernard took a deep breath. "That's not what I mean. You look beautiful—"

"Thank you. That should have been the first thing out of your mouth." She grimaced at herself—she should not have said that out loud.

Bernard pressed his lips together in a tight line before speaking again. "And you are a spinster."

"Well, I am a spinster in search of a husband now. And I must dress the part." Realizing what she had divulged, she had to resist stomping her foot in annoyance at herself.

Bernard's mouth opened and he stammered twice before collecting himself. "I beg your pardon?"

"Vivian." Father patted Bernard's shoulder before stepping forward. "You don't have to go prowling like a cat to find a husband. Why didn't you come to me? I can help you." He rubbed his chin in thought. "What about Mr. Reginald Abbott? I recall him dancing three times with you the first year of your debut."

"He married. Eight years ago."

Father's face went slightly red. "Oh."

Not wanting to go into this any further, Vivian began searching the large room. "Have you seen Mr. McNab, by any chance?" She directed the question to Bernard.

His nose wrinkled. "McNab? The barkeeps? Which one?"

"Mr. Dantes McNab."

"Why would I see him here?" He paused. "Don't tell me *he* is your choice for husband!"

She tore her eyes in his direction. "I said no such thing. Why? Would that be so bad?" Scoundrels knew scoundrels—perhaps Bernard could shed light on Dantes's secrets. Not that she really cared much, of course. It was merely a general curiosity.

"He's not one of us," Bernard replied.

Vivian rolled her eyes. "He's helping me find a respectable gentleman. In exchange for your debt repayment." Vivian glanced at her father, but he was still lost in thought, no doubt searching through his memory for gentlemen he would deem acceptable for his daughter. Men who were likely unbearable—not that he would know this.

Bernard shifted. "Yes. And I can't thank you enough for helping us, Vivian." But he couldn't have said this with less authenticity. Ever since Vivian had paid off all of Bernard's debt other than what was still owed to Dantes, Anne had clearly been more relaxed. But Bernard seemed indifferent to it. Vivian was sure he was merely embarrassed and didn't like to discuss it. "But I still don't understand how McNab can help you."

"He went through some of my calling cards with me and told me which of them were alcoholics, gamblers. Which ones went to *brothels*." She made a point to really enunciate that last word, capturing Father's attention. He furrowed his brows.

Bernard looked away.

"No offense, Bernard, but I don't want to end up like Anne. Maybe *she* tolerates your behavior, but I do not want a life like that. I would rather die alone than be married to a scoundrel."

"Yes, and thanks to you, she told me she's seriously considering a separation. She refused to come here tonight with me."

Vivian's eyebrows lifted. When had Anne decided that? "Well. Something tells me you wouldn't tolerate *her* sleeping with other men and spending all your money on brothels, card games, and horse races."

Father began grumbling and pulled them further into isolation.

Bernard turned as red as a tomato. "He's not supposed to find out about that!" Bernard reminded Vivian.

"Stop the squabbling at once! Bernard." Father took a deep breath and pinched the bridge of his nose between his fingers. "You said you had a small gambling debt to pay. No wonder your wife looked at me like I had turned purple when I told her to expect flowers from you. This is the height of impropriety! If your wife wants a separation, then I'm confident you have absolutely crossed the line. It should never get to that point. You *know* brothels are unacceptable once you marry. I can't even stand the thought, but you can have a mistress if you keep that whole business properly hidden. I can't believe I have to explain that to you." Father's voice was stern and it struck fear in Vivian's heart. She could only imagine how it would feel to be on the receiving end of such anger. "How much debt do you have?"

Bernard was clenching his teeth. "It doesn't matter. The debt has been covered." Of course, Dantes's portion remained, but Vivian was not about to bring that up.

Father pulled back. "If *you* couldn't manage to cover it, then how did—" His attention flew to Vivian. "You covered up for him."

Vivian swallowed.

Father took in a deep breath and let it out slowly. "This reflects on me. Both of you and your actions reflects on *me*! Did that happen to escape you?" Father looked Bernard squarely in the eye. "You quit all vices now or so help me—"

"I will." Bernard's voice cracked.

Father turned to Vivian. "And, Vivian, a lady does not speak on such matters, especially so bluntly! For heaven's sake, what has become of this family?"

As Bernard and Vivian glared at each other, a gem-encrusted woman and her male companion, both of whom were gray-haired and regal, slowly walked by. Father gave them a friendly smile and nod, but his scowl returned once they had passed.

Father let out a sigh. "How did I raise you two to be like this?"

Bernard went rigid. "You *didn't* raise us. You suddenly appeared one day and ever since have acted as if you had always been there." And with that, Bernard fled into the crowd.

Father's face went stark white as he watched his adult son disappear. He turned back to Vivian. "Do you feel that way, too?"

She didn't respond. She couldn't.

Father looked crestfallen, and guilt began to pull at Vivian's stomach. "Well," Father began, "I believe I will be heading home, then."

She grasped his arm before he could turn to leave. "That isn't necessary. I didn't mean to make you feel badly."

But he shook his head. "No, you misunderstand. Like I said, you have too much time on your hand." Father glanced around the ballroom. "There's a list I'd like to make, a ranking of to whom to re-introduce you. You did say you were hoping to marry, didn't you?" The duke gave her a wink before quickly disappearing, no doubt lest she object.

Lovely. This was the exact type of meddling she'd been hoping to avoid.

Now feeling off-kilter, Vivian began to weave through the crowd in search of champagne and people began noticing her again. At first, they nodded in her direction, both men and women. But as the nods became verbal *hellos*, those verbal *hellos* quickly turned into "Lady Vivian!" and Vivian began to run through the crowd as those infernal, unrelenting bachelors began chasing after her once again. She recalled Queen Victoria's promise to send gentlemen her way, but Vivian hadn't been expecting this!

She glanced back to find men shouldering through the crowd after her, their hands waving high up in the air. "Lady Vivian! May I have one dance?"

She accidentally ran into a woman, nearly knocking her over. Oh, blast, it was Her Royal Majesty, and the queen's diamond crown nearly flew off her head. "So sorry, Your Majesty!" Vivian shouted back as the woman righted herself with a face of severe offense.

The exit was just ahead, and beyond that was freedom. That was it. She was going home. She couldn't tolerate this madness. The night had barely begun and was already unbearable. What had she been thinking in coming here? A worse idea couldn't have been had.

But as she broke through the crowd at a run, she came to a halt as she spotted Dantes and his brother Ollie approaching from the hallway that led to her freedom.

For a moment she almost didn't recognize Dantes. Where before he'd had a wild, scruffy edge to him—pub-appropriate attire, stubble, thick hair in need of control—he was now as polished as fine silver. Never would she verbalize this to him, but he cleaned up well. *Quite well, actually,* she thought as she quickly glanced over the long lines of him.

Compared to women, men wore identical clothing. Black trousers and jackets, white waistcoats and shirts. And yet Dantes stood out like a beacon amongst the other gentlemen in attendance. Though he was now clean shaven and his hair was styled and oiled, and he was wearing the same clothing as the others, there was still that untamed wildness to him. Though he had ties to the aristocracy, and he may have been trying his best to blend in tonight, Bernard was right in that Dantes didn't fit in at all.

Then, in remembering her silly vision roused by Claudette, she looked Dantes in the eye in search of a reaction. Was he as taken by her own polishing as the rest of the ballroom had been? Did he show any sign of admiration or even surprise? But she found nothing there other than an even, blank face.

He wasn't the least affected by her improved appearance.

Stupidly, her throat tightened and she scolded herself for being so vain. Of course, why should she care what he thought anyway? He would be a terrible choice for a spouse, and the fact that she even had a modicum of interest in his reaction to her in this moment irritated her to no end.

"Lady Vivian! Lady Vivian!" The voices behind her were catching up and she looked back over her shoulder. "A dance, please! Just one dance!"

She turned back to Dantes and went to walk past him. "I'm going home. This is utter madness, and doubly humiliating."

But he grabbed her hand, forcing her to stop. "No."

"Excuse me?" She shot back, eliciting a stifled laugh off to the side from Ollie.

"You can't outrun them, Lady Vivian." And as her chasers broke through the crowd, they came to a halt, watching Dantes lift her hand to his lips, a kiss lingering on the tips of her silk-gloved fingers.

Her face burned in response. "What are you doing?" It came out at as a whisper.

"I'm calling off the dogs," Dantes replied low before releasing her hand and offering his arm to her. Now understanding this was nothing more than part of a game, she took his offering, ignoring the solid feel of him beneath the sleeve, and turned back to the chasers. The men's shoulders fell and they retreated into the ballroom with heads hanging. A few young women walked by, and Ollie mumbled something about champagne and followed them, leaving Vivian and Dantes alone.

"Incredible." Filled with wonder, her eyes fixed on the space the men had vacated. "Can you believe they chased me?"

Dantes didn't respond to the question and instead placed a warm hand over her arm. "We shall walk in together now, and your first dance will be with me. The weakest men will fall away, those who know they have nothing to offer you, the type who think it's acceptable to chase a woman through a ballroom." They began walking and she tightened her hold as they approached the crowd. "And anyone who captures your interest after that, I can tell you if he's a worthy gentleman or not."

While Dantes spoke, he looked over the crowd, his view much higher than hers. But as she watched him do this, he unexpectedly looked down at her, and the vivid greenness of his eyes in the golden light of the room shot a jolt through her. She had to look away.

"Before we go in," he began again, evidently unaware of her reaction, "are you sure you want me leading you in? Perhaps Ollie would be a better man to walk with you."

Vivian looked back up with genuine confusion. "Why would I want him to walk me in?"

He smiled widely at this, the long scar on his face stretching with it. She wondered what had caused it. "I'm not exactly a pretty face," he said. "I may scare them all off."

"Don't be silly. You're perfect." She paused. "For this. And anyway, I'm *Britain's richest spinster*. I can almost do anything, and the sharks in there will still chomp their way through to talk to me."

A deep rumbling laugh rose from Dantes. "Very well, Lady

Vivian. Shall we?"

And together, Vivian and Dantes entered the wolf's den of society: the ballroom. Where hundreds of pairs of eyes picked apart every inch of every person. Where gossip was created and spread. And the reactions to Lady Vivian Winthrop walking in with Mr. Dantes McNab were quite interesting, ranging from surprise, to horror, to disgust. She could already hear them whispering about it: "Who is that frightening man with Vivian?" Or if they knew Dantes, which she discovered many of them did, they disparaged him as a gutter rat, like Mr. Crosby had in her receiving room, according to Heaton. She felt angry and defensive on his behalf. Who did these people think they were to talk about Dantes like that? She wanted to give each and every one of them a good talking to. But she would never be bold enough to do so, and he probably wouldn't be too happy about that, either.

Speaking of Mr. Crosby, there he was, sipping champagne with a blonde woman and a few of Vivian's chasers. He noted whom Vivian was with, but his face gave nothing away. He did, however, give her a nod but didn't wait for a response before turning back to his companions.

Now, the only reason Vivian had even noticed him in the first place was because Dantes tightened ever so slightly. There had been a sudden stiffness in his arm, a barely perceptible stutter in his walk that seemed completely involuntary. It had been a reaction even the harshest whispers so far hadn't elicited. But she couldn't figure out what had caused it. Would Mr. Crosby cause that reaction? Or was it merely a coincidence?

"Has anyone piqued Lady Vivian's interest tonight?" Dantes glanced down at her once again. "Plenty of gentlemen have greeted you since we began walking about the room, but none approach you. I still insist I do you a disservice being at your side."

She wondered if it was a general question, or if he meant Mr. Crosby. It didn't matter, though, because the response was the same. "No one has interested me so far. But it's a breath of fresh air, not being approached after being chased. Don't forget the only reason I'm still here is because of you."

He nodded slightly, and as a tray of champagne slid past them, she let go of him to grab two flutes, handing one to Dantes. Finally, a chance to settle into the night, if only for a few moments.

"Tell me something about yourself, Mr. McNab." Vivian spun the stem of the glass between her fingers. Though it was polite to make light conversation such as this, she found she was genuinely interested to learn more about Dantes. He was so cryptic, so closed off, getting to know him was like trying to solve a puzzle.

Dantes watched expectantly over his glass as he took a sip. "What would you like to know?"

"Why did you receive Dantes as your nickname? It's interesting. Are you a vengeful man?" Vivian assumed the nickname had something to do with his scar, but she would never dream of asking about that.

"I received it as a child, from friends of my grandparents." He seemed to be evading the question, which only piqued her curiosity.

Next question. "Can you tell me more about your parents?"

Dantes clenched his jaw and took time to respond. But respond he did. "My father was the only child of the Duke and Duchess of Invermark." He looked at her as if gauging her reaction to this bit of news. Of course, he didn't know she already knew, so she feigned surprise by letting out a small gasp. Dantes continued. "However, he was essentially kicked out of the family for being too wild. He then moved to London, where he founded the Southwestern Railway Company for fun."

"He founded a railway company *for fun?*" Vivian's eyebrows shot up.

Dantes nodded. "He met my mother, they married." There was a brief hesitation. It was so minute, Vivian was surprised she'd even caught it. Dantes quickly moved on. "When he died, his partners took over the business. Then when it sold years later to a larger railway company, they gave my brothers and me enough money to open the pub. After being split several ways, it wasn't much, as most of the sale went to the partners. We had to find a way to create an income for ourselves."

"How did your father die?"

Dantes clenched his jaw for a moment. "A train derailment. Ollie never met him, in fact."

Oh, what a horrible tragedy! Vivian felt sorrow for Dantes's mother. Pregnant when her husband had died in a horrific way?

Though it hadn't escaped her he was willing to talk about his father but had become guarded at the subject of his mother. "You said your mother died in childbirth, correct?"

Dantes nodded and glanced around the room, as if considering whether or not he should tell her anything.

"She was Irish," Dantes slowly began and again, he seemed to be studying her reaction. "And she became a laudanum addict, getting addicted after giving birth to Ollie. They gave it to her to dull the pain from a difficult childbirth. She was quite melancholy after our father's death, which I think contributed to her overdose later. We ended up moving to the district she was from after my father died. She had some family there who were only mildly interested in us for a short time. They didn't like my father, and by extension didn't care much for us."

"Where in London was this?"

Dantes hesitated again and looked away. "Whitechapel."

Vivian felt herself grow pale. Whitechapel was rife with gangs, violence, disease. And last year, a madman had begun brutally murdering women there. The police were still hunting the man down, and the city was breathing down their necks for it. Everyone hoped the horrific killer would be caught soon.

She couldn't *imagine* three young children living on the streets there. And she had no idea the McNabs had ever been street orphans, either. That explained why everyone called Dantes "a gutter rat." She thought they said that because they didn't like him, to be cruel. But surely, when their father had died, they'd had money? Why had their mother taken them to Whitechapel? Bringing them there because of family who'd been rather uninterested didn't seem a good explanation.

"If you have a problem with that, or a problem with my mother," Dantes said, his voice edged with menace, "then you have issue with me and I will no longer help you."

Vivian felt the blood drain from her face. "I have no qualms."

The tension in his face subsided. "We survived," he continued as if nothing had happened, as if her heart weren't racing with alarm. "After a few years, my grandparents, my father's parents, took us in. I never knew my mother's parents, only a few of her siblings. I don't even know if they're still alive, or where they are if they are." He took a sip of champagne, his gaze vacant as he thought back to some old memory. Whatever it was lifted his spirits enough for him to look her in the eye again. "I'm sure the first year with us was a wild one for my grandparents." A sparkle appeared briefly in his eyes but fell away quickly. "And then we were sent to boarding school."

"Eton, you mean."

Dantes started at this detail. "Yes. Your butler was listening in that day, wasn't he?"

"At my insistence, yes." Vivian gave him a sheepish look. "I apologize for spying on you. Admittedly, I was curious to know what conversations would be had without me around. I suspected your appearance in the room would make for interesting conversation. I had hoped any man vying for my attention would treat any guest of mine with respect. But that didn't happen, did it?"

Fortunately, he laughed, and it made her smile to hear it. As a servant with a silver tray passed by, they placed their empty champagne glasses upon it as music began to play. It was time for everyone to gather for the first dance.

Dantes looked down at her, and the intensity in his gaze created a strange, twisting feeling in her stomach. "May I have the honor of dancing this set with you?"

Why did it surprise her he knew the proper way to ask? "You may." She gave him the expected little curtsy. And a brush of a shy smile she couldn't hold back.

Dantes led her out to the floor, where hundreds of eyes hooked into her back. She glanced around nervously, catching many in stares.

"Lady Vivian." Dantes's low voice pulled her back to him.

"I can't do this." She gripped him tightly as panic rose. She hadn't danced in years. Why hadn't she thought to practice before tonight? How had it not occurred to her to do so? Surely, she was going to trip and fall in front of everyone, her biggest social nightmare.

"Yes, you can," he reassured her, his gravelly voice oddly calming. Despite the building crowd around them, his attention was on her and nothing else.

"I'm going to trip."

"I will take the blame for that."

"I'm going to fall and everyone will gasp dramatically and laugh and tease me about it until the day I die."

"No, you won't. I will catch you before that happens." She could hear in his voice he meant it. And as she shivered—from nerves or from his closeness?—his hand flexed in hers. "Vivian, I've got you."

Her heart leapt at his usage of her Christian name without her title. But unlike the time he'd called her "Viv," which she'd excused as an honest mistake, this time, he didn't appear abashed at all. A surge of warmth went through her as if he had whispered praise into her ear.

"Are you nervous?" She looked up at him now. After all, he hadn't been out here for a while, either.

But Dantes smiled easily back, giving her a sliver of reassurance. "Not at all." And as the orchestra began, he took her hand in his and placed his other hand on the small of her back. The spot he touched heated beneath her corset—why did that happen? She looked up at him again to see if he'd reacted to it too.

But once again, his face met hers with indifference.

Chapter Eight

O F COURSE DANTES was nervous. He was terrified, in truth, and he hated the feeling.

Dantes could be surrounded by men with pipes and knives and he wouldn't feel fear. He'd feel rage, an all-consuming need to fight for his life, but not fear.

But here in a society ballroom, he held Lady Vivian Winthrop in his arms, the woman who commanded the attention of every person in the room, people who hated him and chased after her to gain her affections and fortune. One misstep and he would humiliate her until the end of time. He had no business being here with her, and they all knew it. Why didn't she?

And the fact that Eleanor was here somewhere. A face he hadn't seen in so long—one he didn't care to see, even after all this time.

But now was not the time to think about that. He had to focus on Vivian, and that thought helped the chill.

Dantes glanced down at her hair, where a few small roses had been woven in, and he studied the way the petals surrounded each other before he circled her out and back to him. She made a little happy noise at the movement, giving him a glittering smile when she was back in his arms.

When she'd popped out of the crowd earlier, gilded in gold and skimmed in black lace, the texture of the dress she wore had led Dantes's mind into territory it had had no place going. It had taken everything to keep his face level, to remind himself she could never be his, even if he wanted her to be.

For some infernal, reason he kept having to remind himself of this.

"I'm impressed, Mr. McNab." Vivian's velvet voice brought him back to the dance floor. "You're more adept at this than I was expecting, I'm ashamed to admit. I'm sorry I doubted you."

"Ollie danced with me all week for practice," he replied.

She threw her head back in loud laughter, causing heads to turn. She reddened. "Sorry."

"Never apologize for your laughter. It's a wonderful sound."

"Why, thank you." A private smile. A long pause. He congratulated himself on his fluid movements as he had noticed a few minute stumbles from others, but there was nothing but perfection from him.

Even Queen Victoria hardly occupied his thoughts, though he caught her narrow-eyed study of himself a few times.

As the dance ended, Dantes held Vivian for a beat longer than proper. He found he didn't wish to let go, however, and the confusion behind the cause of this caused him to freeze.

"That was a lovely dance, Mr. McNab. Thank you." Vivian was looking up at him with a gentle smile.

Still holding her, he responded, "You are very welcome."

She let out a small laugh. "You do need to let go of me, however."

Immediately, he dropped his hands. He was acting rather foolish right now. "Sorry."

Vivian gave him a light curtsy and excused herself, leaving him to go dance with other men. Dantes found a spot where he could keep his eye on her. The first gentleman she danced with, Dantes knew visited brothels rather frequently. Truly, these men were scum. It was amazing women married them at all. But, of course, they didn't know the men's true hearts. Which was why Vivian needed his help.

Ollie reappeared and handed over a glass of champagne. "Drink up, Dantes, because I think you need it."

Dantes accepted it. "Why do you say that?"

His brother held up one finger. "Mrs. Gifford." Then a second finger. "Lady Vivian."

Dantes frowned. Why did he have to bring up ancient history? "I don't care about Mrs. Gifford. You know that."

"But you care about Lady Vivian?" Ollie grinned widely, as if he had uncovered some big secret.

Dantes glanced over to the other side of the room, found Vivian talking and drinking champagne with a man she had just finished dancing with, a man with twice the gambling debt Winthrop had. He turned his back to them. "I told you why I'm here tonight. Don't be daft."

Ollie clinked his glass against Dantes's. "Yes, and I came to watch the fun."

"And yet I haven't seen you since we arrived. You weren't watching anything. You were off with some woman."

Ollie waggled his eyebrows. "Defiling the library, specifically. You should find one while Lady Vivian is distracted. Women have been eyeing you."

"No, they haven't. The women who eye me are not found in a ballroom."

"Yes, they are. You just haven't been paying attention, for some wildly unknown reason."

A dramatic waltz beginning, Dantes looked back out toward the dance crowd and caught Vivian's golden blur as she spun by. She was now in the arms of a man with an opium addiction. That would not be a pretty life. "I don't know what you are referring to, Ollie."

At this, Ollie raised his eyebrows. "No? Well, allow me to theorize."

Dantes shot his amused brother a severe look, rendering his brother silent for once.

A few more dances passed and Dantes grew weary. Vivian

hadn't returned once, and he found himself strangely irritated by this. But why should he have been? He knew his purpose in being here. It must have been the familiarity he felt with her, in such an unfamiliar place.

More time passed, more incessant talking from Ollie filling Dantes's head, when he spotted Vivian dancing with a gentleman who looked rather young. If he were out of university, Dantes would have been shocked.

Ollie seemed to have the same thought. "No man here who is unmarried and even close to her age is respectable."

"No. In fact…" Dantes glanced at Ollie. "I can't even think of one, here or not."

"Nor I, and I've been pondering it myself since you told me what she'd asked of you. When will you break the news to her?"

"I'm not sure. I'm hoping I'm overlooking someone."

Their conversation became interrupted by overlapping gasps and even a few smothered laughs. All couples had stopped dancing and the music stilled with them. Something about it bothered Dantes, and he shoved his champagne at Ollie and trudged forward, searching desperately for Vivian to ensure she was all right. He needed to lay eyes on her but unfortunately didn't find her until he'd reached the dance floor.

The young man Vivian had been dancing with had somehow fallen on top of her and was trying to climb off. While the entire ballroom watched and exchanged stifled laughs, the young man's incessant apologies for making such a stupid mistake echoed in the large room.

A mistake that made Dantes see red.

But because Vivian was white faced and horrified, and he recalled the fears she had expressed in private, he became even more enraged when no one stepped forward to help her. Instead, they whispered to each other while staring at her as if she were a carnival attraction. Princes and princesses. Dukes and duchesses. Hundreds of aristocrats stared at her with haughty smirks and whispering giggles.

Dantes pushed his way through the crowd and out to her, and in his anger didn't hear the offended gasps this received.

"What the blazes is wrong with all of you?" Dantes shouted out to the crowd that had gone completely silent, his words echoing in the large, opulent room. Not one person responded. They all continued to stare, thinking their usual horrid thoughts about him. Once again, Dantes felt that familiar shame of being himself. But the shame and anger was replaced with distress when he returned his attention to Vivian. She didn't argue when he clamped his hands around her waist, lifted her up with ease, and wrapped a protective arm around her to take her out of the blasted ball.

A large piece of jagged, black lace hung from her bodice, torn from her fall.

"My dress!" Vivian cried out. Of everything to upset her right now, *that* was what she focused on? To get it out of her sight, Dantes tore the lace scrap off, hastily stuffing it in his pocket.

As Ollie caught up to them in the dimly lit hallway, Dantes realized Vivian had started crying.

And that crying became frantic as the shock wore off. "Something is wrong with my elbow. I think he broke it!"

Dantes noted she couldn't move it and held her arm against her front. He swore and looked to his brother, who hung back with his arms crossed. "Ollie, find her carriage and have it brought to her house—it'll take too long to wait for it."

Ollie nodded and his shoulders loosened before rushing off.

Dantes swept Vivian up into his arms, eliciting a whimper of pain, before shoving his way through the blasted crowd and out of the house. Outside, the cool air provided a brief respite, and he sprinted several blocks to Vivian's home, shocking numerous pedestrians who stared after him.

As they arrived in Vivian's drawing room, Heaton following frantically while directing a maid to light a candelabra nearby, Dantes helped her sit on the sofa as she continued to panic over her broken elbow.

He lowered down to one knee. "Vivian, I'm going to test your arm to find where it's broken so we can call on the physician, all right?" Though inside, he was frenzied, he was able to keep his voice level. Barely.

She nodded through her tears.

Ignoring Heaton's words of worry, he asked her to point exactly to where it hurt. It was her elbow for sure, and he pulled enough of the end of her glove down to expose it. He cupped it gently with one hand. "I'm going to do a quick test, all right?" He waited until she nodded and with his free hand, extended her arm fully and turned her palm up to the ceiling. She whimpered but was doing her best to remain calm. He then began to distract her by describing the look on her dance partner's face when Dantes had come storming out of the crowd, eliciting a tiny, watery laugh—and arced her palm up and back to her shoulder. They all heard a popping sound right as he felt the joint slip back into place.

Immediately, she ceased crying and stared up at him with giant eyes, her mouth open with bewilderment.

"Good heavens." Heaton placed a hand over his mouth.

"Your elbow wasn't broken. Luckily, it was only dislocated." Dantes's attention remained on her. "It happened to Ollie a few times when we were children. I've had to fix his more than once."

But Vivian continued to stare.

Heaton commented he needed a moment and rushed out of the room to settle what was no doubt his weak stomach.

"It doesn't hurt anymore," Vivian finally said, barely noting her ill butler escaping the room. Disbelief was etched all over her face. "At all!"

Dantes asked her to straighten her arm, then bend it, straighten and bend again. When it was clear she was fine, he sat directly next to her and massaged her elbow gently. She didn't ask him to stop and instead sat there in silence, as if the feeling were pleasant to her. Which was ridiculous, of course. She had to be merely glad the pain had stopped.

"Thank you," she finally said. She removed her gloves, tossing them to a side table.

He let go of her to allow her to do so. "Of course."

"Oh, that was so humiliating!" Vivian buried her face in her hands and groaned.

"Not for you." Dantes tried reassuring her. "But the young man you were dancing with, he'll hear about it for the rest of his life."

"No one helped me," Vivian said after a moment, pulling her hands from her face. "They only stared at me."

"Yes."

"But you helped me, didn't you?"

Dantes gave her a small smile. "Of course. I wouldn't have left you like that."

Vivian curled her legs up onto the sofa, and her gilded skirt swallowed her up. It didn't feel right leaving Vivian quite yet, so Dantes watched her as she stared off at nothing, reliving the entire terrible night.

"Did you note the gentlemen I danced with tonight?" Vivian kept her gaze averted.

"Yes," Dantes responded and, knowing what she was trying to ask, listed off the reasons each one was a scoundrel. "Of course, then there was your final dance partner, who was far too young for me to know, but it could be argued he was the worst part of your evening. In my opinion, that mess was evidence in and of itself that a newly of-age gentleman does not make a good spouse for an older woman."

She sighed in frustration, but not surprise. "This was a truly awful night, and I'm ashamed of myself for expecting anything different. I haven't been to a ball in so many years."

"What happened that got you shunned from the aristocracy?" Dantes could imagine exactly zero scenarios that could result in such a severe outcome, especially for a duke's daughter.

Vivian indicated a small oil painting on the wall nearby. It was a portrait of a regal lady, older than Vivian was at the moment, but the resemblance was uncanny. "Apparently, I am the spitting image of my grandmother when she was young. And the queen greatly disliked my grandmother for two reasons: one, because she was American and two, because Prince Albert made advances upon her on numerous occasions."

Dantes choked back a laugh, and Vivian fixed her gaze upon him. He cleared his throat. "Forgive me. But she appears to have no issue with you now?"

Vivian shrugged one shoulder. "Apparently, she dislikes the sheer number of Americans who have married into the aristocracy and because of that, I am now English enough to get back into her good graces. I believe her exact words were, *'We need more English brides!'*"

"Ah."

Vivian drummed her fingers together. "I idealized this evening to myself with silly visions of romance, of being swept off my feet. Not tripping and having a stranger fall on top of me of in front of everyone. What a disappointment."

Dantes was glad he hadn't seen it happen. The lad who'd fallen on her sure was lucky Dantes hadn't seen.

"I even went to a highly recommended dressmaker," she continued. "I wanted a pale-gray dress, but she had the audacity to tell me *no*." Vivian chuckled.

"Why?"

"Because she had decided on the gold fabric for me, claiming I would stand out amongst everyone else there. I'd be more beautiful than even the young debutantes of the season. A fat lot of good that did."

"She wasn't wrong," he said, immediately regretting it. What in the blazes was he doing?

"What do you mean?"

Dantes debated changing the subject, but she wouldn't let him get away with that. Then again, compliments hardly meant anything. "I mean, you *were* the most beautiful woman there." It was true, though he didn't mean anything by it other than that.

Vivian looked nice in her new dress, and there was nothing wrong with telling her so.

For a moment, Vivian stared at him with a stunned expression, but it morphed into amusement. "You're an amusing man, Dantes McNab. Thank you for humoring me."

"I'm serious." He was indignant that she didn't believe him and almost missed her address of him because of it. But the casual address tempted him. He knew he shouldn't continue with what he was about to say but did it anyway. Because it was the truth. She was gorgeous, and she had no idea. "When I saw you pop out of that crowd when those fools chased after you, you quite literally took my breath away."

"Liar." She arched one dark eyebrow. "You couldn't have looked more unimpressed."

He held her gaze. "Not a lie. I am your... What did I call it? Matchmaker. You are not for me to admire, no matter how admirable you may be in the moment."

The humor fell away from her face and she swallowed. In the muted gold light of the one candelabra a maid had lit, coupled with her dress, she looked as if gilded head to toe in gold.

Vivian continued talking, forcing the words out, as if perturbed. "I'm disappointed I was so excited about this silly dress and the night turned out so humiliatingly dreadful. That's what I deserve for being so frivolous and vain, I suppose. I shall never show my face to anyone again and will burn the dress as well because seeing it again will only incite embarrassment. It's ruined, anyway."

Dantes looked down at the ripped lace upon her bodice and reached his hand over to her back. His finger traced along the torn edge of the black lace, studying the feel of it. Slowly, his finger slid along the tear, from her middle back all the way down to stop at her skirt, where the tear ended.

Dantes finally spoke, his voice raspy and rough. "Your dressmaker made a daring choice of fabric. Black lace is wicked, to my eyes, at least." As he said this, he looked into her face, curious to see what her eyes would give away. She was watching him, wordless, her lips parted ever so slightly, caution shining in her eyes. But to his dismay, it was he who was hypnotized by the moment.

Chapter Nine

DANTES WAS KIND enough to study the tear on Vivian's dress that had distressed her so much. Maybe she had been more upset about the tear than she should have been, but it had been the worst way to top off an already awful night. Though she *had* been rushed home in the solid arms of one of London's most famous pugilists, which had been an experience in and of itself. Perhaps the night hadn't been a full loss.

Her skin tingled as his finger slowly traced the edge of the lace. What had he meant by that comment, that black lace was wicked? It felt silly to ask, so she ignored it.

While Dantes studied her dress, Vivian studied his profile in the dim light. His strong jaw was tense, and his hair gleamed in the light. She found herself questioning why he had been so kind to her that evening when everyone else had been so awful.

Dantes had rescued her from being chased, plucked her up from the floor while the entire ballroom had stared and whispered and laughed, and literally run her home and fixed her injury with gentle expertise, even massaging her elbow after just in case. And he seemed to think nothing of any of it. This man she hardly knew had helped her more than her own brother had, this man who, before he had said his first words to her, would have frightened her if they hadn't met in a crowded pub.

He *was* rather intimidating. Any large man was intimidating to a woman, of course, but the untamed wildness natural to Dantes was only enhanced by the deep, long scar on his face, making him look more like a battle-weary medieval Scottish warrior, ready to pillage villages and plunder women, than a modern, nineteenth-century man.

She found herself thinking about his declaration that he'd never marry, if preferring quiet at home was the whole truth of it, then scolded herself for such a silly direction of thought. It was none of her business. And though Dantes may have been kind with her, he remained a wild, scoundrel boxer with a pub; women from every direction; endless, flowing alcohol; a taste for gambling; and who knew what else.

It was, after all, how he knew the darkest secrets of high society men. He was one of them. He shared those secrets with them.

Even if for some silly reason Vivian added Dantes to her list of potential suitors, he would immediately be scratched out. From the little she knew about him, he was absolutely *not* a true gentleman.

He was exactly that which she must avoid.

Dantes finished tracing the tear and a chill went up her back when he pulled his hand away. Vivian noticed the commanding heat of his body, and how close he was to her. There was a darkening in his gaze, and it caused a funny, warm feeling to bloom in her stomach.

At this sensation, Vivial became horrified.

This was worrying. This was real life, not a fantasy encouraged by a saleswoman. It shouldn't have been happening!

Someone rang at the front door, yanking Vivian back to Earth, dissipating the thick air that pulsed between them.

Alarms rang in Vivian's mind. For heaven's sake, Dantes was a scoundrel helping her find a *husband*! How could she allow herself to be so easily affected? She had to put an end to this. Now!

"Ollie." Dantes glanced back over his shoulder with a hint of frustration as, somewhere beyond the room, Heaton and a footman passed the drawing room for the front door. Seizing the opportunity, Vivian quickly slid away from Dantes farther along the sofa, turning her eyes to the floor, too timid to meet his gaze.

He was quiet for a long moment. "When you continue your search for a mate, Lady Vivian, please ensure I'm there." And with that, he walked out, leaving her to wonder on his words.

⇛⇛⇍⇍

IN THE DARK hansom ride back to The Harp & Thistle, and after telling Ollie about Vivian's elbow, Dantes recalled the forgotten scrap of lace in his pocket and pulled it out, mindlessly weaving his fingers through it.

"What is that?" Ollie was briefly illuminated by a passing streetlamp. He leaned over with curiosity. "Is that…lace?"

"Yes, from Lady Vivian's dress."

Ollie threw his head back in laughter. "You're an absolute scoundrel!"

Dantes studied the intricate details of the sheer fabric, and now that it was in his hands, he could see it was a pattern of long-stemmed roses. Just like Vivian's perfume. He brought the lace to his nose, barely picking up the scent he was seeking, and recalled the way she'd retreated from him, disgusted. Guilt and shame ripped apart his insides.

"You're quite the odd couple," Ollie continued.

"We are not a couple."

"Then why do you reek of her perfume, and why are you fondling a piece of her dress in your hands?"

"None of that makes a couple, Ollie. You should know that better than anyone."

Ollie snickered. "Yes, but I am me, and you are you."

Dantes stuffed the lace back in his pocket, strangely comforted by its hidden presence. "What do you mean by that? I may not get around as much as you, but I haven't been an angel, either."

"Very well. When did you last spend time with a woman outside of the building holding our pub and your flat above it?"

Dantes frowned and had to take a moment to think. "I don't recall."

"You don't recall because you never have."

"That's not true. What about…" Dantes thrashed desperately through his memory. How could he not remember? "What about that walk through Hyde Park we took a few years ago?"

Ollie leaned toward him, his eyebrows sky high. "Seriously? Dantes, our pub didn't even exist yet. That was Mrs. Gifford you were with! Of course, back then, she was Miss—"

"It doesn't matter, anyway." Horrified by this realization, Dantes turned to look out the window. "I'm only helping Lady Vivian to get Bernard's debt paid off."

"You told me you didn't need the money—though to be honest, that's a mad amount to cast off."

"Would you accept it?" Dantes sneered. "Accept that mad amount from a woman? It isn't right."

Ollie blinked. "If some nob offers to give me one thousand pounds, yes, I'm taking it."

Dantes didn't respond.

"Right, so why are you really doing it, then? If accepting her money is against your morals, then you have some other motive. Don't you?"

There was a long, heavy pause. "I should have brought Victor tonight instead of you."

Ollie laughed at this, even clapping his hands together. "Victor? He'd be even more irritating than me. At least I'm not insulting you."

"No? Are you sure about that?" Dantes shot a look through the darkness, though in the moment, he couldn't see more than the outline of his younger brother.

For a while, Ollie didn't say anything, and the quiet clip-clopping of horse hooves calmed Dantes. He assumed Ollie's questioning was over. But right as he began to ease, however, Ollie spoke again in an overly teasing tone. "Are you in love with her?"

Though Ollie was clearly joking, Dantes immediately tensed. "Ollie, you know better than to say those words." His voice held a dark warning.

"I wasn't serious. But I thought your issue was with saying—"

"I've spent two evenings with the woman. Don't speak of such things!"

A long pause. "Why are you so defensive right now?"

"I'm not." Though anger boiled in Dantes's blood.

"Since we're on the subject, your behavior was quite interesting tonight."

"How so?" Dantes asked through gritted teeth.

"The way you bolted through the crowd when that fool fell on Lady Vivian? Shouted at everyone? Normally, you would never call attention to yourself like that. Curious, isn't it?"

Dantes kept quiet.

"You know," Ollie said, "not that this is related to anything, but Mum and Dad eloped after knowing each other one day."

"Not related to anything?" Irritation rising again, Dantes rubbed the bridge of his nose.

"Nope." Ollie remained shrouded in the dark, but Dantes could hear the grin in his voice. "Not related to anything at all."

"Then stop talking about them."

"All I'm saying is, *you* could marry Lady Vivian tomorrow and it wouldn't be the strangest thing our family has done."

Dantes lowered his voice to a dangerous level. "She would never and *should* never want anything to do with me. Now drop it!"

"No," Ollie shot back in irritation, and his tone became serious. "You're my brother, and I'm not going to sit idly by while you're being idiotic."

Dantes cursed loudly. Did they really have to go into this? "Look at my face, Ollie! Do you remember why this happened?"

"Yes," Ollie responded with caution. "Because you loved Mrs. Gifford."

"I'm hideous now, and don't tell me I'm not—I can see myself in the mirror. People have always kept their distance from me, but ever since..." Dantes trailed off, not caring to look back upon that day. "I could be rescuing cute, fuzzy kittens from a flood and people would still run the other direction upon seeing me. You know what he said to me after putting the blade to my face? He said, '*Now no one will love you*' and blast it, he was right!"

Ollie let out a loud, exasperated sigh. "First of all, that is utterly daft. Second, despite what you think, no one cares about your scar. Women still go off with you." Of course that would be Ollie's chosen method of measure.

But Dantes had to get Ollie to see reason and drop this insipid subject. "I look like a criminal, a murderer. Any woman with even a shred of self-respect would not go about her life with a crazed murderer by her side." He shook his head at himself. Why was he even saying that? He didn't *want* to share his life with a woman.

"You're not a crazed murderer."

"Fine, but I *look* like one. Tonight, you heard them, didn't you? Plenty of people there know me personally to some degree, and despite that fact still have wariness in their eyes when they see me." Dantes paused. "Could you imagine Vivian's young daughter playing piano at some fancy dinner party while the child's crazed-looking father glowers off to the side as she plays 'Twinkle, Twinkle Little Star'? Or myself at Christmas dinner with Vivian's snobbish nob family surrounding us?"

"Yes, I can, actually, and you want to know why?" Ollie said this as the hansom came to a stop in front of their pub. Dantes, irritated and angry by this far-too-personal conversation, went to climb out. "Sit down, because I'm not done." Ollie blocked the door.

Dantes grabbed the front of his brother's dinner jacket. "Let me through." He growled in warning.

But Ollie was unaffected by his threat. "I saw something interesting tonight. Do you want to know what it was?"

Dantes swore, then grudgingly let go.

Ollie pulled taught the lapels on his dress coat. "While Lady Vivian danced with those fools, she searched for you. She hardly paid them any attention. Her eyes were constantly ensuring you remained where you were. If you moved, she searched frantically for you."

"That means absolutely nothing, Ollie. She was nervous—she admitted that to me. I was there to help her."

"I also saw how she looked when we first arrived and you were all prettied-up."

Dantes went silent and waited. But Ollie wasn't continuing. Dantes rolled his eyes in the dark. "All right, how *did* she look?"

"Enchanted." Ollie patted his shoulder and exited the hansom.

Dantes froze as this simple but heavy word hit him, causing an impossible, tiny flutter within, but he quickly came to his senses and shook his head at himself. What a load of rubbish his brother had given him, just to boost his confidence.

Chapter Ten

DESPITE THE DISASTROUS ball, Vivian received a few invitations to afternoon tea. The aristocracy seemed to be showing cautious acceptance of her again now that the queen had deemed her English enough in these dire times, giving public approval of Vivian by allowing her at the first birthday ball. This gave Vivian a chance to reconnect with many of her old friends, the women she had grown up with, women who were now wives and mothers.

One such defrosted friend was Mrs. Oscar Bishop, whom Vivian had once known as simply Martha. Unlike with the others, afternoon tea with Mrs. Bishop consisted of only Martha and Vivian. And it happened to occur at the same time Martha's husband, Mr. Oscar Bishop, was entertaining friends from Brooks's gentlemen's club—suspiciously, many of whom were her chasers.

"Very well, you've figured me out," Martha said casually from her dark-blue, velvet chair, a table with multi-leveled trays of finger sandwiches and biscuits between the two women. "I can see it in your face. I won't even try to hide it. I figured, since you're back, maybe I could reintroduce you to some people." She'd ended this with a smirk.

Vivian had glanced out the open door to the den across the hallway, where loud, raucous laughter spilled out into the stately home. Vivian had gladly accepted the invitation for tea to reconnect with a friend. But it appeared to include more infernal meddling.

"Oh, I'm not sure I'm too interested in seeking out male attention, Mrs. Bishop," Vivian replied.

Martha had laughed and set her teacup to the side, clearly determined to ignore Vivian's protests. "I'm sorry. I don't mean to parade you around, but I did want to catch up with you and Oscar said, 'Why don't I have the boys over, too?' Two birds, one stone, as they say. Apparently, you're the popular topic at Brooks's."

Caution snaked through Vivian. She'd been wondering if Queen Victoria had been gossiping about Vivian's secret husband search. There was a lot to dislike about the woman, but Vivian would also have been surprised by this. The queen was many things, including being quite competitive. There was no way the queen would tell anyone Vivian herself had agreed to search for a husband, as that would take away her chances to succeed in creating a match. And once the queen set her mind upon something, everyone else followed. And that would decrease the queen's chances of being the one to make the match.

No, Vivian was confident Queen Victoria was not behind this. "I am?" Vivian asked, genuinely surprised at being a popular topic of anything.

Martha had nodded slowly. "Oh, yes. The boys are fighting amongst themselves over who will win you in the end."

"'Win me in the end'?" Vivian tilted her head. "I don't under-stand."

"You're actively looking for a husband now, are you not?"

Vivian's back became rigid. The last thing she'd needed was for that to get out. Time to deflect. "They assume old spinster Vivian is in search of a husband now, do they? I'm no fool, Mrs. Bishop. I know they're only after my money."

Martha's hand rested casually over the arm of her chair and she slowly looked Vivian over. "Of course they're after that—

money's what runs the world, isn't it? And how many of them are close to broke these days? But they aren't merely assuming—they were *told* you were. In fact, and you'll simply die when you hear this, they started a wager book on you. Wagers are being thrown left and right on whom you will end up choosing."

It took everything in Vivian to not claw at her chair. She needed to keep a calm face. "Oh? And who do they think is in the lead?"

"Lord George Stafford. If memory serves me correctly, he went on a carriage ride with your family once about, oh, fifteen years ago, and that got a lot of people talking about you two."

"Really? Nothing happened there." In truth, Lord Stafford was one of the gentlemen who'd called on her multiple times back when she'd been a debutante and before the queen had marked her as off-limits. Back then, Vivian had even thought something could possibly happen there. But eventually, Lord Stafford's betrothment to another woman had been announced. However, if her memory served correctly, that betrothment had lasted several years before being called off, and his fiancée had married someone else. As far as Vivian knew, he'd never married. He was also not one of her chasers at present, which ticked in his favor.

"So the carriage ride did happen?" Martha rested her chin in her hand. "That's likely *why* he's the lead for the wager." Martha then mumbled something about informing Oscar of Vivian's information. "Anyway, you do know who informed them of your search, don't you?"

"Surely not!" Vivian pressed her hand to her heart.

Martha laughed. "Why, your own brother, of course! Lord Litchfield told the entirety of Brooks's one evening, and that was the catalyst of the wager and wager book."

Vivian did her best to force a pleasant smile. Even though it shouldn't surprise her Bernard had told an entire gentleman's club about her husband search, her blood boiled regardless.

VIVIAN CLIMBED THE stairs to the National Gallery, her emerald-green skirt swishing with the movement. She paid the entry and followed the crowd toward the new Pre-Raphaelite art exhibition. After seeing Martha the other day, Vivian had decided to be more resolute in finding a husband on her own terms, and new art exhibitions were always popular social events. This would be a better place to find a potential husband than a ball.

Thankfully, when she'd sent Dantes a note asking him to meet her here, he'd replied the same day confirming he would.

Unfortunately, so much relied on Vivian finding a gentleman who wanted marriage. It wasn't even that Vivian didn't want to move back in with Father, which was part of it, of course. But the hard work of past generations had to be protected by Vivian. Gran used to share stories about Vivian's great-great grandparents immigrating to the United States from France with empty pockets and big dreams, but connections to perfumers thanks to both of them working for one. And wealthy Americans tore each other apart to get their hands on anything en vogue from London or Paris.

Gran clearly hadn't trusted Bernard with her family's fortune, and with everything Vivian had learned about Bernard since the inheritance, she didn't trust him much, either. She loved her brother, but to deny he would be detrimental to generations of hard work would be foolhardy.

As Vivian entered the new art exhibition and began searching through the crowd, she discovered Dantes was already there, standing before a painting, completely engrossed in it.

For a moment, she watched him. His head tilted ever so slightly, his hands knit together behind his back. People were all around him, with numerous conversations occurring simultaneously. And yet he continued to stare at the piece before him, as if he were alone in the room with it. The anxious pit that had rooted in her stomach over the past few weeks began to loosen. Knowing Dantes was nearby made her feel better. Safer.

As she began walking over to him, he suddenly reached into a trouser pocket, as if feeling for something he was afraid he had lost. Keys, or a billfold, perhaps. As he reassured himself the item remained in his pocket, clearly relieved, he spotted Vivian and began to approach her. He took her hand and leaned over while lifting the back of her gloved hand to his lips, throwing her back to that moment by the boxing ring. She swallowed.

"Lady Vivian." Dantes greeted her with a polite smile, letting her hand go.

"You look dashing today, Mr. McNab." Vivian returned the polite smile.

"Thank you." Dantes's face went flat and he turned his attention to the crowd. "I was thinking today you could walk about the exhibition on your own while I watch from a distance, and later can tell you if anyone you spoke to is a worthy gentleman. I didn't help you much at the ball. No one approached you until you were away from me."

"Oh." Now this, she hadn't been expecting. And the thought of husband-hunting more independently made her a bit nervous.

But he was also right.

"You're not here to be with me, anyway." Dantes looked her right in the eye as he said this.

Oh, she wished he hadn't worded it that way. "No, of course not. Very well. I'll do that if you think it's best." As she looked around the room, however, she spotted Mr. Ollie McNab near a large oil painting of three frilly women playing a card game. "I didn't realize you'd attended with your brother."

Dantes frowned and hastily looked over the crowd. "I didn't," he said right after spotting Ollie himself. Ollie noticed them at the same time and gave a friendly wave as he made his way over. Vivian waved back and couldn't help but notice Dantes scowling quite deeply.

"What a surprise!" Ollie approached them with a wide, humored grin, as a woman in an eye-watering orange dress and pink gemstone jewelry clung to his arm. He introduced his companion as Miss Penelope Findlay and as he met Dantes's glare, his face became veiled with mischief.

"What are you doing here?" Dantes's deep voice was edged with irritation.

Ollie put his arm around Miss Findlay and pulled her close, causing her to giggle. "Penelope begged to come by today, and I *thoroughly* enjoy people-watching, so I agreed." As Ollie said this, he shot Dantes an even wider smile and laughed, almost as if this were a private joke between the brothers. "But don't worry, you won't even see me."

Vivian didn't know Dantes's brother well. But to her, the younger man's impossibly good looks and easy charm screamed trouble. She wondered how the far more serious Dantes and Victor managed to deal with Ollie. She suspected he had been a handful his entire life.

Upon this thought, Vivian looked up at Dantes and saw his jaw clench. Ollie seemed to get a kick out of this, because he turned to Vivian and said, "Lady Vivian, I may be the biggest scoundrel of the McNabs, but if you choose me to be your husband, I promise I'll never look at another woman again."

She could see the humor in Ollie's eyes and couldn't help but laugh. Even Miss Findlay mock-scolded him. "Very well, Mr. McNab. I shall add you to the list—however, you may be closer to the end."

Ollie laughed loudly at this and excused himself, playfully punching his older brother as he and Miss Findlay passed by.

After their departure, Vivian began her circle about the room while Dantes went off to the side somewhere on his own. What exactly was she supposed to do next? This was all so strange. It had been so much clearer as a debutante. You got placed on the marriage market, men asked to court you, and then you got married. What was she supposed to do now? Perhaps she should have asked Dantes for advice.

As she continued to meander about, she exchanged pleasant greetings with several people before she finally noticed a lone gentleman observing a painting of a woman in a blue dress sitting in a tree, an open book on her lap. He wasn't tall, maybe even a bit shorter than Vivian, but he had a nice, square jaw and appeared fit. As Vivian approached him, she realized it was Mr. Robert Knowlton, a man who used to play cricket with Bernard when they'd been younger. Would it be inappropriate for her to start a conversation with him? Unsure of what to do, she decided to stop at the painting and observe it too, hoping he would speak to her first.

"Oh! Lady Vivian!" Mr. Knowlton said almost immediately, to her relief. "What a pleasant surprise! I haven't seen you in quite some time."

Vivian gave him a small smile. "It has been a while."

"Congratulations on your, erm…" He twisted his mouth in thought. "On your recent windfall. You know, you should come by for dinner soon!"

That was quick. "Oh, maybe—"

But he turned around and grabbed a petite woman chatting with others nearby, pulling her to his side. She barely came up to his chest. "Sweetums, look who it is!"

Sweetums shrieked out in excitement when she caught Vivian's eye. "Lady Vivian Winthrop! Ahh!" Miss Minnie Proctor—well, apparently, now Mrs. Minnie Knowlton—rushed up to Vivian. As Minnie did this, over the excited woman's shoulder, Vivian caught Dantes hovering nearby, trying his best to cover up a laugh with a cough. Fair enough, it had been a mildly humorous mistake. She couldn't help but shoot him a sheepish grin. Obviously, she'd had no idea Mr. Knowlton and Minnie had married.

Minnie pulled back. "You absolutely *must* come by soon. We have *so* much to catch up on. I'll send you an invitation." She flicked her wrist.

"That would be lovely," Vivian replied.

"Now, we do have to keep moving." Minnie flicked her wrist again. "We're doing a tour with a guide right now, but before I go, I have a question I'm *dying* to ask. Who was that man you were with at the queen's first seventieth birthday ball?"

Vivian was not the least bit surprised she and Dantes had been the source of gossip, especially with the way he'd yelled at them all. What *did* surprise her was Minnie had been the first to dare ask. "Oh, merely a friend of mine."

Minnie closed her eyes and put a hand to her stomach. "Oh, thank goodness because I thought to myself, *Surely, Lady Vivian can do better than* that*!"

Vivian frowned. "What do you mean?"

"Well, and this isn't a judgment on his character, darling, but he's a rather terrifying-looking man. His face, is all." She mimicked a slash across her own face. "And there are rumors he lives under London Bridge which, of course, is silly. But surely, you lovely creature, you could attract a man much more handsome than that! You *deserve* a man more handsome than that!"

Vivian gasped loudly at this, horrified. "Mrs. Knowlton, how can you say such words?!"

Minnie merely laughed, no doubt completely unaware. Had she always been this way? Mr. Knowlton, however, clearly understood Vivian's horror and swept Minnie away just as his wife exclaimed over her shoulder, "I'll introduce you to someone far superior!"

As the couple disappeared, Vivian was left behind feeling rather small. She glanced over to Dantes. He furrowed his brow in concern, perhaps wanting to know what had happened. But she couldn't tell him. Immediately, she shook her head, mouthing the word *Nothing*, but he held the concerned expression. Distressed, she turned away and continued around the exhibition, feeling like a leaded weight.

After another hour or two of mingling, she stopped at a painting of Ophelia just as a gentleman took to her side and said *hello*.

He wasn't someone she would normally have picked out from a crowd, but as they began discussing the contrast of the serene beauty of the painting versus Ophelia's tragic death to follow, Vivian found him rather engaging. He was a polite gentleman, a little soft-spoken, a little round in the belly, but that was a good sign, wasn't it?

But he soon began to exhibit rather strange behavior. Sweating profusely, constant dabbing at his forehead. And his hands were twitchy with nerves. Bizarre.

"I apologize, miss," he said after seeming to realize she had noticed this odd behavior. "But are you familiar with that gentleman over there? I believe his name is Mr. McNab?"

Vivian looked in the direction he had indicated and spotted Dantes leaning back against the wall. Instead of being relaxed and humored as he had been before, this time, his arms were crossed tightly over his wide chest, his jaw clenched. She met his intense, green stare, a stare that didn't falter under hers. She frowned, concerned and confused by this change in behavior.

To add to the strangeness of this, a further distance away was Penelope dragging Ollie around—but Ollie's attention was solidly on Dantes, the younger McNab's head bobbing around anyone blocking his view to keep his eye on his older brother.

Vivian turned back, not sure what to make of all of this. "Yes, I do know him. Why?"

"Are you here together? I'm sorry. It's just, the way he's glaring over here. Like he's ready to rip my head off or something." The man ended this with a shaky laugh.

There was no sense in lying. "I suppose we are. However, he is nothing more than a friend of mine."

The man let out another nervous laugh, wringing his hands as he took one step back. And another. "Well, it was a pleasant conversation, miss. However, I'm expected on the other side of the museum. Enjoy your afternoon!" And before she could respond, he bolted away and disappeared into the crowd.

Vivian stared at his vacant spot, surprised by the sudden

departure. The gentleman—whose name she hadn't even gotten a chance to learn—had clearly been frightened off by Dantes, not that she could blame him. Why was Dantes glowering? The man was right—Dantes did look like he was about to rip the gentleman's head off.

Vivian hastened over to Dantes, planting both feet squarely before him and crossing her arms. "What are you doing?" she asked, low enough so only he could hear her in the loud crowd.

He frowned even more deeply but remained in place. "What do you mean?"

"I was having a perfectly nice conversation with that friendly gentleman and you wouldn't stop glaring at us. You made him so nervous, he asked if I knew you and practically ran for his life when I confirmed I did!"

Dantes pulled away from the wall and clenched his fists. "Vivian, that idiot was arrested for battering a woman a few months ago. One of the women who works in his kitchen! The poor girl was in hospital for weeks. My sincerest apologies for having an issue with you being within his breathing space, but I thought that was the reason I'm here in the first place!"

Vivian stammered briefly. That timid man had beaten a woman? "He did? You're sure?"

"Oh, blast, Vivian, I wouldn't lie to you about something like that!"

"No. Of course not. But, then, why isn't he in prison?"

"Men like that aren't thrown in the clink. The worst criminals of London live in the nicest houses. But they'll never see the inside of a prison cell, and the newspapers will never report a single word on it because they *own* the newspapers! The police are in their pockets. These men"—he jutted his chin out to the crowd—"could kill someone right here, right now, and never even be glanced at by the police."

Vivian swallowed and didn't respond, horrified by this.

The impossibility of Gran's stipulation began to weigh extra heavily on her. "The others I spoke with in passing. Were any of them even remotely respectable? Even the tiniest bit?" It really shouldn't have been this hard to find an unmarried man with morals, who would respect her as a human being! Were all men such scoundrels?

Vivian thought back to Minnie. Even Martha had her moments.

It wasn't just the men, though, was it?

Was *she* awful, too?

Dantes scratched at his jaw, regarding her for a moment. "No. None of them were worth talking to."

"I think I've had my fill of socializing, then." Vivian tasted the bitterness in her words, thoroughly disappointed by yet another failure of a day. At this point, she would settle for anyone she could trust. Forget love—that was *clearly* impossible.

Which she'd already known going into this.

Dantes's face softened at her evident despair. "Let me take a look around, see if anyone stands out to me."

Nodding, she watched as he looked over the room. She found herself wondering what kind of woman appealed to Dantes. What kind of woman did a scoundrel pugilist desire? Vivian imagined loud, wild women. Clearly not from the aristocracy like herself, not prim and boring like her, either. No, Dantes would go for a woman who didn't care what others thought of her and went out and had fun for the sake of having a good time. Vivian imagined a vivacious, laughing woman like Miss Findlay clinging to him after he had won a fight—he, muscular, drenched in sweat as he pulled her close. An oily queasiness rolled through Vivian's stomach.

"The typical," Dantes said after assessing the crowd, unaware of her thoughts. "Lots of womanizers, and lots of alcoholics."

"So not even one?"

"Of the unmarried men? No."

Vivian let out a frustrated sigh. But before she could say anything further, she briefly spotted Ollie watching them once again, and when she caught his eye he looked away immediately.

"Is your brother watching us?" She looked up at Dantes as she asked, confused.

But the fact that Dantes looked in the direction of Ollie, already knowing where he was, answered her question before his words did. "Yes. He is."

"Why?"

He glanced down at her briefly, his face blank, before looking back up and around the crowd. "He thinks I have affection for you."

Her eyes widened. That must have been why Dantes was so irritated to see Ollie here. "Do you?"

He laughed. "No."

"Oh." It didn't seem that funny.

"Disappointed?" When Dantes asked, he looked back down at her with more focus, but his voice was arrogant.

She brushed her hands over her skirt, annoyed by Dantes's demeanor. "Of course not. Why would that disappoint me? You're helping me find a husband, and marriage isn't of interest to you, anyway. If you did have affection for me, it would be rather problematic, would it not?"

"Yes, it would." There was a long pause before he turned to face her directly. "You know what, Lady Vivian, this is a huge load of rubbish your grandmother has given you. I know grandparents are meddling, but holding an inheritance over you like that, forcing you to marry someone you may not want to just so you don't lose it? How is that supposed to be helpful? And what if you did meet the right person for you, but it was just before your deadline? Would you marry someone you hardly know?"

She stammered at the sudden change in demeanor. "No, of course not."

"Would you let go of your inheritance, then?"

What a strange direction he had taken this. "I can't let it go—that isn't an option to me. My grandmother put full trust in me to protect her family's fortune and the generations of hard work that went into it. Bernard would lose it all."

"It bothers me," Dantes continued while shoving his hands in his pockets. "I'm sure your grandmother loved you and thought this was in your best interest, and with the way you people treat marriage as a business deal, it makes sense in that sick sort of way. I just…" He looked away from her and over the top of the crowd. "You deserve better. That's all."

A shocking realization washed over her. Despite his denial, did he care about her?

Everything made far more sense that way. His willingness to help her find a spouse, the way he'd taken care of her after the ball, his worry for her now. He cared for her as a friend would. Ollie had merely misconstrued the friendship, that was all.

"I know," Vivian admitted, relieved to understand what was going on between them. "I knew from the start it would be a disastrous nightmare. I'm trying my best to remain optimistic, think positively, but it's a rather unsettling endeavor. At least I still have plenty of time. That's my only comfort right now."

Dantes looked back down at her, and then he suddenly seemed to loosen up. "You know what? You're right. You *do* have time. Look, there's a fight at my pub tonight. Not with me in it this time, but why don't you come watch it? Forget about this for one night and have an enjoyable evening for yourself. Unless you want to go home—that's fine too. But I'm going to be honest with you right now: I really want you to come back with me."

Something about the way he said this caused Vivian pause. Looking up into his face, she found a brief flicker of hope. Here was Dantes being the good friend he was, doing his best to help her feel better. And he was right to make this suggestion.

Vivian agreed to join. It wasn't as if forgetting Gran's stipulation for one night could change anything. It was a single night. What could possibly happen?

Chapter Eleven

An hour into the fight, Dantes was on the edge of his seat. But it wasn't because of the match—in fact, he was hardly paying attention to it despite the thunderous noise of the packed crowd. No, it was because Vivian had agreed to come watch it with him, and she was right beside him on a bench, not far from where he had kissed her hand for good luck all those weeks ago. He couldn't help but wonder if she was thinking about that moment too.

He wasn't quite sure why he'd invited her in the first place. Even though she had been here with Bernard, it wasn't a place for her. She was a polished, proper lady and this was worn and weary pub. But after spending more time with her at the art exhibition, he'd found he hadn't been ready for them to part when it was over. He'd enjoyed their time together too much.

They couldn't be anything more than friends, of course—not that either of them wanted that. But friendship? That appealed to Dantes. And he could spend time with her tonight, as friends, without being in the role of matchmaker. He would be Dantes, she would be Vivian, and they would be watching the fight as friends.

Nothing wrong with that.

As the night wore on and Cegelski and Martinez pommeled each other, Dantes and Vivian exchanged stories about their childhoods. Vivian and Bernard had been so close growing up, he'd often played dolls and dress-up with her and she'd played cricket with him. And Dantes opened up a bit more about living in Whitechapel. How, luckily, nothing too horrific had happened, but they'd often had to shield Ollie from violence between adults.

Dantes felt at ease with Vivian, and she seemed to be at ease with him as well, as if they had been good friends for much longer than they had been. This ease he felt was a surprising turn of events for Dantes, as he was always guarded around people, even those he considered friends.

As he thought about this, he looked over to Vivian, watched her engrossed in the fight, studied the little tuft of dark hair that hung loose in front of her ear. There was a sudden desire to loop it back around her ear, and as his gaze lingered, a brief scent of roses passed his nose, causing his heart to quicken.

As if she knew his thoughts, she suddenly turned to meet his eye. Their faces were close, but she didn't move away.

"What are you doing?" Vivian's cheeks were pinking, perhaps upon the realization he was watching her and not the fight.

He gave her a wry smile. "Nothing."

"Yes, you are. You're staring at me."

His stomach flipped at being discovered, a feeling somehow both pleasant and unpleasant. "What if I told you I was admiring you?"

Her eyes flashed with surprise, and she turned her gaze back out to the fight without responding.

Now, he felt a bit foolish.

But he should have known better than to say what he had. And he wasn't even sure *why* he had said it. It had come out, like all the other foolish words he'd said to her.

Fool's words. Because he was a fool.

Dantes tried to turn his attention back to the fight, but his mind trailed away from it. Maybe he *had* been admiring her a bit—she was beautiful—but a friend could think that about another friend. It didn't mean anything more than that, and upon reassuring himself of this, he felt marginally better.

As the crowd cheered over something he'd missed, he forced himself to remember she was in search of a particular person, someone who would be far different than Dantes. What kind of wife would Vivian make when she found the gentleman who ticked all her requirements? She was a gentle but wry soul, with an independent streak itching to shine through. Dantes tried to imagine an aristocrat being married to a woman like that.

Night after night, Dantes heard those nobs talk about their wives and mistresses, and they all wanted to marry the same generic type of woman: someone attractive enough to stroke their egos and who could throw parties for elbow-rubbing purposes. But, most importantly, would never question their husbands about anything. A woman who had absolutely no life outside of being a wife and mother and knew not to lament that, either. No boxing matches in rundown pubs, no independent visits to museums, no walking around town wherever she wished, or choosing the books she preferred.

But it also wasn't any of his business. His job was to find someone tolerable enough for Vivian. He could warn her about the man's habits, but that was all he could do.

He glanced around the room. The Harp & Thistle attracted many men of her ilk, as well as men and even women from the working class, and it was possible her future husband sat in the crowd behind them. He secretly relished in the thought that, at least at this brief point in time, she sat beside him. And he hoped the cad saw.

The crowd gasped as one of the fighters was hit and began bleeding profusely from his eyebrow.

"Oh, my goodness." Vivian suddenly turned her face into his shoulder, unable to watch. "This is far gorier than I expected!"

Dantes laughed. "That's nothing. You're lucky they're not spitting out teeth."

She lifted her face up to see him. She was sitting so close. "Does that really happen?"

As she seemed genuinely bothered by this, he decided to ease her worry. "Not really."

"When will *you* fight next? I want to watch you be challenged next time. As long as you don't have to spit out teeth after, of course." She grinned.

He chuckled in response. "A few weeks. I'll let you know when it's scheduled. It's going to be my last fight, though."

"*What?*" Vivian pulled back, all humor gone from her face. "Why?"

"I have to retire at some point. I'd rather retire now while I'm still good. I'm getting too old, too creaky."

She waved a dismissive hand. "That's utter nonsense." A pause. "How did you get into fighting, anyway?"

Dantes watched Martinez's fist connect with Cegelski's jaw. The crowd *ooh*ed as the men began circling each other again. It wasn't lost on Dantes that, while Vivian was no longer burying her face in his shoulder, she remained close to him. He glanced down at her hand resting on the edge of her seat and had the urge to take it in his.

He mentally cursed himself for such a terrible idea. Friends didn't hold hands. What was it about the atmosphere of this place that kept putting these idiotic ideas into his head?

He forced himself back to Vivian's question. "Fighting is all I was ever good at. My grandparents sent me to university, my marks were terrible, and I got kicked out for fighting. Then my brothers and I got our share of the railway sale. Nearly everything we had went into buying and starting the pub—it was a huge risk we took. I began fighting around then because it made good money as I shot to the top. But I learned to fight as a child when we were in Whitechapel. Both Victor and I did, for survival, but I was better at it than him. Quicker on my feet. I started training for real when I was eighteen. And now I'm an old goat."

Vivian laughed and for a bit longer, they watched the match, but eventually, she leaned over. "How much longer will this be?"

"It could be a minute—it could be two hours."

"Do we have to stay the entire time?"

His heart sank. "Why? You want to leave?"

Vivian shook her head before giving him a sheepish face. "I have the most atrocious headache."

ABOVE THE PUB, Dantes watched Vivian meander around his living room with curiosity. He took great care of his home, though it clearly belonged to a single man—all trim and furniture was dark wood, the walls painted a deep, dark green. And his small art collection wasn't of flowers or still-life fruit, it was subjects like war, hunting, and handsome landscapes. Others were a bit more colorful, and he made sure to lead her away from those, not sure what she would think of them and not eager to find out, either. He was quite reserved when it came to his art collection.

"I feel positively scandalous being up here with you." Vivian shot him a sheepish smile before quickly looking away again. "You're sure no one would have seen?"

"The pub doesn't have a view of the stairs. There's no way anyone would have seen." Unwritten rules forbade Vivian from being alone in his home. Personally, he could care less as she had made the suggestion to come up here to escape the noise.

Vivian stopped as she spotted a tintype photograph on a small table beside a leather chair. She picked it up gently, observing it for a moment. "These are your parents," she said while searching his face. "You look just like your father. And you have his eyes, too, don't you? Well, he either had blue or green because they're so pale here. I'm assuming they were green like yours."

Dantes's face burned hot. "You're right. They had that taken right before he was killed. Ollie is in there somewhere, in fact." He chuckled a bit.

Vivian gazed upon the photo for a bit longer before setting it back down. "Why did he become estranged from your grandparents?"

Dantes recalled the many stories he had heard about his father. Death-defying horse races down Rotten Row. Partaking in illegal duels—though he never had gotten an answer on whether or not his father had killed anyone. Disappearing for a year in Paris with no contact. Running away to invest in the railway. Dantes told her these stories, and more. "My grandparents, though their patience wore thin, didn't fully cut him out of their life until he married my mother. That was the final straw."

"The queen mentioned them to me. She said he stole from your grandparents and that's why they became estranged."

"That's not true. Well, he may have stolen from them, but they told that story because they didn't want anyone to find out he married my mother."

"Why?"

"Because she was poor and Irish. Of course, once Victor and I came about, the truth was eventually discovered. One can't hide for too long whom a future duke married." Bile rose in his throat. "Of course, he didn't live long enough to ever see the title."

Vivian came up to him, hesitating before gently placing a hand on his arm. "I'm sorry he died so young," she said in a softened voice. "He sounds quite fascinating."

Far too aware of her touch, he pulled away. "It was a long time ago." He flattened his voice. "I wish it hadn't happened, but it did and there's no bringing him back."

Unexpectedly, and for some unknown reason, he was feeling nervous. So he decided to keep talking. "I haven't told you the reason why I received Dantes as my nickname yet, have I?"

Vivian grinned wide. "No, you haven't, and I've been dying to know."

And so, he told her the story. How a few years into living on the streets of Whitechapel, they'd been swept up by their grandparents.

"Truth be told, I hated when it happened." Dantes laughed,

remembering the fight he'd put up when being dragged to their gleaming carriage. "It'd been scary, yes, but there'd also been no restraints for us in Whitechapel. No adult to answer to. When our grandparents began forcing baths, bedtime—anything with a schedule—we began to act out."

Six months into arriving at his grandparents' house, Dantes—then only Edmond—had been tired of being told what to do. Their grandparents had held a large dinner party one evening and the three McNab boys had been sent to bed extra early against their wishes. Irritated by this, he'd begun plotting his revenge. Led by Edmond, the brothers had crashed the party by sliding down the banisters with loud calls and shouts—though not Ollie, as he'd been too young and run amok as small children did—and run circles around the party while swinging toy wooden swords about. By that point, the guests had been quite drunk and found the entire saga hilarious. Someone had yelled out, "Watch out for Edmond Dantès!" and the name had stuck.

"My grandparents and their friends only referred to me as 'Dantes' from then on out, and the habit was quickly adopted by Victor and Ollie."

Vivian laughed heartily at this story, and the loud sound made his heart skip a beat. But when her laughter died down, there was a funny look in her eye. She was still humored, but warmth glowed at him.

They were just friends, though, he had to remind himself, as that look in her eye spelled trouble. Just friends.

WHEN VIVIAN HAD told Dantes she'd had a headache, it hadn't exactly been a lie. It *had* been a long day and she *did* have a headache because of it. But mostly, she had grown tired of the noise of the crowd and the sounds were beginning to pound inside her head. She'd needed a quiet break but had known there wasn't a fitting space anywhere in the pub.

Dantes would know her being in his private flat would be quite the scandal. And Vivian did feel a bit daring being there. But at the same time, she was nearly thirty. He was already past that. It wasn't like they were eighteen years. They were solidly into adulthood, and no one would find out.

Plus, she'd been enjoying their time together at the fight. But she'd also been quite curious to see the more personal side of the burly man, and she now had one opportunity to do so. Dantes often seemed standoffish, but for whatever reason, he was opening up a bit.

After sharing stories about their lives, their families, and learning more about the way Dantes had grown up with one eye always open, she began to see a more emotional side to him. When she'd first met him, she never would have suspected he had a tintype of his deceased parents in the most prominent place of his private living quarters. And the way he joked, lovingly, about his brother being in the tintype—their mother must have been newly pregnant, as she didn't appear to be with child—had shown Vivian a side of the cryptic man she'd never expected to see.

She enjoyed, too, that he had shared the story behind his nickname, that he considered her a good enough friend to share it with her. How curious it was to go from Whitechapel to living amongst the aristocracy, even though it sounded like his duke and duchess grandparents ran with a wilder circle than her duke father did.

Vivian looked around the tidy, handsome room, aware Dantes watched her every move. Without realizing it, she began to rub her arms, feeling chilled.

"Are you cold?" Dantes asked, worry sitting between his brows.

"A little bit, yes, but don't put yourself out to accommodate me."

"It's not a problem." He went over to the fireplace, where he began to place logs inside. When the fire roared to life, warmth quickly filled the room.

Noticing books sitting atop the mantle, Vivian relished the opportunity for another peek into the standoffish man and studied the spines of the books.

Not surprisingly, there were several Alexandre Dumas books. But also *Les Misérables* by Victor Hugo. Vivian wondered if he felt a kinship with the characters. That, however, would be far too intrusive a question to ask.

As she studied the titles, it occurred to her how being here could destroy not only her reputation, but her family's as well. And that wouldn't bode well for Bernard and Anne, whom she was trying so very hard to help.

She tried reassuring herself once again there was no possibility anyone would find out.

"You have an interesting collection of literature, Dantes." Vivian turned to him. She was surprised to find him standing so close to her, and for a moment, the only sound that filled the air was the crackle of the fireplace.

There was a strange look on Dantes's face, but he seemed to snap out of it and put his attention on the books. "Yes. I enjoy stories in which a poor underdog rises up to get his revenge."

This seemed like an oddly specific story to enjoy, but before she could comment on that, a bright flash illuminated the living room at the same moment of a rather loud explosion. Vivian yelped and jumped.

"Sometimes people set off fireworks after a match," Dantes murmured, looking over to the windows. "Are you all right?"

Vivian let out a nervous laugh while placing a hand over her heart. "Yes. It was just...quite unexpected." Her heart galloped hard, and she let out a breath of air in an attempt to calm it.

As if he could hear her pounding heart, Dantes focused sharply on her, then shocked her by reaching out to touch her. It was an unexpected and intimate gesture, and she looked up at him with wide eyes as his rough hand cradled her cheek.

Something was bothering him. Though his face held no expression, there was an inner turmoil showing in his green eyes. The pain was clear, but there was something else behind that pain, though she couldn't identify it. Either way, it was probably from an evening thinking about his parents or talking about the past.

What was she supposed to do, though? How was Dantes expecting her to react? How did she *want* to react? And why was he touching her cheek in the first place?

She should have been outraged. She should have been slapping his hand away! If a man had ever dared to touch her face before tonight, she would have been terrified, to say the least. Yet Dantes was doing just that with his rough, ungloved hands and she wasn't upset by it. Confused, yes, but not upset.

Why?

Vivian swallowed as she held his gaze and his thumb gently swept across her skin, sending a tingle down her neck and spine.

She needed to put an end to this. Dantes was a scoundrel, and she was clearly too naïve to understand what kind of game he was playing. Irritation rose. She'd thought they were friends, but it seemed he saw her as something to play with. Vivian opened her mouth to say something, but another firework went off, filling the room with a flash of light.

She gasped at the shock of noise filling the silent room. Not to mention it seemed utterly foolish to light fireworks in a city.

"I'm sorry." Dantes dropped his hand and looked away. "I shouldn't be doing that."

Surprised he would openly admit that, all she managed to get out was, "It's fine."

Dantes took several steps back, apparently wanting to get away from her now. The man was confounding. "No. It's not fine." His voice ground with frustration. "You are not mine to touch. You belong to someone else, and above all else, you should not want anything to do with me." He turned and began to walk away, leaving a strange feeling of emptiness within her.

Vivian unwittingly took a few steps toward him but forced herself to stop.

He was right.

A tightness took hold of her throat and she tried to clear it away. "Where can I get a glass of water?"

Dantes gave her vague directions to another room. Vivian closed herself off in the kitchen and leaned against the door to settle herself. But before she had a chance to consider what had just happened, much less locate a glass, a loud explosion shook the building, nearly knocking her to the floor.

Chapter Twelve

DANTES BEGAN TO rush toward the kitchen. In the seconds before the living room filled with thick, black smoke, he spotted orange flames crawling across the ceiling, as if the Devil himself were coming for Dantes. He started coughing and as the smoke filled the flat, he heard Vivian coughing somewhere else now, too. The stinging of the smoke in his lungs made it impossible to think, to remember which direction he faced, to remember where Vivian was.

He heard her cry out for him, her voice pierced with terror, but he couldn't locate the sound. Now unable to open his eyes, but knowing the fire would quickly overtake the flat, he covered his mouth and nose with his shirt and rushed forward with his arm extended, trying to locate the kitchen.

His fingers found the door. It was shut, but because of the heat, the wood expanded. The door was stuck.

"Vivian!" It took everything in him to bang hard on the door and yell out to her and he was punished with the effort with gasping, rib-bruising coughs. Heat crept across his back, and he could hear the wood of the building crackling and roaring, as if they were inside his fireplace. Everything in him screamed to escape posthaste, but he would burn in hell before he would leave Vivian behind.

Dantes shouldered hard into the kitchen door and it flung

open and banged against the wall. And then he found her arm, or maybe her arm found his—he never would remember. But he grabbed her hand and blindly rushed where he believed windows were, praying with all of his heart that he didn't make a fatal error and go the wrong direction. Escaping from the window was dangerous, but there was one window in which a tree grew close enough to attempt to climb down. He had cursed that exact tree more times than he could count because the slightest breeze made it scratch the window at an obnoxious volume. He had been meaning to trim it back but now was quite glad he'd never gotten around to it.

Finding cold glass with his fingertips, he said a silent thanks and shattered the window with one swift kick. The smoke began spilling out into the night air.

"Escape." His voice cracked and he half-helped, half-threw Vivian out onto the tree. She started up a coughing fit again.

Rapid voices and shouts met his ears from below and he was able to open his eyes enough to see Victor sprint around the back corner of the building, his face sweaty and carbon-streaked. Dantes closed his stinging eyes again. "Victor, get her!"

Then someone grabbed his forearm.

"It's me." Through verbal commands, Ollie helped him out of the window and onto a sturdy branch. Dantes mentally promised to ensure no one ever cut down this tree. "Don't worry, Victor has her."

Ollie gave Dantes directions on where to set his feet and hands, and Dantes managed to open his eyes for enough short moments to see two branches that would lead him to a safe height to drop down.

"That's what you get for leaving a fight for a woman." Ollie seemed to be doing his best to sound upbeat.

Dantes appreciated a shred of humor in the moment and began to laugh but was immediately overcome by coughing.

"Sorry, no more jokes." Ollie dropped off the branch after Dantes, then pulled Dantes over to the greenway behind their building, explaining along the way one of the fireworks had gone directly into Dantes's flat.

"How bad is the fire?" Dantes asked, though the overwhelming stench of it told him enough.

Ollie didn't answer the question, but like Victor, he had streaks of dirt and carbon on his face as well. "The fire is at the front of the building. People are out there throwing water on it until the fire brigade arrives."

When Dantes collapsed into the brown grass, a stranger, an elderly woman wearing a dark shawl, rinsed out Dantes's eyes. Though they still felt dry and scratchy, he could finally keep them open. She gave him water, too, which he chugged down and the urge to cough eased. He briefly forgot about the mess around him when he spotted Vivian sitting on the ground nearby. With the fire up front, hardly anyone was back here. The elderly woman went to Vivian and began talking to her. Vivian kept wiping at her eyes but was able to communicate well enough with the stranger that Dantes felt a shred of ease.

Ollie gave Dantes a squeeze on his shoulder as Victor approached. Victor dripped with sweat, and his face was stony. He rubbed a fist over his forehead, where black hair stuck with sweat. "The front of the building caved in. Your living room"—Victor met Dantes's eye—"is probably ruined. The pub is buried under rubble and water. Luckily, despite the sheer size of the crowd, no one has come up missing yet. Because the flying explosive went into Dantes's home instead of the pub, it gave enough time for everyone to evacuate before the ceiling collapsed."

"Thank God," Dantes replied. Human life was far more important than anything else. But he also knew Victor was more worried about their business than Dantes and Vivian, however, so when his brother immediately rushed away after stating the facts, he didn't stop him.

Later, with the help of the fire brigade, they would be able to assess the full damage and go through his belongings with their insurance company. Dantes clenched his jaw at this, thought about the tintype of his parents, his art collection, and hoped they had somehow survived the inferno.

"You're lucky." The elderly woman appeared again with more water. "That you and your lady escaped."

Unsure of what else to do or say, he thanked her and she left, likely to head back out front. Once the stranger was out of sight, Vivian came to sit closer to Dantes, though she kept a cautious distance. Not that he could blame her. If he ever saw her again after tonight, he would be surprised.

They watched in silence as thickening smoke rose into the night sky. He hoped that meant the fire brigade had finally arrived, but it also meant everything inside his home was burnt to a crisp. At the snap of a finger, his life had been completely turned upside down. Again.

And to make it worse, he'd acted like a complete cad. But the way Vivian had studied his home, his art, his books, not realizing she'd been seeing inside his soul... Few people aside from his brothers had been allowed into his personal space. But those who had been had never taken the time to look or study. They'd been there to take, to use him. Vivian was the only person who'd seen Dantes for who he was and hadn't laughed. She hadn't laughed at his art, she hadn't laughed at his books, she hadn't laughed at his face or his scar.

And when he realized this, he had the sudden urge to take her in his arms.

Which, of course, he didn't and couldn't do.

And it was distressing. One day, she would be gone, this woman who treated him like a human being. She didn't care for him as anything more than a friend and never would. And while his mind battled with itself and he came to understand this, he reached out to touch her one time.

He cradled her cheek in his hand, expecting her to be disgusted, secretly hoping she would be happy by this gesture.

But her eyes shuttered, and she looked away.

And thus, he let go.

Vivian began coughing again and guilt tore through him. If it weren't for him and his bad luck, she wouldn't have gone through this. She would have been at home, safe and sound, if he hadn't been so selfish as to bring her to the pub with him.

He really should have known better than to allow himself to get close to someone. He knew better. He knew better!

Handing Vivian water the stranger had left behind, Dantes watched her gulp it down with greed. "I know you're not all right," he said, leaning forward to rest his elbows on his knees. "So I'm not going to ask that question."

She was sitting in the small patch of grass, her green skirt spread like a circle around her, and he noted the way her eyelashes stuck together from her tears. But she didn't respond or even look at him.

If she hated him in the moment, he wouldn't blame her one bit.

"I'm sorry, Vivian," Dantes said. "I don't know what else to say. But I mean it."

She let out a sigh, shook her head with irritation. "Ignoring the fact that we nearly died just now, I don't know what game you're trying to play. I wasn't going to say anything, but now I'm in a rather sore mood and I'm not going to keep my mouth shut about it."

"What 'game I'm trying to play'? What do you mean?"

She let out an irritated huff. "You keep… You keep doing things that don't make any sense to me. I'm not the most experienced woman in the way of the world and it is very confusing to me."

"What things?"

She looked over at him with exasperation. "I thought we were becoming friends. But then, you touched me in a way I'm rather sure is not a way friends touch each other."

He swallowed, not knowing what to say.

"Why do you do that, Dantes?"

Clenching his jaw with shame, he turned his attention back to his building. If she had her reasons to be confused, well, he had his own. Such as her choosing to go up to his flat, and her use of his nickname, something rather personal, while in the midst of telling him to give her space. "It won't happen again," he responded darkly.

"See that it doesn't."

Humiliation coursed through him. Maybe he deserved it. "You're one of the most powerful women in the country," he began. "With more money than I could imagine. Every time I go somewhere with you, people stop what they're doing to watch you walk by. You could literally have any man you could ever want on this planet. A duke? A prince? A king? The president of America? Probably married, but if you went up to him, he'd stammer like a fool and do anything you asked."

"What are you trying to say, Dantes?"

He ran his hands through his smoke-smelling hair and felt small and insignificant. "Forget it."

Vivian let out a single laugh, but it lacked humor. "Well, it's not at all like that, believe me. And even if it were…" There was a long pause. "I chose to come here tonight, Dantes."

It was tempting to ask what she meant by this. Obviously, she meant as a friend, but saying those words after his claim she could have any man she chose?

It was tempting to continue this conversation and clarify it. But it was also pointless. For so many reasons.

But would their friendship be salvageable after tonight? He wasn't sure of that, either.

Vivian handed over the water and Dantes accepted it to take another deep gulp. A breeze kicked up, and the stench of burnt wood singed his nose.

"I was engaged once." He forced the words out before he could change his mind. "A long time ago." Out of the corner of his eye, he saw her head swing toward him.

A long silence. "Oh?"

"Yes. To Miss Eleanor Crosby."

"Mr. Thomas Crosby's sister?" Her voice hitched.

"Yes."

A pause. "Do you still love her?"

Dantes looked directly at her, concern pulling at his brow. "Christ, no."

"Then why are you telling me?"

"Because it feels like something I should tell you."

She seemed to mull this over but offered no other comment and changed the conversation. "What did your brother have to say about the damage?"

Dantes glanced up at the smoke again. "The front partially collapsed. A firework hit my home directly." Panic rose, but he forced it back down. "It's all gone. My home. My business. Everything."

Outside of his brothers, Dantes had never told anyone about his paintings before. He'd had the paintings because he liked them, because they'd felt familiar and real, and that had been that. He didn't really want to talk about them otherwise.

He hadn't possessed anything wildly famous—no Claude Monet, no Berthe Morisot, nothing like that. His favorites had been by Gustave Courbet, a French artist known in the art world, but most people passing by on their way to work wouldn't recognize his style.

The artist had been extremely controversial. Over his career, Courbet had been frequently called a narcissist and had shocked French society with dark subject matter, as opposed to the sickly-sweet romanticism paintings of his predecessors. Dantes had found himself drawn to the man's work, perhaps a bit humored by the man as well. But the art was just…realistic. He'd shown working-class people, he'd shown death. So many people lived each day in a desperate ignorance of the realities that made Dantes a gutter rat instead of a high society gentleman, but Courbet had captured the essence magnificently.

The last few years of Courbet's life, the two men had exchanged letters. Dantes had seen Courbet's painting *A Burial at*

Ornans, a depiction of a rural French funeral. It was dark and bleak, evoking a feeling of despair and ugliness, and critics had despised it. But it had reminded Dantes of Whitechapel, of his own mother's funeral. It had hit him so deeply that he'd written to the artist about the painting's effect upon him, opened up about his strange life that had begun under a laudanum-addicted mother, to living as an orphan on the streets, to boarding school with Britain's richest sons. Courbet had responded and ignored the comments about *A Burial at Ornans*, hadn't said a thing about Dantes's life, yet despite the seeming lack of care, had continued to write Dantes until his death. During that time, Dantes had bought and acquired a few paintings from the artist, none of which had ever been displayed to the public.

There'd been other paintings, too, that had not been by Courbet, but Dantes had loved each one for its own reason.

Now they were all gone. Forever.

Dantes thought about this as he met Vivian's eye. "Almost everything can be replaced. But the photograph of my parents, and my paintings? I'll never get over losing them."

Chapter Thirteen

"D O YOU NEED more water, dear?" Father leaned forward with a furrowed brow. The fresh April air swept at his white hair sticking out from beneath his black top hat. The Winthrops were out for yet another drive through Hyde Park in the landau carriage, the soft top folded down so Vivian received maximum fresh air for her healing lungs.

But before she could tell him *no*, Anne jumped in. "How are the pillows I grabbed from the house? Are you comfortable?"

In the days after the fire, her family had learned what had happened. However, Vivian hadn't told them the full truth, as Father would have had a conniption if he knew she had been alone with Dantes in his flat. She'd admitted to being at a fight when the fire had occurred and how she'd been helped out by the pugilist Father had met before. Vivian also suspected Father did not believe the full story by the way he'd looked down his nose after the story had ended. He'd seemed to believe her up until the part where Dantes had helped her escape, after which his frown had deepened severely. Before he could scold her or remind her about proper behavior, she'd hurriedly told him who Dantes's grandparents were. All Father had said after that was, "Hmm."

Bernard had found the entire saga riotous.

But Anne had believed her story. Later on, when they'd been alone, Vivian had admitted the truth to her friend. Anne had been utterly tickled Vivian's life had been saved by a pugilist. Her favorite part was where Dantes had broken down the door to get to her.

Bernard interrupted her thoughts. "Are you warm enough, Vivian?" He tucked the wool blanket wrapped around her even tighter, to where now she couldn't even move. Only her feather-hatted head stuck out, and she gave him an unamused look.

She wanted them to stop fussing. *Please.*

"The physician told you to keep up with water intake. It will help with healing," Father began again. "I have more if you need it."

But Vivian was having none of it. "If I have one more drop of water, get half a degree warmer, get slightly more comfortable, I will simply explode like that firework!" She said this much sharper than she'd meant to. But it had been days of this fussing, and she could not stand another minute of it.

Her family exchanged hesitating glances with each other, then removed the blanket and pillows around her. Father dropped the discussion about water.

Vivian let out a long sigh of relief, feeling much less restricted. "Thank you."

"We're only worried about you, that's all," Father said, his gaze dropping to the floor.

She couldn't help but give him a bit of a smile. "I know, but I'm fine. Really."

The Winthrops continued the drive in glorious silence and Vivian's mind began to trail off with the relaxing sway of the landau. In the constant state of inanimation of late, she found her mind often lingered toward the final moments with Dantes before the fire.

That entire night had been quite awful, and she felt terrible for even feeling that way. After all, she'd been able to leave and recover in the comfort of a luxurious Mayfair house, whereas Dantes had no home now, no business, and he had to stay with Victor for the time being.

And between that and the strange encounter they'd had, where she'd told him to essentially leave her alone and never touch her again, she was sure that was the end of their newly formed friendship.

And she found herself melancholy because of it.

But to her abject surprise, Dantes had begun writing letters. First, he'd sent a brief one inquiring after her health. When she'd responded the same day, he'd written another. They'd begun to send chatty letters twice a day. She confided her frustration with her well-meaning, fussing family.

Dantes, meanwhile, kept her updated on the daily happenings of the fallout from the fire.

The McNab fire had hit a soft spot of the residents of London. It was a big city with a small-town heart and anytime a family or a business experienced a tragedy, strangers came out in droves to assist in any way they could. Each day, they came with no expectation of receiving anything in return, refusing any offers the brothers gave because it would be paid forward someday. The brothers refused to accept this as an answer, however, and invited everyone to the upcoming reopening, whenever it was, with the first two rounds on them.

Journalists had even stopped by one morning, and in the evening edition, Vivian had found a photograph of Dantes standing with Victor and Ollie in front of their building, the exterior of which was covered with a tarp. There was also a photograph of Dantes on the second page when he'd been younger, highlighting his boxing career and his narrow escape from death.

She breathed a sigh of relief when there was no mention of a woman being seen with him that evening.

But she'd found herself staring at Dantes's picture for a long time. And she'd been forced to admit she missed him dearly. A few times, she'd debated stopping by the pub site to see how Dantes was faring with the cleanup, but it hadn't felt right. The rift between them was too great. And it wasn't like Dantes had stopped by, or indicated in a letter he wished to see her.

She was not going to act like her chasers.

But she also couldn't overlook the fact that she missed him, as much as she would have liked to. Thus, two days ago, while writing his second letter of the day, she took a chance and blatantly confessed to missing him. Maybe this could be a nudge toward seeing each other in person.

However, she didn't receive a reply.

"Oh, look, Vivian!" Bernard pulled her from her watery thoughts. "It's the Staffords!"

Something unpleasant shot up within Vivian and she tore her attention in the direction of the white landau stopped beside theirs. Seated inside was the Earl of Havenfield and his adult children. The earl's eldest son, Lord George Stafford, was staring at her.

Vivian turned to look at Bernard with a hard, unblinking stare. Lord Stafford was the man currently blessed with 'best odds' of marrying Vivian at the wager book at Brooks's. The wager book created by Bernard. When her stare did not break, Bernard's wide grin melted away. And before Lord Stafford could get one word out, Bernard made an excuse to leave and they were off again, leaving Lord Stafford and his family behind in evident bewilderment as they exchanged rapid, wide-eyed glances.

Vivian sharpened her hard stare. "Mrs. Bishop told me about your Brooks's wager book."

"Your *what?*" Anne exclaimed before Bernard could respond.

"Would you relax?" Bernard hissed back to Anne. "I didn't put any money in it. I'm only managing it!"

Vivian kicked him, though not as hard as she would have liked. "It's wagers on who I will end up marrying, Bernard!"

"It's just a bit of fun, Vivian." Bernard grimaced as he rubbed his shin. "Don't take it so personally."

But before she could respond, Father had something to add. "Now, Bernard, Vivian doesn't exist to be a source of entertainment for you."

"Why, thank you, Father." She pulled her head back with a bit of surprise.

"And on that note," Father continued. "Lord Stafford? Come now, Bernard. The man is an utter scoundrel, not someone you should want to marry your only sister."

Vivian's eyebrows raised high.

Father leaned toward her with a grin. "I pay more attention to people than you give me credit for. Now, why don't you and Anne ditch the two of us and go shopping? Try getting on your feet again. I'll have Adamson drop you off at the millinery you like on Grosvenor Street and he'll come back to fetch you after dropping Bernard and me off at home. That should give you about an hour or so."

This may have been the first time throwing money at a problem actually helped.

VIVIAN AND ANNE were admiring spools of hat ribbon when Anne brought up Bernard. "He's been on his best behavior lately," she said flatly while petting a spool of pink velvet. "I think hitting rock bottom, then your *mishap*"—she whispered this because no one outside of their families knew Vivian had been at the fire. And even among her family, only Anne knew she'd been in Dantes's home, alone with him—"it might have been the thing to knock some sense into him. He's even been helping with the children, which is unheard of."

"That's wonderful, Anne." Vivian held out hope for her brother's marriage. "It sounds like he's finally turned a new leaf."

Anne put the spool back in place. "We shall see. He seems to think acting as he always should have been erases everything, however." She paused, as if weighing whether or not to continue. She decided not to. "Again, we shall see."

Understanding the conversation was meant to be over, Vivian made her way to the sample hats. Nothing in particular tickled her fancy. It was strange—she was looking at beautiful hats, knew they were beautiful hats, yet nothing inspired her.

Anne gasped, lifting one hat gingerly. It was of pale-blue velvet that rouched on one side, with a large, bow-shaped crystal adornment centered on the rouching. A complicated array of feathers splayed out from behind it. "Vivian, this is the most beautiful hat I've ever seen in my life!" As Anne continued to gush over it, the shop owner, who wore a jaunty, black hat resembling a tiny top hat, began to hover nearby.

"It is beautiful," Vivian agreed. "That blue matches your eyes perfectly."

"It's too bad it would take a while to make." Anne pouted playfully.

The shop owner took the sale opportunity and stepped forward. "I made one recently and the purchaser changed her mind about it. It's never even been tried on. If I had to guess, your hat size is six, seven-eighths?"

Anne's pale eyes went wide. "Yes."

The shopkeeper smiled and excused herself, asking the two women to meet her by the mirrors in the other room. Moments later, she returned and set a hat box down on a chair, lifted the lid, and removed the hat to tie upon Anne's head.

"Anne, that hat is stunning on you," Vivian said with admiration. "Your coloring is so fair, I would normally pick a darker color because of that, but my goodness, it's as if you and the hat were made for each other."

Anne laughed and admired herself in the mirror, turning side to side numerous times, her eyes twinkling at her reflection. She met Vivian's gaze in the mirror. "I feel like the most beautiful woman in the world. How silly am I?"

"Not silly at all. I know the exact feeling. It's a good one to have." Vivian watched as Anne continued to stare at herself, almost with wonder, and for the first time in many years smiled so genuinely, it reached her eyes. It hit Vivian that Anne had been struggling in her marriage, not for months, but for years. In fact, the last time she recalled Anne smiling with such brightness was when her second child had been born and introduced to the family. They never did have any other children after, and that had been five years ago.

As the milliner untied and removed the hat, she informed Anne of the price. Anne's face immediately fell. "Perhaps another time," Anne said forcefully with a pained smile following. "It is a beautiful hat, though."

"Thank you for the compliment." The milliner gave a small curtsy then walked out of the room with the hat now snug in its hat box.

Anne's face twisted with disappointment. "Would you mind giving me a moment?"

"Of course not." Vivian gave Anne a kiss on her cheek and left without a word. Out in the main shop area, Vivian searched the bustling room for a woman with a jaunty little top hat and found it a moment later. The milliner had a large, flat box out to show a customer different types of feathers.

"Excuse me," Vivian said once she'd caught the milliner's attention.

The woman smiled, her eyes crinkling with the movement. "Lady Vivian, may I help you with something?"

"The blue hat Lady Litchfield tried on. Could you put it on my account?"

The milliner bowed her head. "Of course."

Vivian bit her lip. "And also, if she asks about the box when I collect it before departing, could we tell her it contains a hat I ordered weeks ago?"

"A gift," the milliner replied, holding up a finger. "I will follow your direction if she asks."

After thanking the milliner, Vivian toured the room and eventually stopped at a round table in the middle of the floor where numerous kid gloves were laid out. She lifted a pair in pale pink, set them back down, and as she did this, made eye contact with the woman on the other side of the table. They both paled at the same time—it was the blonde woman who'd been with Mr. Crosby at the queen's birthday ball. His sister, Miss Eleanor Crosby. No, that wasn't right. She'd married a few years ago, if Vivian remembered correctly. Wasn't she Mrs. Corbin Gifford now? Either way, Mrs. Gifford clearly knew who Vivian was. But was it because her brother was trying to woo Vivian into marriage, or did she know about Vivian and Dantes?

What were they, anyway?

Before either of them could say anything or rush away, though, Mr. Crosby appeared at his sister's side and asked her to pick between two pairs of gloves. Apparently realizing his sister was distracted by something, he looked over to see what had caught her attention and finally noticed Vivian. Mr. Crosby looked almost as surprised as his sister and hid the gloves behind his back.

"Lady Vivian!" Mr. Crosby said with forced enthusiasm. "What an unexpected surprise. Your butler told me you were feeling unwell and wouldn't have visitors for quite some time."

Blast, she would do anything to be able to disappear right now. "Yes, Mr. Crosby, that's correct. But as you can see, I'm feeling much better already." She forced the enthusiasm right back to him.

He smiled. "I apologize for my overt surprise upon seeing you. I'm afraid you caught my sister and I searching for a get-well-soon gift for you." He held up the gloves with a boyish guilt. Mrs. Gifford, meanwhile, turned to give him a wide-eyed look of astonishment.

Vivian responded with polite laughter and cleared her throat at the feel of an alarming tickle. "That's not necessary, Mr. Crosby, though I appreciate the thought."

"It's nothing. Truly. I shall bring your gift by tomorrow, if you're accepting visitors again."

Vivian paused, unsure how to respond. Before she could say

anything, however, a rather severe coughing fit threatened to rise. She tried choking it back, but it forced itself out so violently, she had to steady herself against the side of the round table. The aching in her already sore ribs meant she couldn't look up to see the faces of alarm on every shopper in the store, though truly that was a blessing in disguise.

"Hay fever," she squeaked as the shop owner rushed over. Vivian, still coughing deeply, stumbled her way over to the mirror room, the shop owner guiding her along and into a chair. As Vivian took in a gasping, wheezy breath before coughing severely again, she overheard Mrs. Gifford say from the other room, "Oh, do give it up, Thomas."

Anne rushed over to crouch at Vivian's side and with a gentle hand, patted her back. "Are you all right?"

But Vivian couldn't respond as the hard coughing continued. The shop owner reappeared with a glass of water and Vivian gulped it down. Immediately, the coughing subsided and she felt better.

"Perhaps we should get you home after this," Anne said, her brow furrowed.

Vivian wholeheartedly agreed. "Good idea."

The shop owner took the glass back. "I'll gather up your purchase then, Lady Vivian."

Anne blinked at Vivian. "You bought something?"

"It's a beautiful hat she ordered several weeks ago." The milliner then shot a private wink to Vivian as she left the room.

"My ribs are in agony." Vivian sunk back in her chair. "I wonder if lungs can bruise. It sure feels like it."

"Should you call on the physician on your way home?"

But Vivian shook her head. "That's not necessary. Just give me a moment to gather my bearings and we can leave." She closed her eyes. Her heart rate had shot up alarmingly, but the dry itch in her lungs was beginning to subside, and her heart calmed along with it.

Until she heard a new voice. "Smoke inhalation, by chance?"

Vivian's eyes flew open to see Mrs. Gifford walk into the room.

Panic slammed into Vivian. Did Mrs. Gifford know Vivian had been at the fire? Oh, she must have known. Why else would she say that? This was bad. Very bad.

But how would Mrs. Gifford have found out?

Dantes must have told her.

A sick feeling snaked through Vivian. Dantes must have lied and was still secretly involved with Mrs. Gifford. The woman did have children of her own, including a son. Though rare, it wasn't unheard of for some wives in the nobility to be allowed attention outside of marriage once an heir was provided. Dantes had history with her. Had Mrs. Gifford approached him about rekindling their past with her husband's blessing?

Dantes was a scoundrel, and that was definitely something a scoundrel would get involved in.

But, upon a closer look, Mrs. Gifford wore a humored expression. "Don't worry. Your secret is safe with me."

Anne was watching Vivian, but Vivian ignored her, not wanting to give away the true discomfort she felt in the moment. "I'm assuming you know what that means," Vivian began. "If you're saying that."

Mrs. Gifford laughed, but it wasn't malicious. "I knew the moment you began coughing."

"Rather humiliating."

Mrs. Gifford took the chair next to Vivian, and Anne said something about grabbing Vivian's purchase and meeting her out front, then hurried away.

"If anyone should be humiliated, it should be Thomas. We are here to find birthday gifts for our mother, not to buy gifts for you. No offense." Mrs. Gifford smiled widely.

Vivian surprised herself by smiling back. "I find that rather amusing. Poor Mr. Crosby, exposed by his own sister."

The two women laughed together, but a heavy silence soon fell between them.

Mrs. Gifford spoke first after briefly hesitating. "I'm sure you will be unsurprised to know that people are whispering over your relationship with Mr. Edmond McNab. I had also seen you together as well at the queen's birthday ball, and later at the National Gallery." She gave space for Vivian to jump in but continued when she didn't. "I'm assuming you know by now Edmond and I were once engaged."

"Yes." Vivian was cautious, expecting a secret affair to be divulged.

"Has he told you anything about that?"

"No, he hasn't. Why?" She forced the awful words out. "Are you still in love with him?"

But Mrs. Gifford merely chuckled at this. "Not at all. It was ages ago, and I'm mad for my husband."

"You're not still—" Vivian shifted, realizing she couldn't ask about an affair outright. "Is he still in love with you?" She prepared herself to hear something she didn't want to.

But why did she care in the first place? Dantes was only a friend.

"Goodness, no." Mrs. Gifford said this quite seriously. "We haven't even crossed paths since I broke off the engagement. He stopped going to society events after that."

"Why did you end it?" Unfortunately, the fact Dantes had *not* been the one to break off their engagement did not make Vivian feel any better. Despite Mrs. Gifford's reassurance, Vivian couldn't help but wonder if Dantes remained in love with her.

Mrs. Gifford looked down at her gloved hands, clearly weighing what to say. "My family didn't like him."

Knowing Dantes's background, and what she knew about his so-called friendship with Mr. Crosby, Vivian wasn't in the least surprised by that.

"He's a good man." Mrs. Gifford gave her a small smile. "He's rough around the edges—or at least he was. I imagine that didn't change."

"No."

"I will say, both times I saw the two of you together, I was thrilled."

Confused, Vivian asked why.

"Well, because it's obvious you're happy together, and I've always hoped he would one day find his perfect match."

Now Vivian understood. She laughed. "Oh, no. You've got it all wrong. It's not what you think. He's a mere friend, and nothing more."

"Well, a good enough friend you were in his flat the night of the fire," she teased. Vivian felt the blood drain from her face and Mrs. Gifford gave her a knowing look. "You are not very convincing, Lady Vivian."

Vivian let out a sigh. She hadn't explained that well at all.

"Anyway, I came over to talk to you, to tell you something about him." Mrs. Gifford's brow furrowed in concentration. "Even though he made the effort to propose all those years ago, he never once told me he loved me. I think he did, but he never said it."

"That's odd. Why not?"

"He refused to explain it to me, but I think he plain fears it. He lost his parents at such a young age, and I know his grandparents sending him away hurt him. I don't think he knows how to even say the words, either. I doubt those three brothers exchange them. It's harder for men to state their feelings. They have no issue *showing* it." She let out a small laugh. "But saying it? That's entirely different."

Vivian considered this, thought about her unanswered letter in which she'd confessed to missing him, and felt a rush of embarrassment and regret.

A group of young women came giggling into the room and began to gossip. "Anyway," Mrs. Gifford began again. "You need to get home and get better. But remember what I told you. It may come in handy someday."

They stood at the same time. "Why are you telling me all of this?" Vivian asked. Growing up, she and Mrs. Gifford had been rather distant acquaintances. They had never really known each other, so there was no loyalty between the two.

Mrs. Gifford considered this for a moment. "Guilt," she finally decided. "You need to hear the story from Edmond when he's ready, but I still feel incredible guilt over it, and if I can do my part to ensure he does find his happiness, I want to do that." She began to turn to leave, but Vivian was desperate to get this woman to understand she was wrong, that there was absolutely nothing between her and Dantes. Not in the way she thought, anyway. But who was Vivian really trying to convince: Mrs. Gifford, or herself?

She decided to shove that question far, far away.

"Wait," Vivian called after her. Mrs. Gifford turned back. "You don't understand. This is going to sound ridiculous, but he's helping me find a husband. Ever since my inheritance…" She trailed off before shaking her head. "Anyway, I'm seeking a true gentleman, one who doesn't go to brothels, doesn't have a mistress, doesn't have addictions. They're unfortunately difficult to find, and he knows these things about gentlemen."

Mrs. Gifford forced back a smile. "Well, Lady Vivian, I look forward to reading your wedding announcement in a few months, then." And with that, she turned and left.

Vivian gave her time to leave the shop with Mr. Crosby before meeting Anne out front as planned. As she climbed into the carriage and sat beside Anne, it was clear Anne hadn't looked inside the box. Thus, once they'd arrived at Anne's house to be dropped off, Vivian let her climb out before handing over the box and shutting the door before Anne could react. The carriage went off, and Vivian watched out the back window with a laugh as Anne remained in place, a deep frown on her face.

Chapter Fourteen

IT WAS WEEKS before Dantes was able to safely access his flat and assess the damage. And when Victor and Ollie led him in—along with their insurance adjuster and a member of their fire brigade to ensure safety—he felt he could collapse.

The living room was destroyed. Every single exposed surface that hadn't burned away had either turned carbon black or became gray ash. He located the table that held his parents' tintype and found nothing atop it but a smoky, black rectangle. It was the only photograph the brothers had of their parents, and under his care, it had been destroyed.

He couldn't bring himself to touch it. That would make the disaster real.

"Maybe it can be fixed," Ollie said quietly, no doubt hoping it would help.

"Don't bother. You'll only upset yourself." Dantes nudged a pile of soot that, he assumed, had once been a small, wooden table before heading over to his paintings.

There, he was met by an equally terrible sight, and he shouted out a string of curse words and threw a heavy but unrecognizable object across the room in anger. He couldn't care less about anything else in the flat, save the tintype, of course. And his paintings. And here they were still hanging on the walls but completely black from soot and smoke. The scene was a mockery, like a monument to his destruction. Looking at them in their sorry state, it felt as if a part of him had died.

"I don't care about the rest," Dantes said to the group of men hovering by the door as he trudged through the mess and left for the pub below. No one followed him as they continued looking around with the adjuster, so for a while, he sat alone on the floor behind the derelict bar with a bottle of whiskey that had managed to survive unscathed. He took a few swigs but lost interest quickly. It wasn't hitting him the way he would have expected.

But then he remembered something.

For the first day since the fire, he'd worn the same trousers as that fateful night. Fortunately, he'd been able to otherwise collect a few pieces of clothing from Victor and Ollie to hold him over, only throwing these old fire clothes on when the extras had been sent out to be laundered. He shoved his hand in his pocket with a small shred of hope. His fingertips immediately felt the texture of lace and he pulled the black scrap out. In the madness of his life as of late, he had forgotten all about it. He often carried it with him, an admittedly strange habit, and by some stroke of luck had happened to have it with him the night of the fire. Otherwise, it too would have been lost forever.

He held the piece of black lace in his hands, rubbing it gently between his fingers. A few days ago, he'd received a letter from Vivian and she'd written that she missed him, something so simple, so innocent. And yet, he hadn't been sure what to make of it.

It caused a minute flutter in his heart that had sent him into a panic, he couldn't stop thinking about her letter and what it meant.

And after her absence, the happiness her letters had brought him, that final letter from her, forced him to realize the fluttering in his heart was a growing affection for her.

But the fact remained their entire relationship centered around her finding a husband. A gilded, aristocratic husband who would be happy to go riding in Hyde Park with her, go to balls, yachting, all those events she may not have liked but would be required to attend. Dantes had only been on a horse a few times, didn't know a thing about boats, and didn't want anything to do with all of that socializing. And unlike her, he wasn't expected to join in. And he was quite content with that fact.

She knew he wasn't in love with her. She knew he wasn't remotely interested in ever marrying. And that was what she was looking for.

So to tell him she missed him? It was torture to his heart.

Confused and unsure of what to say, he hadn't responded. But what was he supposed to do? Ignore her letter entirely? Admit he missed her too?

But that would be a lie—he didn't miss her. He *ached* for her. And this made him exceptionally vulnerable, a dangerous spot to be in. He needed to keep his distance.

All of this ran through his head while he sat on the floor with her lace scrap, with the memory of her cheek in his hand as she'd stared up at him with wide, beautiful eyes.

He lifted the lace to his nose, but it had lost Vivian's scent and now smelled like smoke.

He swore to himself and stuffed it back in his pocket.

"Dantes." Victor's voice echoed across the room. "We need to talk."

That didn't sound good. Dantes fingered the lace scrap in his pocket one last time for the comfort it provided and stood up from behind the bar. Victor was waiting for him, alone.

"Where's everyone else?" Dantes asked, feeling uneasy.

"Out back."

They met in the middle. "I'm going to get right to the point." Victor looked around the derelict room. "Insurance is not going to cover your flat."

Dantes felt like he were being shoved underwater. "*What?*"

Victor shifted with discomfort. "I said—"

"I know what you said." Dantes rubbed the inner corners of his eyes. "You need to explain why."

"Insurance only covers the pub, the actual business."

"But that *is* part of the business. It's part of the whole building we own. As a business."

"Yes." Victor nodded and finally met Dantes's gaze. "But because you decided you'd prefer to crawl upstairs after work and not buy a proper home like Ollie and me, and pay me a monthly rent for the flat and not a nightly rate like one would for a saloon, it's a separate entity. Not part of the business. A home. A personal dwelling."

Dantes's heart galloped with panic, but the dread was quickly replaced by a boiling anger. He stepped forward and stuck a finger against Victor's chest. "When I took that place, you were constantly after me about paying rent. You didn't need it, the business didn't need it. I had no money of my own, as my part of the railway sale went entirely into the pub, and I wasn't big in boxing yet. You had already been working for years, had some money already. And you wouldn't give me a break to help me out."

"I know."

Dantes turned away, raked his fingers through his hair, then turned back to his brother, now half-crazed. "Do you remember that time of my life? I had just been kicked out of Oxford. Eleanor left me. And you, my own brother, wouldn't help me. And now you're telling me after all of that, I've lost everything again? Because of *you?*"

"Look, if you need money—"

Dantes got into Victor's face. "I don't want your filthy money! It's going to cost me a ridiculous amount to get clothes again, to find a new place to live, to get furniture, to rebuild everything! But I'm confident I will manage it. The thing is, there isn't enough money in the world to bring me back the photograph of Mum and Dad, or my paintings. Those are irreplaceable. And I will *never* forgive you for losing them."

Victor frowned. "I had nothing to do with that part of it."

"I don't care." Dantes poked Victor in the chest hard enough to make him step back. "You like to bill yourself as the patriarch of the family, the leader, the one who runs everything. Mr. Responsibility. Then you should have put a stop to those blasted fireworks a long time ago."

Dantes turned, unable to stomach Victor's fallen face, and stalked toward the exit. He was going to hire a hansom out on the street, as there was only once place he wanted to be right now. However, he paused to call back over his shoulder. "You can take care of the cleanup. I'm never stepping foot upstairs again. And then, when you rent it out, the money goes directly to me."

"We always survive, Dantes," Victor shouted after him. But Dantes was already out the door.

Chapter Fifteen

V IVIAN WAS READING in the drawing room when someone rang at the door once again, and after dropping the book in her lap, she let out a groan of frustration. Her chasers had heard she'd been spotted out shopping and had begun filling up her receiving room after several weeks of peace. The men had been a mere nuisance before, but now her patience was thin and she was enraged by them. And it drove her mad that she couldn't simply tell them to go away. It was an infernal rule, that she couldn't tell a visitor where she *really* wished for them to go.

For a long while, Vivian waited for Heaton to bring the calling card of her newest visitor, but when several moments passed and he didn't show, she closed her book and set it to the side, confused. Who was here, then?

Suddenly, a man roared in anger, "Get out!" and the front door slammed shut soon after. The door to the drawing room flew open, banging into the wall, and Dantes stood there looking like a wild man.

"Dantes!" Vivian jumped to her feet in surprise. Briefly, behind him, was a flash of Heaton's face of astonishment, and perhaps even a shred of respect, before Dantes closed the door and locked it to send a message to the butler. Do not disturb.

"I kicked them out." Dantes turned back around, crossed the room with long intentional strides, then stopped before her.

She remained rooted in place, shocked by the way he'd just barreled into her house like this. "My chasers? You kicked out my chasers?"

"Yes. For today, at least. They're a pathetic lot I'm sure will return tomorrow." Dantes stared down at her with his intense, green gaze.

As her heart began to thump in response, he stepped away, leaving that strange, empty feeling behind, and angled over to the lit fireplace. It was this moment Vivian realized he didn't have any sort of jacket on, only a brown waistcoat over his white shirt, as if he had rushed over in haste.

Nor had he shaved lately, either.

Curious, Vivian followed him and watched as he rubbed his palms together in thought, his jaw clenched tightly. His normally wild hair was absolutely feral. As she made this observation, Dantes rubbed his hands over his face before raking his fingers through his hair.

Ah, that was why.

"Is something wrong?" Vivian asked.

Dantes continued to watch the fire, chuckled. "The insurance adjuster came by today. I lost everything. In the most literal sense. Everything but the clothing I had on my back that evening is gone forever." He glanced down at what he was wearing. "These clothes, specifically."

A log in the fire popped as despair rose in her throat. "The photograph and your paintings?"

"Nothing more than charred rectangles now." He gave her a half-crazed grin. "Want to hear the best part?"

Unease roiled in her stomach. "Do I?"

"Insurance won't be covering it. Any of it." Dantes explained what had happened, what Victor had done that had led to this.

Vivian listened as a good friend would but also wondered what she should do. Should she try to give him a hug? No, such contact would have been improper. "What are you going to do?"

"What *can* I do? I have to replace everything. Everything

that's *possible* to replace, that is."

"That'll be rather costly, won't it?"

"Yes, it will."

Was that why he was here? She looked down at her hands, ashamed to be such an oblivious fool. Of course that was why he was here. Dantes's lack of response to her last letter, in which she'd written she missed him, was loud and clear in its silence. She forced a grin, though it hurt. "How much do you need?"

Dantes turned to fully face her. "What are you talking about?" But then his face reddened. "Oh, blast, Vivian, I didn't come here to ask for money!"

"Then why are you here? I'm sorry for everything that has happened, Dantes, and I mean that wholeheartedly. It's awful and no one should go through that. But..." That was it—she'd had enough of this confusing man. "Oh, you're driving me mad! We leave on an argument, and when I'm sure I'll never see you again, you start writing me letters. And I tell you I miss you and never hear back? Then completely out of nowhere, you come bounding into my house like a madman on a mission? What does that all mean?!"

He stepped closer to her, his face tight and grim. "*Why* do you miss me, Viv? Why do you have to go and miss me when you're looking for someone else?"

"See, this is what I mean!" This was exhausting. "What are you saying there, Dantes? We are friends, are we not? I do miss you, and I..." She swallowed. None of this was making sense.

"Why do you miss me, Vivian? *Why?*" Dantes's gaze sharpened, as if expecting Vivian to say something specific.

"I...I don't know!" She threw her hands up. "I like when I spend time with you, even though those days often end terribly." After shaking her head, she looked toward the window.

"That's because I'm bad luck," he growled low.

Vivian frowned at the strange comment but ignored it. "When I think of our time together, just you and me, those days always seem like favorite days, despite near-death experiences, despite injuries and public humiliation."

"Because we're friends, right?" There seemed to be a hint of sarcasm in his voice.

Her attention went back to him. "Well, yes. Maybe I'm being silly, but after these past few months, I feel as if we are good friends now. I dare say, you may be my dearest friend in the whole world."

Dantes's shoulders slumped, and he began watching the fire again. Maybe those were the words he'd needed to hear.

Feeling a little better about his demeanor, Vivian took a few cautious steps toward him.

"I think about you all day long," he said, surprising Vivian and causing her heart to skip. "And I feel like a fool for it."

Vivian smiled at his confiding in her. "Oh, Dantes, that's nothing to feel foolish over."

Dantes looked over at her with a blank face, but the worried lines, the wild hair, the unshaved stubble made him look tortured. "Of course it is. I've missed you, too."

"You have?" Her voice hitched at this unexpected turn. She had assumed, based on his lack of response, that he hadn't thought much of her at all. This admission created a strange light within her heart.

"Yes, but this wasn't supposed to happen." His eyes were becoming wider, wilder. "I'm supposed to help you find some *gentleman* who's not a complete idiotic, useless cad, wave goodbye as you go off to your happily ever after with him, then return to my hole-in-the-wall pub and live happily ever alone for the rest of my life. Because that's what I want. Do you understand? I want to be alone!"

She wrung her hands and nodded hard. She had felt similarly but was now wondering if she still wanted that at all. What did that mean? "I understand."

"I'm not going to fall for you. I'm not going to marry you." He put his palms to his forehead, as if he had a terrible headache. "I'm not doing any of that!"

Vivian's heart hammered so hard in her chest, she could feel it in her ears. But as she stared up at him, this impassioned man, big and strong, a bit hairy, the embodiment of raw masculinity, instead of being irritated or boiling over with anger, it felt like warm honey was beginning to coat her insides. And it was bizarrely pleasant.

"Since the moment I first laid eyes on you…" Dantes took a step toward her. "I have been enamored of you. And I deny it to myself every single day. What's the point of admitting it to myself? To you? But right now, with everything going on, I'm weak. And I can't deny it anymore. I can't deny it to me, or to you."

"D-Deny what?" she asked on a whisper.

"I need you. Do you understand?" He pointed inward to himself. "*I need you*, Vivian. Today. Right now."

Dantes took another step closer to her, and her chest began to rise and fall hard with her breathing. Her head felt light under the almost predatory look in his eye.

"Someday, Viv." Dantes tipped her chin up with a gentle hand. His heavy-lidded eyes studied her mouth. "You will marry someone else. But today, you are mine."

Before she could even begin to think of how to respond, his hand fell away from her chin and his arm circled around her waist to tilt her back while his other hand cradled the back of her head. Vivian released a small gasp at this unexpected movement and Dantes angled his face down to hover warm lips over hers, lingering for a moment. It was like the time he'd kissed her hand, when he'd left space for her to protest. But far, far more intimate.

But there was no protest from her. Her mind melted into a puddle, and she dove headfirst into the moment.

Threading her arms back around his neck, she lifted her lips to his and Dantes pressed his mouth down hard against hers. She didn't know what she was doing, and it seemed a bit strange when he opened his mouth, but she followed suit. On paper, dancing tongues seemed strange but right now, all she felt was that she had never experienced something so wonderful. But after a long, fiery moment, he stopped suddenly and put her back upright.

She faltered, but he held her steady.

Dantes stared down into her eyes. He had that strange, pained look again. "Your eyes. They're blue."

She couldn't help but smile. "Yes, silly, you didn't know that?"

"They're so dark, I couldn't tell until the sunlight hit them just the right way." There was that flickering light inside of her again. A faraway warning.

She wasn't foolish enough to ignore it. And as reality hit her, that Dantes had kissed her, that she had kissed him, panic began to rise. She was sorry he was in a bad spot, but what had just happened? She had to put an end to their flirtation. Like he'd said moments ago, he didn't want to marry.

Not that she would ever entertain marrying a scoundrel, anyway!

This entire moment needed to be redirected. For both their sakes. And then, she would go on pretending that kiss had never happened. That was for the best. "After what happened with the insurance company," she began, her voice sounding a bit too loud, "will you still be staying with Victor?"

"Yes. I can't stay with Ollie. I would be a frequent...interruption. No, thank you."

She laughed. "Well, you're welcome to stay here. There sure is enough room."

Upon these words, the remaining heat around them seemed to chill.

Dantes studied her with a sudden stony face. "Don't you think that would be a terrible idea?"

Obviously, she wasn't really serious. Of course Dantes couldn't stay here. She may toe the line of propriety now and then, but even she wouldn't cross something so blatantly scandalous. But that his reaction was so serious, instead of recognizing the obvious joke, bothered her. "Why?"

"I don't think your future husband would be happy to know his wife has another man living at her house."

She searched his eyes, having trouble believing what she was hearing. The obvious concern in such a scenario was it would make her and her family the laughing stock of the nobility. Yet Dantes's concern was what some husband, who doesn't even exist yet, would think of it.

But wasn't this all silly of her? This stemmed from their agreement. One kiss, no matter how passionate, didn't change that. There *was* a future husband out there. And her reputation *did* matter for that, because it was her goal, after all.

Yet minutes ago, he'd called her *mine*.

Goodness, the man was confounding and clouding her head.

"Very well." Suddenly, she turned to the fireplace, doing her best to ignore the hurt that shouldn't even have been there in the first place. "There is a flower show in May. Two weekends from now. I'll be going. It's up to you if you wish to accompany me."

Vivian was hoping he would take this opportunity to slip out of her house without another word. She was wrong.

He came up behind her and placed heavy hands on her shoulders. "What do you want, Vivian?" he asked in a low voice.

It was foolish to deny to herself that he was growing on her. Recognizing that was protective, because she could navigate her mind and heart around it. But she also could never, ever, let Dantes know.

She wasn't going to humiliate herself by answering his question. What would she even say, anyway?

"As I said…" She pulled away from him. "I shall be at the May flower show. I do have numerous letters I must get to immediately, Dantes. It's time for you to go."

But Dantes came around to face her, hands shoved in his pockets. With a face as hard as granite, he studied her for a moment. It appeared he had something else to say but then decided against it. He pulled his hands out of his pockets before leaving the room without another word.

As she watched the door shut behind him, she noticed something had fallen from his pocket. Curious, she went over to it.

Crouching down to snatch it up, Vivian gasped upon realization it was the black lace that had been torn from her ballgown.

Chapter Sixteen

T HE THREE McNab brothers sat together in Victor's parlor after a heavy dinner. It had been yet another day of demolition, and the nearly two months since the fire were starting to blur together. Victor's housekeeper ensured the cook prepared a feast for the starving men that would rival a twelve-person multi-course meal. Now full and satiated, they sat with whiskeys, regarding each other in exhausted silence. In the last few days, Dantes had noticed Victor was out of sorts, more so than usual. His worst characteristics—his broodiness, lack of humor, general bitterness—had only worsened. As Dantes was still reeling from the days-old news that Victor's greed had screwed him over with insurance, and his brother's lack of care over the blasted fireworks led to losing irreplaceable possessions, he had no sympathy for his anguished older brother and found he really didn't much care what had caused his mood.

Ollie's voice cut into the heavy silence. "I'm thinking about crossing the pond and joining up with the Barnum & Bailey Circus."

Dantes tore a narrow-eyed look in Ollie's direction. "What in the blazes are you talking about?"

Ollie grinned, nodding over at Victor, who hadn't reacted. "The world's strongest woman proposed to me and we're going to elope." A long pause. "I'm thinking about becoming a lion trainer, or perhaps an acrobat. What do you think about that, Victor?"

Victor grunted an approval.

Dantes and Ollie exchanged grins of amusement; however, the conversation quickly died again. But unlike Dantes, Ollie clearly couldn't stand the silence and began talking again. "So, what is the news with Lady Vivian?"

Dantes took a hasty sip of whiskey, wishing the conversation had gone any other direction. "Not sure. Haven't talked to her in a few weeks."

Ollie tilted his head. "I thought you wrote to one another twice a day."

"Not anymore." Not with the way they'd parted last, when he'd visited her. When he'd kissed her, and then she'd all but kicked him out. Dantes shoved the memory away.

"I see. Are you going to meet her at the flower show tomorrow, then?"

Why had he made the mistake in telling Ollie about that? "No."

"Why not?"

Dantes let out a frustrated sigh. "Christ, Ollie."

"*I'll* meet her, then."

Dantes glowered but didn't have a retort.

So, Ollie continued. "I'll take her, charm her, entice her home with sweet words under the starlight. Since you aren't staying with me, that shouldn't be an issue." He grinned in his usual easygoing manner. "Do her kisses taste like strawberries? Or mint? Personally, I think she looks more like the strawberry sort."

Red rage exploded and Dantes dove over to Ollie, pulling him up from his chair and off the floor by the front of his shirt. Veins popped out of Dantes's neck and Ollie responded with a cool gaze and a smug smile. Dantes realized in this moment he'd been had and released his brother. He pointed an angry finger at Ollie. "You're lucky you're not dead," he said with a growl.

Ollie rolled his shoulders at being let go. "I was testing my theory. Which stands, by the way. Especially after that."

"What theory?" Victor had decided to finally join in this family discussion.

Ollie looked over to him. "That Dantes is in love with Lady Vivian."

Victor eyed Dantes from his chair but didn't say anything further.

"The funny thing about your theory," Dantes said as he turned to Ollie with resentment, "is you're the last man in all of Europe who would know what love is."

Ollie's eyes flashed darkly, but he covered it up with a laugh. "And why is that, Dantes?"

Dantes wouldn't say it, but Victor had no problem doing so. "It's because you're a whore, Ollie." The words came out so easily, even Dantes felt the knife.

For a moment, Ollie stared with a bit of shock, but it didn't render him silent. Not for long, at least. He did, however, turn his back to Victor and rose up to Dantes, all humor gone from his face, his own green eyes McNab wild. "Fine, I like women. I think they're beautiful, and I can't get enough of them. But you want to know something else? I only take women who want exactly what I want, who know what our relationship entails—a few tumbles in the sheets and that's it. I don't take women who want more than that. Unlike you, Dantes, I don't deceive and mess with their hearts and heads. Maybe I'm a whore, but I'm still a better man than you." And without another word, he left the room, the townhouse's front door slamming shut behind him seconds later.

Victor pressed his fingertips together in evident thought, ignoring everything that had just happened. "Whatever you do, Dantes, don't make Lady Vivian angry. Not yet anyway."

Dantes was still staring at the spot Ollie had vacated. "Sorry?"

"Don't make her angry. I need her help with something."

This got his full attention. "Absolutely not."

But Victor ignored him. "The insurance payout for the fire damage isn't going to be enough to cover everything. I need to get a loan and they are difficult to get, especially with an inoperable and damaged business."

Dantes couldn't believe his ears. "You want her money?"

Victor let out an irritated sigh and tented his fingers together over his lap. "I don't want her personal money, Dantes. I want to talk to her about getting help with a loan. That lot is always cozy with banks. I need her father to vouch for us if she can convince him."

Dantes gave him an exasperated look—he couldn't deal with this new load of rubbish from Victor right now—and went outside to find Ollie before he got too far. Fortunately, his younger brother was standing out on the sidewalk with his hands shoved into his pockets, staring up at the moon. Dantes took the spot at Ollie's side, and for a while, neither of them said anything.

"Victor shouldn't have said that," Dantes finally said.

Ollie didn't respond.

"And I'm sorry."

"Okay." It was the most any of them would have said. "Well, I won't bother you about it anymore."

"Why does it even matter to you?" It was something Dantes had been wondering. Ollie had never cared about any of the women Dantes had courted casually before. Why did he care so much now? Why was he so involved?

"Because I like Lady Vivian," Ollie replied. "And the way you are with her, I've never seen you like that before. At the ball, you didn't let your eye off her and I accused you of being jealous then. But at the museum? You were *bleeding all over the floor* with jealousy over the lads she was talking to! I went there to watch you, admittedly for my own amusement, but your behavior took me aback. The entire time you were off to the side like some vigilant, spiteful gargoyle." Ollie imitated Dantes leaning against the wall, glowering and growling.

"I don't look like that."

Ollie merely lifted one eyebrow.

"And she was talking to someone who beat a woman. Yeah, I

was vigilant and angry about it."

"You were jealous."

Dantes scoffed, shaking his head.

"Look, you're my brother." Ollie stared off into the distance. "I don't want to see you mess your life up because you're afraid of something. That's all."

Dantes laughed. "I'm not afraid of anything."

But Ollie didn't find it amusing. He crossed his arms and gave Dantes a sidelong look. "Yes, you are. If Lady Vivian marries someone else, would you accept it?"

"No." Dantes surprised himself by admitting this aloud.

"Then do you want her to marry you?"

Dantes didn't respond. Because the truth was, being faced with this question by his own brother, he didn't know. For so long, he'd been steadfast in his wish to never marry. It wasn't even a question anymore at his age—it was a solid fact of his life. But he had to admit that Vivian was making him at least question that decision. He didn't want her to marry anyone else, but did he want her to marry him?

Ollie let out a long sigh. "This is what I mean. You're going to ignore the question at hand until it's too late. You may have all the time in the world to get used to the idea, but she doesn't. While you're hemming and hawing about whether or not you're really in love with her, someone else will come along and sweep her away and then for the rest of your life, you'll have to live with your own stupidity. So. You either admit to yourself that you want more from her and talk to her about it tomorrow, or leave her alone. If you can't do either thing for yourself, then at least do it for her."

Dantes glowered. He was going to have to go to the infernal flower show.

After a long bout of silence, Ollie turned to him. "I'm going home, and I better not see you tomorrow."

"You won't." Dantes spoke as if his insistence didn't hold all the answers to Ollie's irritating questions.

And Ollie grinned wide in understanding, waving down a passing hansom cab. He put his hand on the large wheel and informed the driver of his address. But he didn't climb in yet. "Good." Ollie looked back to Dantes, still gripping the wheel. "Now, earlier you said I couldn't know what love is because I—"

"Look, Ollie—"

"No, listen. I just wanted to say I know what it is because I love *you*. And I love Victor, when he's not being this way, at least. I know we don't say that, but I decided I'm going to now." And before Dantes could react, before he could stop his brother, Ollie climbed in and the hansom left.

Terror thrummed through Dantes as he watched his baby brother disappear, the fear quickly replaced by dread when he was completely out of sight. Because anyone who had ever said those words to him, he ended up losing. Sometimes through death.

DANTES FOUND VIVIAN at the Jensen Gardens exhibition, where she asked him to meet her if he decided to go. Immediately, he understood why she had picked it—Jensen was a rose breeder.

The exhibition was large, with numerous rosebushes for sale, but they were set up in a way where it looked like an actual ornamental rose garden at an expensive botanical garden. There were so many different colors and sizes, and with hundreds of rose plants together, the air smelled heavenly.

Vivian meandered in a pink-and-white day dress with a matching parasol to protect her from the hot sun. Dantes took a moment to watch her in her element, solitude and roses, and noted how happy she was amongst the flowers. Occasionally, she stopped to observe the plants, smell the blossoms, or gently pet the petals like a cat with a finger. A white-haired gentleman—Dantes assumed Mr. Jensen himself—approached Vivian and they began to converse. He gave her a cut, yellow rose and they began to study and discuss it in great detail, though Dantes couldn't hear what they said.

He approached. Vivian stilled as she set eyes upon him and smiled widely, clearly surprised by his arrival.

"Dantes!" she called out to him. "Come see Mr. Jensen's newest rose. He named it Lady Luck." When Dantes reached her she tipped the bloom to him so he could smell it for himself, then brought it back to her own nose with a smile just for him, sending his heart aflutter.

"Very nice," Dantes replied, not sure what else to say. It was yellow, and it smelled like a rose. But he also knew it would make her happy to hear he liked it and if smelling one rose made her happy, then he would happily put three hundred of them to his nose for her.

"The blooms," Mr. Jensen began, "open as a deep butter yellow, but as they age, they fade to cream. When you have a mature plant covered in flowers, they're of many different shades of yellow and it looks quite beautiful."

Vivian gushed over the new rose. "When I plan out a new rose garden, Lady Luck will definitely find a home there."

Mr. Jensen smiled at her kindly and turned to Dantes. "Lady Vivian's mother was once a member of the rose society, of which I am the current president. She had a most impressive rose garden at her home that I know Lady Vivian adored as a child."

Vivian smiled at this. "My father will never rid of it. It's his favorite part of the garden, in fact. I never knew my mother, but we feel her presence there."

"I can understand that." Dantes held her gaze. "Personally, roses will remind me of you for the rest of my life."

Vivian's smile fell away, her cheeks blushing at these words as Mr. Jensen chuckled knowingly. "Ah, so you are smitten with Lady Vivian, are you?"

"Yes. Rather smitten, actually." He didn't look away from her, and Vivian's blush turned scarlet.

"I shall leave you two to your flower show, then." Mr. Jensen began to walk away. "And, Lady Vivian, please let us know if we can help with your garden at all." He gave her a friendly nod and went to speak to other show attendees.

Vivian turned back to Dantes. "What has gotten into you?"

Before he'd found Vivian, Dantes had noted a tunnel made up of archway after archway of a symphony of flowers. He took Vivian's hand in his, to her utter surprise, and began leading her in the direction of it. "Nothing has gotten into me. Why do you ask?"

She gave him a sidelong glance but didn't respond to the question. "There's a butterfly garden here somewhere I'd like to see at some point. Water plants, too, featuring giant lily pads."

"Whatever you wish to see today, Vivian, we shall see it."

She regarded him again with vague disbelief but continued to keep her thoughts to herself.

"Your mother's rose garden," he continued. "Is that why you like roses so much?"

"You noticed that? Yes, though now it's partly out of habit. Her rose garden was a mainstay of my childhood, and as I became older, I found myself naturally drawn to them. Soap, perfume, cut flowers—"

"And you put them in your hair, too, sometimes." He looked down at her as he said this, squeezing her hand.

She blinked back and her mouth fell open for a beat. "Yes. That too." A pause. "I sometimes feel strange that I have this connection to my mother through her favorite flower. Like a fraud, I suppose. I have absolutely no memory of her, nor does Bernard, yet I speak of her as if she held a place in my life."

"She did, though. I have more memories of my mother as a laudanum addict than healthy, but that doesn't negate who she was before."

"What was she like?"

"Like Ollie, now that I think of it. Good natured. In a good mood, even when they're truly not."

They both laughed, but guilt hit him again for the way he'd spoken to Ollie last night. He knew Victor found their brother frustrating for being so laid-back, and he knew Victor blamed it on Ollie never having to struggle. Dantes, personally, never really knew what to make of Ollie's stark difference to Dantes and especially Victor. He supposed he blamed the same cause as Victor—it did make sense. But in talking about this with Vivian, he realized that might not truly be the case, or at least the full explanation. Ollie may have inherited their mother's nature, as she'd been quite similar. The two of them probably would have been inseparable if she hadn't died.

"Your father's death took her, Dantes. She was gone long before the laudanum. And it doesn't define her."

His chest tightened at her thoughtfulness, so he put the back of her hand to his lips and kissed it, winning a shy smile in return.

As they reached the tunnel of flowers, he led her inside and noted with relief that, at least for the moment, they were alone. Surrounding them were bursts of purples and pinks and yellows, like they had stepped inside of a rainbow, and the sun peaked through to throw dappled shadows across them and the ground. Dantes turned to Vivian and took the Lady Luck rose from her. He brought it to his nose again before brushing the soft petals to her cheek. "I meant what I said to Mr. Jensen. For the remainder of my life, anytime I see or smell a rose, I'll think of you. Think of your voice, your laughter. Hopefully, you'll be next to me as I think about that."

Her eyes searched his face.

"Do you know why that is, Vivian?"

She swallowed. "Why, Dantes?"

He set the yellow rose back in her hand. "Unfortunately"—Dantes looped a stray lock of hair behind her ear—"I can no longer uphold my end of our deal. I cannot help you find a husband. Because I don't want you to marry someone else."

She blinked. "You don't?"

"No. Truthfully, I can't even stomach the idea of it." He

ended this with a crooked grin.

"What are you saying?"

But as she waited for his response, Dantes found he couldn't say it. He wanted to—he wanted to more than anything—but it was as if there were a wall between his mind and his voice. And as the seconds passed, his heart began to sink down into a watery abyss as he watched the moment with helplessness.

"Dantes."

He didn't respond.

"Do you love me?" Vivian's voice was quiet, private.

He looked down to the ground, crestfallen at his cowardice. "Last night, Ollie surprised me by telling me he loved me. None of us have ever said that before."

"Why not?"

"Because when those words are said, we lose people."

She frowned. "How?"

"I'm incredibly unlucky—have you not realized that? Look at my life. The fire is only the most recent event of many and it won't be the last. And that bad luck, for whatever reason, particularly extends to those I love. When those three little words are said, I always lose the person who says the phrase. It's to the point that I'm too afraid to even say it myself. My mother and father died." He stopped for a moment. "My grandparents took us in, only to send us off to boarding school right after they said it. Victor said it once in his life, then ran off at sixteen to be on his own and work on the docks. Eleanor said it and then..." He sighed. "Well, I'm glad we didn't end up getting married to her, but it was hard to go through that. But ever since Ollie said it last night, I've been terrified something is going to happen to him. I just know something will."

"Nothing is going to happen to him because he said three words, Dantes." Vivian began to spin the rose stem between her fingers. "After the fire, I saw Mrs. Gifford while I was at a millinery. I had a coughing fit and she immediately knew I'd been at the fire with you."

He frowned. He didn't like this.

"She went out of her way to warn me you refused to say those words. I wasn't even sure if I should believe her because why would anyone refuse to say that? But it was true, wasn't it?"

"What else did she tell you?" Who did Eleanor think she was, stepping into his life like that?

"Nothing. Why? What else would she tell me?"

He looked away, afraid she could somehow see the story in his face, though the remains of it were there.

Vivian let out a sigh, no doubt understanding he wasn't going to discuss it further. "Well, Dantes, I hate to tell you this, but I must insist you say the words if that's how you feel."

"Vivian, I can't."

Her face fell. "You're really that serious about it? You won't say it to me?" Her voice cracked.

He reached up to cradle her cheek. "But if I feel it, isn't that all that matters?"

"No." She suddenly pulled away from him. "All it tells me is you're a phony!"

His heart nearly stopped. "What?"

Chillingly, her face remained calm. "You don't want anyone else to have me, but you don't love me, either, and you don't want to marry me. You want to use me. I guess I shouldn't really be upset with you—you've been clear from the beginning what you wanted and obviously, that wouldn't change with me. Blast it all. I got myself too swept up in you, too swept up in a *scoundrel*." She said that word as if it were filth.

"I'm not a scoundrel, Vivian." Surely, she didn't really believe that? Think he was the worst kind of man, the type of man she hated and desperately wanted to avoid?

But she scoffed and readjusted her hold on the parasol. "Oh, please, Dantes. How else do you know the worst secrets of all of those men?"

"Because people talk about it at my pub. Some of them tell me directly, too."

"You must think I'm painfully stupid. No, it's because you go to the same brothels, because you gamble with them. Stop trying to convince me otherwise. Although I do believe you that you all discuss your womanly conquests over beer and whiskey."

He stood there in shock.

"By the way…" She pulled something out of her dress pocket, shoving the scrap of black lace he'd thought he had lost at him. "You dropped this at my house when you came over last week. Do you carry this around with you?"

He didn't answer.

"Why?" She waited a while for a response she wouldn't get. Her one final effort.

Vivian looked him straight in the eye as she broke him. "My search for a husband continues, then."

Chapter Seventeen

A WOMAN'S VOICE called out through the corridor of flowers, ending the moment. "Vivian! Is that you?"

It was Anne.

Vivian let the parasol fall away and turned her head to find Anne standing at the tunnel entrance. Earlier in the morning, Vivian had learned her family would be at the flower show as well and would be searching for her. She hadn't had a chance to tell Dantes, or a chance to tell him his brothers were expected later at the house, though the purpose of their visit remained unknown to her. Thus, she was planning on having everyone for dinner later and couldn't send Dantes away now. But in this moment, she was angry.

And she felt utterly foolish. Foolish for thinking he was trying to tell her he cared for her, that she could be special to him.

What hit her hardest, though, was she should have known better. She *did* know better. A knot formed in her stomach at her idiocy.

"Vivian, wait." Dantes grabbed her hand as she began walking toward Anne, but she pulled it away from him. "Do you want me to leave?"

As Vivian struggled with how to respond, Anne reached them and seemed to mistake Vivian's silence as nerves. "Of course not!" Anne laughed playfully. "Don't be silly. There's plenty of room for you to join. But come now." Anne gave Vivian wide eyes. "Before your father finds you like this."

Just then, Father's profile appeared at the entrance. He called out to Vivian. "Are you coming from the lily pads, dear?"

The trio began walking toward him and she noticed he was with Bernard and another gentleman she didn't immediately recognize. "The lily pads?"

"That's the direction of the water plants."

"Oh!" She responded a bit too brightly. "Of course! Fascinating. Like floating dishes."

Father laughed and pulled her in for a hug. "My darling Vivian. And who is this gentleman?" The duke eyed Dantes.

She briefly looked back at Dantes, noted how stiffly he stood, and guiltily felt a bit good about that. "This is my friend, Mr. Edmond McNab. You remember him?"

Something flashed in Father's eyes, and he studied Dantes for a rather long moment, his brow furrowed and gaze sharp. It was the way every suspicious father looked when he saw a new man with his daughter.

"Friend," she repeated quietly.

Her father gave her back a gentle pat to show he understood and let her go. "Vivian, do you remember my old friend from Cambridge, Mr. Henry Tewksbury?"

She turned to Mr. Tewksbury to say *hello* and remembered him now. Mr. Tewksbury wasn't a titled aristocrat, but he was quite wealthy, as he owned a bank, which was how Father knew him. Mr. Tewksbury had become a widower when Vivian had been a debutante—it was terribly sad. At the time, he'd been thirty, and his wife had been killed in a tragic ferry accident. But even at eighteen, Vivian had recognized how despite the age difference, he was quite handsome, for an older gentleman. Of course, this was before his wife had been killed; Vivian wouldn't have admired a widower in mourning. But even now, the fine lines and a bit of gray in his dark hair only enhanced his appearance.

"Lady Vivian." Mr. Tewksbury stepped up to her with a small bow, his eyes genuine and friendly, unlike those of seemingly every single gentleman she had spoken to since her inheritance. But of course, her newfound fortune would barely be of interest to him, unlike the spoiled sons of the near-penniless aristocrats who chased after her. No, Mr. Tewksbury held enough of his own fortune that Vivian's would garner nothing more than a polite smile and nod from him.

He was the exact type of gentleman she *should* have been going for.

"Mr. Tewksbury." She gave him a small curtsy. "Truly, I cannot recall the last time I saw you. It's been a rather long time."

"Ten years, almost exactly." He smiled. "I was here in London for the same reason as I am now, a rather boring financial conference."

She laughed politely as the group began walking, but Vivian and Mr. Tewksbury naturally began strolling together on their own. Briefly, she glanced over her shoulder and found Father and Bernard talking. Anne followed behind, demure. Dantes kept a distance from everyone but walked directly behind her, his attention squarely on her and nothing else. She held his stare for a brief moment until whipping her head back around and placing the open parasol over her shoulder.

"I heard there's a butterfly garden here," Mr. Tewksbury said, recapturing her attention.

Vivian forced a smile through the unsettling feeling that Dantes continued watching her. "Yes! I was hoping to see that next."

The elder gentleman held out his arm. "Shall we, then?"

For the tiniest moment, she stilled, surprised at the offer. But what harm was there in accepting Mr. Henry Tewksbury's arm to walk about a public place? He was a widower being polite. There were plenty of chaperones around. And so, she accepted the offer of his arm, feeling four pairs of eyes staring into her back, and realized perhaps this wasn't so innocent, especially since her parasol concealed them both.

The butterfly garden, to Vivian's great excitement, was positively brimming with butterflies of all types and hundreds of late-spring- and early-summer flowers that attracted them. It was crowded in the large, netted space, yet everyone wore faces of joy, looking up as beautiful, winged insects fluttered by, or down to the flowers, where they rested.

Mr. Tewksbury led her over to a nearby group of flowers. A butterfly fluttered up to her and landed on her forehead, causing her to squeak in surprise, then laugh when it crawled up to her hair.

"Looks like you made a new friend." Mr. Tewksbury put his hand up to her hair and brought it back down so she could see the butterfly that now sat atop his finger. Its wings opened to reveal several dramatic cream circles. She set the Lady Luck rose on a nearby bench and promptly forgot all about it because Mr. Tewksbury took Vivian's free hand in his own and gently put the butterfly to her knuckles. It walked over to her finger and she couldn't help but smile in sheer delight.

It was called the speckled wood butterfly, he explained. "I became a bit butterfly-obsessed after my wife died. She had set up a corner of the garden with plants that attracted butterflies and it became a sort of sanctuary for me those first years of mourning."

Vivian glanced up. "My father did the same thing with my mother's rose garden."

"Yes, that's where I got the idea from."

They exchanged a smile and returned to watching the butterfly. It opened and closed its wings several times before flying off to find more nectar. "Goodbye, little creature," she said after it. She turned her attention to the rest of the group. Anne and Bernard stood nowhere near each other, more like strangers to one another than husband and wife, and Dantes and her father were talking, though she couldn't hear them. Dantes caught her eye again, but his face gave nothing away.

A few hours later, the group, including Mr. Tewksbury, returned to her home. Vivian had not been expecting him to be a guest but was cautiously pleased by it. The hours spent together at the flower show had been filled with engaging conversation about gardens and butterflies. She'd also learned more about his personal life. He'd made a curious point to mention he and his late wife had been unable to have any children, though he held hope it could still be a possibility for him. And he'd seemed genuinely interested in learning more about her, asking questions that required detailed answers, giving her his full attention as she'd replied.

Everyone gathered in the drawing room, where Anne began playing the piano.

Vivian did her best to remain outwardly cheerful, but despite the time spent with Mr. Tewksbury at the flower show, she was still swimming in a storm of emotions. Dantes was standing in the spot where he had kissed her, and it irritated her because she knew he stood there on purpose. She kept feeling his gaze upon her, caught him a few times watching with that intense stare of his, all while standing in that spot. She did her best to ignore it, but every time she met his eye, the hair on the back of her neck stood up.

She wasn't sure what to make of him, what to make of Mr. Tewksbury, what to make of any of this mess. Truly, she wanted nothing more than to go lie down in bed.

"Vivian." Father's voice cut into her thoughts as Anne's song ended. Vivian turned to find him with Dantes and Mr. Tewksbury. "Do you still have the photograph of you and Bernard out in the grass? It's a favorite and I'd like to show them."

"The one where he's doing a cartwheel, you mean?"

Father nodded as Anne jumped up. "I know where it is. It's in the receiving room," Anne offered. "I will retrieve it."

Anne rushed out of the room, her face oddly flushed. Concern twisted within Vivian and she looked to Bernard to see if he, too, was concerned for Anne. However, Bernard did not notice his wife's departure as he gulped down yet another cognac.

⇶

DANTES FROWNED DEEPLY when Vivian's butler, Heaton, appeared with Victor and Ollie following. Vivian went to greet them warmly, but her smile fell away when Victor said something into her ear and handed her a photograph Dantes assumed was the one Lady Litchfield had meant to fetch.

Victor meandered over to a chair Winthrop lounged in with another drink, when Vivian announced Lady Litchfield had become ill and left for home. Winthrop said, "Oh, should I go check on her?" and began to rise from his chair when Victor forced him back down into his seat, causing the man's drink to slosh over the edge.

Dantes furrowed his brow as he watched Winthrop lick spilled liquor off his hand. What had happened when Lady Litchfield had left the room? She'd seemed perfectly fine only minutes ago.

His interest in the photograph now lost—not that it was for him to see anyway, it was for whoever the blazes this Tewksbury was—he went over to Victor.

"What are you doing here?" Dantes muttered darkly.

"I told you, I need to speak with Vivian about a loan."

"And I told you *no*."

"Tough."

They glowered at each other and Ollie did his best to break up the tension. "Who's the old chap?" Ollie nodded over to Tewksbury, standing with Vivian and her father. As the three brothers watched, Tewksbury said something, and Vivian laughed.

Ollie raised his eyebrows at this and Dantes gave him a deeper scowl than he had Victor and went to sit on the sofa. They would figure it out soon enough, and he would never hear the end of it.

The flower show had been utter torture. Even Lady Litchfield had asked what had happened between him and Vivian. He'd given her a non-answer, of course. But, blast, only he could profess his affections to a woman and have her walk away convinced of the opposite.

But nothing could top the butterfly garden. While Tewksbury had wooed Vivian with a butterfly, her father had asked Dantes how, if Vivian had been inside the pub with him when The Harp & Thistle had caught on fire, where had the newspapers had gotten the idea he'd escaped from his flat?

Dantes, completely caught off guard by this, stammered like an idiot before giving the nonsense answer of, "ah, you know how the newspapers are."

The duke didn't respond, but he did give Dantes a drawn-out, studious look over. Not the first one, either.

Truly, this day couldn't get any worse. Unless Tewksbury proposed to Vivian at the table. It would be just his luck.

As they were seated in the dining room, Tewksbury sat to Vivian's left while Dantes couldn't have been farther away. As Winthrop and his father began to talk with Ollie and Victor about the railway business the McNabs were no longer a part of, Dantes realized he didn't know a single thing about Tewksbury except that he was a widower. He could have been a decent person, aside from getting in Dantes's way. Nothing about Tewksbury seemed off. He wasn't even pompous.

Dantes shifted uncomfortably in his chair. Vivian hadn't said a word to him since their argument, though they had caught each other's eye a few times. What he was going to do about all of this, he hadn't the faintest idea. Ollie's question had been poking at him all day, however. Did he love Vivian? He couldn't answer that. But, using Mr. Jensen's words, he knew he was smitten with her.

As the main course was set before everyone, Ollie leaned toward him. "What did you do?" he whispered.

Dantes ignored the question as he cut into the meat on his plate, paying no attention to what the food was. Ollie dropped the subject, at least for the moment, because everyone began talking about their plans for the summer holiday next month. Well, everyone who wasn't a McNab. The brothers didn't go away for holidays, and they had to focus on getting the pub back up. But Vivian had inherited her grandmother's seaside cottage in Brighton—if a mansion could really be referred to as a "cottage"—and her family would be joining her down there. Soon, she would be gone for several months. He tried his best to ignore the dread that filled him upon this realization.

"Lady Vivian," Tewksbury said farther down the table. Dantes couldn't help but overhear. "Unfortunately, my visit to London ends tomorrow and I rather enjoyed our time together today. I do, however, summer in Brighton, and I hope to get better acquainted this summer."

The duke studied Tewksbury, then Dantes. When he looked down at his plate he shook his head with apparent pity.

Dantes choked on his food. Ollie, alarmed, gave him several swift hits on the back, dislodging it.

"Heavens, Mr. McNab, are you all right?" Vivian asked with evident alarm from the head of the table. Everyone else stared. Dantes cleared his throat and did his best to act like nothing had happened.

Blast it all. This turn of events was more blasted bad luck, and it seemed the day would not end.

Chapter Eighteen

ASIDE FROM THE McNabs, everyone had departed for the evening. Father complimented her hostessing while two footmen guided a stumbling and inebriated Bernard out to his carriage. Mr. Tewksbury left a polite kiss to the back of her gloved hand when he left, though Vivian privately noted it left no feeling behind. It was clear Mr. Tewksbury intended on courting her this summer, but she wasn't sure what to think of that. Deep down, she didn't like the idea, but there was no good reason why, especially now that she understood Dantes's intentions in using her. But Mr. Tewksbury was an agreeable man, handsome, and he wasn't desperate for her fortune. He was simply a widower who'd found interest in a spinster, and really, she should be so lucky.

Yet she found throughout dinner, instead of being absorbed by Mr. Tewksbury's conversation as she should have been, she kept looking over at Dantes, who appeared as miserable as she felt. She missed him, though he was mere feet away. But his heart didn't meet hers, and she couldn't do a thing about it.

Victor approached her, pulling her back to the present. "Dantes and Ollie are leaving now. However, I still need to speak business with you."

She glanced over at the brothers hovering near the door. "Very well. Give me a moment and I'll be right back. Help yourself to a drink if you wish." She glanced in the direction of Gran's old trusty bar cart and followed the brothers out into the hallway and to the large, carpeted entryway. Ollie gave her a hasty thanks before dashing outside as fast as he could. Dantes remained behind.

Vivian took a deep breath. All evening, she had been going over what to say upon his departure. She wanted to be angry with him, wanted to blame him for her unhappiness and for their disagreement, but the only person to blame was herself. "Dantes, I want to apologize for earlier. You have been clear from the beginning where your heart is in all of this. It was foolish of me to hope that would change and I should never have expected you to."

After preparing herself for that apology, after all of the intensive word crafting she'd done to ensure she was clear in her communication, all he did was ignore it. He merely looked at her with his forced blank face and changed the subject. "You're going to marry Tewksbury, aren't you?"

She shook her head in an attempt to shake away the irritation. "That's a rather bold assumption when I haven't received one single proposal from anyone."

A muscle in his jaw ticked. "Very well. Marry me, Vivian."

She gasped and her eyes went wide.

"You heard me. You want a proposal? Then marry me." Dantes stepped forward, now so close even in the low light she could see a single loose thread from a buttonhole.

Her eyes closed at the sensation of his nearness. She wanted nothing more than his touch, but it was his heart that she needed. It was so tempting to say *yes* to his offer, but she couldn't do it. It broke the only rule she set for marriage: never marry a scoundrel.

"Why do you insist on torturing me?" Frustrated, Vivian asked the question louder than she'd meant to, her voice cracking in the desolate space. She had to take a few steps back because his closeness was fogging her mind. "You would go so far as to marry me, just to keep someone else from loving me? You don't love me, Dantes—you don't really want to marry me. Why stand in my way of happiness, then?"

"Vivian—" Dantes's eyes flashed with something she couldn't place, and he turned away. But why? What was it this infuriating man wanted?

She shook her head again with disbelief. "No. Stop. If you do love me, tell me. Please. Because I'm not talking about this anymore."

"You know I can't do that."

"Why?!"

He spun back around. "Because I'll lose you!"

"You're already losing me!"

His jaw clenched and he shoved his hands into his pockets.

"I know how I feel," Vivian continued. "And if you asked me to, I would run around Hyde Park yelling it out to everyone, not caring what anyone thought. And you know what? It would be *easy* for me to do—meek, little old me!"

"Don't say you're meek. You aren't, by any stretch of the imagination."

She ignored him. "That's how I know no matter what you say to me, you and I are in two vastly different places. And that is unfortunate, but it isn't good for anyone to pretend otherwise."

A long pause stretched between them. "Do you love me, Viv?"

"I thought you didn't like people saying that."

"A *yes* or *no* would suffice."

How was she supposed to answer this? Why would she expose herself to further hurt merely to prove a point?

"One hundred years from now…" There was a faint shake in his voice. "You and your family will be remembered, locked into Britain's history for eternity. I'll be forgotten and lost to time, along with my pub. Here I am, some lad who grew up in the slums, with the face of a monster, trying to figure out what is going on with the daughter of a duke, a woman who could find a gentleman far superior to myself. Why would *you* hold any affection for *me?*"

"Surely, you don't see yourself like that!"

"Of course I do. It's the blasted truth, isn't it?"

"No, it's not!" Vivian shot back sharply. "And people only talk to me now because of what my grandmother gave me. I mean nothing to this aristocracy you keep insisting I'm so important to. And, anyway, what do you care? You don't really want me anyway! You'll get over it quick. Go find comfort in one of your other women!"

Dantes narrowed his eyes. "'Other women'? What in the blazes are you talking about?!"

"From the pub! You own a pub and I'm sure they're just crawling all over you every day!"

"There are no other women!" He growled. "Ever since you walked into my pub, I haven't even wanted to *look* at anyone else!"

Her mouth opened ever so slightly, but she quickly shook it off.

He continued with a leveled voice. "Now, you say you would run through Hyde Park declaring how you feel for me, but you can't even give me a simple *yes* or *no* about it. I need to hear it from you, Vivian. I need that run through Hyde Park."

Everything was swirling in her head at once, her heart racing with emotion, with confusion. Why was he asking her to do this? Why couldn't he go be a scoundrel and make this easier?

Vivian broke eye contact. "I must go speak with your brother. Have a good evening, Dantes." And she spun around and rushed back to the drawing room without a glance back.

Upon her return, Victor poured a glass of whiskey and handed it to her. "You look like you could use this."

She took it, thanked him, and shoved the last few minutes out of her mind. "I'm not one to spend an entire day socializing and it's taking its toll."

"And also, my brother is idiotic."

She couldn't help but give him a small smile at this.

They sat in facing chairs and Victor, thankfully, got right down to business. It was rather simple, really. He needed a loan to cover the remainder of what insurance wouldn't.

"And are you hoping I will loan the money to you?" Vivian sipped her whiskey, wanting to be sure she understood what he was looking for.

Victor shifted in his chair. "I was hoping you could give me advice on approaching the bank. It's a large amount."

She studied him for a moment, then set the glass down. In truth, Vivian had enough funds to gain miniscule respect at the bank. However, she remained a woman, and her father—who would be happy to help—was a duke. It would be far more prudent to enlist his help, as much as she hated to admit that. "Did you speak with my father at all tonight?"

"Not about this, but yes. We talked over dinner."

"Good. I'll set up an appointment for you to meet with him. He will be happy to help you get what you need."

Briefly, Victor smiled. He was always so grumpy but was rather handsome when he allowed himself to show through. Vivian wondered why he held the weight of the world the way he did.

"May I ask you something?" she said suddenly. "Is it true none of you verbally express love for fear of losing people?"

Surprisingly, Victor immediately knew what she meant. "No. Dantes is superstitious about it. I don't say it because I don't want to. Why Ollie doesn't say it, you'd have to ask him, but it's likely the same reason. We're not affectionate men, and for that, I apologize."

The conversation was suddenly interrupted, however, when a loud *rat-tat-tat* echoed out from the street. As Vivian rushed over to the window to see what was happening, Victor flew to the ground and yelled at her to "Get down, you foolish woman!"

Before she could respond, an alarming whinnying of horses rang out. Shrieks and shouts came from people down on the sidewalk with their hands over their heads. Two horses were bucking while the driver of the carriage tried consoling the animals. But it wasn't working. The driver ran to the sidewalk when the horses turned sharply, toppling the carriage with the incredible force only frightened horses could create.

Realizing this must be the carriage Dantes and his brother were waiting for Victor in, Vivian screamed.

As Dantes walked outside and headed toward Ollie, he took one last glance over his shoulder at Vivian's grand Mayfair home. He felt rather pathetic in this moment—he had no home, no business, and he was trying to convince the woman who owned this place that yes, he did care about her and no, he wasn't really a scoundrel.

Of course she'd said *no* to his proposal. He offered her nothing.

But he'd been so sure an offer of marriage would be a happy medium. He could learn to be happy to be married, couldn't he? He could if it meant not losing Vivian. That way, he could get used to the idea of marriage, figure out the whole love business and expressing it. And once he was sure nothing would happen to her, maybe he could finally say the cursed words. But how long would that take? Months? Years? Decades?

Would he *ever* be able to say them?

Dantes sighed to himself as Victor's carriage driver climbed down from the coach box to open the door. Dantes gave a nod to the driver as he climbed in.

Women were impossible to understand. He felt in his heart for Vivian. So what if it took time to say those words? They had their entire lives to figure it out. If she loved him, wouldn't she be more understanding of why he hesitated? Victor always called him superstitious, and maybe he was. But he also had several good reasons to be.

"All right, Dantes." Ollie climbed in, too, and sat on the opposite seat. "Tell me what happened today. Best go about it before Victor gets in if you don't want to take the mickey from him."

Dantes swore at his brother. Ollie crossed his arms in response. Knowing it was futile to argue any further, Dantes told him—a less pathetic version of it, at least.

"You're an idiot." Ollie shook his head. "You really are."

"Thanks."

"Well, you know what…? Christ. You're helpless."

A knock on the door caught their attention and it flew open. Dantes's heart stilled when he realized a man pointed a gun at their driver…and then them.

"Good evening, fellas." The man had a thick Irish brogue. "Hand over your money. Watches. Whatever you have, and we'll all get out of this alive." The weapon was held rather lazily—the man didn't intend to use it—but that wasn't what held Dantes's attention. "Tommy Malone?" he said with caution.

The robber's bushy eyebrows flew up to the heavens upon hearing his name. "Jesus, Mary, and Joseph! Edmond McNab?" His eyes flew over to Ollie. "And baby Oliver!" He giggled quite loudly at this, even patting his now-round belly.

"Who is this man?" Ollie hissed.

But before Dantes could explain, Tommy replied with glee. "Your brothers and me was in the same street gang, wee babe, back before your grandparents stole you all away."

"'Wee babe'?" Ollie replied with offense. "I'm bigger than you!"

But Tommy only found this to be funny, patting his belly again as his body shook with his high-pitched giggles. Tommy looked around the cabin. "Aye, you would be, as a McNab. But anyway, looks like you've done all right for yourselves. The wife is expecting me home soon. Hand it all over." He held out a palm with a grin.

"Is he serious?" Ollie asked Dantes without taking his eyes off the robber.

"Yes." Dantes pulled out his wallet, shooting a look to Tommy. "You know, I just lost my business and my home."

"Aye, I heard. Better you than me." Tommy shrugged, the gun still ready.

Dantes and Ollie handed over their belongings—luckily, nothing worth too much—and Tommy thanked them in earnest. "I have five wee babes of my own now. How about you, Edmond?"

"I never married," Dantes replied darkly.

"And he sure won't after tonight." Ollie laughed. Dantes shot him a death stare.

"Ah, that's too bad to hear, fellas. It's been the best years of my life."

Dantes lifted one eyebrow of disbelief. Tommy had been feral when they'd been kids and Dantes didn't believe for a minute this man was happy with settling down into family life. If any of their group had been going to get killed before they hit adulthood, it would have been Tommy. He'd been the most unpredictable one of the bunch. Untamable. In fact, he'd done what he did now, walking around with a gun, pointing it at anyone and everyone to get their belongings.

"I don't believe you, Malone," Dantes retorted.

"'Tis the truth. Believe it or not, Edmond. Settling down with a sweet lass every night, knowing she's always going to be there to love you? That's the best part of it. Maybe I've gone soft, but every night before I fall asleep, I tell her how I love her so much, I'd steal the moon from the entire world if she asked."

The man had become goose feathers. "If you say so, Malone. When we open back up, come by with the wife. I'd love to meet the woman who tamed you."

Ollie shot him a look of alarm. "Are you serious right now?"

"Why not? He's an old friend."

"He's pointing a gun at you, if you didn't notice!"

Dantes merely shrugged. "You can keep an eye on him, then,

if that bothers you." Both Dantes and Tommy laughed at this.

Once their belongings were secured in Tommy's pockets, he let the gun fall away. "Well, got to get on to the next carriage, fellas. Give Victor my regards. You know, he was the only one of you who really scared me." And the door slammed shut.

A huge, mocking smile took over Ollie's face.

"Don't," Dantes said with a deadly warning, knowing he was going to get an earful of Tommy and his moon. "I really don't want to hear it." Dantes slammed a fist into the seat. "Blast, I can't believe Tommy Malone robbed me!"

"I can't see you and Victor running around with him. And he was afraid of *Victor*?" Ollie let out a bark of laughter.

"We were all different back then."

"Apparently."

A loud, ear-splitting bang cut through the air, causing panic and fear to slam through Dantes. Everything moved slowly as he threw himself over Ollie, who shouted in alarm. But just as Dantes covered him, something slammed into his body and screaming pain reverberated. The horses cried out and the two men were thrown to the floor and began to tumble around in the cabin.

In that moment, Dantes thought of his parents laughing together, Ollie as a cooing baby, Victor's rage as he'd seen the stitches on Dantes's face. But the final image he saw, the last thought he had before he was sure he was dead, was Vivian holding the yellow rose to her nose and smiling up at him.

Chapter Nineteen

VIVIAN RUSHED OUT of the room with Victor following, shouting after her to stay back. The scene she came upon when she burst through her front door was more horrific than she had expected. A rather well-dressed man had his arms secured behind his back by two determined bystanders as he shouted he'd meant to kill the Paddy robbing him, not the people in the carriage. As the man continued his protestations, the driver made his way from the crowd and untethered the spooked horses. Thankfully, he was quickly successful, and the horses galloped off to a desolate Hyde Park to calm.

A crowd had gathered around the overturned carriage and everyone, both men and women, worked together through collaborative shouts and movements, trying to break in and get the people inside safely out.

Victor clamped his hands on her shoulders to make sure she stayed in place.

"That's your carriage." Her voice cracked. "Isn't it?

Victor's hands twitched. "Yes. But you need to stay back. Let the people get them."

Vivian stayed at the top of her stairs that led from her front door to the sidewalk, her chest heaving with panic. A loud, wooden crack rang out into the night and she gasped as they pulled the first man out.

Victor let her go and rushed forward, shouting, "That's my brother!" before throwing an unconscious Ollie over his shoulder, then taking him to a spot on the sidewalk the crowd had vacated. He gently laid Ollie out on the sidewalk, checked for blood and injury. Vivian watched without blinking, worried Victor would uncover something fatal. But after a moment, Victor met her eye, mouthed, "He's all right," then pulled Ollie close as if he were a child.

Vivian returned a nod to show she understood what he said.

They then waited with bated breath for Dantes's extraction.

Vivian covered her mouth with both hands, as if that could calm her breathing, keep her last nerve from escaping. The people beside the opening of the overturned carriage began shouting out for a physician.

Terrified, she rushed forward as Victor yelled her name in warning, but she shoved her way through the crowd anyway, sure all of this was simply a bad dream and she would soon wake up. "Dantes!" she cried out. "Where is he? Let me see him!" And she was right there when they pulled him out, covered in blood. Someone caught her elbow when her knees weakened.

A spectacled man in a top hat and eveningwear cut through, his commanding voice bellowing that he was a surgeon and to let him through immediately, and even he stilled at the sight of Dantes. Vivian grabbed his arm. "This is my house," she said with a shaking voice and he nodded before ordering four men to grab the bloody gentleman, and four men to grab the other victim.

Heaton was at the door and held it open to let them through. In the entryway, Ollie and Dantes were laid out on their backs for a quick examination. Because Ollie was merely unconscious, the surgeon quickly put his focus on Dantes. A woman, also dressed in evening wear, took to the surgeon's side, and together, they searched for the source of the blood. Unable to find it on his front, it took several people to roll Dantes over to find the blood had originated from the back of his shoulder.

The woman pulled off her shawl to put pressure on the area

while the surgeon ran off in search of a washbasin with soap to wash his hands. Heaton rushed away to gather a hasty list of supplies, including clean sheets, alcohol, a sharp knife, plate, and a thread and needle.

"I apologize for your carpet," the crouching woman said up to Vivian. "There will be quite a bit of blood to clean up."

"I don't care about the carpet," Vivian snapped harsher than she'd meant to. "You can have the whole house if that's what it takes to save his life."

The woman shifted her position to have a better hold, unperturbed by Vivian's abrasiveness. "You know him," she said, and Vivian nodded curtly, her throat too tight to respond.

When the surgeon returned with a footman and a pale Heaton—who promptly rushed away, citing his weak stomach—there was a flurry of activity. Together, the surgeon and woman cut Dantes out of his shirt, washed his wounds with alcohol, and began to extract the bullets. They worked expertly together, silent except for a few guiding words here and there.

As they removed the first bloody bullet and dropped it onto a white, porcelain plate, Victor appeared at Vivian's side and suggested she go elsewhere for now. The woman helping the surgeon turned to Vivian with a kind face and agreed. "It will be harder on you than him right now. He isn't feeling a thing, I promise you."

Vivian hesitated, looking up at Victor with worry. "If anything happens, you come get me immediately."

"I will."

"And when it's over—"

"Yes."

She glanced once more at Dantes and took sanctuary in her drawing room. She paced, unable to do anything else. Five minutes passed. Fifteen, thirty, an hour. Finally, Victor came in and went straight to Gran's old bar cart to pour himself an extra-large drink.

"He lost a lot of blood." Victor's voice was quiet, tinged with exhaustion. He studied the glass for a moment before taking a deep swig.

Vivian stood rigid, desperate for more information but too terrified to ask. The surgeon and his companion came into the room. No one else joined them.

"They are both upstairs resting now," Mr. Wegner said after introducing himself and his wife, Mrs. Wegner. "Your friend Mr. Dantes McNab was hit by two bullets, which we successfully extracted. He lost a significant amount of blood. He will likely be in and out of consciousness for the next few days and he is at grave risk right now, especially as we wait to see if an infection takes hold. I am not trying to make you worry further, but please understand, he is not out of the woods yet. We washed the wounds with alcohol, dressed with honey—an antiseptic—and cotton, so we have done everything we can. Mr. Oliver McNab received a concussion but is otherwise fine besides significant bruising. He came to moments after you left, Lady Vivian, but refused to leave his brother's side."

"Thank you," Vivian replied. "Both of you, I am truly in your debt."

But the surgeon waved it off as if it were nothing. "When he does regain consciousness, he will be in immense pain. I recommend a spoonful of laudanum—"

"No." Victor immediately cut in, crossing his arms.

"Mr. McNab—"

"There is no discussion around it. He is not to receive laudanum, under any circumstances whatsoever."

The surgeon turned a worried, quizzical look to Vivian. It would have been expected of her to agree with the surgeon in this instance, and normally she would have. But Dantes's health was more important than her social discomfort, and the surgeon wasn't aware of his family's history with laudanum. She lifted her chin in a show of defiance to her own personal nature. "I agree with Mr. McNab," she said. "And I also agree it is not up for discussion."

"Very well, then." The surgeon clasped his hands, seeming to realize there was no breaking through their barrier. "I realize this creates an unusual circumstance that puts you in an awkward position, but I strongly advise against moving the patients out of your home for the time being. It would be an especially great risk to Mr. Dantes's health and life. With your permission, I'll have two nurses sent over. It would be prudent for one to be present both day and night. This would be beneficial to the patients, but it would also protect your reputation."

Vivian, of course, had to nod to that.

Mr. Wegner continued. "My wife and I will come by tomorrow morning and the next few days to check on both patients and Mr. Dantes's wound dressing."

After thanking them again and showing them to the door, Vivian discovered Victor standing in the entryway with her, staring at the floor. A large, fabric tarp had been laid over the spot where the surgeon had worked on Dantes. She tried not to imagine the carnage that lay beneath.

"Thank you," Victor finally said after a long moment.

"I don't think he would be very happy with us if we gave him laudanum."

"No."

A long silence. "May I see him?"

Victor nodded and led her upstairs to the room Dantes and Ollie were sleeping in. The room was quite dark, aside from muted moonlight that cast a faint, silver glow. Vivian went to the foot of the bed Dantes rested in, and even in this light, he was deathly pale, like a ghost of himself. The door clicked shut somewhere behind her, Victor giving her a moment alone in the room.

Nervous, she first went over to Ollie and felt at his forehead, gentle so he didn't wake. When she had convinced herself he would be fine, she returned to Dantes's side to feel his forehead, too. To her relief, there was no fever, and she crouched beside him and took one of his hands in both of hers, rubbing her cheek against it as tears threatened to fall. His hand was warm but limp, almost lifeless. After setting his hand back, she climbed onto the bed to lie alongside him. With her hand on his cheek, she studied his face, almost hoping he would wake as she watched him.

Regret and despair roiled within her. She was frightened, so frightened, and there wasn't anything she could do about it. As she watched his ribs rise and fall, her eyes became heavy. What felt like seconds later, a gentle nudge woke her. Realizing she had fallen asleep in the same bed as Dantes, she sat up quickly and blinked several times. Victor stood over her, his lips pressed tightly. "You should go to your bed," he whispered. "Before any nurses show up."

Too embarrassed to say anything, she hurried out of the room.

To everyone's relief, Ollie was able to get around a bit on his own the next day despite the bruising that covered him. Vivian, Victor, and Ollie spent the day in the drawing room and library, waiting in an all-consuming silence for the hours to pass, wondering when the nurse would inform then Dantes had awoken. Vivian tried to pass the time by reading the newspapers, but the front-page news covered the carriage accident. She didn't like the attention she attracted once again, but because the man injured was famous pugilist Dantes McNab, not long after the fire at his pub, and it had happened in front of the house of *Britain's richest spinster*, it had captured the attention of the entire city.

By yet another stroke of luck with regards to the newspapers, journalists hadn't uncovered the bit that Dantes was recovering at her house. It was incredible how, for a second time, they'd failed to discover a sure scandal. Even though there was always a nurse with Dantes, and moving Dantes was a significant risk to his health, Vivian also knew people would still be up in arms if they knew three unmarried brothers were under her roof.

Of course, she had to tell her family when they came by to check on her after the events. It was now the second day Dantes slept. Vivian explained to her family, her hands shaking with nerves, the surgeon's opinion that moving Dantes would be dangerous. Anne remained silent about the whole ordeal while Bernard didn't seem to listen at all. In fact, he looked as if he were ill and likely wanted nothing more than to go home. And though Father was not too keen on all three McNabs being at her house, he accepted the surgeon's directive and understood Victor and Ollie wanted to be near their brother.

The duke *did* insist on speaking privately with the brothers. When Father left the back library the brothers were in, Vivian glanced in the room as she shut the door. Both of the men were quiet with tense faces. She suspected Father had thrown scary but empty threats at them to ensure their best behavior.

Halfway down the hallway, Father was waiting for her. Understanding he wished a private conversation while no one was around, Vivian stopped and ignored the unease in her stomach.

Father grumbled, then said in a low voice, "If you think it best the McNabs stay here, so be it. But there best not be any funny business."

Vivian felt her cheeks heat. "I don't know what you mean, Father."

"Oh, pish posh. I have twice as many years of life as you, and, despite what you think, I know you've been into mischief with the one abed. I do not want to know what that mischief entails, but I could see as plainly as my own hand"—he held a hand out and looked at it—"that you were both intentionally avoiding each other the way only two people in a lover's quarrel do. *Behave.*"

She gave him a hasty curtsy but couldn't look him in the eye. And, as she was already testing his patience, thought it best to bite back her denial of the *lovers* bit. "Of course."

"I will, naturally, deny all gossip if somehow this gets out. But, please, send him home as soon as possible to ensure it does not."

Vivian promised.

"We would not want this to reach Mr. Tewksbury's ears, either." Father looped his hands behind his back and held a bored expression. Vivian knew well enough this was not meant to come off as a casual, off-hand comment. This was how he looked when he meant business.

She swallowed. "Mr. Tewksbury? Whatever do you mean? I've spent one afternoon with the man."

Father turned and began strolling down the hallway, his hands still behind his back. After a few paces, he paused and added, "I quite like that Mr. Tewksbury, Vivian. If my opinion matters at all."

Of course his opinion mattered to her. Though she wished he wouldn't share his thoughts on the subject of matrimony so freely. She would do as she pleased in that regard.

On the third day, Dantes slept. Vivian received a respite from family, which was a relief. As much as she loved them, they could sometimes be too much.

However, the relief was short-lived. The receiving room filled once more.

Her chasers were back.

Over the past few weeks her chasers had, one by one, started losing interest in her. Apparently, months of ignoring them had worked.

Or so she'd thought.

Now they had an excuse to swarm her receiving room once more by pretending to be concerned for her after the frightening carriage event. And swarm they did.

The servants reached their limits. Heaton and the rest did everything they could to keep Victor and Ollie concealed at the back of the house and their mistress's secret safe. But being on high alert for days on end took its toll.

Meanwhile, Victor and Ollie were sick of being stuck inside, sick of the constant fear for Dantes.

Ollie stood at the window like a forlorn tot on a rainy day. "Look at it out there! The sun is out—when does that happen? What do you think that feels like, having the sun on your face? The fresh air in your lungs?" He turned around to face the room, and Victor scowled at him. "I haven't felt it in days now. I'm going to go mad soon if I don't get out of this blasted room."

Victor dug his fingers into the arm of his chair. "Fresh air? In London?" He let out a sarcastic laugh. "There're more pressing matters at hand, Ollie, than enjoying sunshine and smog. Did you forget your brother upstairs? The one who might die at any moment? Or does that no longer concern you because you're being inconvenienced?"

Ollie rushed his hands through his hair. "This is like being in prison!"

Vivian slammed her book shut. "Stop it! I can't listen to you two any longer! I'm sick of your fighting, I'm sick of you talking about Dantes dying, I'm sick of all of you men pestering me!"

A switch seemed to flip on in Vivian and she decided she'd had enough. She shoved her book aside and stormed out of the back library, rendering Victor and Ollie silent, then stomped down her hallway, where Heaton smartly jumped out of the way.

With as much strength as she could muster, she threw open the door to the receiving room, so packed with men now the floor wasn't visible anywhere, and immediately shouted at the top of her lungs, "Get out!"

The chasers didn't budge, but they did stop talking to stare at her.

"Get out, the lot of you!" Her chest had heaved. "I don't want you here anymore, you are not welcome here, and I will not be marrying a single one of you. You can close out your insipid wagers in my brother's wager book!"

Surprisingly, the men began to file out, giving her nervous glances as they passed by. But they were taking too long.

"I said, *get out*, are you all daft? If you aren't out in one minute, I shall call for the police!"

Mr. Crosby happened to be filing by at that moment. He stopped, causing others around him to stop as well to watch. There was a cocky smirk on his face. "How unfeminine of you, Lady Vivian. A woman should be graceful and delicate, not bellowing like a foghorn."

For a moment, all Vivian could do was blink back. Who did this blasted man think he was, deciding what women should be? Her anger did not cool, however. "Delicate?" She scoffed then held up a fist, recalling the moment Dantes had knocked out Sullivan. "Oh, I can show you *delicate.*"

Mr. Crosby paled but quickly collected himself. He then let out a "hmph," closed his eyes, lifted his nose in the air, and kept walking.

The rest of the men, thankfully, evacuated posthaste as they now wanted to get away from the madwoman who didn't want to marry them.

MEANWHILE, DANTES STILL slumbered on.

Vivian and the healthy McNabs were more concerned than ever and they began taking turns sitting with him. When Vivian was with Dantes she stayed at his side to talk to him in case he could hear her, though she spoke low enough so the nurse couldn't listen in. Mostly, she tried to keep it light, sticking to funny, little quips from Ollie.

But it felt forced.

Other times, the sorrow and guilt weighed so heavily upon her, she demanded through her tears that he survive for his brothers, for her, so they could make everything right again.

A few curious instances, she inadvertently reached out to hold his hand, recoiling at the last moment as she realized what she was doing. This silly mistake, however, forced her to face what she had been trying to ignore over the past few months.

All this time, she had been confused over the affection she felt for him, trying to convince herself it was nothing more than a friendly fondness. But their parting words from that horrible night kept playing over and over in Vivian's mind, both her Hyde Park declaration and those said in frustration. And she realized, she would never *accidentally* reach out to hold another man's hand.

Vivian couldn't deny any longer the cold hard truth.

"I love you, Dantes," she decided to whisper into his ear. Saying it out loud for the first time sent a rush through her, but the moment was blanketed in a heavy sadness. "I know you'll get mad if you ever find out I said that to you, but I don't care right now. I do love you, and I'm going to say it while you can't do anything about it." She almost hoped he would be so furious, he would wake up, but he remained asleep.

One evening, the night nurse had an unexpected family emergency and another nurse was not available. Thus, Vivian refused to leave Dantes's side despite Victor's protests. Normally, she would do as told without complaint, but the thought of being away from Dantes when there wasn't a night nurse was unfathomable.

"I'm not leaving." She surprised herself by digging in her heels and arguing back with Victor. "If you think I'm going to sleep in another room while he's in here like this, you're mad."

"It's extremely inappropriate, Vivian, especially with the two of us sleeping in here, too." Victor pointed between himself and Ollie, who was climbing into the other bed with a bear-sized yawn. "I can get you if something happens."

But she wasn't having it. "No," she replied simply, and she climbed on the bed to lie beside Dantes, wearing a housecoat tied around a nightgown. "You'll have to drag me out of here if you want me to leave."

"I'm about ready to do exactly that," Victor said with deep frustration. "I don't need the wrath of your father on top of everything else."

"So don't tell him." She lifted her head to glare at him, and he glared back, but he seemed to realize it was fruitless. He grumbled to himself and grabbed a spare blanket, tossing it to her. "At least stay above the covers."

Their worst fear was realized when, the following morning, an infection took hold. Mr. Wegner and his wife confirmed it during their morning visit and were incredibly worried by this turn of events. Losing so much blood was already hard enough on Dantes's body; the added infection meant his life now quite literally hung in the balance.

And there was nothing they could do but wait more and see if he survived.

While the surgeon and his wife observed Dantes, speaking to each other in low but rapid voices, there was a knock at the door. Victor went to open it—it was Heaton.

"Your brother is here," the butler whispered to Vivian. "I think something is wrong." He shot an intentional look of worry to Victor, and when Vivian said she would meet Bernard in the drawing room Victor insisted he join her. It seemed a bit silly, but she didn't have the energy to argue with him on one more thing.

So while Ollie sat vigil with Dantes, the day nurse keeping close, Vivian and Victor went into the drawing room. When Bernard walked in, she rushed over, so happy to see him, hoping for one of those giant hugs he used to give her where he would sweep her off her feet and swing her around.

But the sour stench of alcohol clouding him caused her to stop in her tracks.

"You ruined my life," was what Bernard opened with. Not asking about Dantes, not saying he was sorry about the accident, not giving her a shoulder to lean on or a simple hug. No, he gave her a drunken accusation.

"What are you talking about?" Vivian asked, taking a few cautious steps back without even realizing she had done it. "Are you drunk?"

Bernard stepped closer with rage in his reddened eyes. Out of her view, she sensed Victor edge closer to her, clearly concerned by Bernard's state as well.

"Anne separated from me." Bernard's words slurred and he swayed on his feet. "She told Father I'm getting worse and lied that I scared her and the children!"

There was a sinking feeling in Vivian that this may not have been a lie, and she feared Anne's claim may have even been worse.

Bernard continued. "Father put me in the empty townhouse of some insipid baron friend of his this morning and threatened to throw me onto a ship for America if I contact my family before Anne allows me to. She has the children, Vivian. But they belong to me! The children, the money, the house is all mine! That blasted woman doesn't deserve anything!" He took another step toward her. "And this is all because of you. You ruined my life, Vivian!" Bernard shouted this so loudly, she flinched while his words echoed in the room.

"I had no idea she was going to do all of that, Bernard." It came out desperate. But it was the truth. Vivian had admittedly made the mistake of mentioning separation to Anne, but she had no idea Anne had been pursuing it. "Last she told me, everything seemed to be much better since I paid off your debts. Anne said you were helping her out more. I even heard you playing with the children one afternoon. I don't understand. What happened?"

Bernard continued his glare, his nose flaring with his rage. Her brother's normally neat hair and clothing were uncharacteristically messy. "She changed her mind. What do you *think* happened?"

"Did you come here only to yell at me? I can't help what Anne does or doesn't do!" Vivian paused. He was here for something, wasn't he? He wasn't here to confide in her. A queasiness roiled in her stomach. "Why are you really here, Bernard? Why are you staying at some baron's townhouse when Father has other properties you can go to?"

Bernard smiled, but nothing about it was friendly. "If it

weren't for you, I wouldn't be losing my family! Gran's estate would have gone to me! And now you owe me big because it's all your fault I'm in this position!"

"None of it makes sense." It was Victor. "Why would your wife want a separation so badly if you were simply a pathetic drunk who spent too much money? What did you do to your family, Winthrop?"

Vivian looked up at Victor to find a dangerous tension on his face. She was surprised he dared step into this conversation, but he was right. There *was* something more going on here. She looked back to Bernard, waiting for his response, because nothing was adding up. And he kept ignoring questions.

"This is a family matter, McNab, and has nothing to do with you. Now back off." Bernard stumbled toward Vivian as he said this.

"No. I'm staying right here," Victor shot back. "I don't trust you to keep your hands off of her, not when you're this drunk and angry. I'm not a fool, Winthrop. I know what you're capable of."

Bernard swallowed and decided to ignore Victor. "I need your help, Vivian." Bernard pleaded, his voice ringing weak and pathetic. "You're my sister, and I need your help. Please." And he requested a large sum of money.

She gasped. *"How much?"* Gran hadn't trusted Bernard with any money, and this request was concerning.

Bernard stammered. "Father is still furious you covered my debts and refuses to lend me anything. And this morning, when he threw me out of my own home, he put a hold on my accounts. I can only pull a tiny amount of money out each day now. Not nearly enough to sustain anything."

"That still doesn't explain why you're staying at a baron's house and not one of the other properties under the dukedom."

Bernard had the good sense to look sheepish. "Father let all of our empty properties to repay you."

Vivian's eyebrows lifted up to the ceiling upon that unexpected twist.

"However, there is a newly renovated place a few blocks from here—"

"You should be staying where Father put you."

"But the baron will be back at some point! And then I'll have to go live with Father!" Bernard whined.

"What's wrong with that?" She'd done it her entire life until recently; it wasn't *that* bad. And obviously, it wouldn't be permanent, just until he got back on his feet. Bernard living with Father wasn't a terrible idea. He clearly needed help and support from family right now. Father could make sure he didn't succumb to temptations that could only hurt him and his family further.

But Bernard laughed in her face. "Come on. I'm not that pathetic."

Vivian frowned. If he hadn't said that, she would have done *something* to help him. Perhaps have him over for dinner often so he wasn't dining alone, or so she could ensure he was avoiding his temptations. He was her brother, after all, and she didn't want to see him falter. But to insult her as he asked for money? And despite what he claimed, he was far from innocent in the matters of the separation, and it bothered her that he seemed remorseless over his actions. On top of that, when she'd paid off his debt before, he'd never said a word to her about it. He thought she owed that to him, too, didn't he?

She really shouldn't give him a dime. And she didn't care to have him over more often if he was going to act this way. But she was more concerned about what would happen if she didn't help him at all.

"I'll send two hundred pounds to you tomorrow to have on hand in case something comes up," she decided. It was enough to be an emergency cushion if or when Bernard needed it. Or, if there was something he did need unexpectedly but couldn't take enough out to cover it. Father wouldn't be happy about this, of course, but it wouldn't garner fury. And she knew she could convince him of the importance of Bernard having a financial buffer. Then, if Bernard burned through it quickly and came back begging for more, she could remind him she already had helped him.

"That's it? You could buy me an entirely new life and you wouldn't even feel it. Are you serious right now, Vivian?" He slammed a fist into his palm. "I'm your brother! Gran didn't leave me *anything*. If she had, I wouldn't be in this position right now!"

No, you would have squandered every last coin and still ended up here, anyway. But she didn't say that. "I'm not going into this with you right now. You know, you haven't once asked how I'm doing, how Mr. McNab is doing, how his brothers are doing. Did you realize that? Do you even care that Mr. McNab is upstairs fighting for his life right now while we wait around helplessly to see if he pulls through?" She fought back the hot, angry tears forming at her eyes.

Bernard stepped away, looking hurt. "My life is spiraling out of control, and you're the only one who can help me. Forgive me for bothering you when I needed help." And with that, he left. Vivian watched, wracked with guilt, too upset to move from where she stood. She struggled to understand his lack of compassion, but wasn't her refusal to help him just as bad? It might have even been worse. Her issue with Bernard was based on emotion, but she seemed to be lacking in loyalty to her brother. They were family, and family was supposed to help each other and she was well in a position to be able to do that. And she liked helping the people she cared about. It was why she'd paid off his debts without a second thought. She loved her brother.

"Bernard is lying to you," Victor said, causing Vivian to turn.

"About what?" She gulped back the upset that had threatened to rise in her throat, wiping at her tears without a second thought. Victor had already seen her cry plenty in these last few days. There was no point in trying to hide it now.

He ignored her question. "You shouldn't have given him anything."

"He's my brother. What am I supposed to do?"

"He's using you."

Victor's words cut through her. She had accused Dantes of using her, though for much different reasons, of course. And while there was no denying Dantes had hurt her, Bernard was hurting her, too. Yet she was always giving him a pass simply because they were family. Was that right or wrong? She wasn't sure. But now she had two important relationships to work through and understand. Her relationship with Dantes and whatever they were, and her relationship with her brother that was threatening to fall apart.

Chapter Twenty

DANTES COULD PERCEIVE light, and he wondered why he felt like death but couldn't open his eyes. His shoulder and back screamed in pain and he wanted to shout out because of it. But he couldn't move, couldn't talk.

"He's running a fever," a strange woman's voice said, and it seemed to echo from some out-of-reach place.

Some male voice swore. "He's already been through enough. This isn't good. This isn't good at all. He hasn't even begun to recover from blood loss yet."

Dantes felt dizzy, turned inside out almost. He didn't know where he was, who these people were, why he hurt so much. Was he dying?

He came to again, this time perceiving darkness. The room was silent, but he wasn't alone—though he didn't know how he knew that. His ears reached for anything, any sound at all, so he could understand what was happening. He heard someone nearby breathing deeply, slowly. The sound and sensation caused vague images to swirl in his mind, but they didn't materialize.

Lightness. Darkness. Lightness again. He didn't know what was happening, why he felt so awful, why he couldn't move. How much time had passed? Was he even alive? He sometimes heard voices but didn't understand what they were saying. They were frantic, and this was when he felt fear. But otherwise, he felt nothing.

Something wet spilled down his cheek from his mouth. He smelled something pretty. Something deep inside began to stir.

Cold metal touched his lips. A woman was talking. He liked her voice. It was familiar and made him feel safe. Liquid hit his tongue and spilled out of the corner of his mouth.

"Lady Vivian," a faraway male voice said, and his familiar voice coupled with that name stirred him inside a bit more. "It's no use. We need to accept he's not coming back."

A third voice, this time a woman he'd never heard before, added in her agreement. "Patients generally do not come back from this, Lady Vivian. I'm sorry. It's time you take care of yourself."

"He simply needs a little water," the familiar woman said desperately. Dantes felt the cold metal at his mouth again, then liquid spill out. "He's dehydrated, and the fever might go away if he has water."

"But he's not swallowing it," the man responded. "He needs to swallow it. The nurse hasn't been able to get him to swallow it, either. You've both been trying for days now." The man was quiet for a long time. "It's a miracle he's even still alive." Another pause. "The priest is coming today."

"No!" She whimpered as the cold metal came to his mouth again and the liquid spilled back out. "Try talking to him," she said, her voice shaky and high-pitched. "Maybe he'll respond to you. Tell him to swallow."

"Lady Vivian..."

"I know it's not going to work, but we have to try. We have to try, Ollie. It's not over yet! I'm not giving up!"

"I'm not giving up, either!" Ollie shot back with anger.

"Then *talk* to him!" She went quiet. "It's all we have left. Maybe he'll hear your voice, follow you. I don't know."

Dantes sensed someone at his side. "Dantes, it's Ollie," the man said into his ear.

Ollie. Oliver. His brother.

"You need to swallow the water. If you don't, you're going to die, do you hear me?"

Dantes couldn't respond and water spilled out of his mouth again. Ollie swore, then took a deep breath. "You know, Dantes, you have to get better. You need to be there when we reopen The Harp & Thistle. And I need you. I can't deal with Victor by myself for the rest of my life. Lady Vivian needs you, too—for the rest of her life, but watch, she'll deny it."

"*Ollie*," the woman's voice warned.

But Ollie kept talking. "Even Victor needs you, more than I think either of us can understand. Right now, Victor is passed out cold in a chair because he hasn't slept in a week. Do you hear me? We all need you, Dantes. For God's sake, wake up or swallow the blasted water."

"I need more," Vivian said and there was a clatter of silverware against dishware.

"All right. We'll get it. Keep talking to him while we're gone."

"All right." A scratchy, wet towel was pulled away from the side of his face. A soft hand touched his cheek, then fingers brushed through his hair. It felt nice and he wanted her to do it again. "Dantes." Vivian began to speak. "I know you can't hear me, but in case you can, I want you to know I've never been so terrified in my life as I am right now. You've been fevered for a week, won't wake up no matter how hard we try, won't take down any liquids, and I don't know what I will do if I lose you. I don't know what was happening between us before this madness happened, but I want to work through it and figure it out with you. It's going to be the biggest regret of my life that I didn't tell you how I feel soon enough. I would give anything for you to get mad at me right now for telling you."

He wanted so badly to reach out and touch her.

"And Ollie, he remembers the accident and said you saved his life by jumping on him and taking the bullet. If anything, you can't die because of that because he will live with immense guilt for the rest of his life and blame himself. I can already see that he does." She was quiet a long time. "Dantes, come back to me. Please. Come back to us."

A door opened. "I have more water. Anything happen while I was gone?"

"No."

"Let me try giving him the water, then." It was Ollie's voice. "See if he swallows it for me."

"All right."

Dantes's throat felt like desert sand, so dry and scratchy, it felt closed off. And when he felt a cold spoon against his lips again, the water pour into his mouth, he tried to get his throat to take it. But he couldn't move it. They tried again, but he started feeling faint. Their voices started to fade away. He was tired, so tired, and he just wanted to go away now.

Everything began to turn gray. He started to follow the empty blackness sitting in front of him.

But then a gentle hand touched his throat, fingertips stroking from under his chin all the way along and down. They did it again. And again.

It was such a strange sensation that he swallowed in response, as if his throat now remembered what to do.

A gasp pulled him back up from the emptiness that lured him. "Oh! Oh, it worked! Ollie!"

"Brilliant work, Lady Vivian," the nurse said.

"Do it again," Ollie responded frantically.

The spoon went to his lips, and he swallowed the water when it poured in.

Vivian began crying and kept massaging his throat as someone else poured a little more water in. Dantes was able to take in a gulp this time.

While the nurse directed Ollie to hold the container of water, Ollie told Vivian to wake up Victor. A second later, Dantes could feel another presence. Though the person didn't speak, everything felt a little more tense, a bit darker. Through this silence, they gave him more water. He realized how parched his body was. Like dry, cracked leather being dunked into a pool and plumping back up.

He began to succumb again—not to the darkness as before, but to humanly exhaustion.

Sometime later, Dantes woke up and his eyes were able to open. He felt horrid and his shoulder was killing him. "Ow," he said quietly.

Vivian's face appeared above his along with a sharp-chinned woman wearing a nurse's cap. "You're awake," Vivian said with wide eyes, but he merely squinted back up to her. As the nurse took his wrist and commented she would be checking his heart rate, Vivian disappeared from view and ran out into the hallway. "Ollie! Victor! He's awake! Come quick!" She rushed back to his side, too stunned to say anything more.

"Mr. Wegner should be here any moment," the nurse said to Vivian. "I'll go down to meet him so you all can have a moment."

Vivian nodded at the woman as Ollie and Victor appeared in Dantes's view.

"He said, 'Ow,'" Vivian explained with excitement. "And then his eyes were open."

Victor spoke. "Dantes, can you hear me?"

Dantes looked over to Victor, wondering why he had seen a nurse. "What's going on?" His voice felt weak and scratchy. "Where am I?"

The three smiled widely at this response. "You're in Lady Vivian's house, Dantes. Do you remember anything?"

"No. But my shoulder is killing me." He moved to sit up and at once they all shouted, "No!"

"You were in a carriage accident," Victor explained. "You were shot, too. Two bullets in your shoulder."

Dantes closed his eyes. "It *feels* like I got shot with two bullets."

"Hello, everyone." A vaguely familiar voice interrupted and Dantes turned his head to see an older man with glasses following the nurse. The nurse took a few steps back to let the man pass her and put her hands behind her back.

"I've heard you before," Dantes said with wonder, as he had never seen this man before in his life.

Mr. Wegner smiled and began examining him. "You still have a fever, Mr. McNab, but it's finally going down for the first time this week. You lost a lot of blood from the gunshots and you immediately developed a fever. You've been in and out of consciousness for a week now. Do you remember anything at all?"

"Lightness, darkness, and sometimes voices." He spoke quiet and slow, it took a lot of energy to talk.

"Do you remember anything that was said to you?"

"No."

"Do you think you could eat anything?"

"Maybe. I can try."

Mr. Wegner turned to the nurse and asked her to ask the kitchen for some broth. Dantes closed his eyes for a bit and Mr. Wegner woke him up when the broth was ready. The first sip was difficult, but he eventually finished off the entire cup and fell asleep again.

Next thing he knew, it was dark outside. He opened his eyes and turned his head with a bit of difficulty but found Vivian asleep next to him on top of the blankets and in a day dress. There was a different nurse here now; she was reading something but seemed to sense he was awake. She met his eye before looking at Vivian with a deep frown.

However, she didn't say anything and went back to reading.

Vivian slept on her side and drooled in her sleep, and for whatever reason, that was making him misty eyed. Maybe because he almost hadn't learned this about her. He wondered if she had slept nearby every night, but somehow already knew she had. Vivian had been there with him the entire time. They all had.

The following morning, he woke up drenched in sweat, the bed completely soaked. The fever had broken.

Chapter Twenty-One

"I DON'T UNDERSTAND why, of all places, you wanted to come here." Ollie was beside Vivian as they climbed the stairs to the National Gallery. "Wouldn't you rather get fresh air, walk around the park? We've been stuck inside for over a week."

"No," Vivian replied, and when they entered the museum she began looking around for something. "I came here with a purpose, not to dilly-dally."

"What purpose?"

She turned to Ollie and realized how tired he looked. She probably looked no better. "Yesterday, you took me to Dantes's to see if there was anything that survived the fire we could bring back for him."

Ollie stared, waiting for more information.

"I want to save his paintings."

Ollie blinked. "Vivian, they're destroyed beyond repair. You saw them yourself."

"Then they can tell me that." She nodded out to the museum and began walking again to the front desk. "Now that he's on the mend, with a long road of recovery ahead, I need a project to keep my mind from going over the edge, knowing how awful he feels right now."

"Don't most women, you know, sew or read? Perhaps you can take up photography."

"You know what, Ollie? I'm doing this." Vivian gave him a smile that was pleasant but final.

They arrived at the front desk, and she met eyes with a young, freckle-faced gentleman behind the counter. "Hello. I need to speak with the director about a collection of artwork in my possession."

The young man looked at her as if she had three heads.

"Well?" Vivian didn't have the time or patience—or energy—to beat around the bush.

"Do you have an appointment? Or…"

"No. But it's essential I speak to him."

The young man scoffed. "I'm not risking my job to tell him some random lady wants to talk to him."

Vivian resisted the urge to react, offended. "Tell him this *random lady* will be making a three-thousand-pound donation, then."

Ollie let out a low whistle.

But *that* caught the young man's attention, and he exchanged a look with another employee beside him. He rushed away without another word, looking over his shoulder one last time before disappearing behind a door.

"Demanding today, are we?" Ollie said with bemusement.

Vivian looked at him with seriousness. "I learned something over the past week."

"What's that?"

"I no longer care what other people think. If I want something done, I'm going to make it happen, not wring my hands over it."

Ollie laughed, no doubt because he knew she was completely serious. "I noticed—when you refused to leave Dantes's side every night despite everyone's protests."

"I made sure to sleep above the covers as asked."

"Good for you, then. I wager you'll be a force."

"I intend to be."

The young man to whom Vivian had spoken returned, followed by an older gentleman with a mustache. He introduced himself as Sir Frederic William Burton.

Vivian spoke. "A dear friend of mine has several priceless paintings and a tintype photograph that were damaged in a fire. I would like to discuss your conservation department looking at them and restoring them if at all possible."

The director was clearly stunned for a moment, staring with hesitation. "Miss…" He trailed off, no doubt realizing he didn't know her name. "I'm not sure what you think we are, but we're not a restoration business."

Hiding her embarrassment, she finally introduced herself properly to the director. "May I be frank with you?"

Sir Frederic looked at Ollie, as if asking for help, but Ollie merely shrugged. "Very well."

"Good, because I haven't slept in a week, I'm rather tired, and I dislike long conversation. My name is Lady Vivian Winthrop, and I am willing to donate three thousand pounds to the museum if you agree to help me. Another place simply won't do because I only want the world's best."

His eyes briefly widened before narrowing. "Four thousand."

"Three thousand remains. However, I'll cover the cost of supplies."

The director held out a hand to shake hers. She watched the maneuver with surprise—no one had ever offered to shake her hand in a business manner before—but she returned the handshake as if she had done it hundreds of times. Sir Frederic asked them to follow him and led them through the doors from which he had emerged.

"I have the perfect person in mind to lead this," he said over his shoulder as they continued walking. "She came to us from the Louvre." They went through another set of doors and climbed stairs to the third floor. Soon, they entered a large, sunlight-filled, high-ceilinged room with numerous giant tables and easels, each one covered with paintings in various sizes as well as conservation paraphernalia Vivian could hardly begin to identify. The director looked over the room, passed a few people, and made his way toward his destination. "We have several different conservation departments, but, obviously, you'll be working with the Department of Paintings. Miss Sparrow?"

A willowy, auburn-haired woman was leaning over a painting in deep concentration. When she looked up upon hearing the director's voice, round magnifying eyeglasses made her eyes comically large, and she blinked several times through them. She removed the glasses and blinked again to refocus as she set them to the side. "Apologies. I forgot I was wearing those." She seemed unsurprised to see Sir Frederic, but upon seeing Vivian, she squinted, perhaps wondering if she should know her, and then her eyes trailed to Ollie. Her cheeks flushed crimson and she hastily looked back to the director.

"Lady Vivian, this is Miss Evelyn Sparrow, one of our conservators. Miss Sparrow, Lady Vivian Winthrop." The director indicated toward his employee before putting his attention on Ollie. "And this is Lady Vivian's...erm..."

Vivian jumped in. "This is my friend Mr. Oliver McNab."

"Hello." Miss Sparrow nodded as she rapidly looked back and forth between Vivian and the director. No doubt she was wondering why they were there.

Sir Frederic explained the nature of their visit. Miss Sparrow listened with proper interest, her hands looped behind her back, absorbing every word.

"This is a bit..." Miss Sparrow began after he had finished.

"Unorthodox?" the director added with a nod. "Lady Vivian will be donating three thousand pounds to the museum, half of which will go exclusively to your department. She will also be covering cost of supplies."

Miss Sparrow's mouth fell open, but she quickly slammed it shut. "Oh. Oh my." She had to take a moment. "Of course, I will need to see the paintings first, and art conservation and restoration aren't really the same, but I *have* worked on fire-damaged artwork before. Plan on at least a month per piece, more or less depending on the size. And I may need help from my colleagues, if necessary. But I'll oversee everything."

"However long it takes, I don't care, as long as it's done right and well," Vivian replied, and they discussed plans on how the museum would retrieve the artwork the following day. Once satisfied it would all be transported safely, Vivian had other questions for the young woman. "I would like to know more about your background, however, Miss Sparrow. I hope you understand, this is not only a large investment I am making, but the owner of these paintings is very dear to me, the brother of Mr. McNab here."

Miss Sparrow nodded, though she looked a bit nervous. "I was born and raised in London and have had in interest in art since I was quite young. My father has a library filled with books about the subject and I would spend hours with those books each day. I received a degree in Art History at Vassar College over in New York, as women's universities are almost non-existent here. After I graduated top of my class, I took an apprenticeship at the Louvre, and now I am here."

"That is quite an impressive background. But how long have you been here?"

Miss Sparrow reached up to her hair. "Six months."

"That's all?" Vivian turned to the director. "I was hoping for someone with a little more experience, for the money I'm spending."

"Once again, Lady Vivian, this is a museum and not a restoration business. I have full faith in Miss Sparrow, which is why she is here in the first place, and I think you will be satisfied with her expertise."

Vivian turned back to Miss Sparrow. "Very well. Can you show us what you've been working on?"

Ollie, evidently curious as well, took it upon himself to take to Miss Sparrow's side to see the painting. Vivian couldn't help but notice Miss Sparrow found Ollie rather distracting—she kept fidgeting and reaching up to fuss with her hair. Ollie appeared not to notice any of this.

"My word." Ollie let out a sharp laugh upon seeing the painting. "Is that baby smiling as he urinates on a nude woman's stomach?"

Miss Sparrow gasped loudly and tried covering the baby with one hand, and the woman with the other. "This is *Venus and Cupid* by Lorenzo Lotto, painted in the 1500s," she explained rapidly. When she realized the woman in the painting was still exposed, she moved her second hand from the baby to the woman. Miss Sparrow's hands did a hovering dance over the painting trying to figure out what to cover before she accepted it was futile—there were more spots to cover than hands available—so she found a piece of fabric and hastily covered the painting, her entire face bright red with embarrassment.

"This painting…" She closed her eyes as she spoke, as if trying to regain her composure. "Was likely a wedding gift. Cupid is…urinating through a laurel wreath onto his mother and that…used to symbolize fertility. For some reason."

"I see." Ollie covered his mouth with a fist and made a choking sound. Vivian shot him a look and his humor fell away. He cleared his throat and laced his hands behind his back. "So, tell us what you've done with this one."

"Why don't you show them something a bit more innocuous, like a pastoral landscape?" the director said blandly.

Miss Sparrow nodded and led them over to another table. "This is a Dutch barnyard scene likely from the 1600s. However, it is unsigned, so that's only a guess. It came to us covered in dust and its varnish was aged dark yellow. After identifying the type of varnish, I was able to remove the varnish without damaging the paint. Then I inpaint and repair any damaged areas, and re-varnish it when finished, this time with something that will not yellow over time."

Vivian went around to the woman's side and noted the whites of the painting were as white as they were meant to be. The work was spectacular, and she said as much. "I look forward to working with you, Miss Sparrow." Vivian held out a hand to the woman, receiving a rapid succession of blinks from Miss Sparrow. But she accepted and shook Vivian's hand.

"Come by in two days' time," Miss Sparrow said. "I'll be able to do a quick conditions assessment of the whole collection and we can discuss what's next."

DANTES CLENCHED HIS teeth as he tried to push through a wave of pain. He had been out of his fever for a full day now and it had been nothing but agony. His appetite was still minimal, but he did his best to keep up with water intake to the incessant demand of Vivian, Ollie, Victor, the nurses, and the Wegners. And of course Heaton and the rest of the household. The house was filled to the brim with people watching his every move.

Pain made him groan and he rolled to his side.

The door opened and Victor came in carrying a bowl and spoon. Victor dismissed the nurse for her luncheon, and the door shut upon her departure. "You need to eat something, too." He watched his writhing brother. "And then you need a bath so they can change the bedding. You reek to the high heavens."

Dantes weakly told Victor where he thought he should go.

But Victor merely pulled a chair to the bedside and set the bowl on the nightstand. "Mr. Wegner tried to convince us to give you laudanum. Both Lady Vivian and I fought him on it."

Dantes swore loud with a grimace. After what had happened to his mother, he should have been grateful, but right now, he was in agony and wanted it to end. "It feels like I was beat to death with a hammer."

"Eat and then bathe. And you'll feel better."

Dantes waited until the pain had subsided to a more tolerable level. Once the excruciating moment was over, Victor gently helped him sit up before handing him a bowl of buttered mashed potatoes. "I thought this would be more palatable than yet another cup of broth."

"Yes. Thank you." Dantes took a huge spoonful and for the first time in a while, felt sort of human again.

Victor watched his younger brother for a few moments and leaned forward with his elbows on his knees. "We haven't really had a chance to talk yet."

Dantes paused. "All right." He continued eating.

"What do you remember about that night?"

"Not much. Tommy Malone robbed us."

Victor nodded. "Yes. Tommy is in hot water for robbery. Do you remember anything after seeing Tommy?"

"Something slamming into me. I'm assuming that was the bullets."

"Tommy Malone went to rob another carriage. The owner of that carriage, instead of cooperating, wrestled away Tommy's gun. Tommy ran away and the man shot at Tommy. As he had never shot a gun before in his life, his aim was terrible, and two of three bullets went through the carriage and into you. The first shot—they don't know where it went, probably into a tree."

Dantes stopped eating, but his eyes remained on his bowl. "What happened to him? The one who nearly killed me?"

"Police let him go, said it was self-defense, so he wouldn't be charged."

Dantes shook his head.

Victor continued. "Ollie told me you identified the noise of the first bullet, that you threw yourself on top of him to get him down. Obviously, you knew what gunfire sounded like and he didn't."

"No, he wouldn't."

Victor looked down at his hands. "If you hadn't done that, Ollie would be dead right now. You nearly sacrificed yourself for him."

Dantes's jaw went tight. "It's his own fault."

"What are you talking about?"

"The night you called him a… Well, you know. He told me he loved me."

"Oh, come on, Dantes," Victor said with evident exasperation, of course knowing what he was getting at.

"I knew something was going to happen to him." No longer having an appetite, he set the bowl back on the nightstand. "Every single time. Something happens."

"Nothing happened to our grandparents," Victor pointed out.

"Nothing happened to them, but they got rid of us immediately. Well, you and me at least. And then you left, too."

"I wouldn't have survived a week in boarding school. Working on the docks was less torturous."

They were silent for a while, each reeling about the subject.

"Where are Ollie and Vivian?" Dantes asked after a while, so used to his room being crowded with them.

"They went to the museum. I told them to get out of the house. I figured you wouldn't want her seeing you writhing about."

Dantes leaned back against his upright pillow, and at the mention of Vivian, remembered something.

"What is it?" Victor asked, evidently seeing the strange expression on Dantes's face.

"I, um…" Dantes looked away. "When the carriage tumbled, a bunch of memories ran through my head. I just remembered that. I thought I was dying."

"What did you think of?"

"Vivian was my last thought before I blacked out. And I thought I would never see her again."

Victor leaned back in his chair, letting out a deep breath. "What are you going to do about that?"

"I don't know."

"She refused to leave your side the entire time and slept beside you every night, if you could even call it sleeping. Whenever I woke up in that chair"—he nodded over to the chair that had been his bed for the last week—"she was checking your breathing, her hand against your forehead to see if you still had your fever, watching you to make sure you were still alive. The night nurse hated it, but she never said a word, either. I think she didn't know how to tell such a high-ranking woman what to do in her own house." Victor paused. "You do know you nearly died? I mean, once we got you in here."

Dantes tore a look in Victor's direction. He knew he had been in bad shape but had had no idea it had become that severe.

"You went almost a week without water," Victor explained, "while fighting a fever and blood loss. Mr. Wegner told us to prepare for the worst. We even called a priest for last rites."

Nauseating guilt twisted in him knowing he had put everyone through such a horrid scare.

"Lady Vivian saw it all happen, just so you know."

The guilt became too much, and Dantes put his full focus on anchoring his view on the foot of his bed. The focus acted like a dam to emotion.

"We heard a gunshot, and of course I knew what it was. But like Ollie, she had no idea. Like a fool, she ran to the window and saw the carriage get dragged and thrown about. I never..." Victor's voice cracked. "I never again want to hear someone scream the way she did."

Dantes looked up to Victor and for the first time in his life, through everything they'd survived together, this was the first time he'd seen his immovable brother struggle to hold it together. Victor leaned forward, rubbing the heels of his hands into his eyes. It was a long time before he could sit back up with nothing more than a sniff.

Victor continued. "I knew something bad had happened when she screamed like that. Immediately felt it in my bones. She ran outside, I followed. And strangers from all over rushed over to help. They didn't give it a second thought. All I could think about was: *that's my life in there.* That's all I have, what I live for."

"Victor," Dantes said softly.

"It's true. But I'll never admit it again." He let out a small laugh.

"You want to know what else I saw when I thought I died?"

"Yeah."

"Your face when you saw my stitches."

Victor frowned as he recalled. "The stitches on your face?"

"Yes. I've never seen you so angry in my life, before or since. Now I think it's funny that would be my last thought of you."

Victor found this amusing as well. "I'm glad I left an impression." He shook his head. "I still can't believe he got away with that."

"Of course he did. He always got away with everything. And he always will." Dantes paused. He had yet to tell Vivian the story of how he'd gotten his scar. Was it time to tell her, time to open up to her about the darkest moment in his life?

Dantes scratched at his jaw, noting how long the facial hair felt. "And my memory of Ollie was him as a baby."

"We're always going to see him as a baby, aren't we?"

Dantes gave his brother a small smile and grabbed his bowl of mashed potatoes. "Yes. We are."

Chapter Twenty-Two

VIVIAN AND OLLIE agreed to keep the art restoration from Dantes for the time being. They didn't want to get his hopes up that his artwork could be saved, only to find out it couldn't be and let him down. So when they found Dantes and Victor upon returning, they acted as if they had gone through the new Pre-Raphaelite exhibition once more now that it wasn't as crowded.

"Mr. Wegner stopped by." Dantes shoveled a spoon into a bowl of mashed potatoes. "He excused the nurses now that I'm up, but it'll be a few more days before he can take the stitches out. The blood loss should be fully recovered a month after the injury. Same with the bullet wound, as it was a muscle injury only. In other words, everything should be as good as new in a few more weeks."

"That's wonderful news," Vivian said with relief.

Victor jumped in. "Mr. Wegner also said Dantes was incredibly lucky the bullets only hit muscle. Bones, tendons, organs would have been much worse. Recovery could have taken up to a year."

Dantes swallowed a bite of mashed potatoes. His appetite had returned with a vengeance as well, but he could only handle small amounts of food at a time. He had woken ravenous at nearly two in the morning. "None of what happened was *lucky*."

Ollie rolled his eyes to Vivian and she had to suppress a smile.

"When will you be able to eat full meals again?" Vivian asked. She had not wanted to wake the servants at such a late hour simply to get the mashed potatoes made for him to eat throughout the day. Ollie, instead, fetched them without a thought. But also, she greatly missed Dantes's presence at the dining table. Those first few days after the accident, none of them had eaten much, but since his recovery from fever, Vivian had had her meals with the healthy McNab brothers in the dining room and it felt empty without Dantes. It was unsettling as well because she would stare at empty chairs and remember how close they had been to losing him. Probably within hours, Mr. Wegner had said.

"He said I can try tomorrow, if my appetite is up for it. I can start walking around a bit too, as long as it doesn't hurt too much. But honestly, all I want right now is a bath. I've never felt so disgusting in my life."

"Oh," Vivian said thoughtfully. "I don't really want to wake Heaton or any of the footmen this time of night." She looked expectantly at Victor.

Victor glowered back. "I'm not bathing my adult brother."

"Well, I can't do it. You didn't even like me sleeping next to him above the covers."

Ollie spoke next. "Yes, but that was different."

Vivian gave a small laugh while Dantes watched the entire scene with amusement. "How is *that* not appropriate, but washing him is perfectly fine?"

Ollie grinned widely. "Because we don't want to do it."

But Victor wasn't having it. "She's right. I suppose I'll do it, then."

"No, no," Vivian said in a singsong voice. "I don't wish to upset your delicate sensibilities." She motioned for Dantes to follow her and he began to slowly rise.

"But—"

"It's already decided, Victor." She gave him a triumphant smile, winning a severe frown in return. Deep down, though, she *did* want to be the one to help Dantes. And beyond *that*, the prospect of seeing Dantes lounging in a tub, bare chested and wet, was quite the temptation. Not that she could fully admit this to herself.

"Whom do you want to help you?" Victor, determined, shot the question to Dantes. "Me, or Ollie?"

"Vivian," Dantes replied with a roguish grin.

Ollie let out a bark of laughter. Victor narrowed his eyes. "At least let me help you walk to the bathroom. If you fall into her, she'll be crushed."

AS THE LARGE tub filled, Dantes watched it with wonder. He had heard about hotels and wealthy homes getting running water installed but had never seen a hot, running bath for himself. The late dowager duchess, Vivian had to explain, had put it in about a year ago as she'd started taking multiple baths per day to help with joint pain.

Pulling his attention away from the tub, Dantes tried his best to gently undress. They had never put a shirt back on him after his clothing had been cut off, but he remained in the same trousers as that fateful night. Out of the corner of her eye, she could see him struggling.

"I'm here to help you." She stepped up to him and looked into his face. "There's nothing wrong with asking for help, Dantes." She waited until he'd given her a small nod and glanced back down to the task. There were a few buttons on the front of his trousers he was struggling with. She should have been embarrassed to help with something like this, but the moment wasn't exactly brimming with intimacy. Swallowing her nerves, she began unfastening each button.

If one of the servants woke and came in here, though, that would be the end of her reputation. Even Father wouldn't be able to cover up servants' gossip around something so scandalous. She pushed this thought aside.

"You can't soak your stitches," Vivian said, keeping her mind from focusing too closely on the task. "Keep that in mind when you get in." Her heart was beating hard, and she looked up once more and found him watching her intently. His hand reached down and gently brushed against hers.

"I can finish these last few, if you're uncomfortable," he said in a low voice.

Taking in a sharp inhale, Vivian nodded and turned away, hearing the sound of rustling fabric.

"I can take those." Over her shoulder, he handed her the clothing he had discarded. Vivian's face heated.

Considering everything that had happened the day of the accident, and whatever was between them was as murky as ever, Vivian decided to take his trousers and fold them with more care than necessary, her eyes focusing solely on that task.

"I finally purged the chasers from my home," she began, needing something other than heat and tension to fill the air. Her palms pressed a crease in the dark fabric. "Even after the accident, they continued flooding my receiving room. I was utterly mad with worry and exhaustion, and I finally went in there, screamed at them like a madwoman to get out, and swore if any of them ever returned, I'd send for the police." From the corner of her vision, she could see Dantes staring at her. "It worked."

"How did Crosby take that?"

With a bit of embarrassment, Vivian recalled that moment and cleared her throat. "He told me as a woman, I should be delicate. Not bellowing like a foghorn. I held up a fist and told him I'd show him *delicate*."

Dantes made a choking sound and Vivian had to bite her cheek to not grin to herself.

Of course, it also decreased her marriage prospects, as now none of those men wanted anything to do with a woman who'd acted as she had, but she didn't want to marry any of them, anyway.

She continued. "Poor Father has done his best to uphold my image despite his own irritation with me—he visited several times while you were asleep to ensure I was well with your brothers here—but everyone is having a lark gossiping about a woman who threatens to stick police on England's most elite men." She paused. "It does sound rather silly when said aloud."

Dantes's vague form went over to the sink. "Do they know I'm here? Or my brothers?"

Vivian swallowed. "No."

"Does it bother you, that they talk about you like that?"

Vivian had to force her eyes to remain averted. "No one likes to be gossiped about. But it bothers me more when they talk about *you*. They laugh at me for being foolish, but I've heard what they say about you. And I don't like it one bit." Of course, she didn't need to tell him what she'd heard because he'd been hearing it for years. Examples of what she'd overheard had been people calling him grotesque, the Devil, surmising he was a monster who lived beneath the London Bridge and came out to attack women at night. She'd overheard such comments from passersby while she'd walked into a shop to fetch new stockings and shoes. Or while at tea with a reacquainted friend, from the other women in attendance. It was clear these comments were whispered in such a way she could overhear. Anne had been hearing those comments as well, even when Vivian wasn't around. Their words were appalling and upset her greatly. But she genuinely didn't understand their contempt for him, either.

"Ignore them. That's all you can do." Dantes said this without any emotion, clearly numb now to their words. "I have a full-grown beard." He chuckled at his reflection. "I look like a wild man, like I should be panning for gold in California."

With his attention away from her, Vivian allowed herself a quick, safe glance of his towering profile. He had clearly lost weight, which caused a brief moment of worry, but his broad shoulders and arms remained rugged and strong.

Embarrassed of herself, she hurried to find soap Victor or

Ollie used. "Truthfully, I think you look quite handsome with the beard. I hope you at least keep it for another day or two."

Vivian felt his eyes bore into her as she turned off the bathtub faucet and set a bar of soap in the soap holder, a rather comfortably domestic moment, she thought.

"You like it?" he asked.

She crossed the bathroom to pull a clean washcloth and towel from a drawer in the built-in. "I do. Don't do anything on account of me, of course, but I like when you have a bit of grit to you. At first, I thought I liked you polished like silver, but grit suits you much better. *I* think, at least."

A strange stillness settled over the room. Had she said the wrong thing? "Well, you can climb in now." She was eager to change the subject.

Moments later, water splashed, indicating Dantes had climbed into the tub. Knowing she should not turn around, she did anyway. Dantes sat hunched in the bath, wet up to his midback, and she observed his muscular forearms, the hair now dark from being wet.

He placed a hand under the running faucet. "I can hardly believe such novelty. Hot water with a mere twist of the wrist."

"It is brilliant, isn't it? Not even Father has it."

Dantes let the water fall over his hand for a moment longer before leaning back. "I can't believe you've been sleeping near me all this time," he said with a hint of humor. "I smell something awful."

She laughed. "Dantes, you could smell like a pig farm right now and I wouldn't care. The only thing that matters is you're here." There were several different ways he could take those words, but she wasn't going to clarify. Because, really, she meant all variations of it.

"Have you ever smelled a pig farm?" He was ignoring her comment.

"No."

"You would keep several miles from me, then, if that were

the case." As she chuckled, he picked up the bar of soap. "What is this?"

After leaning forward a bit for a better look, she shrugged. "Victor's or Ollie's soap."

He looked it over but held it out to her. "Can I use yours?"

She took it, one eyebrow lifting at his request. "You want to use *my* soap? Why?"

"I want to smell it. I have no memory of anything over the past week, but I somehow knew you were next to me each day and night. I'm curious if it was because of your scent."

Not sure what to make of this, she grabbed a fresh pink bar for him and inserted humor into the moment. "You can keep this one for yourself. You're quite hairy and I don't want your man hair getting stuck on my soap."

This made him laugh loudly, the happy sound echoing in the humid room, and for the briefest moment, her heart swelled. Dantes was safe and, bit by bit, returning to normal. A heaviness began to lift from her. She turned away, close to breaking out into tears.

No doubt oblivious to what she was going through, Dantes held the soap to his nose. "This is definitely you, my little rose."

The floodgates broke and she began to sob loudly. She would have been fine if he hadn't gone and said *that*.

"Blast, Vivian, I'm sorry." Dantes's voice was low and quiet now. He let out a sigh. "I'm sorry I scared you like that."

She mumbled something watery and incoherent, keeping her back toward him.

"Victor told me you saw it happen."

Vivian took in a deep, shaky breath, patting her face dry with a plush towel. "Yes."

"Come here. I need to tell you something."

Following his request, she crouched next to the bathtub. The hot, steamy room now smelled like roses. She watched Dantes scrub at his face with soapy water using the hand he could, but all his weary-eyed focus was on her. "That night, before I was knocked out, I thought I was going to die."

"Oh, Dantes." A sob rose again as hot tears stung her eyes.

He set the soap down on its holder and put his dripping-wet hand on hers resting on the edge of the bathtub. Her stomach fluttered at his touch. "You were the last thought I had before I lost consciousness, when I thought it was all over. I thought I would never see you again after being a foolish idiot. I have no idea what happened that day between us, and I know we can't jump back in, either, but I'm not giving up yet. You wanted me to leave that day, but I'm not going to." A pause. "I'm hoping you don't still want me to, at least."

Tears began to roll down her cheek and she wiped them away with her free hand. "No, I don't. I don't know what's going on, either, but I want to figure it out, too."

His strong, wet hand lifted to her cheek to wipe away new tears. "That didn't really help, did it?"

They both laughed.

"There's something else I need to tell you," Dantes said after a moment's hesitation.

Vivian held her breath, sensing in his voice something big was coming.

He pulled his hand away, leaving that empty feeling behind. "When I was twenty, Eleanor and I were seeing each other in secret because, as you know, Crosby and I weren't exactly on good terms. People always say *hate* is such a strong word, but yes, that's pretty appropriate here. And because Crosby hated me, by default so did their parents. I don't think they would have been fond of me anyway, but Crosby's hate of me made it an easier decision, I suppose."

A droplet fell from the faucet, sending ripples over the still water. "Anyway, we got engaged and I tried to convince her to elope, knowing her family wouldn't approve of us. But Eleanor wouldn't, even though she knew my history with her brother, and convinced herself her parents would love anyone she loved.

"Of course, she was wrong, and one afternoon after classes, I received a hastily written note from her ending it. No explanation, no apology, only that it was over. I hadn't even known she'd been *going* to tell them, just that she'd wanted to."

"Oh, dear," Vivian replied, dread banding her stomach.

"That night..." Dantes trailed off, and the air seemed to thicken. He motioned toward his throat. "I can still feel the grass against my neck. Crosby pulled me from my bed in the middle of the night, gagged me, and with the help of his weasels, dragged me out to the grounds in front of our building. He kicked the back of my knees to knock me down and the weasels laid me out flat and held down my arms and legs so I couldn't fight back." Another pause. "Crosby revealed a knife. I thought he was going to kill me at first. He placed the tip of the blade over my heart, pushed it just enough for it to hurt but not enough to pierce skin, and slowly twisted it back and forth as he threw out rhetorical questions like, '*Who would find you here? Who would even care?*'"

Vivian swallowed. He must have been so frightened.

"He then placed the blade to my face, told me Eleanor would never marry a Paddy, that I should go back to the slums where my mother had known I belonged. But above all, he wanted to mark me to make sure women could see what I really was beneath the nice clothes, that they would always look at me with disgust. He wanted to make sure no one would ever love me again. And with the entirety of his strength, Crosby sliced across my face, torturously slow, and left me to bleed in the grass."

Vivian gasped.

"I'm lucky I didn't lose an eye." Dantes stared across the room with a vacant expression. "And he smiled when he did that, too. It took years to not see that horrific smile in my nightmares." His attention returned to her, and life seemed to lift in his eyes. "But a month later, I got my revenge. I beat him so badly, he missed an entire semester of university. I did it in between classes so everyone could see it happen. I'm not going to lie, Vivian. It felt really good and to this day, I don't regret doing it."

"Is that the fight that got you kicked out?"

Dantes nodded.

"Did Mr. Crosby get kicked out, too?" Surely, he had been! How could Mr. Crosby do something so horrific and never receive punishment?

But Dantes laughed sardonically. "Absolutely not. He never once got in trouble for anything he did to me."

"Did his parents go to the police?"

"They threatened to but ended up covering up the whole thing. I don't know what truly happened, but I wouldn't be surprised if my grandfather had something to do with it. He and I may not like each other much, and my relationship with my grandparents was pretty much over after that event, but the man is absolutely terrifying when he wants to be. And I'm sure wanted the whole mess over with."

A sick realization came over Vivian. "That's why you called Mr. Crosby the worst of them all, isn't it?"

"Yes. I was not about to let Crosby, of all people, take you away."

Vivian's lip quivered. Dantes had exposed the rawest, most vulnerable part of him, a part of him that may never fully heal. He trusted her wholly, and it was a gift she held dear.

Now wasn't the time to bring this up, but Vivian decided right then and there to bring Dantes to Brighton for the summer. There was plenty of room at Summerwood for him and her family. They could finally spend time together, good time together and not her seeking someone else or recovering from injury. They could figure out what was going on between them.

Perhaps, dare she even think it, start planning a future.

Though she was getting far ahead of herself, the thought sent a rush through her. A future.

Could it be possible?

Plus, it would be good for him to get away for a few months after the fire. And it would work out well with Gran's timeline. Vivian was nearly halfway through the year Gran had set for her. And time was flying by.

"But I have to live with the reminder every day," Dantes continued in a quieter voice, bringing Vivian back to the present. "Every time I see myself, I remember the raw terror I felt that day. And I'll never get used to how people react to my face. It could be off of my mind in the moment, but then someone will gasp when they come up to the bar for a drink. I know it's surprising to them and they usually don't mean anything by it, but that doesn't make me feel any better." He moved to rest his arm on the edge of the tub. "I wouldn't blame you, Viv, if you didn't want me around because of it. If you're with me, it will affect you too. You would experience those same stares, those same comments, everywhere we go."

"I've already had those stares and comments. My only concern is it bothers *you*. Otherwise, they can go eat dirt."

But he didn't find her comment funny and confessed something heartbreaking. "I'm afraid that someday, you'll see me the way they see me."

She searched his eyes. "Dantes, you're the most beautiful man I've ever seen in my life. When people say such ugliness, I truly don't understand what it is they see. You are lovely." Her finger gently traced the scar. It was smooth and warm. "It's a part of you, and I wouldn't want anything about you to change."

Dantes's green-eyed gaze softened, and tears began to well.

AFTER THEIR TENDER discussion, Vivian helped Dantes wash his hair and disappeared to fetch him clean clothes. It left him briefly with his thoughts, and how her kindness and words hugged his dark and broken heart.

Once more, he took her soap from the soap dish, put it under his nose, and inhaled her scent.

There was no longer any question that the affection he felt for Vivian was far beyond being merely smitten. Vivian brought a lightness to him, to his heart and soul. Joy. That morning, he'd awoken in immense pain, yet he'd also felt peace simply because she'd been the first sight he'd seen when he'd opened his eyes.

He wanted to wake up like that every day.

But he didn't know how to make that happen.

Because to Dantes, the gunshots and the carriage accident were further proof he was unlucky and loving him was dangerous. No one had believed him, but he'd *known* something would happen after Ollie had said those cursed words.

And he'd been right.

For whatever reason, bad luck still followed Dantes, and those three little words remained cursed. If something happened to Vivian because of him, he would never forgive himself.

He wouldn't survive. That's the only certainty he held about that.

Vivian returned and did her best to help him redress while keeping her eyes properly averted. Well, as proper as one could in the situation. Dantes found her concern about propriety a little endearing.

There was no point in putting a shirt on yet, as it would only cause him discomfort. And as he needed to begin moving around more during the day, they began to slowly walk up and down the hallway together, arm in arm for balance.

Meanwhile, Victor and Ollie stood nearby, wanting to be close just in case.

As they had to walk quite slowly, Vivian updated Dantes about the previous week to keep his mind off how terrible he still felt.

"Anne asked Bernard for a separation and my father forced him out of their house," Vivian explained. "It's rather curious. I didn't know it was something she had been seriously pursuing, and my father's involvement causes me pause. I tried asking my father what had happened, but he refused to indulge my curiosity and told me it was none of my affair."

"A separation?" Dantes paused momentarily. He didn't know

Lady Litchfield well, but in their limited interactions, she'd seemed like a sweet woman. That her husband's father had come in to swoop up his son was curious. Had something happened? Or was he simply being supportive?

Victor's dark voice interrupted. "Tell him about the visit."

Dantes caught Vivian glaring at Victor. "Tell me." Dantes spoke a bit harsher than he'd meant to. But clearly, the visit had concerned Victor enough he thought Dantes should know about it.

Vivian sighed. "One of the days after your accident, my brother showed up quite drunk and angry—"

"He better not have laid a hand on you." Dantes's hands twitched at the thought.

"No," Victor replied. "I made sure of it."

Dantes met his brother's eye, giving him a nod of thanks.

"Anyway," Vivian said loudly to get his attention back, "Bernard blamed me for the separation, then asked me for money. An exorbitant amount I won't even tell you."

Dantes frowned deeply.

"I only gave him two hundred pounds."

Only? He pushed that thought away. Her money was her business. But her brother taking advantage of her? That was absolutely his concern. "He's taking advantage of you. He's using you, Vivian."

Her gaze faltered. "That's what Victor said, too."

"He was right. And so am I."

And she surprised him. "I know. I'm not giving him anything more. He was so broken when he showed up, though, and he's my brother and needed my help. No matter what he has done, I still love him, you understand?"

No, he didn't understand. But kept his mouth shut on that.

"I think this summer will be good for him. Summerwood is such a happy place. It will lift his mood immensely."

So, Winthrop was still going to be in Brighton that summer. Dantes had never really liked the man, but after everything he'd just heard, the final shred of respect for the cad as Vivian's family fell away. Dantes thought Winthrop was nothing more than an idiotic scoundrel. But the man's behavior was becoming more erratic, unpredictable, desperate. It was escalating. To what, he couldn't say. But the idea of Winthrop having months to hurt and manipulate Vivian without Dantes there to protect her was concerning.

At least Vivian had come to accept Winthrop had been using her, so hopefully, she would pick up on anything her sneaky brother would try. All Dantes could do was hope her two hundred pounds satisfied the greedy man and marked the end of his deception. What remained to be seen was if the separation would cause Winthrop to try to improve himself to win back his family, or multiply his behavior and destruction. And Dantes had a sick feeling it would be the latter.

Chapter Twenty-Three

OLLIE HELD THE door open for Vivian as they went to see Miss Sparrow. While they walked down the hallway toward their destination, Vivian recalled the day she and Dantes had been at the museum together, how that trip had been meant for her to mingle with other gentlemen and yet, deep down, the only one she'd wanted to be with had been Dantes.

Vivian had been so sure Dantes was a scoundrel, she had been avoiding the nagging feeling that maybe she was wrong. She couldn't imagine him going behind her back to do something hurtful. Nothing about him was evasive or untrustworthy. In fact, he went out of his way to be truthful, even if that truth put him in a vulnerable spot. Then again, she hadn't known how to identify a scoundrel a few months ago.

Why would she know how to recognize a scoundrel now?

She stopped walking. "Ollie, please be honest with me. Is Dantes a scoundrel?"

Ollie faltered to a halt. "Is he what?"

"You know, a scoundrel. How often does he go to brothels?"

He gave her a funny look. "I've never known him to go to one."

"What about gaming hells?"

Ollie thought about this, then shook his head. "I mean, you know he bets on fights sometimes. But that's it."

"I don't understand," she said, conceding defeat.

"Don't understand what?"

Vivian shifted with discomfort at opening up to Ollie. "While he was helping me…you know, find a husband. He knew which of the gentlemen were scoundrels."

"So?"

"How would he know that, unless he was one, too?"

Realization seemed to dawn on Ollie's face. "Vivian, those idiots come into the pub and brag to us about it. Well, they don't *all* go there themselves, but men gossip worse than women and they tell us about everyone else's escapades too."

Could she believe him? Or would he lie to cover for Dantes? Then again, Dantes had said the same thing when she'd confronted him previously.

"When we open back up," Ollie continued, seemingly understanding her thoughts, "just sit at the bar for one night, a little out of sight, and you'll hear all about it." They began walking again. "You know, Dantes knew they all were scoundrels from the beginning. There really aren't that many unmarried gentlemen in your social circle and they're all unmarried for good reason. My brother knew you would never give any of them the time of day. He only helped you to be with you."

Vivian's heart fluttered. "Really?"

Ollie grinned widely. "Of course. He's a bit of a strange bird, that's all. It's something you'll learn to live with."

"Well, I like strange birds." She returned his smile.

"As do I. Now, let's go see what's happening with his artwork and get back before he wakes up."

Miss Sparrow was working at the same table as before. At the sound of their arrival, she turned in their direction, wearing the magnifying spectacles that made her eyes giant in the glass.

"Lady Vivian, Mr. McNab, good afternoon." She removed the glasses and set them down. "I'm glad you're here. I've begun on the first painting. Come, let's talk." She came around her table and waved them over.

Vivian took a deep, nervous breath. "Do you have good news or bad news?"

Miss Sparrow smiled brightly. "I have the best news, in fact. I haven't had a chance to deeply inspect each painting, but I was able to give them a quick look over and I'm confident they all can be saved."

Vivian's eyes widened. "All of them? Are you serious?"

Miss Sparrow smiled again. "Quite serious, Lady Vivian. It will be a long process, but yes, your dear friend will have his collection saved."

Immediately, Vivian placed a hand over her quickening heart, relief spreading over her.

"This is absolutely brilliant news, Miss Sparrow!" Ollie, in his own excitement, gave Miss Sparrow a hug, lifted her, and spun her around.

"*Ollie!*" Vivian shrieked. "Put her down!"

He did so instantly and knew well enough to look bashful. "Sorry about that," he said, scratching his jaw. "Got a bit exuberant there."

Miss Sparrow, the poor dear, merely stared back at him with an open mouth of shock. Finally, she shook her head at herself. "I almost forgot something." She suddenly ran off and out of view.

"Ollie." Vivian watched the spot where Miss Sparrow would reappear. "Please do not go after the woman working on Dantes's art collection."

His head flew in her direction. "Excuse me?"

"Oh, please. Must you play coy?"

His mouth hung open briefly. "I honestly have no idea what—"

But she shushed him as Miss Sparrow reappeared. Was it an act? For a self-proclaimed scoundrel, Ollie seemed oddly, and genuinely, confused by her accusation.

"I already completed this," Miss Sparrow said as she approached them, clearly oblivious to their conversation. "It was rather simple to clean the soot away. I did that by—"

Vivian stopped her. "Thank you, Miss Sparrow. We trust you know what you are doing."

Miss Sparrow handed over the object.

Vivian's free hand flew to her mouth as she realized what it was. It was the tintype of Dantes's parents. And it was in perfect condition. "Oh, Ollie, look at it." She handed it to him. "Of everything, he was most upset about this being damaged."

"I swear it looks better now than it did before." Ollie's voice cracked. He looked up at Miss Sparrow. "Thank you. You don't realize…" He took in a shaky breath. "It's the only photograph we have of our parents. They had it taken not long before he was killed. She passed not too long after. I never met my father, and I have no memory of my mother."

Miss Sparrow seemed to understand the gravity of these words as she gave him a small smile. "I'm honored you all entrusted me with it."

Quickly, Ollie knuckled at his eyes. "Can we leave it here for now? I would like Dantes to see it when he comes here himself." When Miss Sparrow took it back with care, he turned to Vivian. "Perhaps he will be up for it in a few weeks. Then he'll see for himself what she does." Ollie angled his head in Miss Sparrow's direction.

"That's a fantastic idea," Vivian said. "That works out well, actually—it'll be right before we leave for Brighton."

Ollie started at this. "Wait, are you saying he's going to Brighton with you?"

She shook her head. "I haven't talked to him about it yet. I figured he could go for a few weeks—I doubt he would want to be away from you and Victor and rebuilding the pub for the entire season."

"No, he wouldn't. And once he finds out about this," Ollie said as he looked around the room, "I'm sure he's going to want to pop in all the time."

"Oh." Miss Sparrow furrowed her brow.

"Don't worry. I won't let him." Ollie was trying to put her at ease. "He's going to be thrilled by this, though."

Vivian smiled wide in agreement. "I can't wait to see his reaction. He's going to be so surprised."

Chapter Twenty-Four

"I'M GOING HOME tomorrow." Victor didn't look up from the invoices when he heard Dantes step into the drawing room. "You're not at death's door any longer, and Ollie's nearly ready to leave, too, but he can keep an eye on you two for a bit longer while I refocus on the pub."

Dantes swirled his whiskey, humored, and went over to sit on a sofa. "'Keep an eye on us'? And you believe Ollie the best choice for the job?" He watched Victor's pen scribble across a check. The paper tore off loudly, and Victor set everything to the side.

"I was able to secure a loan with a bank with Lady Vivian's help." Victor's attention was fully on Dantes now. "As you know, we had to get a loan to cover what insurance wouldn't. Outside of your flat, I mean."

Dantes narrowed his eyes. "I told you twice not to do that. I have a say in these matters too, you know. Ollie and I both do."

"You were unconscious and Ollie was injured. It couldn't wait."

Dantes held his brother's eye. "I don't want to take advantage of her kindness. She already let us live here for the last few weeks."

"She was happy to help, Dantes, even knowing the risk it put her in. We're not taking advantage of her."

Dantes scoffed. "What, so every time we need something,

we're going to turn to Vivian? Like Winthrop does?"

Victor looked away, tapped at his knee, and changed the subject, never one to do well with familial conflict. "Are you planning on chasing after her when she goes to Brighton?"

Dantes pulled back at such a bizarre question. Victor seemed bitter about something, but Dantes couldn't figure out what. "No, what kind of a question is that?"

"Good, because we need you here. Like you said, you're a part of this all, too. Just because you've got your eyes set on a woman now doesn't change that fact. I still expect the same hours and work out of you."

Dantes had to resist rolling his eyes at his brother's dig.

Off in the distance, the front door opened, and the loud, rapid conversation of Vivian and Ollie echoed as they made their way to the drawing room. When they entered, they were visibly surprised to see Dantes. For the last few days, Dantes had taken long afternoon naps, only waking when his appetite for dinner had roused him, but those naps had been tapering off. Today, he felt pretty good and had only slept for twenty minutes.

Though Vivian's surprise over seeing Dantes awake and mobile lasted for a beat, she began crossing the room toward him. A warmth built in him as he watched her approach, smiling widely, a brief jolt of happiness cutting through the ever-present caution.

As she walked past him to sit on the other end of his sofa, the desire to touch her was too strong and Dantes covertly reached his hand out to brush hers as she walked by. It appeared to startle her, but when she met his eye, she gave him a private little smile.

"Where were you two causing mischief today?" he asked casually, as if that little moment had not happened.

"Oh." Vivian waved a casual hand from her seat. "I had to go take care of some things before we leave for the summer. Ollie was bored and came with me."

"Ah," Dantes said, taking another sip of whiskey.

"Is it all right for you to be drinking yet?" Concern pulled at her brow. "You won't have the same tolerance as usual."

"I know. I'm only having a few sips. I can only tolerate so much of Victor each day and he's been a constant for far too long. There's a reason we own a pub, Viv, because we have to drink in order to tolerate each other for more than a few minutes. A barbershop, for example, would not have ended well."

She laughed at his joke, and his heart swelled. "That worked out well, then," she said, still smiling before turning to Victor. "How is everything going with the pub, by the way?"

"Good. Now that we have secured the complete funds, we need to move forward with renovations. It should be smooth sailing, aside from any city inspector delays. Waiting for inspections is taking a bit longer than anticipated but, if we're lucky, we should be opening again this fall. Definitely will be reopened by the end of the year."

"Oh, wonderful. I'm glad it's all coming together as best as it can."

Dantes turned to look at her. "You didn't have to help us with that loan, Vivian. Really, Victor shouldn't have gone to you about it. I told him not to."

Vivian frowned. "Why shouldn't he have gone to me about it? It wasn't like he was asking me for my own money."

"I know, but I don't want you to think we're going to come to you for every little monetary thing."

"Well, I know you're good for it," Vivian continued. "That's really the biggest hurdle in getting a loan. I've been to The Harp & Thistle, and so has my father. We've seen you have a large and steady customer base. And I know you three to be good men who will repay it. Anyway, my father is good friends with Mr. Henry Tewksbury, who owns a bank, and together, they were able to vouch for your pub."

Dantes studied her for a moment, irritated Tewksbury was involved. And once again, the man had everything in his favor. Even kindness. Dantes felt extra surly. "All right."

Vivian seemed satisfied by this response, but he didn't feel better about it.

Victor was clearly eager to move on from this. "Anyway, Lady Vivian, I was telling Dantes I'm going back home tomorrow. Dantes's health isn't at the risk it once was, and I need to focus on the business now."

"Oh, no, Victor, you can't be serious!" She gave a slight pout. "Of course the circumstances for you all being here were not good, but it was nice having other people in the house."

Victor stammered. "Well, I know this an impossible ask, and I shouldn't even be asking…" He rubbed a palm over his cheek and grimaced. "But I do worry it's too early for Dantes to leave. If it isn't too much trouble, I think Dantes would benefit from staying here a bit longer with Ollie. I know that's asking a lot, but I won't be at my house much because of the pub, and I only have a housekeeper and a cook. I don't have a large staff like you, and he's getting excellent care from them, and I know so far his stay here has been concealed well, and—"

"It's fine, Victor. Really."

Victor tilted his head. "Are you sure? Absolutely sure? Because it's a major violation of propriety, and I'm ashamed to even put forward the question."

"It really is fine. I think the staff enjoy having them here and have proven themselves trustworthy. I wouldn't fret. But you leaving is making me a bit sad." She gave him a small smile and Dantes could tell Victor was increasingly uncomfortable by the attention. His older brother hated any shred of affection, especially from a woman.

"I wouldn't have made it through those first few days if it weren't for you," Vivian continued. "And I will never forget how kind you were to me."

"'Kind'?" Ollie grimaced with exaggeration. "Are you sure that was Victor and not an impostor?"

Vivian laughed. "Yes. And I will always be grateful for it." She jumped up to hurry over to Victor and gave him a big hug.

Victor shot a look to Dantes, who was thoroughly amused by

this moment. "Get her off of me."

"Aw, but she likes you!" Ollie had a big toothy, grin plastered on his face.

Vivian began to laugh, letting Victor go. "I'm sorry, Victor. I think you need to be hugged more. Affection is important to one's happiness."

"I'm fine." Victor was doing his best to hold back a scowl.

"And I know one day, you shall meet a pretty woman and she won't like it very much if you don't hug her."

Victor suddenly began piling the invoices and checks together. "I should gather my things," he said rapidly. "I'll see you all at dinner." And he rushed out of the room.

VIVIAN WATCHED AFTER Victor, biting her lip before returning to Dantes's side. "Oh, dear, I shouldn't have said that."

Dantes shrugged. "He'll get over it."

"I didn't mean to upset him."

"You didn't upset him."

But she wasn't convinced. Dantes had only seen his older brother's usual hard shell. But Vivian had seen the flicker of sadness in the man's eyes when she'd spoken and it broke her heart to have caused that hurt. In a flash of a moment, she'd seen he was exceptionally lonely, seen more of him than his brothers seemed to see. Maybe because they couldn't, maybe because they didn't want to. But she also knew Victor well enough to know he would never, ever admit to it and likely hadn't even admitted the loneliness to himself.

Maybe that was why he was so dedicated to the pub—it was so loud and crowded there, it blocked out the emptiness. Wasn't that sort of why she'd gone there the night of the disaster? And he hadn't had a loud, energetic atmosphere for quite a while now and was spending so much time with Dantes and Ollie, even

Vivian. Victor was finally being forced to face his feelings.

"Why has he never married?" Vivian asked after a moment.

"He doesn't want a family."

"Why not?"

Dantes took the last sip of his whiskey and set the glass to the side. He exchanged a look with Ollie before looking back at her. "Some people simply don't want to marry, don't want children. I figured it's because he has a black heart." He ended this with a grin.

"That's not funny, Dantes. I was with him after everything happened and…" She recalled Victor holding the unconscious Ollie against him like a father with his child. "Please. Don't."

Dantes glanced over at Ollie again, but this time, Ollie was staring at the ground, his brow pulled together.

"I remember that night, after I woke up." Ollie's voice was uncharacteristically quiet. "He was terrified of losing you, Dantes. I've never seen him so scared. It was worse than the fire. Not even comparable, to be honest."

Dantes let out a groan of frustration. "How long are we going to look back on the carriage accident?"

"It *just* happened!" Vivian said with a bit of offense.

"I know, but I'm sick of hearing about how much I made everyone worry. I don't want to hear it anymore. I feel awful enough about it already, like I had a choice in the matter."

"Fine, we'll drop it." Her fingers began to pluck at something invisible on her skirt.

But Ollie's mind was elsewhere. "The night of the fire, he told me why he doesn't want a family."

Dantes couldn't mask his surprise. "He did?"

"Yes. He told me it's because he already raised a family. You know, after lambasting me for being a spoiled cad. He told me he, and you, risked a lot to keep me safe."

"We did." Dantes stared off unfocused, probably remembering those days.

"What was it like?" Vivian asked.

"We were orphans living on the streets. There were rats, we slept in dirty outdoor corners each night, we never bathed, we never ate. Well, Ollie ate—Victor never did. We had to sleep with one eye open for rivals or opportunists. We pickpocketed drunk men passed out in the middle of the sidewalk, or literally in the street gutter. You can create your own stories from everything I said, and those stories probably happened."

Vivian remained quiet, not sure what to say.

Ollie stood up. "I'm going to go talk to him."

"You know that's the last thing he wants," Dantes warned.

Ollie shrugged, but as he reached the door, Dantes shouted after him. "Don't go telling him you love him—you'll just lose some teeth." Without turning around, Ollie gave Dantes a rude gesture over his shoulder and left the room, the door clicking shut behind him.

"They're quite different, aren't they?" Vivian said after a moment.

Dantes nodded. "Our childhood was such a contrast to Ollie's. Imagine someone like your brother as a young boy being dropped off in the slums. We were lucky because we were bigger kids, but we still had to learn fast how different life was in Whitechapel, how to fight and defend ourselves. Blend in. It's why we took up with the other boys that we did when our mother died; they were on their own too and we all protected each other. Safety in numbers."

"I'm surprised your father's background didn't cause you any problems."

"Our mother was from there, so we were able to blend in. By the time we had to move there, she was so deep into her addiction, no one believed anything she said about our father or our old life and Victor and I knew to keep our mouths shut about it. We didn't have anything to show for it, anyway."

Vivian looked over at the fireplace.

"After she died," he continued, his voice quieter, "we were afraid an orphanage would split us up, so that's why Victor had us live on the streets. We could run when they came looking for us. They were like dog catchers, but for kids. Just snatching them up, didn't matter if they had parents or not. But in a tenement, you could be cornered. Outside, we could run away."

"I'm surprised your grandparents were accepting of all of that."

"They weren't," Dantes responded gravely. "But they didn't know, either. They didn't support my father's decision to marry my mother and cut contact with him over it. But one day, after my father's death, they went to our old house to find it abandoned and starting to fall apart. We didn't know, of course, but my mother had no idea how to pay the bills. How to pay taxes on the house. She was too melancholy to care to find help, too deep into her addiction, and creditors and the tax people bled her dry. It then took a few years for my grandparents to track us down."

"How did your parents meet?" There had to be good memories amongst the bad, and Vivian wanted to know about them. "They had such wildly different backgrounds."

Dantes chuckled before leaning closer. "Believe it or not, they met at a pub."

Vivian's mouth made an 'O.' "Really?"

"Yep." He was grinning from ear to ear now. "My mother, though quite the funny woman with those she was close with, was also rather introverted. I'm guessing that's why my father took to her, and she to him. She was quiet initially, while he could talk to anyone. They had met at the pub, happened to sit beside each other at the bar, and found they fit well. He figured she wouldn't run around on him, maybe, and after they left the pub that night, they immediately left for Gretna Green and eloped. They just knew." He shrugged. "I remember how he used to look at her with awe, but she loved him right back. I never found out if she knew who he was before they married. If she did, I'm sure she liked the thought of his money, but it wasn't because she wanted to show off with jewelry and whatnot."

"I know what you're saying. It was more that she wanted it to get out." Even though Vivian lived a far more privileged life, she could still understand the unique relief a woman would feel upon an influx of life-changing money.

"Yes." He looked off across the room with a brief smile of remembrance. "Anyway, Ollie doesn't remember those tough years. He grew up with my grandparents, and he still talks to them, in fact, whereas Victor and I don't."

Vivian wondered what Victor thought about being the heir to their grandfather's dukedom. Considering none of them had yet mentioned it, she wasn't going to be the one to bring it up.

Dantes continued. "Ollie's entire life was gilded. But he always wanted to be with Victor and me, no matter what we did. He was the only one of us who finished university, but he still went to the pub with us, anyway."

An intense, warm glow overtook Vivian's heart. That Dantes trusted her enough to expose another puzzle piece of his life meant so much. She recalled saying those three little words to him when he wouldn't wake up. But was that truly how she felt?

Yes, she decided. It was.

That being said, it was one thing to say the words while he'd been asleep. She knew the curse wasn't real, but she also knew he didn't want to hear them.

But did he *feel* that way, too?

There was only one way to find out.

And so, she made an unexpected but big decision. It was a major risk.

She took a deep breath and a big chance. "Dantes…" She briefly hesitated. If she was going to turn back, now would be her only chance. She moved forward. "I don't need to say the words."

Something in Dantes seemed to still.

It was rather unsettling, and she braced herself. "Did you hear me?" She glanced toward him, but he kept his eyes averted. What would she do if he got upset? If he told her he did not, in fact, feel that way for her?

She braced herself.

But Dantes smiled. "I heard you. I'm too happy to say anything. You're sure, though? You think you can do that?"

"Yes. I've been thinking about it and, in the end, for me, words are just words. But to you, those words hold a lot of fear. It doesn't make sense to lose you over a simple phrase."

Worry began to snake through her veins, though. Had she said too much too soon? And how would this all fit into Gran's stipulation? Was Dantes still against marriage despite what was growing between them? He had asked her before, but she didn't for a second believe he wanted it. Did *she* even want marriage after all?

Vivian tucked the sudden explosion of questions back in—they could all be answered later. Dantes was clearly a man who took his time for something like this, and she had plenty of time before her stipulation deadline for them to discuss everything.

"But you're leaving," he said after a moment.

Something in the way he said this caused her pause. "Well, I have to, silly. That's why I want you to join me and my family."

"You want me to go, too?"

"Yes, wouldn't it be lovely?"

"Can't you stay here?"

This wasn't going the way she had hoped. Why was he asking her to stay? Didn't he want to go away for a few months?

"No, I can't. This house gets closed up," she explained. "And it's the first chance to have any work done on it in years, as my grandmother became more frail over the years. The house will be filled with workers. Summerwood is already being prepared, and my family will be there too. I can't cancel it on them."

Dantes leaned forward, resting his elbows on his knees. "I can't, Vivian. I can't leave Victor and Ollie to bring the pub back up alone. Especially after everything they've done for me."

To Vivian's alarm, Dantes, the moment, seemed to be slipping away. She began to panic. How could she go an entire season without seeing him? Three months without him? She had already begun imagining him holding her hand and sneaking kisses at the beach.

But he had only ever kissed her that one time and had never tried again.

How had this not concerned her before now? Now that she had given her heart over to him? Oh, she was a foolish, foolish woman!

But to her abject relief, Dantes wasn't fully off of the idea. "Maybe I could visit for a few weeks. I'm not sure how well I can travel yet, so it would have to be later in summer."

"Of course." Relief washed over Vivian. She had to resist the urge to close her eyes and place her hand on her heart. Instead she smiled and gently set her hand upon his arm. "I couldn't go an entire summer without you, you silly man. I l—" She barely caught herself in time, her heart stopping in panic. "I like being with you far too much."

Alarmed by her near-error, she snuck a quick glance to Dantes, expecting him to be red with anger, or his lips pressed tight with disapproval. But to her relief, his face held no expression. It appeared he had not picked up on what she'd almost said.

Chapter Twenty-Five

SEVERAL NIGHTS LATER, Dantes found himself tossing and turning, struggling to sleep, and looked over at the empty bed on the other side of the dark room. Earlier, Mr. Wegner had said he was close to releasing Dantes as a patient, then removed the stitches, and upon the good news, Ollie had gone home.

It was the first quiet night for a long time and he had secretly been looking forward to it. Ollie talked his ear off every single night and Dantes wound up falling asleep to that, having no other choice. But now? The silence he had always treasured was keeping him awake. It was strange—for years, he had fallen asleep daily to such silence, alone in his home, and it was comforting. Now, in having it again, it was eerie. Unsettling.

He didn't like being alone anymore. And the realization hit him like Sullivan's fist.

Immediately, his thoughts went to Vivian. On the other end of the hall she lay curled up in her bed, sleeping peacefully. He wondered if he could go to her in the middle of the night, what she would think of that, if it would be overstepping.

A few days ago, she'd given him the surprise of his life by promising not to say the cursed phrase. He'd been stunned because he knew she didn't believe in the curse, but more importantly, the meaning of what she was saying in those unspoken words wasn't lost on him.

And the realization she felt that way sent a wave of terror over him. And that wave of terror remained cemented in place when just minutes later she'd almost slipped.

She probably thought he hadn't caught her near-error. But he had.

And it had caused nightmares. Vivid nightmares, almost as if they'd been omens. He had visions of her falling from the cliffs in Brighton, visions of her in a sinking boat, getting into her own carriage accident. He kept trying to convince himself they were nothing more than bad dreams—after all, she never once uttered the cursed phrase. But the fear lingered and clung to the air.

How could he go the rest of his life this terrified?

And yet, the alternative was worse. A life without Vivian in it.

That, he was realizing, wasn't even an option.

He needed Vivian in his life. She made him want everything he had sworn off. He had sworn off marriage, sworn off a family. He had sworn all of that off, thinking he didn't want that kind of life. But Vivian had made him realize that wasn't true. The real reason—the reason he wouldn't admit to himself all this time— was he was afraid he wasn't deserving of that kind of life. But wanting her overpowered his hesitation and doubt.

He wanted a life with *her*, to have a family with *her*, to grow old with *her*. Everything. With Lady Vivian Winthrop.

And admitting this to himself sent a thrill through him. It was a cautious thrill, but it was there. Scary, but in that life-altering anticipation big change brings.

But despite this, the fear of the curse remained. In fact, it was magnified. Vivian being in Brighton without him there to keep her safe made him uneasy. Plus, Tewksbury would be there. Could Tewksbury, who was arguably a far better mate for her, tempt Vivian away from Dantes in his long absence? Would she come to realize this on her own without him there?

No.

No more pushing away in fear. Dantes was going to have to do something about it. Do something to make sure that couldn't happen.

He had to go talk to her. Immediately. He couldn't go another night with everything as clear as mud.

Thus, he climbed out of bed and hastened into the sleepy hallway, barely lit by dimmed gas sconces.

Quickly, he hurried down the hall without making a sound. Up ahead was her bedroom door, the final one all the way at the end.

He approached it. Stopped. Raised his fist.

Hesitated.

Questioned if he lacked intelligence by being here.

Despite this, he moved his fist back to rap on the door gently—when the door opened instead.

Vivian appeared in the doorway and shrieked upon seeing him, then covered her mouth with wide-eyed realization they were both sneaking around in the middle of the night. But seeing her beautiful face after the big decision he had made moments ago reassured him.

"Hello." She used a proper voice, as if it were the middle of the day, not the middle of the night. As if they hadn't almost collided at her bedroom door. In the dark.

"Hello," Dantes responded with a crooked smile he couldn't hold back.

"What are you doing here?" Vivian asked as innocently as she could.

"I need to talk to you."

"Did anyone see you?"

"No."

Vivian nodded and stepped back to let him in. A candle was lit, allowing enough gold light for them to see.

"Dantes." Vivian shut the door and followed him farther into the room, where he stopped upon hearing his name. She moved to stand in front of him, wringing her hands. "I simply cannot spend another night away from you. And I know you said you would only kiss me that one time and—"

Anticipation hit. "No."

She blinked. "And also I know I said something a few days ago that was a rather big deal and we haven't talked about it again." A pause. "I'm sorry, when you say *no…*"

Dantes separated her wringing, clasped hands and weaved his hands in with hers. They stood in the middle of her bedroom, both hands clasped between them, the glow of the lamp surrounding them. It was such a warm, intimate moment.

"Your hair is down," Dantes realized with a bit of wonder. Vivian's dark hair, which for the first time he saw was thick and wavy, reached all the way to her waist. He released one hand and ran his fingers through that hair. It was soft, silky, and he was overwhelmed by the desire to make it wild.

But he had to move past this distraction because he had a life-changing question to ask.

VIVIAN SHIVERED UNDER Dantes's admiring gaze. He was here, in her bedroom! Seeing her in her nightgown. Seeing her hair down!

What had possessed him to come seek her out?

What had possessed them to seek each other out at the same time?

The emptiness she always felt when he wasn't with her had become so much stronger since they'd made the decision to never say the cursed words. Their feelings for each other had been made clear—as long as they didn't *say* them, of course.

But this new step made their summer separation that much more difficult. It would be so hard to be away from him for so long, especially now that they had confessed their feelings to each other.

His thumb swept over her hand, sending tingles up her arm. All this time, she had been waiting for him to kiss her again. It had been weeks of waiting. With many opportunities for him to do so.

Yet he hadn't.

Vivian had hemmed and hawed over this fact. Did it mean something?

Maybe. Maybe not. But she could always do something about it herself.

"Were you coming to find me?" Dantes asked in a low voice, as if knowing her thoughts. She looked up to find a curious, warm glow in his eye.

Her cheeks became hot at how close they were in this intimate of the moment. "Yes, I was."

"Scandalous to visit me in the middle of the night," he teased, but then he moved his hand to caress her cheek. "Why were you coming to me?"

This was her chance. She forced the words out, lest she cower and change her mind. "I want you to kiss me again." Her heart galloped at hearing those words with her own ears.

Dantes tilted her chin gently to see her better and ran his thumb over her bottom lip. "You want me to kiss you again?"

"Yes, please," Vivian replied, hypnotized by his touch.

Dantes let out a breathy chuckle before leaning down, cradling her face gently in both hands, obliging her with the slowest, softest, most sensual kiss she was sure ever existed in human history. It felt as if gooey caramel flooded her body, delicious and sweet and warm and lovely. Surely, those bursts of light she felt in her heart were fireworks going off around them.

Dantes pulled back and grinned before holding her close. "You taste like mint toothpaste."

Vivian, slightly embarrassed, grinned against him. "I will admit I brushed my teeth for a second time knowing I was coming to see you. Now kiss me just like that. Again."

He grinned and obliged, and Vivian was sure they were floating up to the ceiling.

Dantes broke the kiss, but his face remained close. "For some reason, I don't know, I really like that. It feels right. This feels right." Dantes wrapped his arms around her waist. "Seeing you in your nightgown, tasting your toothpaste. It feels right to be together at night like this."

"Oh." Vivian was disappointed as she imagined what she looked like through Dantes's eyes. When envisioning romance, she'd always pictured herself dressed in a ballgown with hair piled atop her head perfectly, her neck perfumed and nose powdered. But here she was, in an old, too-frilly nightgown, her hair unkempt. "That isn't the most romantic setting, is it? I wish I looked nicer."

"Nicer? No. I wouldn't change anything about this moment. You are absolutely stunning, Vivian. In your nightgown, or a gold-drenched ballgown, no one else on this Earth compares to you. To me, you are perfect."

"I have a too-large freckle on my shoulder I rather dislike," she deflected before looking up with a small smile. In the dim light, Dantes's scar was more obvious by the shadow it created. She tried to imagine him without it, but it would be like the Mona Lisa without her private smile.

"Nothing on you is a flaw," Dantes retorted.

"Nor on you." To make sure he understood what she meant, her hand reached up to touch the scar upon his face.

"You are reaching for my heart," he said. "You don't know what you do to me, do you, Vivian?"

"Tell me." She rested her head against his chest and could hear his heartbeat.

"I think about you far too much," he explained. "Every single day, every single night." He pressed his cheek to her hair. "You make me feel…worthy."

Surprised by his raw admission, she had an overwhelming urge to say the off-limit words. They were in such a tender moment, but she couldn't say three beautiful words?

Maybe that promise shouldn't have been made.

"You *are* worthy, Dantes." The words came out a quiet promise. "You're worthy of so much. You're worthy of everything."

Dantes put his forehead to hers. "You are mine." His voice strained. "And I am yours."

"Yes," she whispered back.

"Always."

"Yes."

"Forever."

Hot tears began to well in her eyes. "Yes!"

"Vivian…" He paused, as if there were more words to follow.

"Yes?"

"Marry me."

Shock tore through her. Had she heard that right? "Marry you?"

"Yes. Marry me. For love."

Her eyes widened at this. Though it wasn't the off-limits phrase, hearing him say that word filled her with pure joy. "Oh! Oh, Dantes." She threw herself on top of him and nuzzled into the crook of his neck, overjoyed.

His arms wrapped around her tightly, a warm embrace. He pressed his cheek to the side of her hair. "Is that a yes?"

She laughed. "Yes, of course, yes!" She paused as emotion continued to flood her. "I want to say it so bad. I won't, but I need you to know I want to say it so bad right now. I feel it for you, in my heart and in my soul."

Dantes didn't respond to this and instead placed her in bed, and to her amusement, tucked her in. He climbed in next to her and for a long while they lay there, snuggling close, coming down from the joyous moment. He kissed her hairline gently again as she drifted off to sleep, ignoring the ache in her heart.

Chapter Twenty-Six

T HE LAST ROOMS of the Mayfair house were closing as Vivian set to depart the following morning for Summerwood. Father would be traveling with her. Bernard and Anne, in their separation, had agreed to split their time at the cottage. As Anne remained close to Vivian like a sister, Vivian insisted she continued her stay at Summerwood each year.

The first half of the summer season was granted to Bernard while Anne stayed home with the children, and halfway through, they would switch. Instead of the children going to Bernard's lodgings at the baron's, though, he would return home as long as Anne wasn't there. Doing it this way was least disruptive to the children. And it kept up appearances to the aristocracy as well.

Vivian wished she could see her niece and nephew. But her father, who came up with the split-time idea, thought it best for the children to stay in familiar surroundings while they adjusted to the new version of their family. Vivian didn't disagree.

However, it was all for later consideration because the present day was a rather important one. It was also Dantes's departure day as he was now well enough, though still slightly weak. However, that wasn't why the day was so important. That had to do with their engagement.

Vivian and Dantes were regaled to the library, as the drawing room had already been shuttered, the furniture covered to protect it from dust.

They weren't quite sure how long the absence between them would be, but it would be at least a month. A sense of dread had been eating away at Vivian, getting stronger as each minute went by, but she did her best to ignore it.

Dantes watched Vivian flit back and forth like a hummingbird, preparing armfuls of books to pack in her overnight trunk. There were already books at Summerwood, of course, but she had a few mainstays she read each summer and wanted to ensure she had them on hand. And she was adding *The Count of Monte Cristo* to the list As Vivian set the books down on the corner of a large, oak desk and prepared to hurry back for more, Dantes wrapped an arm around her waist, lifted her up, and perched her on the edge of the desk. She elicited a small shriek of surprise that turned into laughter.

"Nothing will happen if you forget one or two books, Viv." He wrapped his strong arms around her, and she closed her eyes to listen to his heartbeat.

Being away was going to be difficult. They were in the throes of a new romance, where even a few hours apart felt like an eternity. Maybe she was trying to run from that thought. "I know. I always worry right before going on a trip. Worry I'll forget something important, worry I'll leave an entire trunk behind, worry, worry, worry."

"Everything is already packed up," Dantes promised in his comforting voice. "Now, I want to be selfish and have you pay attention to me." He punctuated this by showing her an over-bright smile.

She giggled and returned to burying herself against him.

"It's going to be hard with you being away so long," Dantes admitted. "I'm going to miss you."

"I'm going to miss you, too." She was trying not to think about it too much, though, as she was already feeling emotional as it was.

"But we will be together again at the end of summer," he

added with a promise. "And, we will be able to officially post the wedding banns."

Her throat feeling tight, she nodded against him but couldn't lift her head to look him in the eye. It would hurt too much.

The clock indicated their final hours together were flying by, and Victor and Ollie were moments away from bringing Dantes back to Victor's. As Vivian checked her reflection in a small mirror, making sure her eyes weren't giving away the distress she felt, Dantes reached into his pocket and pulled out the black lace scrap. With it over his hand, he cupped her chin and tilted her face toward him for another kiss, then gently rubbed the lace behind her collar, where she applied her perfume. He pulled the scrap away and brought it to his nose and smiled at her.

"You still carry that with you?" Charmed, she grinned to his reflection.

"Sometimes, yes, but I will each day you're gone. I find it comforting, like a part of you is with me. I'm sure that sounds ridiculous coming from a grown man." His hand dropped to his side, but he continued to rub the lace between his fingers.

"I don't find it ridiculous at all. I find it rather romantic, rather. When I miss you I'll think of you with my lace."

Previously, they had promised to exchange letters twice a day like they used to, though instead of getting their letters the same day, it would be a few days between replies, but that didn't matter. As long as there was daily correspondence, they were sure they could get through the difficult absence.

"Whatever happened to that dress?" Dantes asked, referring to the gold ballgown. "Did you really burn it?"

Satisfied nothing was giving away her inner turmoil, she faced him. "No. I couldn't bear to get rid of it and put it in storage. I'm not sure what I'm going to do with it, but I'll find a purpose for it at some point."

Heaton appeared to inform Vivian that Victor and Ollie had arrived. She left the library, with Dantes following, and met them in the entryway not far from where the carpet had been torn up, the full replacement planned while the house would be empty. Now that Dantes was better, it didn't bother them nearly as much as it once had, but it was still hard to look upon the place where Mr. Wegner had saved Dantes's life. With purpose, Vivian led them all into the receiving room because of the carpet, though there was no usable furniture.

Victor and Ollie exchanged a vague, confused look.

"Before we leave…" Dantes said to his brothers, who had both tensed, no doubt realizing something was amiss. "We have something important to share with you." Dantes glanced at Vivian, and she gave him a nod to go ahead. "After summer, we're getting married."

Ollie let out a whoop and immediately hugged Dantes, then Vivian. "See? I told you!"

Victor remained the usual grump, but Vivian caught a small twinkle in his eye as he shook Dantes's hand. "Congratulations. I'm sorry I doubted you."

"What do you mean?" Dantes asked.

Victor placed a heavy hand on his shoulder. "I was sure you were going to muck it up."

"Thanks for the confidence." Dantes couldn't help but offer a sideways smile.

Ollie gave Vivian a reminding nudge, as if she could possibly forget all about it.

"Dantes." Vivian's voice was full of excitement. "I have a surprise for you before you leave."

His brow furrowed. "A surprise? What is it?"

WHEN THE CARRIAGE rolled to a stop in front of the National Gallery, Dantes was at a complete loss. He had no idea what Vivian had planned, but based on the excited whispers between Vivian and Ollie, whatever this was, they were both the architects. He shook his head in amusement, feeling really lucky in the moment that his soon-to-be wife got along so well with his brothers.

Wife.

The thought sent his hardened heart singing. He truly hadn't believed a woman would ever love him, would ever want to marry him. He knew he was a bit rough, gruff, that he had an unorthodox lifestyle of fighting and owning a pub, especially to a high-society woman.

While thinking this, he rubbed a palm over his scar, thinking back to the day it had happened. It had taken a while to get here, but as long as it had always led to Vivian, he would do it again and again. And to his surprise, he realized that yes, that even included getting slashed with a blade. After all, that was part of his story. Part of his life. For the last twelve years, he had wished it hadn't happened. Wished it wasn't upon his face. While he would still get rid of it if he could, if it hadn't happened to him, he may not have met Vivian. Vivian, the most perfect fit for him.

Their plan in telling family about their future wedding was to tell his brothers today and her family in Brighton whenever he arrived, hoping somehow Lady Litchfield could be there for the announcement, too. Lady Litchfield was still Vivian's family, Vivian insisted, even with the separation. He wanted her to tell them and get it over with, but she argued it was important he be there for the discussion. And she was right, he knew she was, but deep down, it would make him feel better. He still didn't like the fact that Tewksbury was going to be there when Dantes wasn't. He knew it was a foolish fear, as he trusted Vivian completely. But he was still a man, and he just plain didn't like his future bride being so far away from him for so long while another man lurked nearby.

This time next year, they'd be preparing to leave together. He kept having to remind himself of that.

After climbing out of their carriage, Vivian took his hand and led him up the stairs to the entrance of the museum. Oddly, when they arrived at the desk, everyone seemed to recognize both her and Ollie, even joking with his brother as if they were friends. But he was completely floored when they went through back doors and up to the third floor, without anyone escorting them. They walked into a large, high-ceilinged room with what seemed like hundreds of windows. Dantes noted numerous worktables with paintings lying on top, others propped up on easels.

"Did you…buy me a painting?" The thought was spoken out loud. Could one even buy a painting from a museum? Maybe for a high price? But weren't they often on loan?

Vivian only responded with a giggle.

Dantes kept looking around with increasing curiosity as Ollie told them to wait there before crossing the room with an easy and casual gait, as if he belonged there, as if he dropped by all the time. Ollie approached a woman seated at one of the desks, her focus homed in on something lying across the tabletop. Upon hearing someone approaching, she looked up and removed magnifying eyeglasses from her eyes.

Ollie leaned down into her ear to say something, and she tore a look in their direction. First, her eyes studied Victor, then Dantes. Finally, she exclaimed, "Oh!" as Ollie continued to speak low. And when he stopped talking and pulled back, she rose to greet them.

This seemed to be Vivian's cue because she looked up at Dantes, her face filled with child-like excitement, and she led him forward with Victor following.

"Dantes, darling." Vivian indicated toward the woman when they came face to face with her. "This is Miss Evelyn Sparrow." The woman did a proper little curtsy. "She works for the museum's conservation department; her specialty is in paintings. Miss Sparrow, this is Mr. Edmond McNab."

Everyone looked at him expectantly, as if he were supposed to understand why this woman was being presented to him. "And?" Dantes replied slowly, still confused.

Vivian shifted. "She's restoring your paintings that were

damaged in the fire."

It took a moment for him to fully comprehend what she was saying. His paintings? From his flat? The paintings he didn't like anyone to see were now here under scrutiny of one the most prestigious art museums in the world? This woman whom he didn't know was going to be inspecting and judging his dreary collection, in extension judging him? Dantes suddenly felt exposed, vulnerable, like some deep-seated humiliating secret had been thrown out to the wind for the entire world to laugh at. Panic set in and his palms began to sweat.

"She is *what?*" That last word hit hard, like two stones slamming together. Miss Sparrow's proud smile immediately fell away and she seemed to shrink.

He could feel how severely his face twisted from fury, but he didn't care. This was a major violation of his privacy. Surely, the woman who was supposed to marry him, and his own brother, would have known better!

Vivian swallowed and shot a brief look of concern to Ollie. "Dantes—"

But as she was about to launch a defense, a horrifying thought crossed his mind. This was the Met. How had she gotten them to agree to this? It wasn't like someone could waltz in and hire them for this kind of service. And it wasn't even one mere painting—he had several. Surely, it would take quite a long time to restore the collection. He interrupted her. "Vivian, how much are you paying them to do this?"

The room stilled.

"Vivian." He ground his teeth together. "How much did you have to offer the museum to get them to agree to restore my paltry art collection?"

She straightened her back and lifted her chin. She knew there was no ignoring this. "Three thousand pounds."

"Three…." His hand slapped to his forehead. "Are you kidding me? What were you thinking?" This question was given to both Vivian and Ollie, the pair looking like children caught trampling their mother's flower garden. "What gives you the right to do anything with my belongings without my knowledge?" But this next question was directed at her. "Did it not occur to you to *ask* me before you did this? My God, Vivian, *three thousand pounds!*" Not sure what to do with himself, but needing to move, he began to pace away. But he quickly doubled back. "This is foolish, Vivian. I didn't ask you for your help. I don't need your help. I can take care of my things by myself. Do you think because you have endless money now, you can do everything for everyone? That anytime I or we need help, you'll come save us?"

Vivian's bottom lip began to quiver as she let out a tiny whimper.

"*Dantes.*" Victor's deep voice cut in, no doubt attempting to stop him for a moment to calm.

But Dantes wasn't having it. "Victor, don't even get involved in this. Do. Not." His eyes were sharp with warning, and Victor took the hint by placing his hands behind his back and looking at the ground.

"I'm sorry." Vivian's small voice shook. "I knew how much it all meant to you. I was so scared after what happened and…and I wanted to do something for you!" In her rising anger at his reaction, her voice strengthened. "And how *dare* you tell me what to do with my own money! I like to help people I care about— there's nothing wrong with that! This was meant to be a gift. And it isn't only to support this incredible department, but the museum as a whole. Are you against gifts now? Gifts with a good, charitable purpose?"

"If it costs three thousand pounds, *yes*, I'm against it!" He buried his face in his hands and let out a frustrated sigh. "Why do you do these things? First your brother's gambling debt." Though he would accept the part of that he was owed, not from her.

His eyes met her unblinking glare. Boy, was she boiling mad. "You helped us get a loan for the fire, let us live with you for a time, helped me recover under your roof with nurses and a physician paid for by you, and now this? Did you ever stop to think maybe it's embarrassing I have to work myself to the bone to reach those amounts while you merely sign off a check and you're done?"

"You had no problem agreeing to help me in order to get your wager money in return!"

Dantes inhaled deeply through his nose and turned his eyes up to the ceiling. "That's not why…" He rubbed his forehead. She was getting him off-track. "Why do you *do* all of that?"

"Because I love you!" She shouted back immediately. And in the seconds that followed, her face contorted from shock to fear to indignation.

It felt like the floor had dropped out from under Dantes and he was falling, falling.

No.

No, she had not just said that. Surely, he hadn't heard her right! But Ollie's and Victor's obvious discomfort confirmed his fear. And at the back of the room, Miss Sparrow and two men huddled over a large book, seemingly doing their best to be invisible.

Dantes's hands dropped to his side as his heart seemed to stop beating, the room now so quiet, he could hear a conversation outside, three floors below.

"You swore to me you would never say that!" His voice was rapid with panic. "Do you remember what happened only a few weeks ago?" He gestured between himself and Ollie, who looked rather eager to disappear.

But Vivian stepped up to him with defiance, though her face was etched in pain. "Yes, well, I've already said it to you. When you were feverish. And I nearly let it slip every single day. I tried, Dantes, but I can't keep it to myself anymore that I love you. You're asking me for something that is quite literally impossible. I can't do it and I won't do it anymore. I'm sorry."

"I forbid you from saying those words, Vivian." Elation from the fact she felt this way was drowned out by mortal fear. "I don't care how ridiculous you think it is, the bad luck is real, and the words are cursed. You've witnessed for yourself what happens!"

A haughty laugh came from her. "You *forbid* me?" She crossed her arms and opened her mouth as if she were about to continue speaking but decided against it. Instead, she took a deep breath. "I've said my piece and will not discuss it further. Miss Sparrow, thank you," Vivian called out to no particular direction. And without saying goodbye, without looking at Dantes one last time, she walked past him and left, though she did give a curt nod to Ollie and Victor before doing so.

Dantes remained as still as a statue, listening to her clicking footfalls fading away into the depths of the museum until a distant door opened and closed. He ignored his brothers, who smartly kept quiet, and went to sit in a nearby vacant chair to turn away. Low, indecipherable discussion from Miss Sparrow and her colleagues filled the thick air.

The desk had a large, dark painting on an easel, the background black and the foreground a hazy vase filled with flowers. Amongst the flowers of various darkened but bold colors, there was one white rose. He stared at the infernal flower for a long, unblinking time. Beyond the terror that pounded into his heart, a pain began to rise, like someone was squeezing it and ripping it out of his body.

Chapter Twenty-Seven

DANTES DIDN'T KNOW what to do. He knew he wasn't wrong for being upset something of this magnitude had been done behind his back. Something like this, you didn't hide. And he also knew he wasn't wrong in being upset that she had said those cursed words. It was something they had talked about, and while he knew she didn't understand it, she'd fully respected his genuine fear of those words and had agreed to not say them. Now, he was going to be living each moment of his life terrified that somewhere Vivian was hurt and he didn't know. Or that something dangerous loomed over her and he wouldn't be able to protect her.

He continued to study the white rose in the painting, wondered how in its lack of color, it stood out against the richly hued flowers surrounding it. He sighed. He shouldn't have gotten as angry as he had. But really, didn't Vivian, didn't Ollie, think this might surprise him a bit too much?

"Dantes." Ollie's voice interrupted that thought and Dantes spun in the chair to see Miss Sparrow had rejoined them. The slight woman was now holding a small object wrapped in tissue paper, looking quite uncomfortable to be there. Ollie turned to say something to her and headed over to Dantes to lean back against the desk. "I'm sorry."

Dantes grunted back.

"I take responsibility. I should have known you wouldn't like this."

"Yes, you should have."

But to his irritation, Ollie became animated. "But she was so excited about it! I didn't even know what she was up to until she brought me here and then, I don't know, I saw what they could do and I saw how eager she was to do this. She partly did this for herself, too, you know. It was right after you woke up and she wanted to do something for you, some kind of project, to distract her mind from worrying about you so much. Because she loves you, remember that part?"

Dantes tapped the desk in thought. "No more of this. I want my paintings returned to me in whatever state they are in." He finally looked up at his brother, noting Ollie's stunned silence.

But after a moment, Ollie found his voice. "Why don't you at least give it a day's consideration? Make sure that's the right decision? You were already horrific to Vivian. At least take a day to think about it before you make it worse."

Dantes stood up, the chair creaking at the sudden release of weight. "No," he said sternly. He had already made up his mind and wasn't going to change it. He made his way back to Miss Sparrow, noting Victor was keeping his distance from Dantes.

"Miss Sparrow," Dantes began as he came to a stop in front of the willowy woman, "I appreciate everything you've done. However, I'm going to have everything returned home." Though he wasn't quite sure where exactly home was, he would figure out that part later.

"They can be saved, Mr. McNab." Miss Sparrow surprised him not by cowering from his brutish behavior, but by tilting her chin up. As if preparing to argue. "They have water damage, which is highly destructive. The acidity in the soot can destroy the paint. If you delay any further—"

"Please. I've made up my mind."

Ollie had rejoined them and exchanged a look with her. "Before you decide," Miss Sparrow said to Dantes. "Perhaps you should look at this." She handed over the tissue-wrapped object and he scowled at the delay to his departure. All he wanted was to leave. But grudgingly, he took the object from Miss Sparrow, setting it down on a desk nearby and peeling it apart. Once opened, the tissue paper revealed the tintype of his parents. Unmarred. Clean. Perfect.

"What in the blazes is this?" he asked with a growl, angrier than he'd meant to. Was this some kind of sick joke?

"This is the tintype of your parents," she explained.

"But it was destroyed. Burned to a crisp!"

She gave him a small smile. "It was only soot, though there was a rather lot of it. It was quite simple to clean. All it took was a vulcanized rubber sponge."

A what? Never mind. He held the tintype at eye level, staring at it in disbelief. "You did this, Miss Sparrow?" He gave her a blank look.

She nodded.

Inside, emotions roiled. He'd been so sure, so confident, that this tintype had been turned to charcoal, that he would never see his parents' faces again for the rest of his life, afraid he would forget what they'd looked like. This little photograph had been the real reason he'd refused to return to his flat, why he'd never wanted to see those paintings again. They would only remind him of the photograph, lying there on the table, destroyed forever. And how could he have such useless expensive paintings when he'd only wanted this cheap, little photograph? Forgetting it had been the easiest option for him amongst the heavy guilt he carried.

But now he had it again. Because of Vivian. And Miss Sparrow, of course.

Miss Sparrow's voice grabbed his attention. "I've already begun one of your paintings, if you could follow me." Though her voice was pleasant, she wasn't giving him a choice, not really. So he followed her over to another desk, where an easel cradled a painting covered by cloth. She lifted the white cloth up and over the back to reveal a large painting with severe soot and water damage, and about one quarter of it was immaculate.

He took in a sharp breath of genuine shock at the stark difference between the portion she had repaired and the rest of it. Dantes leaned in close, and even from that view, it was perfection. "It looks even better than it did before."

"The varnish had begun to yellow. Once it's completely clean and any necessary repairs are made, I'll re-varnish it again." She appeared at his side, observing the painting at the same distance. "It's an interesting piece, seventeenth-century Italian. Venetian, influenced by Giorgione."

He tore a look in her direction. "You know all that?" What a foolish question. "Of course you would. You work here. You're probably the most educated woman in the world on the subject of paintings."

"She used to work at the Louvre," Ollie added from somewhere off to Dantes's side. At this admiration, Dantes noted the tiniest twitch at the corner of Miss Sparrow's mouth.

Interesting.

"I saw in your collection, Mr. McNab, you appear to be a fan of Gustave Courbet." Miss Sparrow looked up at him.

He cleared his throat. "I am."

"He was a fascinating character. A pioneer, rather. He went against convention, against Romanticism, and was one of the first painters in the Realism movement. He didn't paint frothy pastels of idealized life—he painted what he knew. Working class, the poor, death, prostitutes. It caused quite a scandal back then."

Dantes felt heat rising in his cheeks.

She continued, evidently unaware of his embarrassment. "Unfortunately, I never met him myself. However, many of my friends did. He was a great influence on them, in fact."

"Influence?" Dantes was beginning to warm up a bit to the woman. "You mean friends of yours are artists?"

"Oh, yes!" She smiled widely. "Claude Monet and Edward Degas. They like to joke there wasn't a mirror in France Courbet hadn't gazed into with adoration. Of course, I could say the same for Degas." She rolled her eyes.

Dantes stared at her, stunned. Somehow, she knew the world's most famous artists. Personally! Friends of hers! And she didn't think anything at all about his art collection. In fact, she seemed to, maybe, even admire it. Or at the very least, respected it.

Dantes returned his attention to the Venetian painting before them. "Very well, then. I look forward to seeing it upon completion. As you know, Lady Vivian will be away for the next few months. Since Ollie seems to know more than I do about"—he rolled his hand in the air—"everything, I think it makes sense that he continues to keep up with it instead of me. And update me when necessary. How does that sound, Ollie?" He looked his younger brother in the eye.

Ollie shifted. "Well, if you think that's best…"

"I do." Dantes turned back to the genius woman. "You're rather convincing, Miss Sparrow. Thank you, especially for this." He held the tintype up and smiled. "However, I do need to depart and beg on my knees for Vivian's forgiveness, then grovel and wash myself in her triumph when I tell her I accept her rather undeserved gift." Dantes departed with a hasty goodbye, assuring his brothers he would find his own hansom home.

But when he arrived at Vivian's and Heaton answered the door, Dantes was crestfallen to learn she had made a sudden change of plans and had departed early for Brighton.

"But…" The butler reached into a pocket inside of his jacket and revealed a piece of paper. "She did tell me to give you this letter if you stopped by."

VIVIAN DID HER best to leave the museum without throwing the doors open too hard. And when she climbed into her carriage, she tried her best not to sound too angry to her driver. And when she returned home, she did everything she could to not stomp up into her bedroom.

She tried. She really did. But she didn't succeed.

Heaton followed her upstairs, where she showed her lady's maid, Norris, the last items to be packed. As she did this, requesting far too many different-colored gloves, she explained to the butler what had happened, and he listened patiently and without comment.

"Norris," Vivian said with a sudden decision made. "Have you finished packing your personal items for Brighton?"

The plump woman gently laid out another pair of pink gloves in Vivian's traveling trunk. "I am nearly done, my lady. I only have a few more items."

"Excellent, because I would like to depart as soon as possible. I know this is much earlier than expected, but I think it's high time for some seaside air."

Norris agreed with a curtsy.

"What about Mr. McNab?" Heaton asked as she had Norris wrap up a bottle of perfume.

"We already said our goodbyes." Vivian masked her hurt with curtness.

"What if he comes by, anyway? Would you like to leave a letter?"

"Why should I leave a letter? He was the one out of line."

Heaton nodded slowly, watching as she zipped back and forth across the floor mumbling to herself in frustration. The painting restorations *had been* a great idea. Dantes loved them; she knew how devastated he'd been to lose them. And the photograph she hadn't even had a chance to tell him about! Would he rather not get them back? And it wasn't like her home, her money, wouldn't be his once they married. Would he be dictating how she spent their money? Inspect every receipt from every store and comment on her spending habits? She wasn't frivolous or irresponsible with money and yes, she liked to sometimes treat or help the people she loved and cared about. Was that really so bad? The volume of her voice increased with her frustration.

"And the infuriating paintings aside, how can I possibly go my entire life without telling him I love him? Isn't that the most preposterous thing you have ever heard?" The books she had collected earlier had been brought up and she shoved them into the trunk. Normally, Norris would have been doing this, but she needed to exert her anger somehow.

"That, I will agree with, my lady," Heaton replied.

"He thinks he's unlucky." She shook her head as she explained and began her pacing once more. "That the words 'I love you' are cursed. I tried respecting his odd conviction, even accepted his request that I never say it. And ignoring the fact that I'd said it to him anyway when he'd been halfway to death, I didn't even last a few days before it slipped out! How am I supposed to go my entire life not saying it?" As she said this, it occurred to her that he'd never once nearly let those words slip. It was so hard for her to keep it to herself—why was it so easy for him? She brushed the thought away, but the shadow of doubt remained.

"I understand, Lady Vivian," Heaton said.

But at this, she stopped her pacing, releasing a deep sigh. "Do you really?"

He smiled. "No."

She couldn't help but let out a small laugh. "Nor do I, Heaton. This is all madness."

"Lady Vivian, may I speak freely about something?"

"Please."

He looped his hands behind his back. "Do you think perhaps Mr. McNab may not be in the wrong for being as upset as he was about his paintings? After all, they are his possessions. And that *is* an exorbitant amount of money."

She looked away.

"Here's a test. Put your father in place of Mr. McNab in this situation. Your father's wealth is comparable to yours, at least for argument's sake, so there is no disparity there. And a loving father is much more forgiving to his beloved daughter than a loving husband is to his beloved wife. Or soon-to-be beloved wife. How would your father react to you spending three thousand pounds on something for him?"

As she watched the treetops swaying outside of her window, she tried to imagine. It wasn't too hard. Father would have been absolutely offended if a lady spent that on him, even his own daughter. Even if it was for a charitable purpose.

Guilt and shame ripped apart her insides. She whispered a curse at Heaton.

The butler cleared his throat to mask his chuckle. "Lady Vivian, I would like to add that you're well within your right to feel hurt as well. It's possible Mr. McNab did react too harshly. Perhaps you both did. I cannot say, as I was not there. But regardless, I'm sure at the moment he is feeling terrible. And I know you had nothing but good intentions in your heart."

She didn't respond, as she was far too mortified to.

"So," Heaton continued, "I suggest you write a heartfelt letter in the *apparently unlikely* event he does come by."

"Very well." She tore away from the window. "Please have the footmen bring my trunk out to my carriage."

"Excellent. I hope your travels are without event, and your summer enjoyable."

Vivian gave Heaton a warm smile and a hug that surprised the normally stoic gentleman. "Thank you, Heaton. You're a good man, and a good friend. I appreciate everything you've done for me since my arrival here. I just want you to know that."

He shifted with evident embarrassment, gave her a quick thanks, and departed to leave her to her letter. She swung over to her desk, dipped her pen in ink, and began to write from the heart.

Dear Dantes,

If you have received this letter, then you know I have already left for Brighton. As we had already said our goodbyes, and our departure was rather unpleasant, in my discontent, I hastened my departure.

I wish to apologize for the paintings catastrophe. In your illness, my brain was addled with worry, and upon your miraculous recovery, my nerves became tender and frayed. Wanting to do something for you and also find some kind of diversion, I came upon the idea for paintings restoration. In retrospect, I should have given it more thought, but selfishly, I was swimming with excitement and wanted to be the one who solved the conundrum. Please believe I never intended to cause offense or upset.

Once I am settled at Summerwood, I will post a letter to Miss Sparrow and the museum director to let them know we will no longer continue with the project. Under my expense, the paintings will be sent to Victor's for you to decide what to do with them.

At the bottom of this letter is the address for Summerwood if you wish to write to me.

Before I sign off, there is one further thought I must share. You requested that I do not say those three little "cursed" words for us to be together, and I agreed. Truly, it has been a test of will. I cannot help it, and I have come to understand that verbal expression of love is, for me, as natural and lovely as physical expression.

In the fading remnants of my anger from the museum, I'm finding it difficult to properly describe my love for you without using that phrase. For I do so desire everything about you: your mind, your heart, your body. Never in my life has someone so greatly affected me and I can say with confidence there isn't another person on this fine planet who could replicate those feelings within me.

Thus, I cannot keep the words to myself any longer. Because those three little words are the only way to express what I feel about every facet of you. I know this will anger you, and I know there is a chance you will never speak to me again, but I must take that chance. I simply cannot do what is impossible.

I love you.
Vivian Winthrop

Chapter Twenty-Eight

V IVIAN HELD ON to her hat as she angled her head to look up at Summerwood, thrilled to have arrived at last. The trees that dotted the property towered high above, providing plenty of shade across the large and expansive front yard. The cottage, according to Gran, had been the source of the only major argument her grandparents had ever had. Vivian's grandfather had been a social butterfly and had insisted on adding a bigger ballroom to the centuries-old home so they could host parties and rub elbows with important people. Gran had threatened to leave him over it because she'd hated hosting, and she'd done enough of it in town. Of course, and unfortunately for Gran, it was expected and normal to have a ballroom, to socialize, even in the country, and so a bigger and more modern ballroom had had to be added. Gran had made sure to make it as small as she could get away with, however, and grudgingly hosted parties every year until her husband's death. She'd then holed up the way she'd wanted to.

Vivian smiled to herself as she thought about this, but the smile fell away as she climbed up to the front porch. This house had been a mainstay of her childhood, of her life, really, as she'd summered there every year. Even as an adult. Every inch of this home held memories for her. Almost all good, but there was one bad memory. It was last summer that Gran had learned of her illness—lung cancer. It had been aggressive, and far along. Gran's physician had expected her to make it only another month or two. The news had been devastating to the family, of course, and Father had immediately begun making plans to return home and get Gran back as comfortably as possible. Of course, the stubborn woman had outright refused to leave.

Vivian's misty smile returned as she recalled Gran's reaction to the devastating news. Gran had poured herself a whiskey, put a cigarette in her long cigarette holder, and gone out onto the grounds. Vivian had come across the moment on accident, running outside moments earlier to hide and react to the news in her own private way. Through the hedges, she'd witnessed her grandmother scolding God for making her miss the best season of the year and telling Him He'd better let her live out the summer or she'd be sure to spend eternity being a constant irritation.

Gran had ended up not only surviving summer, but autumn as well, finally passing during winter. Vivian liked to think Gran's scolding had had something to do with that.

Ready to return to the present, Vivian entered the cottage, shivering at the realization that it was hers. A few of the servants came out to greet her, led by the butler and housekeeper, who updated her on the state of the home and then left Vivian to walk through by herself. After, she went out into the yard, closed her eyes, and relished in the feeling of the warm sun upon her face, the expansive and lush lawn that looked out toward the cliffs and the water beyond. The smell of the salty air, the coolness of the breeze. She took a deep, cleansing breath and let it out slowly.

The remainder of the day, she prepared for the season. She planned menus with the cook, checked on the guest rooms, and that night wrote a letter to Dantes to tell him she had arrived, and her travel had been uneventful. And, most importantly, she was safe. She folded it up, sealed it, and set it to the side.

Father and Bernard arrived the following day and she was thrilled to see them, greeting them with excitement. Her first thought upon seeing them was wishing she could share the news that a wedding was in the future, but that would occur later in the summer when Dantes arrived. But then she remembered she'd broken Dantes's one big rule. Perhaps, the wedding may not even happen.

The physical distance from him was hard enough, but now there was a distance in their hearts. That negative voice in her mind told her to expect the worst and start to move on. But the rational part of her kept beating it back, reminding that little negative voice that there hadn't been enough time to hear from him yet. She was sure she would receive a letter from him any day now reassuring her that he may have been upset, but he still did want to marry her.

She hoped, anyway.

The day after Father and Bernard's arrival, Bernard found Vivian outside writing another letter to Dantes. It had been so hectic, she hadn't been able to send any of her letters out yet, being sure to include an apology for this in the newest letter. "It's pretty strange to be back here," Bernard said as he sat in a chair nearby. "Remembering everything that happened last summer."

Vivian agreed and told him about Gran scolding God.

Bernard laughed heartily. "She was quite a presence. I miss her. A lot."

"I do, too." Vivian folded up the letter and slid it into the envelope, turning her focus completely to Bernard. Since even before his separation from Anne, he had been distant and it had only worsened after the day he'd shown up drunk and angry, asking for money. He looked tired and had lost noticeable weight. His skin was sallow, and dark circles had formed under his eyes. Quite frankly, she had never seen him look so terrible. "How are you doing, Bernard?"

Bernard looked over at her for a moment but turned his face back out toward the yard when he understood what she was asking. "The shock is still wearing off. I couldn't believe it when she broke the news to me."

But Vivian found she had to bite her cheek to keep quiet

about his shock. Surely, he couldn't have been *that* surprised? While she didn't know what final behavior from Bernard had led to Anne wanting the separation, she did know about his atrocious behavior beforehand. Granted, a separation wasn't common, but it wasn't unheard of, either. They were hardly the only aristocratic couple in such a situation, though it *was* unusual Father had been involved and ensured Anne had equal time with the children and the house. It was a very American solution, in her opinion. Perhaps Father was influenced by his American heritage.

Regardless, this was her brother, and the separation was over and done. It wouldn't do anything to share these thoughts with him. "How are the children taking the change?"

"They've hardly noticed. We haven't explicitly said anything to them except I'll sometimes be at a different house, and other times they'll be at that house with me and their mother won't be there. They haven't questioned it."

Vivian didn't say this of course, but she wondered if Bernard's old *habits* had kept him out of the house to the point the children wouldn't notice him gone now, either.

A rush of cool, ocean air swept across Vivian's face and the flutter of the letter caught Bernard's attention. "I'm going into town," he said. "To post letters to the children."

"The servants take care of that."

But Bernard shook his head. "It's a reason to get me out of the house, get some walking in. Do you want me to drop that off?"

Vivian lifted the envelope up. "Actually, yes, if you wouldn't mind." She handed it to him as they stood at the same time. "Could you see if I have anything as well waiting for the postman to bring to the house? You'll already be there."

"Yes, of course." He looked down at the letter when he frowned. "You're writing to McNab?"

"Yes." She offered nothing else.

"It's utterly mad how lucky you are no one discovered he was staying under your roof. I was a bit busy with my entire life turning upside down to care about it too much, but I was waiting for the day I walked into Brooks's and the boys all burst into laughter upon my arrival. Though I did hear about you screaming at them to get out of your house. *That* did not elicit laughter from them."

Vivian lifted her eyebrows a bit at this.

"I did stand up for you! Anyway, Father had more confidence in the situation than I did, or maybe he was so tired of me, he couldn't even begin to worry about you. You must have quite the happy group of servants to keep something like that quiet. That or Heaton is secretly a menace." Bernard laughed. "And you think *I'm* the family blackguard? Pish posh, Vivian."

Vivian let out a loud sigh.

"What exactly is going on between you two?"

"Oh, don't be so nosy, Bernard, and send my letter for me." She began walking back to the house and he followed. "Will you be back for dinner?"

As their conversation went into more neutral subjects, the siblings stepped inside right as their father walked through the front door.

"Ah! My adoring children." He gave them each a peck on the cheek. "What devilry are you up to?"

Vivian laughed. "Writing letters and going to the post office."

"I have letters for home that I'm sending now," Bernard added, "if you have anything you need to send out."

"No mail from me, but I just saw one of the footmen collecting this from the letterbox," Father pulled out a few envelopes from his jacket and handed them to Vivian. "I took it upon myself to bring it to you and already took out mine. This is all for you. But I am in desperate need of an afternoon nap. If either of you need me, I'll be upstairs."

Father went up to bed as Vivian eagerly flipped through the envelopes. To her great disappointment, there wasn't anything from Dantes. Though she scolded herself for being silly, she hadn't yet had a chance to send him a letter before the one she had just written.

There was, however, something from Mr. Northcott, Gran's solicitor. She pulled it out of the stack and held it up. That was odd. Why would she be hearing from him?

"Is something the matter?" Bernard asked, evidently noticing his sister's sudden change in demeanor.

"I'm not sure. Don't leave yet. I may have another letter to post." With shaking hands, she ripped open the envelope and hastily read through. Her face paled and she read through it again and again as her heart raced faster with each read.

My lady,

I hope this letter finds you well and you are settled into your holiday. Unfortunately, I have some distressing news. The last time we spoke, I gave you a letter from your grandmother. In the unlikely event you do not recall the letter, your grandmother had a stipulation in her will requiring you to marry within a year for love in order to keep your inheritance. And if you do not, the entire inheritance goes to your brother.

I recently recalled this stipulation, one of the most unorthodox of my long career, and mentioned it to a colleague of mine. As he had never seen such a request before, he asked to see it for curiosity's sake. To be technical, the stipulation is what we call a conditional bequest and a conditional bequest must be fulfilled for the will to be valid. However, my colleague discovered something when reviewing the document. Your grandmother never specified the one-year countdown should begin upon her death. My colleague pointed out that because the conditional bequest is a separate document from the will, the countdown began the date of the document's creation in lieu of a designated start date. Sure he was in error, we brought the document to several other solicitors I hold in high regard, and their interpretation of the document was the same. The conditional bequest was added to the will last summer, not long after her illness was discovered. This is all to say the one-year countdown began on July 30th, 1888, and not upon her death in February of 1889. In other words, you have mere weeks to marry.

Never in my career have I made such an error and unfortunately, there is nothing to remedy this. As love is not a concrete object that can be measured, that portion of the conditional bequest can be overlooked and I would strongly encourage you to overlook it as well, if necessary. As soon as you have a ceremony date and marriage license, please send a copy to me posthaste.

The letter continued further, though it was mostly incessant apologies.

She threw the letter down to the sideboard with the rest of the mail and began pulling drawers open in search of paper and a pen.

"What's wrong?" Bernard's volume had raised and he took to her side.

"Nothing you need to worry about," she replied curtly as she rushed off into adjacent rooms in search of paper and pen. Had they all gone and walked off? "Where is my stationery?" she asked with a frustrated mutter.

"You were writing a letter outside earlier," he responded the from hallway. "Unless it blew away, I would imagine it would still be there."

She pressed a hand to her cheek. "Oh, goodness, you're right. Thank you, Bernard. Give me one minute."

Vivian hurried back outside and went straight to the chair she had been sitting in when she'd written the last letter. Bernard's assumption was right; her stationery was still there. She sat once more and hastily responded to the solicitor, informing him she'd received his letter and understood what needed to be done. Being frustrated or angry with Mr. Northcott would do her no good. The man hadn't acted with malice, so she did her best to keep those feelings of upset level. She also wrote a second letter to Dantes informing him of the news and asked that he join her a few weeks earlier than expected. She sealed the letter.

With worry creased in her brow, Vivian returned to the hallway and found Bernard exactly where she had left him at the sideboard. He straightened as he spotted her, glanced at the letters in her hand, then the one she had left on the sideboard. He still clutched the one letter she'd handed him moments ago.

Vivian handed him more letters for Dantes, and the one for the solicitor.

"Please, make sure those are sent right away," she said, smoothing out invisible wrinkles on her skirt. She wondered how Dantes would react to going from the first letter, relaxed and carefree, informing him of her safe arrival to Brighton, to the second letter of life-altering alarm. Bernard took them with a nod, and she gave him a kiss on the cheek and a hasty *thank you*.

Chapter Twenty-Nine

THE HARP & Thistle was on track to reopen in autumn, and truth be told, it was all Dantes looked forward to. He glanced around at the mess, observed the fine haze of renovation dust over every surface, and tried to imagine it clean and filled with people and loud noise. The place was going to look a lot nicer than it had before, no longer the hole-in-the-wall it once had been, but polished and handsome. There would be more intricate wood detailing throughout, the dingy floor was going to be replaced, the old, banged-up furniture would be new. The front of the building had already been redone and they'd added in larger front windows to entice people inside. That had been Victor's idea, and Dantes thought it was ingenious.

Everything was going to be brand new, shiny. Even his old flat he refused to set foot in, as it made him think of Vivian.

He could still envision her standing in his living room, smiling at the photo of his parents, smiling up at him as he stood so close, the fireplace crackling and warm before the whole place lit up and burned.

It had been three weeks now since Vivian had left for Brighton and he still had not heard from her. Her last word was the letter Heaton had given him.

Not one letter, not one telegram, had arrived since.

Dantes had, of course, written to her after a few days of silence, at first trying not to sound desperate or worried.

No response.

Dantes swiped a finger over the dust upon a table, rubbing the grit between his thumb and forefinger. His heart and mind felt like they were covered with that same dust.

Dantes's dreary thoughts were interrupted when Victor came through the front door and thumped a large catalog on the table Dantes stood beside. A cloud of dust puffed out to the floor. "In having some free time," Victor began talking without looking at Dantes, instead thumbing through the catalog. "I've been looking into other liquor distributors. I discovered this one—their prices are better, and the liquor is better too. Basically, we'll be paying the same price for higher quality." He pointed to an example.

"That's good," Dantes said flatly.

Victor looked up and observed his brother for a long, studious moment. "Have you heard anything from Lady Vivian today?"

"No." Dantes clenched his jaw and recalled this morning, when his worry had seemed to snap him into madness. "In an act of furious desperation, I went banging on the servants' door at her house. Her butler, Heaton, answered red-faced, like he was ready to kill me. He was even holding a pistol and behind him, the housekeeper had a rolling pin raised."

Victor made a choking noise.

Dantes shot him a deadly glare. Though he could only imagine what the poor maids and footmen had thought with his incessant banging.

Of course, when Heaton had opened the door to the mad banging, Dantes had keeled over. He *still* hadn't recovered his full strength and it was easy to find himself winded and light-headed.

"And?" Victor said. "I'm assuming you found out she isn't dead like you feared if you're sitting in front of me, calm." He looked Dantes over. "Sort of."

Dantes ran his hands through his wild hair. "I asked if something had happened to Lady Vivian."

What had truly occurred was Dantes had turned into a wild man, spouting a bunch of nonsense to the butler about cliffs and carriage accidents.

Vivian had said the cursed words and then immediately left. He hadn't had a chance to go with her to keep her close and safe, hadn't had an opportunity to even warn her to keep extra care of herself. She'd said the words and was gone.

Initially, he had considered going after her, even though traveling would take its toll on his body, especially three weeks ago. But at first, he thought she needed space after their argument.

Eventually, he began to think she had disappeared, or had been killed.

That was when the nightmares had returned.

Vivid nightmares of Vivian falling off cliffs into the ocean, a crazed burglar kidnapping her in the middle of the night. Drowning. Run over by a carriage. Getting struck by lightning.

Tewksbury marrying her instead.

He wrote letters, begging her to be careful. Begging her to reply. Even just once. Just once! All he wanted was one reply and he'd leave her be.

Victor crossed his arms and drily replied, "I'm sure when you talked to her butler you were a paragon of calm and not the growling, pacing madman you've been for nearly a month now."

Dantes ignored this. "She is alive," Dantes said, pain stabbing his heart. "Heaton hears from her. He gets responses when he updates her about the work being done at the house." He puffed out a breath. "And then when I came here today, I received a notice from the bank. Vivian sent over the money to cover Winthrop's debt to me. I immediately went to the bank and told them to refuse the money, but they said it didn't work like that."

Victor frowned at this. "She paid the debt?"

"Yes." Dantes's voice was dark. "The final thread between us has been cut."

That action spoke plainly to him. She hadn't disappeared, she hadn't died. Vivian refused to speak to him after his ridiculous behavior, then she'd given him the money owed, though he hadn't fulfilled his part of their bargain.

He hadn't ended up helping her find a husband. Maybe she had done that all on her own with Tewksbury. Tewksbury wouldn't have blown up at her over a three-thousand-pound gift. The man likely had never raised his voice in his life, either. He seemed like that kind of chap.

Giving Dantes the debt money gave her a clean break from Dantes.

She wanted him out of her life.

There was another stab to his heart as he thought about this.

Victor came around the table and gave Dantes an awkward pat on the shoulder, his biggest attempt ever at showing affection. "Three weeks really isn't that long. Maybe she's been busy. Or ran out of ink."

Dantes scoffed and collapsed into a chair.

"I think it's odd you haven't heard anything from her. Nothing at all."

"Because she wants nothing to do with me. She couldn't make that more clear!"

Victor gave Dantes an unamused once-over, crossing his arms across his chest.

Dantes stepped around the table with hands clenched. "Keep looking at me like that, I have no problem taking you down."

Victor gave him a sharp laugh. "You can't, not after everything you went through last month." Narrowing his eyes, Victor solidified his stance to show he meant business. "This is exactly why I refuse to involve myself with women, Dantes. Men become bumbling fools. I know somewhere deep in that head of yours, the logical solution is screaming at you. But your idiotic and emotional heart is drowning you, and that logic, in grief. Pathetic."

Dantes clenched his teeth.

"Lady Vivian apologized in her final letter, did she not?"

Victor was referring to the letter Heaton had given Dantes. "Did it not sound like she was still interested in salvaging…whatever you two are?"

"Yes, but—"

"She doesn't strike me as the type of woman who would put you through this. If it was really over, she would tell you that with her own words. She wouldn't make you guess."

"That's exactly what she's doing, though." Dantes growled with frustration. "What in the blazes am I supposed to do, then, since you seem to know everything?"

Victor tapped his head and his eyes became wide. "Think, Dantes."

Dantes again collapsed into a chair, but this time, he buried his face into his hands. What could he possibly do now? The grief of losing Vivian was too much and it clouded his mind, his world.

After taking a deep breath, though, he tried to move focus away from the way his heart felt. He then put his focus over to his mind, to logic, and pushed aside the clouds until the answer came through like a beacon.

He tensed.

What if he went to Brighton to confront her?

Christ, he could imagine it now. How idiotic would he look banging on her front door, calling to her like some desperate mongrel whimpering to get into the house, after who knew how many unanswered letters and telegrams? Her butler would chase him across the yard shouting at him to take the blasted hint.

What a fool he would look. And be.

But…did he care? Did he really care that much about what they all would think of him? Was it more important than seeing her and getting answers?

Before he could even begin to start considering his next move, Ollie came bounding in through the door talking quite rapidly.

"The weirdest thing just happened, and I had to rush right over!" Ollie angled over to the dusty table Dantes and Victor were beside. "I went to the National Gallery to check on the paintings—"

"Oh? Interesting. You went there yesterday to check on everything, too," Victor said with evident boredom.

"And the day before." Dantes couldn't help but grin at this. Giving Ollie a hard time still gave him a bit of amusement.

Ollie shook his head in evident disbelief at them. "Forget about that. While I was there, Miss Sparrow got a letter from Lady Vivian."

"What did it say?" Dantes demanded immediately as he leaned forward.

"Give me a second to breathe, will you? Lady Vivian dismissed Miss Sparrow from the project and wrote how since you hadn't responded to her letter asking if you wanted the project to continue, she assumed that meant you did not. I told Miss Sparrow something wasn't right, to keep at it, and came here immediately."

Dantes's heart began to race. "I never got a letter from Vivian, much less one asking me about that."

Ollie pointed a finger at him, gloating like he had solved a riddle. "Exactly."

"I'm not understanding."

"Something is keeping your correspondence from reaching each other."

Dantes swallowed as a cautious glimmer of hope, of happiness, winked through the gloom surrounding him. But what could possibly keep them from reaching each other?

The front door flung open again. The brothers froze when Lady Litchfield, steam practically shooting out of her ears from beneath a yellow flowery hat, came storming in and over to Dantes, her two children trailing behind. She was significantly smaller than him, but glared with a furious stare, daring him to go against whatever she was about to say. Her daughter, meanwhile, crossed her arms at Dantes with a similar frown while her son stepped up to Victor, craning his head all the way back to stare up at his height, licking a lollipop as he did this. Victor, however, did not notice the child's awe. Victor stood as rigid as a statue, his gaze fixed upon the boy's mother, and nothing else.

"You!" Lady Litchfield shouted at Dantes before covering her children's ears by pulling them against her and putting her hands to each uncovered ear. They protested and flailed, but she was stronger than she looked. "I expect this kind of behavior from Bernard!" She released them with a huff. "But you…you mean, mean man!"

Dantes exchanged a look of bewilderment with Victor. "What in the Devil are you talking about?"

Lady Litchfield yanked folded paper out of her silver reticule and shook it at him. "I received this frantic six-page letter from Vivian telling me she has sent you"—she hastily unfolded the letter and skimmed through—"*thirty* letters since her arrival at Summerwood, countless telegrams, all begging you to respond to her and you couldn't be bothered to do that! See this page?" She turned it to him and shoved it against his nose. "Those splotches on the ink are tear marks. *Tear marks!*"

Dantes was sure that up until this moment, he couldn't have felt any worse. He'd been wrong. "I haven't received any correspondence from her, Lady Litchfield. Not one shred."

Lady Litchfield stilled, but the anger quickly returned. "You expect me to believe that? No, you're a coward who can't admit you're too scared to commit! You are a liar! I should have seen it in you. I'm an expert in that now, you know!" Her voice was now as frantic as Vivian's letters.

Victor jumped in. "He's not lying, and I know this because he's been grousing about it incessantly."

Lady Litchfield turned her attention to Victor, swallowing when their eyes met. But then, she lifted her nose. "He's not? Are you sure?"

"Yes. My brother has been sending constant letters to Lady Vivian since she left. I've seen him send them off. And he's never received a single response."

"Oh, dear." Lady Litchfield bit her bottom lip, evidently trying to figure out what to say or do next. "Then you don't know yet."

"Don't know what?" Dantes responded with a jolt of fear.

Lady Litchfield explained what she had learned in Vivian's letter about the solicitor's error. "I didn't even know she had to get married to keep the inheritance. But she's in a panic now because she only has one week left to get married and thinks you don't want to marry her anymore. And if she doesn't get married, even to someone else, everything relinquishes to…" Lady Litchfield froze and all the color drained from her face. "Oh, no."

"What is it?" Dantes and Victor said at the same time.

The marchioness's hand flew to her mouth, and she had to take a moment to herself. "If Vivian doesn't get married, everything goes to Bernard."

Dantes could see the answer in her paled face. Bernard had, somehow, found out about the solicitor's mistake and prevented Vivian and Dantes from contacting each other.

Fury like Dantes had never felt before burned through him like wildfire, and he clenched his fists to keep calm. "Winthrop has something to do with this," he said through gritted teeth.

Lady Litchfield glanced at her children, who were fighting over who could jump highest and closest to Victor's shoulder and were not paying attention to the conversation at hand. "I don't want to say that outright but you know his history."

"It would make the most sense," Ollie added. "I mean, her other letters are reaching their destinations. It's only Lady Vivian's and Dantes's letters that are missing." Ollie briefly explained to Lady Litchfield about the restoration project and the letter to Miss Sparrow.

"And the children get daily letters from Bernard," Lady Litchfield added while tapping her chin. "Oh, I guarantee that scoundrel has something to do with this!" Frustration ground at her voice. She looked back to Dantes. "What are you going to do?"

Lady Litchfield's theory made a lot of sense. It could even explain Vivian's unexpected debt repayment. Vivian thought *he* was ignoring *her* and maybe she did see it as cutting the final thread between them, but not in the way he had originally thought.

But how could she think something like that? Didn't she know how much he loved her? Was it not obvious?

He asked these questions out loud.

"Of course it's not obvious to her, you fool." It was Ollie. "First of all, you haven't been getting her letters, either, and have been worrying about the same thing."

All right, Ollie had a good point.

"And second, you refuse to tell her you love her—what's she supposed to think about that? I don't care if she *says* she's fine with it, she's not. No one would be."

"You've never told her you love her?" Lady Litchfield blinked. "I don't understand. She told me in the letter you were going to get married."

"That was the plan."

But Lady Litchfield shook her head at him. "Believe me when I say you shouldn't marry someone you don't love. *Do* you love her?"

"Of course I do!" Dantes shot back, frustrated by this incredibly personal conversation being tossed around out in the open.

"Then why haven't you told her?"

Victor gladly took the opportunity to explain Dantes's belief the phrase "I love you" was cursed for him. Of course, Victor explained it in a way that made Dantes look like a complete cad.

"You must be joking," Lady Litchfield said after hearing the truth. "I'm sorry, but if words can be cursed, I refuse to believe that such wonderful ones, said in truth, could ever cause physical harm."

"You would think."

"No, I *know*," she corrected him as her children began pulling at her skirts in boredom, causing her to wobble in response.

"Curses aren't real, Mr. McNab. You're wrong, and that's that." She nodded her head once. And as the children worked together to pull on one side of her with a single hard yank, she nearly toppled over. Victor quickly caught her as she yelped and looked up at him red-faced. Victor furrowed his brow while searching her face. The marchioness pushed off of him and took two shaky steps back. After a brief hesitation, she then turned away to wave her children off with a scolding. Victor gave his vote on the matter by giving Dantes an infernal smirk in support of Lady Litchfield.

"Sorry, Dantes, but it really is ridiculous and not true in the least." Ollie joined in with further support. "It's always been a coincidence you lose people after they said those words. You haven't lost me so far, have you? Despite what we went through? You're merely afraid of losing her—anyone is afraid of losing people they care about. But if you're truly that worried about it, give her a painting blessed by a priest or something and put it in her house. I don't know."

Dantes laughed at this. A painting blessed by a priest? Now that was ridiculous. But Ollie's suggestion made the gears in his head start turning. And as the thought took hold, the despair that had enveloped him these past few weeks began to crack and fall away, only to be replaced by raw excitement. He looked back up, his decision solidified. "I'm leaving in two days."

Lady Litchfield responded. "Are you sure you want to wait that long? That's rather close to her deadline."

"Yes." Dantes offered no further explanation. He had to take care of something before he left.

"Very well." Lady Litchfield blew out a breath as she helplessly watched her son rub renovation dust on his sister's pristine sleeve. "I'm worried about Vivian, so I'll join you on your trip."

"I'll join as well," Victor added, offering Dantes a grin of arrogant bemusement. "I want to witness this all for myself."

Not wanting to miss out, either, Ollie was going to join, too. "It's not like this place will be open, and they're going to be tearing down the old bar anyway." He said this at Victor's disapproving frown. Victor, however, didn't argue any further.

Two days later, the McNab brothers and Lady Litchfield boarded the steam locomotive that would travel to Brighton. As Dantes watched the city shrink and disappear outside the window, he thought about his life. His future. As long as everything went exactly as planned, the next time he saw London, he would have a wife. A passionate, beautiful, caring woman. A woman he admired, a woman who somehow saw past his scars. And, the best part of it all? She loved him exactly how he was.

He only hoped nothing more would get in his way.

Chapter Thirty

VIVIAN PACED BACK and forth, staring at the floor as she did this. It was a wonder a hole had not been worn in the rug as it seemed pacing had become her default since she'd posted the desperate, frantic letter to Anne. She'd received a short telegram a few days ago from Anne that said she was leaving for Brighton soon, but no other information was provided. And that was driving Vivian mad, coiling her nerves into tight springs. She hoped with all hope Anne would arrive with *something* to share about Dantes. Preferably a story of ripping him to shreds in front of his brothers. She paused for a moment, smiled at the thought, and continued with her anxious pacing.

"Vivian, please, you're going to wear a hole in the floor." Father entered the parlor with his morning newspaper, having had the same thought about the floor as Vivian. "I can't stand to watch you do this to yourself."

She stopped, but her movement traveled from her feet to her hands, where they began to wring together. "I can't handle this anymore, but I don't know what to do." She was getting worked up again, so Father pulled her in for a hug, gently patting her back. All this time, Vivian had kept Gran's will stipulation secret from her family, not wanting it to taint their view of whomever she chose to marry. But yesterday, she could no longer hide it and had tearfully told Father everything, from Gran's letter to her unexpected relationship with Dantes and finally to the solicitor's error. The duke had seemed stunned by the tale, but whatever thoughts he'd had, he'd kept to himself.

"Why does this hurt so much?" she asked with defeat.

"Because he broke your heart, the blasted fool."

Vivian sniffed.

"Do you want to go back home for a few days and go talk to him in person? You could stay in a hotel if needed. I know seeing him again would be hard, but at least you wouldn't have to wonder any longer about why he did this."

If she went back to London now, she would likely miss her deadline. Could she risk her future for a man who clearly didn't love her? Mere weeks ago, they'd been discussing marriage. How could Dantes be so angry about the paintings, about her slip of the cursed phrase, that her pleas and apologies could be so easily ignored? That he could knowingly make her miss her deadline and alter her life so severely? His anger and frustration could perhaps be understandable, but this severe level was not. And it didn't match with the man she thought she knew, the kind and gentle man whom she had fallen for.

Maybe she didn't know him at all.

"I wrote a rather desperate letter to Anne and she's on her way here," Vivian said.

"I think Anne would be understanding in this situation, sweetheart."

"If I go back, I'll likely miss the deadline and lose the estate. If Bernard takes it over, he's going to ruin generations of the hard work of our family."

Father gave her a small smile. "That's a noble concern of yours, but to be quite blunt, Vivian, they are dead. They don't know, nor do they care, about what happens to the money. What you need to figure out for yourself is what is most important to you."

This provided Vivian with a small bit of relief, but it hardly answered the question. Which was more important? Keeping her life-changing gift from her grandmother, one where she always had her own home and need not worry about money? Or losing that to go confront Dantes, possibly get answers, possibly still end up married some day when they figured out what had happened? Of course, in that scenario, they would not have the inheritance and the extra protection it provided her.

Even though it would be quite the conversation, she was sure she could at least convince Mr. Tewksbury to consider marriage. He had, after all, clearly stated he still hoped to have children someday. An unmarried man simply didn't say that to an unmarried woman for conversation's sake. He could get that, and she could keep her inheritance. There would be no love as she wanted, but they would both get something they wished for out of a marriage.

"The next train doesn't leave until tomorrow," Father said. "You have the rest of the day to decide what to do. I understand your heart is struggling right now, but I also know you don't want to lose everything your grandmother gave you. It's not only money you inherited—I know how much you adore this house and the memories it holds. And I know how important our family legacy is to you, our history. I hope you don't mind, but after we talked yesterday, I invited Henry Tewksbury to visit this afternoon. He's a good man and I know he will treat you well. He is a dear friend, and I've never heard a bad word about him from anyone. He doted on his wife before her passing, and I know he would treat any woman with love and respect."

The urge to pace took over Vivian once more. She was sure Father was right in that he was a fine gentleman. And perhaps she would in time grow to care for the man. But she would never love him. She would never love anyone the way she loved Dantes. The way her heart fluttered due to his mere presence, how his voice swept over her like a caress. She trusted him, knew he would be there for her if she ever asked.

No one else on this Earth could be more compatible for her.

Or so she had thought.

But what else could she do? Would it really come down to her having to marry Mr. Tewksbury?

The front door creaked open, and Bernard walked in casually, the day's mail in hand. Vivian rushed to him but didn't have to ask anymore—he already knew what she wanted to know.

As she looked at Bernard and his sad, understanding smile, she couldn't help but meet him with a small one of her own, appreciating that he always fetched their mail early so she didn't fret the entire day.

Bernard had improved significantly since his arrival, and he credited his daily walks to the post office. He was so much happier, looked so much healthier. He hardly drank at all, ate better, diligently wrote letters to Mary and Freddy, even had Vivian include paragraphs of her own where she sent them lots of hugs and kisses. In her unending stress about Dantes, Bernard had been so patient and understanding, listening to her when she blew off steam. He was back to being the brother she had missed and loved dearly.

"I'm sorry." Bernard dropped his head. "Nothing today."

Her stomach fell, as it always did. Each disappointment was a new wound, and each day, the crack in her heart grew bigger. "Just as well." She tried to swallow her disappointment. "Thank you for checking, anyway."

He gave her a quick kiss on the cheek, a gentle squeeze on her shoulder, and when Father handed the newspaper to him, Bernard commented he would be out back if anyone needed him. Vivian smiled after him as he walked away, grateful for his help.

For the next few hours, Vivian solemnly prepared for Mr. Tewksbury's arrival. She put together a small menu of tea and cold finger sandwiches, planning extra food for dinner in case he wished to stay. In the back of her mind, she knew if she invited him to stay for dinner, that meant she had decided to marry him in place of Dantes. She didn't let the thought form too strongly, however.

Go back to London as soon as possible to end this torture? Or stay with Mr. Tewksbury?

Thinking about it made her dizzy.

If only Anne had arrived before today to give some clarity on the situation at hand. But it was now too late and Vivian had to make a risky choice one way or the other.

Forcing away the worry, Vivian rushed off to begin preparations for her possible departure back to London before Mr. Tewksbury's afternoon visit.

Within hours, she would have to make a life-altering decision—marry a decent man she would never love to keep Gran's estate, or lose the estate to go confront the man she did love, possibly salvage what they'd once had. She could not wait any longer for answers. It had already been nearly a month of this torture.

When Mr. Tewksbury arrived later that afternoon, her Summerwood butler, Keane, led him into the parlor, where Vivian and Father waited. Bernard was oddly absent—Father had mentioned Mr. Tewksbury's visit to Bernard, and ever since then, her brother had become scarce. Vivian rationalized it as him not wanting to discuss his separation, as perhaps gossip had begun to spread.

The visit started off well enough, with plenty of polite chatter around their travels to Brighton. The sky had begun to darken with the threat of thunderstorms, and Vivian commented it would be the first rain since any of them had arrived, which meant it would likely be quite the storm. Better today than tomorrow when she would be traveling.

After a while, however, Father made an excuse to leave, and Vivian and Mr. Tewksbury were left alone.

The elder gentleman had given her a few brief glances that afternoon that seemed almost confused, as if he hadn't been sure why he was there. Vivian hadn't known what to make of that, as it was pretty clear when they saw each other last, he was at least mildly interested in her. What that meant, exactly, she hadn't the faintest notion, but she did finally come to one conclusion.

Her mind was made up.

Vivian was going to fight for Dantes, no matter what it took. Despite his intimidating appearance, he was not a man of confidence. Not when it came to love, at least. Dantes was a man who needed reassurance, nurturing, love, attention. That was what all that worry about curses is about. Curses didn't exist, but insecurity did. And she knew exactly what to say to prove to him he wasn't unlucky. Quite the opposite, in fact.

Vivian wanted to give Dantes everything he needed. And if that meant going back to London for a week, or a month, even, to coax him out of the fog, then so be it. Even if it meant losing Summerwood and the rest of the inheritance, as much as it would hurt. Because a life without Dantes wasn't a life she wanted, even if it was a gilded one. She wanted him, love, above all else. Above even Summerwood and the family legacy.

But right now, she had to deal with Mr. Tewksbury and that was going to be uncomfortable.

"Lady Vivian." He furrowed his brow as he knit his hands together over his lap. "I didn't want to say anything in front of your father, as I assume it is a private matter, but I was wondering why he asked me to visit."

"Oh!" She searched for how to respond. "Well, you know Father!" She tried to play it off with humor and her response made absolutely no sense. She winced at herself.

"No, what I mean is…" Mr. Tewksbury paused, probably unsure of how to broach whatever subject he had in mind. He took a deep breath. "Lady Vivian, perhaps we could be straight-forward."

"I would prefer that, in truth."

"As would I. I intended to spend time with you this summer with the hope that, perhaps one day down the road, a wedding could be discussed."

"Yes. About that…"

Mr. Tewksbury continued, saying something that caused Vivian pause. "When I arrived to Brighton last week, I saw your brother at the post office. He seemed taken aback when I called out to him, like he had been caught doing something. But before I could do more than ask after you and your father, he told me you were already engaged to be married."

Vivian frowned, frantically searched her memory for when she had told Bernard. "He said that?"

"Yes."

Glancing down at her fresh glass of iced tea, she watched a drop of condensation slide down the side. "It is true, but I'm not sure how he knew that—I haven't yet told him. Or Father, until quite recently. Anyway, tomorrow I'm thinking about heading back to London because I'm not even sure I *am* still engaged and I need to find out. That is, unless…"

Outside, the dark storm clouds opened, and it began pouring rain. Heavy footfalls crossed the covered front porch, sounding loud through the walls, and Bernard took a seat in an outdoor chair with a book and a glass of whiskey. Vivian envied him, as she adored sitting on the front porch to listen to summer rain. She liked daytime storms, so long as they did not become too violent.

Mr. Tewksbury was regarding her. "Forgive me, but how does one not know if they are engaged to be married or not?"

Vivian returned her attention to him. "It's rather silly. Dantes is supposed to come out here at some point for us to share the news with my family. Right before I left, we had an awful disagreement and ever since then, I've sent him many letters. Not once have I received a reply. I've even resorted to begging, which is not one of my finest moments."

Mr. Tewksbury listened with patience, his mouth then twisting with thought. "And you're sure this is uncharacteristic behavior?"

"Yes. It doesn't seem right, but then again, the actions show for themselves."

"What does your brother think of Mr. McNab? Are they friendly?"

"No."

"Does he like the gentleman at all?"

"Not...particularly."

"Interesting." Mr. Tewksbury looked away, thinking quite deeply about something.

"Why do you ask?" Something in the way he'd said this piqued Vivian's interest.

He looked back to her. "I saw something when I crossed paths with your brother at the post office that, at the time, didn't strike me as unusual. Did you know they replaced their front door? It's made of glass now, so you can see through it."

"I didn't, but it was always rather dark in there."

"They also have a rubbish bin right outside as well. Anyway, the day I saw Lord Litchfield, we talked briefly just as he was leaving. After we said our goodbyes, I watched him go and, once outside, he tossed a few letters into the bin. I figured they were advertisements, as I toss those myself. But that's rather curious under the circumstances, don't you think?"

The blood drained from Vivian's face right as a heavy boom of thunder shook the earth. The pouring rain was now a torrential downpour, coming down in heavy sheets. Surely, Bernard had not been throwing out her letters to Dantes. His letters to Vivian. "Oh, hellfire," she whispered as it sunk in.

"You see where I'm going with this, then."

But why would Bernard make such a concerted effort to keep their letters from each other? And how in the world had he found out they had planned to marry? None of this made any sense. Did Bernard assume so? No, that was far too big of an assumption to make to then go around telling people. There was no way Dantes and Bernard would ever socialize, so Dantes wouldn't have told Bernard. Additionally, Bernard's dislike of Dantes wasn't so strong that he would put this much effort into preventing their marriage. If anything, he would ask her why in the world she would pick Dantes, and that would be the extent of his commentary. So why go through the effort of keeping them apart, unless he got something out of it?

Her heart stilled.

Gran's will stipulation.

No. Surely. Surely, he wouldn't have done that to her!

But he needed that money. And he'd been devastated, angry even, that Gran had snubbed him. But how would he have found out about all of this? The solicitor would never have shared it with Bernard—he'd been the one who'd told her to keep it secret.

She gasped. The letter. He'd read the letter! She'd left it out when she'd gone to write Dantes about the change in deadline.

As this all ran through her mind, she realized that outside, Bernard was standing and looking out toward the drive that led up to the front of the house. She leaned forward to better see, and through the rain could just barely perceive the outline of a carriage. It was tilted, as if it were stuck in the mud. Bernard began to jog out there to help whoever it was. But a moment later, there was shouting. It was a woman's voice, and next thing Vivian knew, Bernard was running back toward the house with Anne chasing after him.

Chapter Thirty-One

THE CARRIAGE BEGAN to sink and lean to the side, and they all groaned with that special frustration long travel instills. They were so close to their destination, it felt like a cruel trick. Dantes watched out the window as the driver leapt off and sprinted toward the house to escape the downpour.

"Look at it out there." Ollie jumped as a frightening boom of thunder cracked above and shook the ground. "No way I'm going out there right now. I'm waiting here until it stops."

"I'm glad I had the children wait out the storm with the governess and my lady's maid back at the station." Lady Litchfield peered out the window at the storm. "Their carriage surely would be stuck right behind us!"

Dantes sank back in his seat and watched the rain pour. The drive leading up to Summerwood was quite long, with tall trees lining it. They all seemed to be hoping the rain would let up in a moment.

But before Dantes could decide if he should run to the house like the driver had, Lady Litchfield let out a shout of surprise and pressed her nose to the window.

Following her line of sight, Dantes spotted a male figure coming toward them in the rain.

"That bloody…pigeon-livered…wagtail!" Lady Litchfield shouted out. And then, the woman surprised them all by jumping out into the rain and running toward the figure. Dantes lifted his eyebrows sky-high at this. Lady Litchfield had not said much about her husband on the train except that she hadn't seen him in quite some time. However, it appeared she had had enough of his antics.

Deciding to follow suit, Dantes rose as best he could to climb out, too. But Victor suddenly shoved Dantes back into his seat and ran after Lady Litchfield. Ollie, happily staying put where it was nice and dry, shot a questioning look to Dantes. But Dantes said nothing, far too curious about the events occurring outside.

Winthrop was jogging toward them but came to a dead stop in realization his wife was coming for him, Victor following not far behind. The cad turned to run for his life. That, Dantes had to admit, was exceptionally funny. He would have to give Lady Litchfield a good pat on the back for that later, perhaps even a toast.

"What are you going to do now?" Ollie asked.

Dantes eyed the distant house, though in the rain and the steamy mist it had created, it was hard to see. "I have no idea. I don't know how upset she's going to be."

"Well, I can tell you. She's going to be hopping mad. With flames coming out of her eyes and steam coming out of her ears."

Dantes let out a laugh, and it felt good. Yes, Vivian was going to be pretty mad. But they would get through it, figure it out, move on. Get married. Hopefully. "I'm going." Dantes went to climb out when Ollie grabbed his arm.

"You're sure?" Ollie looked nervous. "It's pretty bad out there."

"Yes. I'm sure." Dantes pulled his arm away and went to leave again.

But Ollie grabbed him once more.

Annoyed, Dantes scowled over his shoulder. "What are you doing?"

"I, um…" Ollie scratched at his head "I don't like storms."

Dantes lifted his eyes to the sky. "And I don't care. I'm going to the house—right now. Either you come with me or stay here."

Ollie let out a sigh of frustration. "Fine." He grudgingly followed Dantes out into the downpour.

They hurried up the long drive, and through the fog and rain, Dantes could barely make out the shape of the front door, where the driver took shelter in the covered porch. Dantes's lungs and body were still weakened and he soon began to tire, his shoulder started to ache, but he pushed through it. Seconds later, however, Vivian burst out the front door, halting right before the porch stairs, shouting at Winthrop as he bolted past her and into the front door, slamming it shut behind him. And then, Tewksbury emerged.

Upon seeing Tewksbury, Dantes slid to a halt.

The world around him stilled, and there was no sound, other than the millions of raindrops that tapped against the leaves of the enormous trees around him, and his heart pounding in his ears.

Why the blazes was Tewksbury there? And why had he been alone with Vivian?

Winthrop hadn't been with them, and her father wasn't around anywhere.

His heart caught in his throat on a sob. He was too late.

Vivian had probably written to him numerous times to say she was going to marry Tewksbury if he didn't respond to her letters. But she *had* to marry the man, didn't she? He knew how much she enjoyed her freedom after living under her father's roof her whole life. And he knew she worried what would happen if Winthrop got his hands on everything. Honestly, he couldn't really blame her if she had chosen Tewksbury.

It was a desperate situation. And she didn't know he loved her. But oh, how he loved her!

And it was his own blasted fault she didn't know and had married another!

He hung his head and buried his face in his hands. For the rest of his life, he would have to live with his own stupidity.

But then, through the sound of the rain and his shattering

heart, there was a small and distant cry.

He looked up.

Vivian cried out his name. And started running toward him.

A flutter brought his dead heart back to life and he started running toward her, too, the blasted rain pelting his face. His heart revived, beating with life because she wasn't furious with him, or at least not so furious she went into the house and slammed the door in his face. And even better, she wasn't standing at Tewksbury's side, nor by her father, who had emerged to see what the commotion was.

No, she was running toward Dantes, crying out to him in front of her family, the family she hadn't wanted to tell yet about their betrothal. This was her moment of running through Hyde Park that he needed, the confidence from her, the declaration that she did in fact love the frightening Dantes McNab and she didn't give a blasted care who knew it! The most stunning relief washed over him, and the interior pocket of his jacket heated against him as he recalled what lay safely inside.

But as Vivian came closer, there was a bright flash of light as lightning struck the tree she was passing. And then she screamed.

VIVIAN RAN AS fast as she could. He'd come to her, Dantes had come to her—she'd been so sure he'd never want to see her again, so sure she had ruined everything by saying those cursed words, by the paintings. And here he was, rushing to her!

Had this been Anne's doing? Was Dantes angry with Vivian? Was he hurt? Had she hurt him? The mere thought of it struck her heart.

Whatever happened, she didn't care. She wanted to be in his arms again. Kiss him again. Hear his voice. The rain felt like needles on her face, but she hardly noticed.

"Dantes!" she shouted with all her might, and he went from a run to a sprint. Her arms extended out to him in joy as she got closer to him.

Lightning flashed.

The world went white.

The light was so bright, it sent an electric quake of shock through her. Sure she'd been struck, she screamed out with pure terror. That white light was immediately followed by the most ear-splitting crack of thunder she had ever heard in her life. It vibrated the marrow in her bones.

Snapping wood echoed out and when she realized she hadn't been struck, she opened her eyes and looked up in the direction of the noise. An enormous branch was tumbling down from the top of a towering tree. Right above her.

"Vivian!" Dantes screamed as her body reacted by raising her arms protectively to her face. A loud, rustling crash slammed into the ground and she held her breath as she realized the branch had only missed her by a few feet.

A cacophony of shouts from every direction began to descend upon her, shouts of fear and then relief as they all found her safe, the mud and puddles not the slightest concern to anyone.

Her family.

His family.

Their family, really.

Dantes's sprinting didn't slow, and he launched over the branch without a thought. Breathing hard, he easily lifted her from the ground and searched her for injuries, and once he'd seemed to convince himself that she hadn't died, that she hadn't gotten hurt, he pulled her desperately against him and pressed his mouth to hers for a kiss. Her heart pounded so hard in her chest, she was sure he could feel it. She buried her fingers into his wild hair, and for a few minutes, she forgot where she was, all of her senses and feelings and awareness only around him as they kissed each other with fear, with relief, against all odds at finally being back together.

"You scared the life out of me." He finally pulled away, but only a few inches, his hands remaining on her face. His green eyes were bright with fear. "I've never been so scared in my life, Viv. I almost watched you get crushed by a tree."

She started crying, and it irritated her. She had never been a crier, and she seemed to always be crying now, her heart so sensitive to everything. Or maybe that was the way it was supposed to be. Dantes breathed life and warmth back into her. "Bernard…" She couldn't even say it out loud. The devastation she felt at her brother's deception and betrayal was too much.

"I know. Lady Litchfield figured it out. I don't care anymore. Forget Winthrop, and that's the end of it. This is all I want. I only want you every day, forever. Now, please tell me you didn't marry Tewksbury."

She gave him a misty laugh, surprised that was a concern of his. "No. I was going to get on the train tomorrow, go home, and give you a piece of my mind. And then," she continued, "I was going to convince you that you don't have bad luck, that the curse isn't real."

His smile fell. "You don't believe in it even after what just happened?"

She shook her head. "Even after what just happened. You know why?"

He waited for her to continue, looping a loose strand of wet hair behind her ear. But his eyes were filled with skepticism.

"I realized you're not unlucky. In truth, you're possibly the luckiest man in the entire world."

Dantes gave her a sidelong glance. "All right, I'd like to hear this."

"Well…" She took a deep breath and noticed the rain was letting up. "Think about it. The fire, for example. We escaped unharmed despite being taken by surprise and not being able to find each other—you remember how bad the smoke was. Thankfully, no one else died in that fire, either. In the carriage accident, Ollie didn't die because you knew what a gunshot sounded like, because of where you'd lived as a boy. And then you were mere hours from death and miraculously came back from it. You never lose fights, you didn't marry the wrong woman, you have a successful pub with your brothers. Of all the pubs Bernard could have gone to, he went to yours. And even though you and your brothers all irritate each other, you really do genuinely love each other. You know you can trust and rely on each other completely. I didn't get struck by lightning, or crushed by the tree, even though I came pretty close to both. And best of all, you get to marry *Britain's richest spinster*." She ended this with a shy smile.

Dantes tilted his head in thought, and she could see he was deeply considering everything she'd said, that she had finally reached something deep inside of him that had been closed off forever.

"Yes, but what about my parents?" Dantes replied. "My father getting killed in a derailment, my mother's addiction and death, living on the streets—though thanks to that, I learned what a gunshot sounds like. Getting sent off to boarding school, which comprised the worst years of my life, and all I wanted were my grandparents then. The knife to my face, and everything else Crosby put me through? And yes, we survived those events you laid out, and this one just now, but those events sure aren't lucky."

But she shrugged her shoulders. "Bad things happen, Dantes. To everyone. And no one is immortal. That's all it is, darling."

For a long while, he stared at her, his eyes boring into hers, but a softness came over him, a softness she had never seen in him before, almost like something had been released from deep inside of him. "Maybe you're right," he said simply, as if it weren't the biggest deal in his—or her—life.

"Of course she's right." It was Ollie. Vivian startled, as she had forgotten all about everyone else. "We've been telling you the same thing, but you don't listen to us."

Dantes grinned as Ollie shook his head and placed an arm around Dantes's shoulders. And while Ollie teased him about it further, Vivian looked around at the faces of relief that surrounded them. Father, Anne, Victor, Ollie. When had Keefe come outside? Even Mr. Tewksbury was there, and a man who was a complete stranger, perhaps the driver of the carriage stuck in the mud. Bernard's absence was not lost on her, but she would deal with that later.

They were her family, her friends, standing in the rain, though it was more of a drizzle now. And each one of them stood with her, not minding that they were covered in mud.

She had never been alone, had she?

"I thought Vivian had been struck by lightning." Anne looked up to Victor, who stood near her.

Victor stared back but didn't speak.

"I saw the branch fall," Ollie jumped in. "I knew the lightning hadn't hit her but thought she'd been crushed."

Now that the fear from the storm had dissipated along with it, there was a lot of "Did you see that?!" and "Look at your clothes!" coupled with laughter and other excited discussion.

With everyone distracted, Dantes pulled Vivian off to the side for a moment of attempted privacy. "Vivian…" He paused in thought. "I'm really sorry about everything that happened."

"I don't want to dwell on it anymore. If you want the paintings home, that's fine. If you want them fixed, that's fine too. Whatever you want. I shouldn't have surprised you with such an extravagant gift, or stormed off the way I did. But it will be your money, too, if you still want to get married."

His eyebrows pulled together severely. "Of course I still want to get married, Vivian. That's why I came out here. I love you." He didn't even flinch, and the words flowed, as if he'd been saying it all this time.

Her eyes went wide at the shock that hit her. "Oh, can I say it, too?" She waited for a denial, but he smiled back instead. "I love you, too, Dantes."

"It's going to be hard for me to get used to that. But I understand now what you mean, that you can't go without saying it.

They aren't mere words, are they?"

"No, darling, they're not. They're everything."

Dantes sealed their love with a kiss, wrapping his soaking-wet arms around her soaking-wet waist. "It's still going to make me anxious, at least for now," he admitted, his cheek pressed against her hair. "But I have something that I think will help me and I hope you like it." He pulled back to reach into his jacket, revealing a wet ring case, and handed it to her.

With eagerness, Vivian opened it and found a gold ring with a four-leaf clover made of emeralds. "It's beautiful," she said with deep awe. "Dantes." She looked up at him with a wide smile. "This is magnificent!"

A faint blush on his cheeks crept up from behind his beard. "It's your wedding ring. I had it blessed by a priest too, to keep you safe. I know it's a bit absurd, and you're probably right about me not truly being unlucky. But you wearing this, I don't know— it will make me feel a lot better."

She admired it for another moment, turned it a bit to watch the rich green and gold sparkle in the now-unclouded sun. She handed it back to him. "I can't wait to wear it."

"What are you going to do about your brother?" Dantes asked after stuffing the box safely back in his pocket.

"I'm not sure. This is our first discussion as a couple, I believe, since his actions affected us equally."

"Very well." Dantes stared off toward the house. "He hurt you. And I'll never be forgiving about anyone doing that."

"No," Vivian agreed. "He tried to keep you from me, even after I'd helped him when he needed it." Vivian looked in the same direction as Dantes, knowing her brother was somewhere inside the house, hopefully packing. There used to be a time when Bernard had been her best friend, and she had always looked up to him because of it. Maybe that was why she'd made so many excuses for him over the years, overlooked the now-obvious signs that something in him had changed dramatically. He wasn't the Bernard Winthrop she had grown up with.

Looking back, she could see he'd begun to turn after his wedding, and that had been over ten years ago. He'd been so young when he and Anne had married, probably too young, not that that was an excuse. But before his wedding, he'd been so carefree and happy, and really had seemed to want to be with her when he'd chosen her to be his wife. Clearly, some kind of pressure as a husband, maybe even as a father, had had something to do with it. How, she could not say and probably would never know. But he had made the decision to marry Anne, he should never have hurt his family the way he had, and it would take her a long time to forgive him for it or trust him again, if she ever did.

She probably should have never paid off his debts in the first place, at least not so easily, but she couldn't take that back. "I don't know if I can cut him out of my life forever. But for the time being, I want to keep my distance. Our distance."

Dantes agreed.

"I'm going to tell him he must leave today. I don't want him at our wedding, either." She finally admitted this with a heavy sigh. "That was really hard to say out loud."

He pulled her close and she felt safe against him. "I don't want him there, either. I'm so glad we're in agreement on that. I know he's your family, but what he did…"

"I know. But you're my priority now, Dantes. You, our future."

"I can't wait to start it."

The sun now shone in a sapphire sky, clouds turned fluffy and happy. The air was quickly becoming sticky and humid. Vivian noticed everyone walking back to the house, and she wondered how in the world they all were going to get cleaned up when there were only two bathtubs. She said this out loud, not really expecting a response.

"You and I can double up." Dantes dipped down to her ear with a daring voice.

She laughed. "You think so?"

"Yes, after we strip off our muddy clothes and toss about the sheets for the rest of the afternoon, locked away while everyone else cleans up. Then we can double up in the bath. You know, it saves a lot of time." He gave her a roguish grin.

Vivian couldn't help but laugh. "I think that's a splendid idea." She paused. "I do have a secret to tell you. I made some wedding-related inquiries after I received the letter from the solicitor. There's a little church here in the middle of renovations. But as it's wedding season, they were the only place with an opening for us in time. Technically, they aren't even holding weddings this year because their building is a mess, but I don't much care about that, do you?"

"No. I don't care where we get married, as long as we do."

"Good. I promised them a nice donation when they told me it would be impossible. Suddenly, it became possible. They even offered to help get a special license once I told them *Britain's richest spinster* and famous pugilist Dantes McNab would be the ones exchanging nuptials." She paused and felt her face go hot. "I got ahead of myself a bit and had them put your name on there."

Dantes grinned. "What would have happened if you decided to marry Tewksbury instead?"

"Oh, dear, that would have been an uncomfortable conversation, wouldn't it?"

Dantes laughed heartily.

"What do you think?" Vivian asked. "You want to marry me tomorrow morning?"

Surprise flickered in Dantes's face. But then he said, "It's not even a question, my little rose."

"I love you," she whispered, no longer needing to hold it back, wanting to say it fifty more times today.

"I love you, too, Vivian." He responded with a smile. "Always and forever."

Epilogue

London
October 1889

THE NIGHT THE Harp & Thistle reopened, they got lucky, as it was an unseasonably warm autumn night. And because of that, the entire city went out to enjoy the last bit of summer before the chill took over. A line went out the door and down the block—something that had never happened before. Victor made one single comment about how the crowd seemed decent, and Ollie was thrilled to mingle and be the big personality once again. And Dantes, he really couldn't have been any happier than he was in this moment. He was making his familiar rounds around the pub, saw old friends, and met the woman who'd tamed Tommy Malone—who had recently finished up a short stint in the slammer for the robbery—and Mr. and Mrs. Malone met the woman who'd finally tamed Dantes.

Dantes received plenty of jokes about being tied down, but he didn't mind. He had a wife, the most spectacular woman in the world, and no amount of teasing would ever get to him about that.

Looping back around, his eyes anchored on Vivian. She was perched atop a tall stool at the bar with Lady Litchfield and they were whispering excitedly about something.

Dantes went up behind his wife and wrapped his arms around her waist.

"Darling," Vivian said low into his ear as his chin rested upon her shoulder. "A few minutes ago, I heard someone say Mr. Crosby had been forced into marrying. He got one of his sister's friends pregnant."

Dantes turned to kiss her neck in a wholly inappropriate way, not caring about Crosby in the least.

She giggled. "We're in public!" And she reprimanded him with a playful pat on his arm.

"Come with me, then," he said low enough to ensure no one else could hear.

Vivian gave him a teasing look of exasperation and excused herself to Anne. He took his wife's hand in his, shot a look to Victor, who had suddenly appeared to ask Anne if she needed anything, and Vivian followed him to the office in back, where he shut the door and pulled her close. He kissed his wife passionately for a long while, something he'd never tire of, and ended it with a gentle kiss on her hairline. "It's hard to work when you're here. You're exceptionally distracting."

"Should I go home?"

"Absolutely not."

She smiled up at him as she played with a button on his shirt. "There's something I've been meaning to talk to you about, and this time is as good as any I suppose."

"Oh?" His curiosity was piqued. "Is everything all right?"

"Oh, yes." The forced brightness in her voice made him arch an eyebrow. "It is. It's just…remember how after we married, we decided to put off having children for a little bit so it could be the two of us for a while?"

"Of course I remember."

"Well, I was wondering. What if we stopped doing that?" She looked up with a lip-biting grin.

A thrill went through him. "What are you saying, Viv? You want to start trying for a baby?"

She blushed at the words, and in this tender moment, he couldn't help but place his hand at her cheek. "Yes." She smiled at his touch. "I think so. I know the pub recently reopened, but sometimes, it can take a while. And the fact of the matter is I'm not twenty anymore. If you're not ready, though—"

"I'm ready. Are you kidding me? Vivian, this is better than the pub reopening."

"Really?"

He laughed. "I can't wait, if we're going to be honest."

She rested her head against his chest as he wrapped his arms around her. "I know Victor is rigid on everyone's work hours, but you all are going to have to consider hiring on more help now. You're a married man, after all, hopefully a father sooner rather than later. And I really don't think Ollie and Victor will remain unmarried forever."

He pressed his cheek to the top of her head. "Who do you think goes first?"

"Oh, that's easy. Ollie."

"Why do you say that?"

"Because he's younger. Victor, he's too disciplined. Stubborn. Used to being alone. Sound familiar?"

"Maybe, but I think Victor would go first. Ollie is too free-spirited to settle down. But enough about that. Let's talk more about making a baby."

Vivian laughed before pulling away and gave him a coy smile over her shoulder as she went to leave the office, reminding him of the time he'd kissed her hand for good luck. Maybe *she* was his good luck, what had turned his life around.

"That happens at home, silly," she said while fluttering her eyelashes.

"Wait." He crossed the room to her. "I love you."

"I love you, too." She took his hand in hers and they went back out and into the happy noise of the crowded pub.

HOURS LATER, AS the sky began to brighten on a new day, Vivian opened her eyes and found the gold dress she'd put on when they returned home ripped to shreds and tossed onto the floor. Remembering their first night of trying for a baby sent a thrill through her and she couldn't help but smile to herself as she recalled the passion it had elicited in them. She turned to her side to find her beautiful husband lying next to her, fast asleep. They had separate bedrooms, but he never did manage to leave her room ever, and she never managed to ask him to.

At some point overnight, the autumn chill must have once again taken over the city. Vivian shivered a bit and snuggled close against Dantes. In his sleep, he mumbled something before putting his arm around her. She drifted off back to sleep, cozy and warm.

ABOUT THE AUTHOR

Born and raised in Chicago to an artist family, Arden Conroy grew up attending museums and played piano and cello for fifteen years. When she isn't writing or reading, Arden enjoys historical fashion, art history, and historical dramas and comedies. She has lived all over the United States from the Hudson Valley, NY to Tulsa, OK. Currently, she resides between Chicago and Pennsylvania with her husband and two children.

Website – www.ardenconroy.com
Facebook – facebook.com/profile.php?id=100083677291622

www.ingramcontent.com/pod-product-compliance
Lightning Source LLC
Chambersburg PA
CBHW070507310726
48976CB00002BA/371